NOVA-STAR
REPUBLIC

NOVA-STAR REPUBLIC

Unholy Alliance

Michael Pinto
Trevor Moore

Full Court Press
Englewood Cliffs, New Jersey

Second Edition

Published in the United States of America
by Full Court Press, 601 Palisade Avenue
Englewood Cliffs, NJ 07632
www.fullcourtpressnj.com

ISBN 978-0-9709477-3-4
Library of Congress Control No. 2011940188

Cover Art by Matthew Pinto
Editing by Arlene Pollack
Book Design by Barry Sheinkopf for Bookshapers
(www.bookshapers.com)
Colophon by Liz Sedlack

Please send your thoughts and comments to:
pintoandmoore@live.com
and visit us on the web at *www.nova-starrepublic.com*
We hope you enjoy reading Nova-Star
as much as we did writing it.

ACKNOWLEDGMENTS

Michael Pinto would like to thank: God, for my gift in storytelling. My wife, Shinnie, for her faith in me. My mom, for loving me and raising me in a Godly manner. Trevor, for his unwavering support—I know it wasn't easy. John, for some great ideas. And Arlene Pollack and Barry Sheinkopf of Bookshapers.com for their editorial and design assistance.

Trevor Moore would like to thank: God, for everything. Michael, for opening up my creative side. And my parents and other family members, who told me to keep going and never give up.

Accessing Historian's Database

Persons of Interest

ADMIRAL JONATHAN PAUL MIKEL
> Species: Human
> Age: 50
> Height: 6'1"
> Race: Black
> Eyes: Right is cybernetic, left is brown
> Hair: None
> Occupation: Exiled officer of the Imperial Guard; Special
> Agent for Measha Station

NOVENA STARR
> Species: Twilight
> Age: 500
> Height: 5'7"
> Race: Star Travelers
> Eyes: Onyx
> Hair: Silver, White
> Occupation: Merged Pilot to a Twilight Heavy Cruiser

GENERAL EUGENE BLAKE
> Species: Human
> Age: 49
> Height: 6'
> Race: Caucasian
> Eyes: Blue
> Hair: Brown
> Occupation: Agent of the Ashlon Republic; Liaison to Measha
> Station

KATRINA TARR-BLAKE
> Species: Tigeras

Age: 66
Height: 5'8"
Race: Humanoid Feline
Eyes: Green
Hair: Varies (Originally Black)
Occupation: Combat Strategist and Navigator; Member of
the Tigeras Royal Family

LIEUTENANT SARA ALBRIGHT
Species: Human
Age: 21
Height: 5'9"
Race: Black
Eyes: Green
Hair: Black
Occupation: Leader of Omega Squadron

ENSIGN WILLIAM BLAKE
Species: Human
Age: 16
Height: 5'11"
Race: Caucasian
Eyes: Blue
Hair: Brown
Occupation: Special Agent for Measha Station: the Infiltrators

LIEUTENANT RYAN BLAKE
Species: Human
Age: 22
Height: 5'11"
Race: Caucasian
Eyes: Blue
Hair: Black
Occupation: Special Agent for Measha Station; Member of
the Infiltrators

ADMIRAL THOMAS J. BLAKE
>   Species: Human
>   Age: 55
>   Height: 6'1"
>   Race: Caucasian
>   Eyes: Blue
>   Hair: Black
>   Occupation: Ashlon Republic; Naval Fleet Commander

ADMIRAL SCOTT T. WRIGHT
>   Species: Human
>   Age: 55
>   Height: 6'
>   Race: Black
>   Eyes: Brown
>   Hair: Black
>   Occupation: Imperial Guard; Naval Fleet Commander

HIGH RULER MEI-LING
>   Species: Human
>   Age: 48
>   Height: 5'4"
>   Race: Asian
>   Eyes: Brown
>   Hair: Black
>   Occupation: High Ruler of the Imperial Guard

NESITHSUL
>   Species: Solien
>   Age: 200
>   Height: 6'6"
>   Race: Reptilian
>   Eyes: Dark Brown
>   Hair: None
>   Occupation: Head Tribal Leader and Co-leader of the Resistance

BROUGTH

Species: Wraith
Age: Unknown
Height: 6'5"
Race: Insectoid
Eyes: Red
Hair: None
Occupation: Commander of the Dark Squadron and Liaison
to the Imperial Guard

TERRA NORA

Species: Human
Age: 250
Height: 5'6"
Race: Native Indian descent
Eyes: Brown
Hair: Raven Black
Occupation: Soldier for the Dreamseeker Council and the
Guardian of the Box

TERRI ALBRIGHT

Species: Human
Age: 50
Height: 5'5"
Race: Caucasian
Eyes: Green
Hair: Blonde
Occupation: Member of the Imperial Council

Weapons Used

PPC—Plasma Particle Cannon: Used by all races except the Wraiths.
Used on capital ships and defense systems. Used against other
capital ships and on armored targets on the surface.

HPLC—Heavy Particle Laser Cannon: Used on capital ships and defense platforms against fighters and small battleships.

PLAS-CRYSTAL CANNON—Used by the Imperial Guard. A tense energy beam designed to break down a ship=s energy field.

ARROWHEAD LASER CANNON—Used by the Ashlon Republic. A cannon that can drain a ship's energy field.

DCBC—Diamond Cutting Beam Cannon: Weapon used by the Tigeras on their capital ships, and smaller versions are built onto their fighters. They can cut through most material and armor.

IAC—Implosion Accelerated Cannon: Used by the Wraiths. The energy beam bypasses the energy field and causes the ship=s hull to explode from the inside out.

FBC—Fusion Beam Cannon: Used by the Twilights. Recreates the power of the sun and focuses it into an energy beam.

STINGER MISSILES—Missiles that are used by the Imperial Guard and the Ashlon Republic. They are smart missiles that can find their own best route to their targets, either automatically or manually.

STARLIGHT MISSILE—Universal use. It is an antifighter missile. Also has heat-seeking capabilities and can be programmed to be used on capital ships.

KCT—Kraken Concussion Torpedo: Used by the Tigeras. Combination of Kraken energy and an energy shockwave that is designed to critically cripple a capital ship or destroy it.

DPC—Devastator Pulse Cannon: Used by the Soliens. Fires energy that is three times greater than the sun.

HIVE LAUNCHER—Used by the Telbin. A missile system that is as smart as a Stinger missile. It launches several missiles at once that can lock on to different targets.

DRONE CONTROLLER—An intelligence system that fires a missile used to gather intelligence.

HRG—Hyper-capacitor Rail Gun: Used by the Telbins and the Historians. It fires an aluminum-based shell at almost the speed of light.

M-9 LASER PISTOL—Handheld weapon used by most species.

MACK-93 LASER RIFLE—Rifle version of M-9 Pistol.

ZACK-33 PLASMA PISTOL—More powerful version of the M-9 Pistol.

ZEUS-T PLASMA RIFLE—More powerful version of the Mack-93 Laser Rifle.

BOARHEAD PLASMA SCATTER RIFLE—A rifle that fires multiple plasma energies at once, striking a wide variety of targets.

PLASBORE LAUNCHER—Launches a plasma energy ball, which has enough power to punch a hole through most armor, most ground-based vehicles, and on fighters.

History of Man

I N THE YEAR 2201, Mankind's future was bright. New technology had allowed the species to colonize outer space. First was Mars. Next, they moved past the asteroid belt into the outer planets and their moons. With every moon came a new challenge to colonization.

When they had colonized Pluto, they knew what their next step would be: to journey out into the unknown universe. Ships were being built, plans made, and crews assembled for the voyage.

Then an amazing discovery was made.

During a routine patrol, a space station of unknown origin was discovered not too far from Pluto. While exploring the station, scientists discovered that they could create a wormhole able to transport a person or ship to another station or destination. Before they could get much further, however, the scientific team made a shocking discovery: the station's advanced scans revealed that two unknown objects were coming towards their solar system. The projected trajectories of the objects indicated that one would hit the station while the other would strike the Earth. The impact would shatter the Earth's surface and cover the sky with enough dust to blanket it and leave the planet uninhabitable for thousands of years.

The military assembled its fleets to try to destroy or derail the unknown objects, but they didn't know if they would be successful. Could their species survive without their home planet?

It was decided to activate the station's wormhole and send through as many people as possible; but since they did not know how to properly sync up with another station, they would be traveling blind, to an unknown destination.

Using the remaining time before the objects struck, they gathered the ships already built for the voyage into space, along with those they had newly built, and situated all outside the station. Despite failures to stop the unknown objects, the military continued its preparations as it counted down the days until Earth's destruction.

Finally, the destructive objects arrived. Earth was hit first. The event later became known as the Destruction of Earth. The station was next. Before it was hit, the wormhole was activated and the fleet of escaping refugee ships jumped to an unknown destination. But billions had been left behind on Earth and the surrounding colonies. The Great Exodus had begun.

IT IS NOW 4201. Two thousand years have passed since the Great Exodus forced Man to leave the home system and find new systems to inhabit. Once resettled, they befriended alien species.

As a result of a conflict regarding how to deal with the new species that had aided them once they came through the wormhole, Man decided to split up into two separate governments—the Ashlon Republic and the Imperial Guard. This reorganization came to be known as The Great Divide. The Ashlon Republic decided to ally itself with the alien species and to welcome any alien group into its fold, while the Imperial Guard chose to have as little to do with the aliens as possible. Both governments have grown enormously in size, becoming two of the most powerful players in the galaxy.

But both the Ashlon Republic and the Imperial Guard are unaware of a serious danger looming ahead: a dark force has appeared on the horizon, threatening all the races in the galaxy.

1

WITHOUT WARNING

THE *TWILIGHT STAR* ROARED through space at faster than light travel, FTL. They had just finished a mission and as everything was going smoothly, they thought there was no rush to get back to Measha Station.

The crew consisted of three people—four, if you included the ship's computer, Novena. The XO, General Blake, and the navigator, Katrina Tarr-Blake, were on the bridge. With Novena, the bridge did not need to be manned at all times. If a problem were to arise, she could alert them, and they would then convene on the bridge; but as a precaution, the bridge was manned at all times. There had been only a few incidences when the whole crew slept while Novena kept watch.

The rest of the crew, which consisted of twenty-five people, did not take part in the mission. Since their presence was not required, they remained at Measha Station for the duration of the mission.

The captain, Jonathan, was sleeping in his quarters, where Novena's attention was currently fixed.

She watched Jonathan from her camera on the ceiling. He was thrashing about, experiencing the same nightmare he'd been having just about every night.

He woke up, screaming, "Cease-fire! Cease-fire!" and started to breathe and sweat heavily.

"Jon? Are you all right?"

Panting, he said, "Yes, Novena. I'm fine."

"Did you have the same nightmare?"

He paused for a short moment. "No."

Novena made what sounded like a snort through the speaker. "You're lying."

Jonathan exhaled. "Guess I can't fool you, huh?"

"Nope, and you should know better."

Jonathan sat up on his bed. "How's the XO doing?"

"He's still piloting the ship, but I think he's scheming to sneak into the main fusion cannon room."

Jonathan shook his head. "That's Eugene for you; he loves playing with big guns. I just wish he would stay away from yours." Both of them laughed. Eugene had been, and always would be, a gun nut.

Out of nowhere, Novena asked, "Jonathan, do you think we would stand a chance if I weren't merged with the ship?"

Jonathan didn't speak. *How can I have feelings for her? She's permanently merged with the ship—not to mention that I'm also in love with someone else. I must have gone crazy. How do I get myself into these situations?*

Before Jonathan was exiled, he had been a much-respected admiral and in love with Mei-Ling, the high ruler of the Imperial Guard. When he was exiled, he broke off his relationship with her.

He had barely seen Mei-Ling in the five years since he had broken up with her, but there was a part of him that still loved her. Yet, he was now forming a relationship with Novena, the ship's pilot. She was part of a species called Twilights, who could merge with ships and become one with them.

It had all started a couple of months before. Jonathan had been alone in his cabin, drunk, and thinking about his life before his exile. He was in love, had a daughter, and was enjoying a great career in the navy. In his drunken stupor, Jonathan had poured out all his feelings to Novena. It wasn't the first time he'd told her what he was feeling at the moment. She had always been a good listener, putting up with all his rants and helping him when he was depressed and feeling alone, missing his sweetheart. He'd also express his love for Novena. They could have just chalked it up to his being drunk, but it wouldn't have worked: they both knew that he'd meant every word of it.

For five years, they'd been there for one another, sharing their feelings and heartaches. She had told him a great deal about her life before her merge, and he had told her much about his own story. In a way, they knew each other better than they knew themselves.

For a while, they'd avoided the subject of their feelings for each other, but now it looked as if she wanted to face it head on.

Jonathan sat on his bed, trying to think of a way to stall this inevitable conversation. "Call up the XO for me," he told her.

He could hear the hesitation in her voice as she said, "Yes, sir." Over the course of the years, Jonathan had come to the conclusion that Novena was also forming an attachment to him. One of the things that made him so nervous was that she might confess her feelings for him.

Jonathan walked up to the table that contained his cybernetic arm. He'd lost his right arm from the elbow down, and also his right eye in a crash five years before. Novena had put him back together as best she could. He might have gotten a brand-new eye and arm, but as punishment for what he'd failed to do, he decided to pass up that option.

He took a look at himself in the mirror and said to himself, "This is what I deserve for what I did to them. I swear that I'll bring them to justice somehow."

His head was bald, and the left side of his face was flesh while the right side was metallic. His left eye was dark brown while his right was a robotic red eye. He was of medium build for his height, with a right arm that was robotic from the elbow down. The image before him was a constant reminder of his failure. He vowed he would make it right one day.

Sensors located in his fingertips and connected to the nerves in his arms gave him feeling. The rest of him was human. No synthetic skin covered his cybernetic parts.

He pulled out the chair, sat down, and started working on the arm. Jonathan was a marksman in small arms and assault rifles, a martial arts expert, and a medical technician, as well as a crash mechanic able to repair a ship in the middle of combat and keep it in the fight.

Novena came back on the speaker. "You never answered my question."

She sighed. *She's never going to let this go.*

"Haven't you gotten hold of Eugene yet?"

She paused for a moment. "I've tried reaching him, but I've had no luck." He could tell that she was a little annoyed because he hadn't answered her, but she didn't press the issue.

Jonathan sighed. "Call up Katrina. Maybe she knows where he is."

A few seconds later, Katrina was on the comm system. "Katrina, have you seen Eugene?" he asked.

"He's uh . . . he's taking care of some business. He should be back soon," she replied.

Jonathan heard Novena chuckle to herself. They both could tell that Katrina was lying. From the way she was talking, it wouldn't take a rocket scientist to realize she was covering something up.

Jonathan frowned. "What kind of business?" he asked.

She hesitated. "Just. . . you know. . .using the head and all that."

Jonathan's frown deepened. *Something is up*, he thought.

Suddenly, it hit him. "Oh shit! Novena, scan the main fusion cannon room."

"Yes, sir." While Novena was doing that, he reconnected his arm and started to make his way to the bridge. Halfway there, Novena called him. "Sir, there's no one in the main fusion cannon room."

Despite Novena's answer, Jonathan knew that something was wrong. He changed direction and headed toward the main fusion cannon room while talking to Katrina. "Katrina, I know you love him, but I need to know what he's up to." She didn't reply. Jonathan sighed with frustration. *Lovesick woman.*

"I promise that I won't hurt him," he told her.

She sighed. "Think, Jon. What's his only other love besides me?"

Great! He's in the main fusion cannon room. Jonathan took off running. "Novena, open the doors to the main fusion cannon room."

"But my scanners don't pick up anything."

"Eugene's somehow masked the sensors. Now open the doors or I'll blast them open!"

"Fine. Fine."

Jonathan continued racing toward the main fusion cannon room. When he arrived, the doors were still closed.

Jonathan screamed, "Novena, how come the doors aren't open?"

"I'm trying, but they've been tampered with. They can only be opened from the inside."

That did it. Eugene had to be in there!

He pounded on the door with his cybernetic arm. "Eugene!"

Eugene Blake was sitting in the captain's chair on the bridge, smoking a cigarette. The bridge was big enough to hold twelve people. In the middle were two command chairs, one for the captain and the other for the executive officer. There were also three major stations, each situated ten feet from the command chairs and able to support three people.

The helm station, responsible for maneuvering during combat, was located directly in front of the command chair, from which the engines, thrusters, and light speed engines were controlled.

To the starboard side was the tactical weapons station, where the crew controlled the weapons, the defensive grid, and the energy field that was designed to absorb PPC, HPLC, and missile attacks.

On the port side was located the navigation and comm station, from which the crew could control the navigation of the ship as it went through light speed, so that it would not hit planets, asteroids, and other space debris. That station also controlled the comms throughout and outside the ship. As long as the ship's A.I. was functional, three people could command the ship.

At the moment, Eugene was monitoring Jonathan, who was experiencing another nightmare. Eugene knew that whenever Jonathan had a nightmare, Novena would direct all her attention toward him, watching over him; now was Eugene's chance to sneak into the main fusion cannon room.

He turned to his wife Katrina. "Honey, I'm going to go for it! Cover for me, will you?"

Katrina turned to look at him. She was a Tigeras, one of the most feared races in the galaxy. Although she was a princess in the Tigeras

Empire, she didn't behave in a way that reflected her status, choosing instead to dye her hair a variety of colors and to wear black leather outfits. That day, her hair was dyed hot pink.

"If Jonathan catches you, he'll kill you," she said with a smile.

Eugene smiled back. "He has to catch me first. If you do this right, he won't find out until it's too late."

"Eugene, you know I'm not a good liar; as soon as they hear my voice, they'll know something is up."

"You can do this. Look, I've been watching those two. Each time Jonathan has a nightmare, I've timed its duration at about twenty to thirty minutes. And I've found a way to mask the sensors—"

"I still don't know how you managed that," she interrupted.

"A magician never tells his secrets," he said. "I can keep the doors locked long enough to finish the upgrade."

"Upgrade? More like an act of suicide."

"Where's the faith?"

"Look, whatever you do, don't rupture the membrane that houses the fusion energy."

"Don't worry. I'll be back in two shakes of a lamb's tail." He stood up and smothered his cigarette in an ashtray. He was about to leave when Katrina grabbed him and kissed him.

After they separated, he asked, "What was *that* for?"

"Just in case Jonathan kills you," she replied.

"Thanks for your faith in my abilities." As he was walking out, Katrina slapped him on the backside. He turned his head, smiled, and walked out, starting to make his way toward the main fusion cannon room.

The task ahead of him would be easy; besides being a major gun nut, he was a mechanic, an electrician, and a specialist in stealth, sniping, hand-to-hand combat, and swords and knives.

It wasn't long before he reached the main fusion cannon room. He punched in the access code. The doors opened, and he slid inside. He quickly closed them. At the main control panel, he took out a disk and inserted it into the slot. For weeks he had been working on a program that would mask him from the sensors and keep the doors from opening. He had finally done it.

Once he finished downloading, the screen lit up. It told him that he had complete control of the room's systems.

He rubbed his hands together in delight, happy as a gunner's mate in a knife-and-gun show, took out one of his cigarettes, and lit it up.

The cigarettes of that time were very different from those of the twenty-first century, which had been filled with nicotine, tar, and countless poisons so hazardous to a smoker's health. The plants used for the new cigarettes were harmless, designed for recreational use. Some came in a variety of flavors. There were even cigarettes prescribed by doctors to help relieve stress.

Eugene tapped the keys of the computer, activating a few commands. The doors locked up; the sensors did not recognize him. He created a loop in the video and shut the audio off.

He looked at his wrist monitor, then re-routed the video from Jonathan's room to the monitor. He saw that Jonathan was still asleep but starting to stir. The nightmare was about to reach its peak. Eugene would have to act fast.

Most people would consider it inconsiderate for a person to use his or her friend's nightmare to further their own objectives, but he and Jonathan had been friends since childhood, and there was nothing that he would not forgive. He also realized that the upgrades would improve the power output of the main fusion cannon. Furthermore, Eugene didn't consider this inconsiderate; he was merely taking advantage of an opportune moment.

Now that part one of the plan had been completed, it was time for part two: the main fusion cannon.

Its housing was made of titanium. The inside of the casing housed the membrane and the magnetic field around it. When the gun was fired, the magnetic field would force the fusion energy into a beam and push it out of the barrel. That barrel reached out to the end of the ship, under the nose. The gun could keep a firing rate of sixty seconds before overheating. If the upgrades worked, Eugene hoped to be able to increase the firing rate to ninety seconds and the energy output up forty percent more, making it the most powerful fusion cannon in the galaxy.

The usual energy output of a fusion cannon was 120 percent. Eugene wanted to push it up to 160 percent. The way to do that would be to tighten the magnetic field and narrow the beam, while at the same time forcing more energy through it. He would have to do this without rupturing the membrane. The last ship to try this had gotten the power up to 130 percent; but when the canon fired, the front end of the ship had exploded. No ship had ever succeeded in amplifying the power without causing an explosion.

Eugene, though, had found a way to succeed. His hands started flying across the keyboard. First, he increased the magnetic field around the membrane housing the fusion energy. Next, he opened the extra intake vent that led to cold space, sucking the cold vacuum, which was colder than ice, directly into the cannon's housing. He had secretly added this on their last trip into Measha Station, using the same sensor-masking program, but that had been an experimental model. The one he was using now was a more advanced model, with an extra vent that would keep the cannon cooler and increase the firing time. Lastly, he focused the beam, making it tighter to increase the power outage. He had to increase the fusion energy from the membrane to the focal point, where the magnetic field forced the energy into a beam.

After he finished the upgrades, he checked to see if the cannon's computer had accepted them. There was a momentary pause. Before the computer answered, however, he heard someone pounding on the door leading to the room. The noise caught him off guard. He could have sworn that he'd jumped ten feet in the air. He turned around and saw that someone was putting dents in the door. It had to be Jonathan. Checking his wrist monitor, he saw that Jonathan was no longer in bed. Eugene had been so engrossed in his work that he had never checked to see if Jonathan was still in his room.

Katrina must have cracked. Figures. He couldn't blame her. She'd *told* him that she was the galaxy's worst liar.

Now, Eugene could hear Jonathan on the other side of the door. "Eugene! Open this door now! Do it, and I promise that I won't kill you—I'll just maim you!"

He turned back to the computer. "Come on, you stupid machine!

Quit chitchatting and confirm my results." As if hearing his commands, the computer screen lit up. "Upgrades have been accepted. Please press enter to initiate."

Eugene was ecstatic. After years of trying to find a way to upgrade the fusion cannon and to get past Novena and Jonathan to initiate the upgrades, he had finally succeeded. Part three would be to test fire.

At this point, several problems would come into play: one would be Jonathan; the second would involve firing the cannon and possibly causing the ship to explode. Time would tell if such a catastrophe would occur; the third problem involved the fact that they were currently in light space, but that situation would soon be rectified.

"Katrina, I'm ready. Drop us out of FTL."

"Eugene, I don't think that this is a good idea," she said worriedly. *Oh, honey, don't do this to me now.*

"Honey, please hurry. Jonathan is about to blow the door open."

"He's going to beat the crap out of you."

"That's *my* problem, not yours."

"Fine. It's your funeral."

A few seconds later, Eugene felt the ship lurch forward very gently. It was now in real space.

He went to the fire control panel, turned on the targeting system, and selected a nearby asteroid. He took a deep breath. *This is it, the moment of truth.*

Before Eugene could press the firing button, Jonathan blew the door open. Pointing his finger at Eugene, he shouted, "Step away from the firing panel!"

Eugene took the cigarette out of his mouth and threw it on the deck. *Shit! Here we go again!*

KATRINA WATCHED EUGENE LEAVE the bridge. She did have faith in his abilities to get the job done, but she worried that Jonathan would kill him when he discovered what he was up to. She knew that Jonathan would not kill her husband; he would just injure him. Badly. And Jonathan wouldn't escape without a few injuries himself. Whenever those two got into a serious fight, it would end with both of them in the medical bay. The last real fight they'd had was the last time Eugene'd tried to upgrade the fusion cannon. They'd beaten each other unconscious. She'd found them in the main fusion cannon room, bloody and bruised. They'd been hospitalized for several days.

Thanks to technology, it would take only hours and days to fix injuries, unless those were too intense. They could regenerate body parts, but some people refused the treatment. She didn't know why Jonathan elected not to have his arm and eye grown back. She tried to get Eugene to explain the reason for Jonathan's decision, but when it came to keeping Jonathan's secrets, Eugene was absolutely tight-lipped.

Ah, Eugene . . . amazing man . . . crazy and a little bit psychotic, but a great man. She'd first met him almost thirty years before. He had been a lieutenant in the Imperial Guard and on a secret mission when she stumbled onto him.

The Tigeras were one of the most feared species in the galaxy—a fighting species that loved to wage war. At the same time, they were an honor-bound species, with a code of ethics and a sense of honor unlike that of any other in the galaxy. They had a humanoid body, golden orange skin, catlike ears, and feline teeth hidden within their mouths. The males had black stripes, while the females had white ones. They had the reflexes and the agility of cats, and, by dislocating their joints, they could fight on all fours. In this form, they were one of the most dangerous forces in the galaxy. The females were extremely calm, unlike the aggressive males. Anyone with a mission to do battle with Tigeras males would have to be very tough—or very suicidal.

Eugene and Katrina had met again several times over the years and begun working together shortly after Eugene left the Imperial Guard to join the Ashlon Republic. During the time they knew each other, they'd fallen in love and married. This had caused a stir in the Tigeras Empire—not because Eugene wasn't a Tigeras, but because he wasn't from a royal bloodline. There was a debate about whether or not, if the king died and Katrina took the throne, Eugene would become king. She and Eugene didn't care; they were just happy to be together. Soon they would celebrate their tenth wedding anniversary. Katrina couldn't wait for that day to come.

Suddenly, Jonathan came on the comm, interrupting her thoughts.

"Katrina, have you seen Eugene?"

She braced herself. *Come on, girl. This should be easy. Just tell them what Eugene told you.* "He's, uh . . . he's taking care of some business. He should be back soon," she replied. *Please let them buy it.*

"What kind of business?" Jonathan asked.

Katrina hesitated, praying that Jonathan wouldn't press her any further. "Just . . . you know . . . using the head and all that."

Jonathan didn't reply. She hoped that he'd accepted her answer. Suddenly she heard a bleep emanating from her console. She looked at it and saw that Novena was scanning the main fusion cannon room. *Oh, man! They must know what Eugene is up to!* But the scan turned up empty; Eugene's program must have worked. Hopefully, Jonathan would let this go.

But luck was not on her side.

Jonathan came back on the comm. "Katrina, I know you love him, but I need to know what he's up to."

Don't crack, girl. Don't crack!

"I promise that I won't hurt him," Jonathan assured her.

"Think, Jon. What is his only other love besides me?" She *had* cracked.

She looked at the monitors and saw Jonathan running all the way to the fusion cannon room.

She listened and watched as Jonathan tried to enter. It took him a few minutes, but he finally got in. Since Eugene's program was masking the cameras, she couldn't see what was happening.

Novena came on the comm, "So—Eugene is in there, isn't he?" It wasn't really a question.

"Yes, Novena, he is. And now those two are probably beating the crap out of each other. We'd better get things ready at sick bay."

"Way ahead of you, Katrina," Novena replied. "Everything is ready and waiting. The Medi-bots are standing by with the hover-stretchers. When we decode Eugene's program, we'll be able to see how much damage they've done to one another."

That was hardly reassuring to Katrina. She hated it when the guys went at each other. Sometimes they didn't know when to quit.

"Men," she said.

"Yeah," Novena agreed. "Men."

There was a moment of silence.

"Katrina, can you tell me when you and Eugene fell in love?" Novena asked.

"Again?"

"I like that story. Please tell it," Novena pleaded. Katrina smiled. Ironic that she'd just been thinking about their first meeting.

She couldn't resist telling Novena the story. She was aware that Novena had feelings for Jonathan. Eugene also had his suspicions that something was going on, but he wasn't one hundred percent sure. Katrina knew that, because Jonathan was still in love with Mei-Ling, if Novena ever allowed her own feelings to be known, the situation would become "one big soap opera drama," as Eugene would call it.

Katrina was about to begin when she heard an explosion and felt the ship shake. Someone was firing on them.

"Novena, who's shooting at us?"

"No one."

"What do you mean, 'no one'?" Being shot at was the only explanation for the ship's shaking and the explosion. "Somebody just shot at us!"

"I'm not arguing with you on that one," she replied. "But the sensors are saying that no one is out there."

"Must be a cloaking device." Katrina knew that some species used cloaking devices that completely shielded their ships. There was serious trouble ahead. "Novena, will you be a dear and break up the boys' party?"

"Sure."

JONATHAN SENSED THAT HE had a big problem: Eugene was at the firing control console, which meant that he had finished uploading the upgrades. Maybe he didn't have a target; if he didn't, there was a good chance that Jonathan could stop him. He glanced at the targeting screen. Eugene had an asteroid targeted. Great! That stripped his odds of stopping him down to almost zero. He would have to play this carefully.

Jonathan drew his M-9 from its holster and set it to STUN. "Now listen, Eugene. The last time you tried to upgrade the cannon, we had to jettison its core; the upgrades caused the membrane to rupture because you had too much pressure on it. So just back away from the cannon, and everything will be fine."

"Come on, Jonathan, just give me one shot. I've done it right this time. Really I have. The pressure is perfect now."

"You said that last time, and the front part of the ship was almost blown up because of it. So just back away!"

Jonathan could see that Eugene was struggling over what to do. He'd known Eugene long enough to know that he would press the button sooner or later. He decided to take Eugene out before he could do it. He pulled the trigger on the M-9, but Eugene dodged it easily.

"Not a bad sh—"

Eugene never got the rest of the words out. As soon as Jonathan shot his pistol, he lunged for Eugene, tackling him to the floor. When they landed, Eugene flipped Jonathan over onto his back. They both jumped to their feet and settled into their attack stances. They moved in a circle, keeping their eyes on each other. These two were the best of friends, but when Eugene started a project, he had to finish it; no one could stop him, not even his best friend. Jonathan knew that he would have to play hardball on this one.

Jonathan took a swing, and Eugene blocked it. Then Jonathan tried to sweep his feet out, but Eugene jumped above Jonathan's leg and, still in the air, kicked him in the head. When Eugene landed, he quickly kicked Jonathan in the chest and then backed away. Jonathan could feel blood oozing from his lip. Eugene had already recovered and was waiting for him. Jonathan decided to finish the fight quickly.

He took out his stun baton, and Eugene retrieved his Taser. They charged each other. Jonathan swung his baton down onto Eugene's shoulder, while Eugene hit underneath Jonathan's chin with the Taser. Both fell to the ground like a sack of potatoes, unable to move.

After a few minutes, they regained motion in their arms, but not their legs. Eugene started to crawl his way to the firing console.

Jonathan couldn't believe that he was still going for it.

"Eugene, what are you doing! We've both lost movement in our legs, and all you want to do is blow up something, mainly us!"

"Oh, ye of little faith. It'll take more than this to stop me. I will crawl thousands of miles, if that's what it takes, to press that button."

"We'll see about that. You'll have to crawl past me first."

"Any time, chrome dome."

The two friends crawled toward each other, ready to continue the fight. Just when they reached each other, they heard a large explosion and felt the ship shake. They looked at each other with worry in their eyes.

Suddenly, Novena came on the comm. "Guys, I hate to interrupt this friendly conversation, but something just hit us."

"A stinger," Jonathan said. He had been in enough battles to know what the impact of a stinger felt like.

Stingers were the nastiest missiles around. A stinger's warhead had a titanium tip capable of penetrating almost all hull types. Energy fields could barely defend against them, except to slow them down. Their basic design was to destroy or cripple large vessels and to destroy military installations on a planet. They were also the smartest missiles in the known galaxy, with an onboard AI that allowed them to react to different targets and to find the best means to destroy them.

"We need you both here on the bridge."

"No problem. We'll be there in—" Eugene looked at his watch. "Give us five minutes. Ten tops."

"What the hell!" Katrina yelled. "Why would it take you both five minutes?"

Jonathan looked at Eugene, annoyed. "We stunned each other. We can't move our legs."

"Again?" Novena asked, sounding exhausted.

"We'll talk about that later," Jonathan said, crawling toward the door. "Just hold them off until we get there."

"Great, stingers!" Eugene mumbled, following Jonathan. "This should be fun."

AMBUSH

JONATHAN AND EUGENE CRAWLED out of the main fusion cannon room. They didn't get more than a few feet before Eugene became frustrated.

"All right, screw this."

Jonathan looked at his friend and asked, "What? You got a better idea?"

Eugene smiled, "Actually, yes. I do." He took out a small injector gun and stuck it in his leg. Jonathan knew what the gun was: an adrenaline booster.

"Great idea."

Eugene nodded as he injected the substance. "I know." Eugene jumped to his feet as the drug did its job, giving him the ability to use his legs.

"We need to get to the bridge." He picked up Jonathan and, putting the 220-pound man over his right shoulder, ran down the hallway and made a right toward the elevator.

Before they could reach it, there was a large explosion that shook the ship, causing Eugene to drop Jonathan, who landed on his head.

He looked up at Eugene, rubbing his head. "If I could walk, I would kick your ass."

"Quit whining. You landed on your chrome; you should be fine." Eugene looked up and saw a fireball heading toward them from the fusion engine room. "Looks like we'll have to do this another way."

"And what way would *that* be?" asked Jonathan.

Eugene smiled and grabbed Jonathan's feet. He started running to the elevator, dragging Jonathan behind him. Eugene could hear Jonathan cursing and felt the heat from the fireball behind him. Finally they reached the elevator. Eugene threw Jonathan inside and jumped in behind him. He hit the button just as the hallway was being filled with the fireball. The doors closed and they headed for the bridge. While going up, they felt and heard the fireball slamming into the elevator doors.

Jonathan looked angrily at Eugene while he massaged his sore skull. "I'm going to kick your butt after this is over."

"Relax," Eugene said. "We can just buff up your chrome later."

The elevator stopped. By this time, the effects from the stun devices had worn off, so the two friends ran for the bridge. "Do you think that we'll make it to Measha Station?" Eugene asked.

Jonathan looked at him, trying to mask his worried face. "I don't know, my friend. . .I just don't know."

Jonathan and Eugene ran onto the bridge. Katrina was frantically pushing buttons at her station, trying to get the weapon and comm systems back online. She shot a look at Jonathan and Eugene. "Where the hell have you two been?"

"Sorry we're late, honey," Eugene answered.

"There was a fireball that wanted to dance with us from engineering," Jonathan said as he jumped into the helm station. Eugene positioned himself at the weapons station, and Katrina focused on navigation and comm. He called out, "Novena, give me manual control!" There was no response.

Katrina shouted at Jonathan, "We lost Novena a few minutes ago! We only have partial control of the helm! If you want it, it's yours."

This was not good. As long as Novena was active, three people could control the ship. Now the three-member crew was doing the work of six people.

Jonathan's hands raced across the controls, trying to stabilize the ship and keep it from rolling. It was moving too slowly and was leaning heavily to the right.

Eugene yelled at Jonathan, "I've got some bad news!"

"And I've got some more bad news!" Katrina added.

"Terrific," Jonathan mumbled. "Lay it on me, guys," Jonathan said as he finally stabilized the ship.

"We've just lost weapons," Eugene said.

"Great! Well, we can't find any targets anyway. What's the other bad news?"

Katrina looked out the forward viewport and pointed at an approaching object. "There's a missile heading straight for the bridge."

Eugene and Jonathan looked out of the plassteel viewport, and then at each other. "Ah, crap!" they said in unison.

CID STARLIGHT, THE COMMANDER in chief of Measha Station, looked out the viewport of its command center, waiting for the arrival of the *Twilight Star*, which would be returning shortly.

"Sir, we have a ship coming in," the radar operator, Mark, announced. Cid turned his attention to the radar screen. There was indeed a ship coming in.

"Operator, identify the ship."

"Identifying it. The computer identifies it as the *Twilight Star*. Resignation #021DBM."

Cid smiled. "I'm glad that the kids made it back home. Now let's see if anybody followed them. Scan the area."

"Scanning, sir. There's a small blip fading in and out. Looks like we might have a ship with a cloaking device."

Cid walked up to the sensor station. "Concentrate on sector 2.2, just starboard forward of the *Twilight Star*. Change frequency of targeting sensors to 8.2 and do a flash point sensor on my mark—3, 2, 1, *now*." The secondary blip suddenly appeared on the three-dimensional radar. The *Twilight Star* appeared as a teardrop-shaped ship with six cylinder engines, three on the starboard side and three on the port side.

The other ship appeared to be an Imperial Guard vessel, a battle cruiser, made up of two and a half spheres. One sphere was connected to the next by a huge cylinder-shaped tube. The first sphere housed the bridge, four missile launchers, twenty-five PPC turrets, and fifteen HPLCs. The second sphere housed four squadrons of twelve fighters each for a total of forty-eight fighters. It also housed fifteen PPCs and fifteen HPLCs. The third sphere was actually half a sphere. It housed forty HPLCs and two six-pack engines, as well as two plasma cannons mounted on the starboard and port sides. It was the workhorse ship for the Imperial Guard, who usually came in packs of two to four ships per task force. *Why is this one by himself?* Cid wondered.

To the comm officer, Jennifer, he said, "Lieutenant, contact the *Twilight Star*."

"Yes, sir," Jennifer said. After a few moments, she remarked, "Sir, I can't raise them. The Imperial ship must be jamming their signal." Cid had a bad feeling about this and ordered the *Twilight Star* scanned for damage. Much to his shock, she was in bad shape. The damage report was read out loud by the station's computer; they had lost their starboard engine, and comms were damaged.

"How far away are they from our air space?"

"At their current speed, fifteen minutes," replied Elijah, the tactical officer.

"That's too long."

Before Cid could give another order, Elijah shouted, "The Imperial ship just shot a missile at the *Twilight Star!*" He looked up at Cid with a shocked expression. "It hit the bridge, sir."

No, not them. Cid was worried, but only mildly so; the gang had gotten out of bigger scrapes than this. For now, he needed to find a way to get them safely to the station, but first things first. That S.O.B. in the Imperial ship had to be dealt with.

"I want you to alert Omega Squadron and tell them to launch ASAP. Ready all missile launchers and turrets. Fire as soon as you have a lock on the Imperial ship." He looked at Elijah. "Lieutenant, I want you to send a stinger straight into that Imperial vessel!"

Elijah gave Cid a thumbs-up and activated the targeting sequence, trying to get a lock on the enemy ship. The cross hairs turned red, showing that he had a lock on the ship, but then he lost it; thanks to the cloaking device, he couldn't keep a solid lock on the ship. He would have to guide the stinger in manually. He brought up the ship's last known location and possible trajectories, then fired the first missile at its present location. Whenever the ship's sector changed, he changed the missile's course along with it. On the screen, the missile got closer and closer to the ship.

Twenty seconds after the launch, the stinger hit the Imperial ship. The cloaking device must have failed, because the ship stopped blinking in and out on the screen. Measha's PPCs opened fire as soon as the cloak went down. When they were finished, Omega Squadron would have their fun.

SARA ALBRIGHT WAS SITTING in a fighter squadron's lounge, watching an old classic TV show from the *Hall of Man* with her squadron, Omega, the *Twilight Star*'s personal squadron, the best of the best, containing a total number of thirty fighters.

Instead of accompanying the *Twilight Star* on their latest mission, her squadron had been told to stay behind on the station, as they weren't needed. Previously, there had been a couple of missions when they hadn't been needed, so it didn't bother her too much.

All of a sudden, the alert lights flashed and the alarm sounded. Before the speaker came on, the pilots started running for their fighters. "ATTENTION, ATTENTION! ALL OMEGA PILOTS, TO YOUR FIGHTERS! I REPEAT, ALL OMEGA PILOTS, TO YOUR FIGHTERS! THE *Twilight Star* IS UNDER ATTACK! I REPEAT, THE *Twilight Star* IS UNDER ATTACK!"

Sara's heart began to race. Her father and the rest of her friends were in trouble.

She ran out of the lounge and headed for her fighter, which was waiting for her in the nearby hangar bay. She climbed the stairs and jumped into her seat. She strapped herself in, put on her helmet, and did a preflight check before takeoff. She spoke into the Omega's comm channel: "All squad members report status." Everyone reported their status to be "hot and ready to burn," their call when they were ready for battle.

Sara called Measha's command center: "CC, this is Omega 1. All fighters are ready for launch."

"All fighters are ready, aye. Please stand by while missiles and PPCs fire on ship."

"Roger." Sara didn't like to wait, but she didn't have a choice.

Looking through her canopy and out of the hangar bay opening, she saw missiles fly outward, toward infinite space. Shortly after, the PPCs opened fire. She watched as blue and silver particle plasma energy fired from Measha's guns and hammered the Imperial ship from an extreme range. Since the Imperials were out of their firing range, they couldn't inflict the maximal damage they wanted, but it caused damage nonetheless. This went on for almost a minute.

When the firing stopped, Cid came on the comm. "Omega Squadron, launch your fighters. Cover the *Twilight Star* while you pull her into our air space. Protect her at all costs."

"Roger, Chief. Omegas 1-12, launch now!" The squadron of fighters launched from the bay, flying at incredible speeds to reach the wounded *Twilight Star*.

Omega's fighters consisted of sub-light engines. They used a miniature fusion reactor to fuel the engines and the rest of the fighters' systems, and they carried HPL auto cannons. All the fighters were also equipped with FTL drives.

When the Omega squadron reached the *Twilight Star*, Sara could see that the ship was in pretty bad shape.

She tried to raise them on the comm, but there was no response.

"Damn! Omegas 2 and 3, come to heading 523 and get a closer look at the *Twilight Star*."

"Aye, ma'am." Omegas 2 and 3 circled the *Twilight Star* once. "She looks like she's in pretty bad condition, Omega 1," declared Omega 2. "She has several hull breaches, and where her engines used to be on the starboard side, there is now a big hole. There is another breach in the hull directly underneath the bridge."

Definitely bad. "Did you get all that, Chief?"

"Yes, I did, Omega 1," Cid answered. "Crash units are standing by in hangar bay 12. Do whatever's necessary to get her here."

"Aye, Chief. Don't worry. We'll bring them home."

"Thanks."

"All right, Omegas, here's the game plan: Omegas 2, 3, and 4 will grapple the *Twilight Star* and tow her back to the station. The rest of us will engage the Imperial ship." Sara knew they wouldn't be able to get the *Twilight Star* to Measha Station fast enough with only three ships towing it. All they would have to do would be to get to Measha space, and then they'd be safe. Whoever was in Measha space would be in range of the station's full defensive and offensive weaponry. They were among the best weapons in the galaxy. Whoever entered Measha space looking for a fight would be at war with Measha Station, and they would lose.

Omegas 2, 3, and 4 flew toward the *Twilight Star*. They shot their grapple hooks onto the ship. Once the hooks were secured, the two Omegas started for Measha space while the rest of the squadron headed toward the Imperial ship. "Omegas 5 and 6, come up behind me. We're going to launch an attack on the starboard side. I want as many of their weapons out of commission as possible."

As the Imperial ship began its attack run, it started to fire its HPLCs at the Omegas. Suddenly, a stream of red with blue particles came at the twelve fighters, forcing them to separate from their attack run. Sara and her two wingmen pulled hard to the right to evade the laser fire. During the attack, Omegas 6 and 7 were hit, exploding into balls of fire. Such fighters had energy fields that absorbed energy attacks and deflected missiles, but they could not stand up too long against the firepower of a battle cruiser.

"Crap! People, how many times do I have to say it? Be careful!" Sara yelled. Her display screen lit up. Her scanners showed some damage around the hangar bay on the central sphere. "Everyone, listen up! There's a weak spot in the armor near the hangar bay on the central sphere. Omega 8 and 10, I want you to fire on that location. I want the rest of you to cover them while 5, 9, and I try to attack the starboard side once again."

The rest of the Omegas headed toward the central sphere while Sara and Omegas 5 and 9 headed for the starboard side of the battle cruiser. "There are a few weak spots near the energy batteries. We have to fly one after the other. Stay close on my 6; I want you two to fire your missiles after me." They closed in on the energy batteries. The ship started to fire its HPLCs and missiles at the fighters. They deployed decoys to take the brunt of the fire, and EMPs to counteract the missiles. They were able to evade the missiles and cannon blast that didn't hit the decoys or the EMPs. Soon, they were in range of the energy batteries.

"Omegas 5 and 9, get ready to fire on my command." She targeted the energy batteries. "Fire now!" The other two fighters fired their missiles, striking the hull. A big explosion of white-and-blue fire erupted from the openings in the hull. "That's a direct hit! Pull back for another pass!"

Suddenly, the ship fired several of its cannons. "Incoming fire! Evasive maneuvers!" The three fighters went into a spin to evade the fire, but they were too close. Sara got hit in the right wing, where it connected to the fuselage, severely limiting her maneuverability and making her an easy target. Omega 9 fired a grapple onto Sara's fighter. He towed her away from the battle cruiser. Suddenly, a huge explosion came from the center sphere.

"Look at that!" Omega 9 shouted. "Eight must have hit the hangar bay." The hangar bay was at a position where only a pilot could get to it—and even if one *did* reach it, the bay was heavily guarded with HPL cannons. Even stingers had trouble getting through; but once in a while you got a lucky shot. Suddenly, explosions were taking place all over the center sphere. It was starting to collapse on itself. That could mean only one thing.

"Omega 8, did you hit what I *think* you hit?" Sara asked.

"You got it, Omega 1. I got one in the hangar bay."

"All right, she's going up like a roman candle."

"Omega 1, we have entered Measha space."

"All right, then. Everyone fall back. Let the station finish her off." The Omegas started to clear out of the station's line of fire, but before they could fire, the ship started to turn away. Soon, it went into an FTL jump.

"Whoa! Did they just go into FTL?"

"Yep."

"That's *crazy*! Are they *insane*?"

"Obviously." The Imperial's ship was seriously damaged; going into an FTL jump would just tear it to pieces.

"Oh, well. Come on, guys. Let's head home." Omega Squadron turned around and headed home, with a seriously wounded *Twilight Star* in tow.

WHAT THE HELL IS THIS?" Mei-Ling yelled as she slammed a pile of datachips on Admiral Wright's desk. Wright uttered a weary sigh. He was not in the mood to fight with the high ruler.

"Ms. Ling, I'm very busy, and I'm not in the mood for this."

"Well, then, *get* in the mood!"

Wright sighed again and looked at Mei-Ling, sizing her up.

Mei-Ling was a small woman, but one that could never be underestimated. She was an excellent and popular leader, an expert in martial arts, and rumor had it that she was one of the best hackers in the galaxy.

"Make this quick."

She picked up one of the data chips, inserted it into her PDA, and read the information on the screen. "I was going over the fleet stations. Can you tell me why the sixteenth and seventeenth fleets are in the outer rim of Imperial space? They're almost on the outer part of Ashlon territory. We've just signed a treaty with them. Are you trying to start another war?"

Wright gave her an annoyed look and said, "There have been reports that Ashlon's fleets are gathering on the outer rim of our borders. I'm just making sure that we have enough ships out there to counter whatever they might be up to."

"Why didn't you inform me of this beforehand?"

"According to protocol, if the head of the military feels there's cause for concern, he or she can distribute forces without consulting the high ruler. I was within the scope of my authority. Don't worry, I would have told you. Eventually."

Years before, when he became the head of the military, he had used the council to add this back-door policy so that he wouldn't have to go through Mei-Ling. It wasn't perfect, but it gave him the freedom he needed to operate his special project. He gave her a smile and started back to work.

"Oh, *please*," she said. "We all know the *real* reason you sent those fleets out in the middle of nowhere."

Wright stopped smiling. He looked up at her, cocking one eyebrow. "And what reason would *that* be?"

She smiled. "You sent them out there because you know that they're still loyal to Jonathan. You don't want them anywhere near you!"

In the Imperial Guard, loyalty and influence controlled the government. Those who had the highest influence were in charge, even if there was someone else on the throne, or if someone was in exile. Mei-Ling was the high ruler of the Imperial Guard. She controlled all the political aspects and ruled all the planets in the Imperial Guard's territory. The navy fleet admiral was appointed by the Guard's high ruler to handle the military aspects, in order to help ease the pressure of governing the hundreds of worlds that made up the Imperial Guard. Usually the high ruler would appoint the navy fleet admiral, the last of which had died fourteen years before, and Jonathan was set to take his place. But Shin-Ling, Mei-Ling's father and high ruler at the time, was assassinated. Through his influence, Wright was able to take control of the naval fleet. He wanted to become the next high ruler of the Imperial Guard, but Mei-Ling was next in line for the throne. Not even Wright could take that from her. Even without the throne, Wright stole a great deal of power from Mei-Ling, but after Jonathan's trial and successful escape, she was able to use that incident to discredit Wright. With that, she was able to reclaim the power Wright had stolen; but because of his influence, she still couldn't remove him as head of the naval fleet.

Wright was becoming more and more annoyed. "You need to stop with these delusional fantasies; they could get you into trouble." He leaned back in his chair. "Is there anything else?"

"Yes, there is one more thing." She ejected the data chip from the

PDA and inserted a second one. "I have been going over the prison barge data sheets. They tell me that you have dozens of barges assigned to systems that are inhabitable for humans. Tell me, Admiral, what is the purpose of this?"

How the hell did she find out about that? he asked himself. "These prisoners are very dangerous. They are being taken to more secure locations."

Mei-Ling just stared at him for a moment, studying him. Then she got so close to his face that their noses almost touched. Her eyes narrowed. "Don't bullshit me, Admiral! We both know that you are lying! I know that you are up to something—and when I find out what, I will expose you to the council, have you removed, and have the rightful admiral installed in your place." Wright got so angry that he started to grind his teeth.

She turned and started to leave his office. Before she left, she turned back to Wright with a huge smile on her face. "And by the way, I know that those barges are full of female prisoners, and female prisoners are good for only two things. Slavery and breeding." The door closed behind her as she left. For a moment, Wright did nothing, his anger simmering to a boil.

When he couldn't hold it in any longer, he screamed, fury spilling out of him. He grabbed his PDA and slammed it on the desk repeatedly until it shattered. When he finished, he heard someone clicking their tongue against the top of their mouth. "Temper, temper, Admiral."

Wright looked into the darkest corner of the room. The Wraith called Brough stepped out into the light. Wraiths, an alien race with humanoid bodies mixed with those of insects, had two legs and four arms. Their two upper arms had two hands with three long fingers and an elongated thumb, while their lower arms were shaped like a praying mantis's and were razor sharp. Their heads were humanoid in shape, with pincers that were hidden in their mouths, and their eyes were fiery red. Their average height ranged from six to seven feet. This Wraith's height was six feet five inches. "Is this how the 'soon to be leader of humanity' is supposed to act?"

The Wraith walked toward the admiral's desk while Wright was speaking. "I have to take over the Imperial Guard first, and Ling is not making it easy for me." Wright plopped down in his chair and heaved another long sigh. "And I have to take down the Ashlon Republic, but if I do that, the Tigeras will move in—"

"That's why we have to strike them first, right at the heart of the empire," Brough interrupted. The Ashlon Republic had a host of allies. With the Tigeras, they had a back-door treaty; this treaty allowed any Ashlon fleet to seek refuge in Tigeras space for protection or regrouping. If they inflicted great damage to the empire, the Tigeras wouldn't be of much help to the Ashlon Republic. "Did you find the heart of the empire?"

"Yes, we did," Wright answered. It was not easy finding the Tigeras Empire's home planet. With the help of the Wraiths' technology, they had been able to follow a Tigeras royal vessel to its main home world. "When do we attack?"

"In one week. By that time, the Shadow Fleet should be ready." The Shadow Fleet was a joint fleet of Wraith and Imperial Guard vessels. "Soon, the Wraiths and the humans will rule the galaxy."

Wright smiled and nodded in agreement. Then his smile turned into a frown. "But now we have a new problem."

"Are you referring to your conversation with Mei-Ling?"

"We have always suspected that she was spying on us, but her outburst about the fleet positions and the prison barges confirms it."

The Wraith was silent for a moment. He leaned back in his chair. "What do you propose that we do about it?"

"Take her out of power."

The Wraith sat up straighter at hearing this. "Really? Is that wise?"

"We don't have much choice now, do we? We're about to attack the Tigeras, so we can't have her snooping around, causing trouble."

Brough fell silent.

"And besides, we knew that it would come to this sooner or later. It might as well be sooner."

After a few more seconds of silence, Brough nodded in agreement. "You're right. Do you have an idea of what to do?"

Before Wright could answer, his comm beeped. "What is it, Ms.

Weeves?"

"Admiral, there is a long-range communication from Captain Albright."

Wright looked at Brougth. "This is the call we've been waiting for." He turned back to the comm. "Patch it through to me."

A screen came up from the floor to the right of the desk. Wright pressed a few keys on his desk, and the screen lit up. On it was a six-foot-tall Caucasian man with green eyes, a clean-cut face, and black hair streaked with gray.

"Admiral, I wanted to inform you that we have crippled the *Twilight Star*. We are going to board her in ten minutes."

This pleased Wright enormously. "Captain, did the cloaking field work on the *Gorgon*?"

"Yes, it did, sir. They never saw us coming, and the information we got on the *Twilight Star* was correct. They almost immediately stopped dead in space."

Brougth gave Wright a smile—or what passed for a Wraith smile. "I *told* you that the information was correct."

Wright gave Brougth a sarcastic smile and turned back to Albright. "Captain, did the Omegas give you any trouble?"

"We have yet to meet any resistance from them, sir."

"They must have split from the *Twilight Star*. We got lucky," Wright said. "Congratulations, Captain. Give me a status report when you reach Imperial space."

"Will do, Admiral."

Before Albright could sign off, his radar officer shouted, "Captain, we have an inbound stinger coming our way!"

"What's the source?" Albright asked.

"From Measha Station, sir." There was a look of disbelief on Albright's face.

"How can that be? They shouldn't be able to see us."

"It's coming in fast and hard, sir."

"Engage evasive maneuvers."

"We can't, sir. The missiles are too close to us."

"Throw up the shields and brace for shock!" Everyone on the ship held onto something as the *Gorgon* was hit. The ship shook violently, and Wright and Brough could hear a loud explosion over the comm.

No. This can't be happening. We can't allow Jonathan to escape again.

"Captain, destroy the *Twilight Star*."

Albright looked at Wright, wondering if his ears were working correctly. "But, Admiral, he's your *brother*."

Even though Albright had it in for Jonathan, he had been given orders never to kill him or to destroy his ship if he came across it. Admiral Wright's new orders puzzled him greatly.

"Sir, the cloaking field is failing. Incoming PPCs from Measha Station!" yelled the radar officer.

Communications started to break up as the *Gorgon* began to take damage. Soon, the comm screen went blank.

The Wraith looked at Wright. "I take it that wasn't the news you were waiting for?"

All Wright could say was, "Nope." He was still in shock. His perfect plan had been literally shot to hell.

Brough smiled and said, "I believe the human saying is, 'Good help is so hard to find.'"

3

THE HARD WAY HOME

JONATHAN SLAMMED HIS HAND on the console, activating the vertical thrusters and thereby enabling the ship to move enough for the missile to hit below the bridge. The fireball from the missile came up through the front deck, the concussion sending Jonathan, Eugene, and Katrina across the bridge. Jonathan was blasted into the command chair, and parts of the helm control console fell on top of his leg, breaking it. His cybernetic eye shorted out from the explosion. Eugene hit the ground and rolled against the wall. His hands got flash burned from the explosion. Katrina hit the wall and landed hard on the deck. She broke a couple of ribs and an arm. All in all, things were not looking good.

"Roll call!" Jonathan shouted. "Is everybody all right?"

"This is Eugene. I'm okay. My hands are a little burned, and I've got a few bruises. What about you?"

"My cybernetic eye is out, and my left leg is broken."

"Which leg?" Eugene asked with a smile.

"No jokes. Where's Katrina?"

Eugene looked around but didn't see her. He stood up and climbed to the upper part of the bridge. She was there, lying on her side. He ran over to her.

"Jonathan!"

"What is it?"

"She's unconscious! She also has a broken arm!"

"Unconscious?" It was not easy to knock a Tigeras unconscious. "Eugene, she'll be fine. Right now we need a damage report."

"I'm on it." Eugene reluctantly left Katrina's side. He raced to one of the consoles and did a scan of the ship. "That blast took out all the forward weapon launchers and the turrets— and worst of all, the main fusion cannon is down."

"Is the core stable?" Jonathan asked.

"Yes," Eugene answered. "It wasn't ruptured."

"That's the best news so far! Help me to the Nav computer."

"Sensors are almost completely down, and we can barely see out through the viewport. What do you plan to do, fly the ship blind?"

"As a matter of fact, yes."

"And people say *I'm* crazy."

"You *are*." Jonathan turned to the overhead and shouted, "Novena! I need you, girl! Come back to us."

"Don't worry, guys. I'm here," Novena said wearily. "One of the blasts knocked me offline for a moment. My scans tell me that we're in bad shape. The whole starboard section is compromised. The magnetic field is barely keeping it together; if it fails, that section will fall to pieces in minutes. We need to get to Measha Station. *Now!*"

"Can you tell us what's going on around us?"

"From the sensors that are still working, I detect several fighters. Scans tell me that they're from Omega Squadron." There was a short pause. "They've fired several grapples onto the ship and are now towing us to Measha Station."

"I love those guys," Eugene said. "Is there anything else out there?"

"Yes, there's also an Imperial Guard ship. Scans tell me it is the *Gorgon*."

"Albright!" Jonathan shouted. "He's never got us this bad before."

"Boy must have got himself some new toys," Eugene added.

"Like a cloaking device and the schematics to the ship," Jonathan said. "He knew exactly where to hit us. Can you get me comms?" he asked Eugene.

"I'll try." There were a few seconds of silence that seemed to last forever. "I have comms with Omega 2."

"Put him on." A few seconds later, Omega 2's voice came on through the speakers.

"*Twilight Star*, this is Omega 2. Come in. Is anybody alive, over?"

"This is the captain, over."

"It's good to hear your voice, sir. Can you tell us the condition of the crew?"

"We have one who's out cold, my XO has a couple of bruises and some burns, and I have a broken leg and a shorted-out eye. Other than that, we're good."

"You guys are lucky. Our scans tell us that your ship is barely holding together. Do you think you can land?"

"No problem. Piece of cake."

"Good. We'll bring you guys as close as we can to Measha Station. Then you're on your own."

"Thanks, Omega 2. Keep us posted. *Twilight Star* out." As soon as Jonathan stopped speaking, the Medi-bots came onto the bridge. "It took you guys long enough to get here."

"Hey, man, this whole ship is falling apart. We had to find a safe route to get here in order to help your sorry asses," said the robot.

Jonathan just heaved a big sigh. "Eugene, we need to have a talk about the robots' personality programming."

"Oh, come on, Jonathan," Eugene groaned. "These guys would be dull without *some* kind of personality."

"Yeah, but did you have to make them so sarcastic?"

"Yes."

Jonathan just shook his head and gave up as the Medi-bots dressed their wounds. The robots could only clean wounds and set bones; other than that, they would need the ship's or Measha's medical facilities to complete the job. "Novena, what's the condition of sick bay?" Jonathan asked.

"*What* sick bay?" Novena asked.

"Great!" Eugene said. "Hey, bot, how's my wife?"

"Don't call me 'bot.' And she's fine. She'll be awake in a few moments."

As Katrina began to stir, she shook her head and rubbed her right hand against it. "*Man, do I have a headache!*"

"That *would* happen after being slammed into a wall," stated the robot.

"Oh, great, it's these guys." Katrina didn't exactly agree with the changes Eugene had made to the Medi-bots either, but she put up with them more than Jonathan did. "Can someone tell me what I missed?"

"The short story is that we got our butts kicked by the *Gorgon*—"

"Albright!" Katrina screamed with disbelief in her voice. "I can't believe he got us!"

"It was only a matter of time. And it's personal," Eugene said as he, Katrina, and the Medi-bots turned their eyes to Jonathan.

"Don't even say it, guys; I didn't know."

"Ignorance is no excuse," Eugene said as he sat down beside Katrina.

"If it hadn't happened, we wouldn't have Sara."

A while back, Jonathan had had a brief fling with Admiral Albright's daughter, Terri. It hadn't lasted long, and the two former lovers had became friends; however, when Terri found out that she was pregnant, the two had talked the situation over and agreed not to get back together just because of the pregnancy, realizing that having a forced relationship was not going to be healthy for them or for the baby. They'd also agreed to share custody of Sara and help each other raise her. It had worked out well; their friendship remained close, and Sara had turned out to be a smart, healthy, amazingly talented woman.

However, Albright had wanted the two to get married; when they refused, he had developed a hatred for Jonathan.

"Still, you should have known the consequences."

"I don't want to talk about it."

"Fine, but we will later."

At this point, an explosion rocked the ship. "Guys," said Novena, "we just lost a section of the starboard hull! The magnetic field can't keep it together much longer."

Omega 2 came on the comm. "*Twilight Star*, a part of the starboard hull just broke off."

"Oh, *really*," Eugene said, his voice full of sarcasm. "We didn't *know* that. Thanks for *informing* us."

"You're welcome. We're going to have to disengage. You're only a few minutes from the Measha Station. We've got you lined up for hangar bay 12. All you have to do is keep her going straight. We'll disengage in one minute. Do you copy, over?"

"Yes, we copy you, over," Jonathan said.

"Good luck and Godspeed. Over and out."

"All right, guys, let's get ready." Everyone got up and walked or hobbled to what was left of steering control. "Novena, give me a neural link."

"Jonathan, just let Novena pilot the ship," Katrina said. The neural link came out of the control console and went into the back of the head, connecting with the brain. It allowed someone to have the ship respond to their thoughts. It was designed for Twilights, and so it should only have been used as a last resort, as it could cause brain damage to humans. The last time Jonathan had used it to avoid an asteroid collision; he'd been connected for only one minute, and it'd almost given him a stroke; this time he would be connected for at least two minutes.

"I would turn it over to her, but the ship is too badly damaged, and manual steering is not reliable at the moment."

"Uh . . . guys, the ship is starting to dip low. We'll be out of alignment if we don't do something," Novena warned.

A thin wire with a sharp needle on its end came out of the control console and snaked up Jonathan's left arm and behind his head. The wire lined up with the base of his skull. Jonathan made a fist and grimaced; it was going to hurt like hell. With that, the needle pieced his skull, sending microscopic fibers throughout his brain. Jonathan could feel his senses and his mind expanding. His brain felt as if it were going to explode.

Blood came out of Jonathan's nose, ears, and eye. Eugene came to his side and kept him steady, as Katrina walked over to them and wiped the blood from Jonathan's face.

"Thirty seconds from the hangar bay," Novena announced. "I can't believe he's doing it."

"We better get strapped in. This ride is going to get a little bumpy," Eugene suggested while setting Jonathan into his seat and strapping him down. He and Katrina headed back to their seats. Before they strapped themselves in, they gave each other a brief kiss. "See you after the landing, darling," Eugene said with a smirk on his face.

"If we survive."

"Such an optimist. That's why I love you." They strapped themselves in, and not a moment too soon; hangar bay 12 filled the viewport. Seconds later, the ship bounced off its deck.

CID AND THE CRASH TEAM, along with some medical personnel, were standing by as the *Twilight Star* came in for its landing. The members of the team wore magnetic gloves and boots to help them scale the ship to the bridge. The ship skidded to the end of the hangar bay, turning 180 degrees in the process. The aft end of the ship slammed into the bulkhead. As soon as the ship stopped, they jumped onto the hull and climbed to the bridge, while another team went in through the entrance.

As the team on the hull reached the viewport, they set a special charge specifically designed to break through viewports. After the charge went off, with Medi-bots and a doctor in tow, Cid jumped through the bridge's viewport, with the rest of the team following soon after. Then the crash team went to work, clearing a path to the ship's entrance, while a Medi-bot, with a hoverbed attached to its base, went straight to Jonathan. Its tentacles cut him loose from the chair and set him on the hoverbed as if he were the Medi-bot's own child. It quickly went to work on his injuries as the doctor examined him. The other bots went to work on Eugene and Katrina.

"How are they?" Cid asked.

"How do you think?" replied Eugene as he lit up a cigarette. "We just got ambushed, had our asses handed to us, and crash-landed. So please tell me, how do you *think* we a—"

A Medi-bot injected Eugene with a sedative. He fell asleep in his chair, the cigarette falling from his mouth onto the deck.

"Thank you," Cid said to the robot. "What are his injuries?" he asked as he stamped out the cigarette.

"He has several burns, bruises, and cuts, and a couple of broken bones due to the crash. He'll need a couple of days in the healing tank."

"What about Katrina?"

"No need—" this coming from Katrina herself as she stood up. "My body is already healing itself."

The Medi-bots grabbed Katrina. "I don't care!" Cid said as the Medi-bots set her on a hover bed despite her protest. "You're going to spend at least one day in sick bay!"

"But I'm *fine*," she insisted.

"No buts. I promised your father I'd take care of you, and I will— despite your best efforts." He turned to a doctor. "Put her to sleep." Before Katrina could protest, she was injected with a sedative. She collapsed with a look that could kill on her face.

"She's not going to be happy when she wakes up." It was Novena, speaking to him through his earpiece.

"I know, but we need to make sure that they're healthy for the coming battles, whether they like it or not. Would you like to come to the infirmary?" Novena was silent for a moment. Cid was beginning to wonder if Novena was going to answer him at all.

But she did. "Yeah, I'll come," she said in a whisper.

Cid turned to the Medi-bots and doctors that were tending to Jonathan. "How bad is he?"

"Very bad," the doctor told him. "I don't know why he's still alive. He should be dead."

"That bad, huh?" Cid asked. At this point, the crash team returned to the bridge, accompanied by the team that had started from the ship's entrance.

"Chief, we've cleared a path to the exit. A team from the infirmary is standing by."

"Good work. Start clearing paths to other sections of the ship, so that it'll be easier to get around while fixing the ship." As the crash team left the bridge, Cid turned his attention back to the doctor and said, "Doc, take everyone to the infirmary. We'll talk about their injuries later."

Cid waited until the bridge was empty, then went over to the star board side, and opened a secret compartment, inside which lay a keypad. When he punched in the pass code, a portion of the wall opened. He stepped through, and the wall closed behind him. He walked down a short hallway until he reached a door. There was a smaller room on the other side with several other doors and an elevator. The doors were entrances that led from various sections of the ship. He stepped into the elevator and rode it down; when it stopped, he found himself facing another hallway. He soon reached a door with another keypad and punched in a different set of codes; he then stepped through and entered the Heart of the Twilight.

The Heart of the Twilight was the chamber where a Twilight could merge with the ship, becoming one with it either permanently or temporarily. The chamber had monitoring, medical, and other life-sustaining equipment, as well as other machines that were hooked up to the cocoon housing the Twilight while it was merged. The cocoon was made of titanium and extra durable plassteel. There were also backup systems installed, in the event that any of the main systems were somehow damaged. In addition, the ship had Mecha-Spiders, little robots that looked like oversized tarantulas with multipurpose claws. Their purpose was to spread throughout the ship, helping to keep it clean and make any necessary repairs.

Just then, the chamber wasn't looking good, and because of that, the spiders were going crazy trying to repair the broken equipment. A portion of the starboard side had collapsed, and half of the equipment was scattered throughout the chamber. Cid stepped over the debris and toward the cocoon. Visually, there didn't appear to be any damage, except for a few small sections on the surface. The monitors next the cocoon showed that Novena was still alive.

Cid banged on the cocoon. "Novena, what's taking so long?" It wouldn't take this long to get out.

"I can't open it from this side," she answered. "I think the mechanism is broken."

He sighed, sensing that she was probably right. "Don't worry; I'll get you out of there. Tell me you're all right."

"Yeah, I'm good. The cocoon protected me."

"Okay, hold on." He walked over to the port side and opened a large storage compartment. Inside he found several tools, medical kits, clothing, and other supplies. There was also a Medi-bot equipped with a smaller version of the cocoon. It would be used to secretly take Novena off the *Twilight Star*.

The compartment was designed to protect everything inside, even during an attack, so that the equipment would be ready for use at a moment's notice. Cid grabbed a welder, a crowbar, a towel, and a robe, and walked back to the cocoon.

He called out to a few of the Mecha-Spiders that were nearby. "Hey, come over here and help me!"

One of the spiders stepped forward. "Sure thing, Chief."

Cid nodded at the spider, recognizing who it was by the sound of its voice. "Hello, Eight-legs. How's the rest of the family?" Eight-legs was the main spider in charge.

"We're doing great, man. We would be better if this ship wasn't falling down around us. We've lost ten of our own spiders." The Mecha-Spiders had an advanced form of AI that allowed them to create their own personalities, feelings, and emotions. They could show emo-

tion through their voices. Their eyes were able to change color to describe their emotions—white for calmness, green for happiness, red for
anger, and blue for sorrow. At the moment, some of the spiders' eyes
shone red or blue, and some were a mixture of the two. Eight-legs'
eyes were red.

"I'm sorry," Cid said, and he meant it. "We'll see what we can do
for them later. Right now, we have to get Novena out of the cocoon."

"You got it, boss." Eight-legs turned to a few others. "Let's go,
guys!"

Cid and the spiders went to work on the cocoon's hatch. Within
minutes they had it loosened enough to open it.

"All right, Chief. This is as good as it's going to get, but we should
be able to get Novena out. We'll fix it later."

Cid thanked them, stuck the crowbar into the cocoon, and started
to pry it open. A minute later, the hatch popped open. Cid reached in
and assisted Novena as she climbed out. He dried her off with the
towel and helped her into the robe, because she was still weak.

Cid was about to help her into the cocoon pod, but she waved him
off. "Wait a minute," she said.

"Novena—"

"Just one minute, Cid," she interrupted. "Just tell me about the
others. Have you received any updates?"

Cid sighed and helped her to a chair. "Before I tell you, will you
let the Medi-bot take a look at you?"

"Fine. Go ahead."

Cid motioned for the Medi-bot. As it looked her over, Cid told
her that he had received no new information about their condition. As
far as he knew, Jonathan was still in pretty deep trouble. Hearing this,
Novena started to cry, and Cid looked at her, reflecting upon her race.

Twilights had humanoid bodies, a blue skin tone, white hair, and
their eyes were tear-shaped and as black as onyx. Their bone structure
was twice as strong as that of humans. Males had heights ranging from
five feet five to six feet five. They had genetic tattoos on the right side
of their faces and on the left side of their chests. Each tattoo was different and symbolized their tribe and heritage. They specialized in

hand-to-hand combat, melee attacks, and firearms, and were also excellent tacticians.

The females ranged in height from five feet to five feet ten inches (Novena was five feet ten). They had wings that were folded beneath their skin, behind their shoulder blades, allowing them to fly with great speed and grace. Their genetic tattoos were located on their wings, making them very beautiful. They were thin but strong, and shaped like a butterfly's wing. Because of this, they were masters of aerial combat.

There was one other Twilight characteristic that made them unique: they had the ability to merge with ships. This feature increased the speed, agility, and firepower of the ship with which they were merged. There were two different ways for a Twilight to merge with a ship: the awakening merge, when a Twilight could merge with and disconnect from a ship at will, and during which all abilities of the ship would increase by twenty percent and only the Twilight's conscience would be connected with the ship; and the eternal merge, when the Twilight's mind and life force merged with the ship, at which time its body would die. This merge was rarely done, as that would increase all of the ship's capacities by seventy-five percent and double the amount of damage it could take.

Cid shook his head. "I can't believe the *Gorgon* got—"

"Wait, wait, wait! Hold up!" Eight-legs interrupted. "You mean Albright hit us? *The* Captain Albright? That guy is a complete idiot! We've always kicked his butt in the past. How did he get the jump on us *this* time?"

"Someone gave him a cloaking device and the plans to the ship," Cid said. "They knew exactly where to hit you."

"In other words, he cheated," Novena said.

One of the Mecha-Spiders joined the group. "Jeez. What is it with Captain Albright? We get more grief from him than from the entire Imperial Guard."

"You mean you don't *know*? I thought *everybody* knew," said Eight-legs as he climbed onto Cid's shoulder.

"Knew *what*? What happened?"

"Well, Jonathan used to date Albright's daughter——"

"Shut up, Eight-legs. Don't you even think about finishing," Novena said as she was being placed in the cocoon pod.

"Well, it's the truth."

Cid gave him a stern look. "Let it go. You know how she feels about Jonathan."

Eight-legs gave up and said, "Fine. Fine." He jumped down onto the floor and went back to work. "Eugene is right: you don't let us have any fun."

"You need to stop listening to Eugene. You've been hanging around him for too long." He asked the Medi-bot, "What's her condition?"

"She's suffering from exhaustion and extreme bruising on her right side. Other than that she's fine."

"Thanks." He looked down at Novena. "Do you want us to give you a sedative?"

"Yes. Please," she said, her voice filled with exhaustion.

The Medi-bot injected the sedative and she began to fall asleep. Cid reached down and took hold of her hand. "Don't worry. We'll take good care of them."

Before she fell silent, she said, "Cid, I love him. I love him sooo——" She never finished, the sedative having sent her into a deep sleep.

Cid bent down and kissed her on the forehead. "I know, kid. I know," he said as a tear rolled down his face. He said a short prayer, thanking the Creator for bringing his family back. He closed the cocoon pod and walked out of the chamber, the Medi-bot close behind.

4

FALSE ARREST

MEI-LING STORMED THROUGH the halls of the Imperial palace, barely keeping her anger in check. She reached her chambers and walked in, closing the door behind her. She stood still for a moment, her mind whirling. Then she screamed and threw her PDA across the room.

When it crashed into the wall, she heard a sound of surprise coming from the bathroom. She looked at the doorway and saw the head of her friend, Isabella Rose, peering out at her.

When Isabella realized that it was Mei-Ling in the room, she heaved a sigh of relief. "Your Majesty, what's the problem?"

"Belle, we've been friends a long time. There's no need to call me 'Your Majesty,'" she said, annoyed.

Isabella gave a shrug. "It's just force of habit."

The Rose family had been servants for the leaders of the Imperial Guard for hundreds of years, always by their side. Isabella was no exception. She looked at Mei-Ling, her face full of worry. "What happened?" she asked. Isabella was of Irish descent, with long red hair and freckles. She was about five feet six and a bit toned out, but still with a feminine frame.

During the centuries after the Destruction of Earth, humans had no more home world to call their own. They embraced what was left of their culture, preserving it as well as they possibly could. In the end, there was no more racism among themselves, or against the alien races that they met. Not all humans felt that way; as a result, a decision had been reached to form two separate governments: the Ashlon Republic, which saw aliens as equals; and the Imperial Guard, which saw aliens as a possible threat to humanity's survival. This period of reorganization was called The Great Divide.

Mei-Ling walked over to her desk and sat down. The room, fit for royalty, was filled with fine decorations and furniture. It contained a hidden work station with dozens of computers; Mei-Ling was a big-time hacker, one of the best.

She heaved a long sigh. "I let the cat out of the bag," she said.

Isabella blinked. "Excuse me?"

"I confronted Wright about the fleet and the prison barge placements that our spies had discovered. I could tell that he was surprised I knew about them."

"That's just terrific! If he wasn't onto us before, he is now. He'll be keeping an extra eye on you."

"I know." Mei-Ling balled her hands into fists. "It's just that *he makes me so mad!*"

She pressed a concealed switch underneath her desk, and a hidden doorway in the wall opened up, revealing a room with a supercomputer inside.

"Whoa! Whoa! What are you doing!"

Mei-Ling entered the room and sat down at the computer. "I've exposed myself to Wright. He's going to come after me."

"Are you sure? Wright can be stupid, but he's not *insane*; besides, people spy on each other all the time. After all, this is politics. Why would he come after you for this?"

"Because there *is* something different about this. Whatever Wright has planned, it's bigger than just becoming the high ruler of the Imperial Guard. And I know Wright: If he feels that he's threatened, he'll attack at the first opportunity. There's only one thing left to do."

Isabella was afraid to ask, but she did anyway. "What's that?"

Mei-Ling booted up the computer. "I'm going to hack into Wright's classified files."

Isabella's eyes widened in surprise. "What! That's crazy. Mei-Ling, I know that you're one of the best hackers there is—but not even *you* will be able to keep out of sight if you go into Wright's classified files."

"I know. I just need a few minutes."

"It will only *take* them a few minutes to find us and break down the door."

"Don't be so dramatic."

Isabella crossed her arms. "All right, then, how do you plan to get out of here?"

"Not me. *You*. You will take all of the information from the files, get out through the secret passage, and give this information to Nesith," she explained. Over the years since Jonathan's exile, Mei-Ling had been gathering information from Wright's files but had not taken the chance of breaking into his most encrypted network. Until now.

"Wait a minute. What about *you*? Aren't you coming with me?"

Mei-Ling didn't respond. Isabella took a step back in surprise. "You're not coming with me, are you?"

"Someone has to stay here and hold off Delta Team." Delta Team was Wright's personal guards, who doubled as his death squad. They handled all of Wright's dirty work. They'd had run- ins with Jonathan and Eugene on several occasions.

The screen lit up and Mei-Ling prepared to go to work. "Get some things packed. Travel light; I don't want anything holding you down." When she didn't hear Isabella moving, she turned around. Isabella was standing still, with her arms still crossed. "A Rose has *never* left a Ling in time of need. I'm not going to be the first!"

"I need you to get this information to the Resistance, Isabella. I have no doubt that his files will contain the real recording of what hap-pened on the Freedom's bridge during the Gypsia incident. Don't worry—Nesith will know what to do."

Isabella's face still showed doubt. "He'll have you killed, Mei." She tried to mask the terror in her voice, but Mei-Ling could detect it.

"If he kills me I'll end up a martyr, and that's the last thing he wants. Everything will turn out all right. I promise." She turned back to the computer and started to type.

Isabella still didn't move. As she said her next words, Mei-Ling could swear that Isabella was smiling, even though she wasn't looking her way. "What about Thomas? Aren't you going to tell him what's happening?"

Mei-Ling stopped typing for a second, then started again. "Don't make me force you to leave!"

"Aren't you going to call him up and tell him?"

"No. There isn't enough time," she said, her fingers flying across the keys.

"That's bull!" Isabella accused. "You still have plenty of time, so stop hacking and call him!"

Mei-Ling typed a few more strokes, then stopped. "Too late. I'm already in. Now start packing. In ninety seconds they'll find out some-one has hacked into their systems. It'll take them about a minute to trace it back to me. Then, depending on where they are, Delta Team'll get here as soon as possible and bust down my door."

"Well, that leaves you two and a half minutes to call Thomas and tell him what's going on—though I give you a maximum of five min-utes before everything goes to hell."

Mei-Ling made a few more strokes at her computer, then pressed the ENTER key. A small empty bar appeared on the screen. In a few seconds, the bar filled up with a message on the screen indicating that all the files has been copied. Mei-Ling took out the datachip, gave it to Isabella, and said, "I still have plenty of time to call him, but I need you to take this chip and get out of here. Now go!"

Isabella reluctantly took the chip and started throwing some things into a bag, while Mei-Ling activated the comm unit. She punched in a few commands and waited, hoping that Thomas would pick up before Delta Team came crashing through her door.

ADMIRAL THOMAS BLAKE SAT at his desk, thinking about the meeting that he had held with the president of the Ashlon Republic. He had in-formed the president that Wright had moved the seventeenth fleet to the D-Zone, the border that separated the two governments. No one was supposed to fight in this section of space. The president told him to keep an extra eye on what the Guard might be doing there.

Thomas also told the president that many of the Guard's female prisoners were being relocated to uninhabited systems they yet to be identified. When the president asked why that was so important, Thomas explained that female prisoners of the Imperial Guard were good for either being laborers or breeding, and that, considering their destination, they certainly wouldn't be doing much heavy lifting. The president wanted him to investigate further, but he would have to be careful. Since they were at peace, they weren't supposed to be investigating each other. If Thomas got caught, it would be considered an act of war. The last time the Imperial Guard and the Ashlon Republic had waged war against each other, it had turned into a long and bloody conflict that lasted for a couple of years. They did not want another one so soon.

So here he was, going over the rest of the day's events and having a glass of wine, when suddenly his comm unit went off. He looked at the identification screen. It had the name *Shades* on the display screen. *Shades* was Mei-Ling's code word whenever she called. He pressed a button, and Mei-Ling appeared on his screen.

"Thomas, I don't have much time," she said.

"What is it?" He could tell that something was wrong. He could see Isabella in the background, throwing some things into a bag.

"I've hacked into Wright's classified files—"

"You did *what?* How could you do something like that?"

"Don't, Admiral," she said, holding up her hand. "I've already gotten the same speech from Isabella. I just wanted to tell you that she's taking all the information to the Resistance. They'll make a copy and send one to Cid, then to you."

Thomas thanked her, even though he didn't like the way he was getting it. Then a thought occurred to him. "Wait a minute—you said *she* would bring it to the Resistance. What about *you?*"

Mei-Ling didn't say anything for a moment. "I'm going to stay behind and stall Delta Team."

Thomas dropped his glass of wine. "*What?*" he screamed. "What are you smoking? This has to be—"

"Please, Thomas, Isabella gave me that speech too. I just wanted to call and tell you what's going on–and that—"

"Mei-Ling," Isabella interrupted, "we don't have much time until Delta Team comes through that door! Make it quick!"

Mei-Ling nodded in Isabella's direction and took a deep breath. "I—I just wanted to say that I love you."

Thomas was silent for a few seconds. It was the first time she'd said those words to him. They had developed feelings for each other after the last war ended. Jonathan and Mei-Ling had been an item when they were younger, but they'd broken up for political reasons. Even when Jonathan had started dating Terri, Mei-Ling still had romantic feelings for him. After he and Terri had gone their separate ways and had became friends, eventually they'd decided to get back together, and this time they weren't going to let anyone scare them away from each other.

When Jonathan was framed and exiled, he'd told Mei-Ling that it was too dangerous for her to be involved with him. With her father dead, Wright in charge of the military, and himself now exiled and disgraced, he knew that the Imperial Guard needed her more then ever. After Jonathan had left, Mei-Ling had held onto the hope that he would come back and fight to regain his rightful place in the Imperial Guard. It had been five years since his exile, and Jonathan still hadn't returned. Thomas knew that Mei-Ling still loved Jonathan, but telling Thomas now that she loved him meant that she was finally starting to let go of her feelings for Jonathan.

Suddenly, there was a knock at the door. "Mistress, this is Delta Team. Lord Wright wishes to speak with you."

A nasty look formed on Mei-Ling's face. "I'll just be a minute." She grabbed her pistol, checked the charge, and turned back to Thomas. "Company is here. I have to go. Wish me luck."

Thomas was still silent. So much was happening so fast. He said the only thing he could think of: "I love you too. Give them hell!"

Mei-Ling smiled and said, "Don't worry, I'll make them cry!" She blew him a kiss. Then she raised the pistol and fired it at the comm unit. The screen turned black.

Wasting no time, Thomas dialed Cid to inform him of what had just happened.

After he punched in a few more commands, the screen lit up. Cid's face appeared. "Thomas, my friend, what is it? Has something happened?"

"You could say that." Thomas then told Cid about the call that he'd just received from Mei-Ling.

Cid was silent before finally speaking. "Thomas, I have something that I need to tell you . . ."

THOMAS REMAINED IN HIS chair after Cid had disconnected, musing over the conversation they'd just had and wondering where they should go from there. He got to his feet and started to pace around his office, his panic rising. He quickly calmed himself. He had a lot to do. Things were going to get very bad very quickly.

It looked as if Wright had finally gotten his wish; he was now in complete control of the Imperial Guard, or would be soon. God help the galaxy when Wright was finally in that position! He sat back down at his desk and looked at the mission package that he and Cid had written out for Mei-Ling's rescuer. Then he activated his comm and punched in a series of codes. Seconds later, the screen lit up.

"Hello, Admiral. Are you finally going to tell me why you need me so badly?" asked the young man on the other end of the line.

"Let's cut the formalities for now. It's time."

"Good. I was getting bored." The young man, Ryan Blake, was Thomas' son and one of Measha Station's best Infiltrators. Before the *Twilight Star* left for its latest mission, Thomas had called Cid and asked for help. He didn't know why at the time, but he had a feeling that he would need some standby assistance. Cid agreed and had Ryan sent to his covert base, which was in Imperial Guard space. Ryan had been there a week, waiting for further orders. "So what's the problem?"

"We have a *big* problem," Thomas said. "Wright is going to arrest Mei-Ling and, no doubt, assume her throne. He's already taken on the title of 'lord.'"

Ryan's eyes widened. "Arrest Mei-Ling? That's pretty ballsy of him. Any particular reason why he's doing this?"

Thomas nodded. "She's hacked into his classified files. Delta Team should be knocking down her door as we speak."

Ryan cocked an eyebrow. "*She actually hacked into Wright's files?*" Thomas nodded again. Ryan ran a hand through his hair. "Well, that would definitely stir the grass beneath his feet. What do you want me to do?"

"I need you to infiltrate Earth 2 and get Mei-Ling out of prison."

Ryan shook his head, not believing what he was hearing. "You actually want me to sneak into the Imperial Guard's home world, go into the heart of the capital, break out the most guarded prisoner they have, and then sneak out? Am I getting this right?"

"Yes."

"Well, that shouldn't be too hard. I've only a few questions. First, am I going to get any help? Second, did you have any inkling that this was going to happen? Third, does Cid know about this? And finally— *are you insane?*"

"One, yes, you will have help. In addition to the Resistance, Isabella will most likely lend you a hand. She's Mei-Ling's best friend, and she won't leave Earth 2 without her. You'll probably find her at the Resistance base. The location will be in your brief package; two, a few weeks ago I had a bad feeling that something was going to happen, so I wanted you to be on standby in case something went down; three, I've just talked to Cid, and yes, he *does* know. Apparently, he's known for a while that she would do this; four, according to my most recent psych eval, no I'm not."

"You had one of your 'feelings'?" Ryan asked.

Thomas was silent. A few people had heard about Thomas's 'feelings.' A little over twenty years before, Thomas had gone to a planet called Serene and participated in a spiritual journey. He'd come back one year later a brand-new person. Somehow, while on his journey, he'd gained the gift of foresight. He was able to sense that certain events would happen before they did. His friends and family were skeptical about it at first, but they warmed up to it after they saw that it worked. Later on, Thomas stopped using it as frequently as he had been doing, for reasons that he kept to himself.

Ryan let out a sigh of frustration. "Fine. You got me. But I do have one more question. What means do I have at my disposal?"

"*Any* means," Thomas said without hesitation.

"*Any* means?"

"Any."

Ryan whistled. "You must really love this woman."

"I'd die for her."

"Normally, when someone tells me that, I tell them to go out on this suicidal mission—but I guess that wouldn't work with you. It's nice to see that you still have your head on your shoulders."

Thomas nodded in agreement, knowing what he meant. The Infiltrators were basically a spy network, but they also performed secret ops from time to time. And if the situation warranted it, they also fought with Measha'a marines. Cid had lots of agents in different governments, spying on political figures and sending the information back to him. He loved to keep tabs on everything that was going on in the galaxy.

With Ryan being a member of Measha Station's Infiltrators, there was no way that, if he were discovered, he was doing this on Thomas's behalf.

"Good luck, son."

"Thanks, and don't worry, Dad; I'll get her back." The screen once again went dark.

THE BLAST FROM THE M-9 destroyed the comm unit. "Mistress, what's going on in there? What's that noise?" She didn't answer them. She activated the self-destruct on her computer. After the wall closed, she heard a small explosion. The self-destruct was enclosed in that room specifically so that the blast wouldn't damage the surrounding area. "Mistress, we're coming in." Sparks from their torch started to shoot through the door. They would be through any moment now.

She ran over to the secret passage that was at the back of the room. Isabella had already opened it and was standing by. "Can't change your mind?"

Mei-Ling shook her head. "Sorry. I've made my choice. Now go."

They embraced for a short moment. "'Bye."

"Good-bye. Be safe."

Isabella nodded and stepped through the passage. It closed behind her as she entered the passageway. Mei-Ling turned her attention back to the door. They were almost through. Turning a table over onto its side as a shield, she knelt down behind it, raised the pistol, and aimed it at the doorway. The sparks stopped and the door fell to the floor.

Delta Team stormed through the opening, dressed in black, with masks and body armor. She fired off shots one at a time. The first shot hit the first soldier who came in the door, burning right through his leg. He dropped to the ground, grabbing the leg and screaming in pain. The second soldier didn't stop in time, so she shot him in the leg. He also went down. She was able to shoot the third man in the leg before Delta Team finally gotten bright and stayed outside the door.

Even from her position in back of the room, she could hear Delta Team arguing among themselves. "Weren't we told that she wasn't armed?" the sergeant asked.

"Obviously we got some bad intel," the captain replied. He turned to the second sergeant. "Toss in a concussion grenade."

"Yes, sir." Concussion grenades gave off a small sound blast that could knock a person out cold or disorient them, depending on how close they were when the device went off. The sergeant pushed a button and threw it through the opening they had made. As the grenade flew through the air, Delta Team readied itself to storm the room.

Inside the room, Mei-Ling saw the grenade. She quickly jumped over the table and, while still in the air, kicked the grenade back out the door. It hit the wall and landed on the floor, right in front of Delta Team. The soldiers looked at it in disbelief before quickly running for cover. They hadn't gotten more than a few feet when the grenade went off, knocking out one of them and disorienting another. They ripped off their helmets and covered their ears as Mei-Ling charged out of the room.

Once outside, she went straight to the nearest disoriented soldier and slammed her palm against his face. The force of the blow knocked him out before he hit the floor. She did a spinning kick to the second soldier's chest, knocking the breath out of him as he hit the wall behind him. She charged up to the last two squad members and prepared to take them out, but they raised their Zeus-Ts and fired stun beams capable of paralyzing her. Both beams hit her in the chest, making her fall to the ground on her back.

She started to get up, but she was hit with two more stun beams. She stayed down for a few more seconds. When she tried to get back up a third time, the soldiers looked at her in shock; they couldn't believe that she was still conscious. She made it to her hands and knees and took a few deep breaths, then looked at them with fury in her eyes and said, "Go . . . to . . . hell!" She slowly lifted her hand, raised her middle finger, and smiled. Then she passed out.

AFTER THE TRANSMISSION ENDED, Ryan Blake remained in his seat, thinking about the mission that he was about to undertake. Throughout his life, he had been on dangerous missions for Measha Station. He was an expert in all manners of combat, but the three areas in which he excelled were stealth, disguises, and assassination. Sometimes he wondered how his family and friends would react if they knew all the things he'd done in the past. Yet, the truth was that there were only a few men and women who were ready to go the extra mile to make sure the job was completed. Those few would do whatever it took to protect the ones they loved and the government they had sworn to serve. He was one of those few. They never talked about the specific details of their solo missions, but they all knew that they had, at one point or another, done something that would weigh on their consciences for a while.

"Lieutenant?"

Ryan looked to his left, the source of the voice. An ensign was standing in the doorway at attention, a datachip in his hand. Ryan motioned for him to enter the room. "What is it?"

"Here's your brief, sir. It just arrived a few minutes ago. You can go over it while we prep the ship for launch."

Ryan stood up and walked to the ensign. "Thank you, Ensign," he said, taking the chip from him. "Call me when the ship is ready."

The ensign gave him a salute. "Yes sir, Lieutenant."

Ryan returned the salute. After the ensign departed, Ryan inserted the chip into his PDA and watched the brief.

5

BAD NEWS AND MORE BAD NEWS

THERE WERE SPARKS FLYING *throughout the bridge as he and his wife strapped into a couple of seats. He looked out of the viewport and saw Measha Station coming closer. He gripped the armchair with his left hand and grasped his wife's hand with his free one. The hangar loomed larger and larger as they came closer to Measha Station. Suddenly, the ship entered the bay and hit the——*

Eugene shot up in his bed, breathing heavily and soaked in sweat. For a moment he thrashed around, not knowing where he was. He began to hear the soothing words of Katrina and his son William. Slowly, he relaxed and settled back down onto the bed, then closed his eyes and passed out.

KATRINA AND WILLIAM WERE sitting by Eugene's bed, waiting for him to regain consciousness. For a while, his limbs made sudden jerking movements as he slept. They could tell that he was having a nightmare. He awoke a few minutes later, and they tried to calm him. When he fell asleep again, Katrina quickly turned to William. "Call Cid and the doctors! Hurry!" He gave her a quick nod and ran to the comm unit on the wall. Within a minute, a doctor, nurses, and some Medi-bots arrived. The doctor checked his heart rate and pulse.

"He's fine. He's still just in a little bit of shock from the crash."

Katrina heaved a sigh of relief, thankful to hear that her husband would be all right. "Thanks, Doc."

A moment later, Eugene began to stir. This time, he didn't thrash about. He looked up at his wife and gave her a big smile. "Well, honey, it looks like we made it." She laughed and gave him a long kiss.

About a minute later, they heard William groan, "Jeez, shall I leave the room? It looks like things might get a little *graphic* in here."

Eugene broke away from Katrina and looked over at his son. "Shut up, you smart-ass." But he broke out into a grin as William came to his side and gave him a big hug. He disengaged and slapped William on the shoulder. "Glad to see you. Have you been keeping up with your studies?"

"Of course."

Eugene nodded in approval. "How long have I been out?" he asked Katrina.

"Sixty hours. The doc said that all your wounds are healed, and that you could leave whenever you woke up."

"Thank God!" Eugene threw off the sheet and stepped down from the bed. "Hey, guys, where are my clothes?"

William jerked his thumb toward a door that was off to Eugene's right. "They're in the bathroom. We figured you'd want them the moment you were awake."

Eugene smiled; his family knew him all too well. "Thanks." He entered the bathroom and changed into the clothes that had been laid out for him. When he finished dressing, he left the bathroom and found Cid sitting in a chair. "Good thing you're here," Eugene said. "I was going to hunt you down in a minute."

"I figured you would," Cid said. He stood up from his chair and ran his hand through his hair. "So tell me how you want to hear the news about Jonathan? Do you want it sugarcoated, or do you want the truth?"

Eugene looked at his son, his wife, and then Cid. "Right in between the eyes."

Cid nodded. "The neural link left him with serious brain damage. He's in intensive care right now."

Eugene was both horrified and amazed. "How the hell did he survive, Cid?"

Cid snorted and shook his head. "The doctors said it was because we got to him in time. A priest might say that it was a miracle; personally, I think it's because that guy is just plain hard to kill."

Eugene had to agree with that. Jonathan was one tough mother. "Where's Sara?"

"She's with Jonathan. She hasn't left his side since the doctors placed him in his room."

Eugene raised an eyebrow. "They let her stay after visiting hours?"

"More likely they couldn't get her to leave. They would have called security, but I told them they would have a few more patients if they did." That was the truth. When it came to someone getting hurt in those two families, it was nearly impossible to get them to leave the bedside of one of their own without somebody else getting hurt.

"Can we see him?" Eugene asked.

"Of course. Let's go."

THE GROUP WALKED TOWARD Jonathan's room in silence. William could tell that everyone was nervous, even though they tried not to show it. On the surface they were all calm and quiet; on the inside, however, they were screaming, afraid that they were going to lose Jonathan.

The two families had been together since before humanity left Earth. Over the next thousands of years they had experienced both loss and tragedy, but they'd also had many happy moments together. It was because of this that the families had survived together for so long. Now William prayed for the best.

THEY REACHED JONATHAN'S ROOM within minutes. Inside, they found him lying on a bed, tubes in his nose, mouth, and arms. Sara was sitting in a chair beside the bed. When she saw the group enter, she walked over to them and gave each a hug.

"I'm so glad that you guys are okay!"

Eugene felt the same way. "I'm glad we're okay, too." He looked over at Jonathan and walked toward his bedside. Silence fell over the group as they stood back to give Eugene some space.

Eugene and Jonathan had been best friends since childhood and had remained friends after Eugene left the Imperial Guard to join the Ashlon Republic. They'd been to hell and back together; now it hurt Eugene deeply to see his best friend in such poor condition.

"Has there been any sign he's aware of anything that's going on around him?"

Sara looked as if she wanted to say something that would have a positive effect, but she just shook her head. Silence once again engulfed the room.

The doors opened and Jennifer and Elijah entered the room. Cid spoke to them in a hushed voice. He held up one finger, indicating that he needed a moment with them, and walked outside the room. Everyone waited patiently for them to return. A minute later, Cid came back.

"Sorry about that," he said.

The group let it go at that, but a thought came to Eugene.

"What was *that* about?" he asked.

Cid shook his head. "Don't worry about it."

"No, I think I will." Cid was about to say something, but Eugene cut him off. "Does it have anything to do with my nephew?"

Cid didn't say anything for a moment. Before the *Twilight Star* left, Ryan had been pulled away to do a mission. They'd been told nothing about what it was, and now a week had passed since he left; there had been no word from Ryan, or any information about what he was up to.

"Yes, it does." The group waited for him to continue. "Thomas asked for him."

"And?" Eugene asked.

"I'm sorry, Eugene, but I can't say anything else."

"Oh no," Eugene said, shaking his head. "Don't give me that 'classified' bullshit! I want to know what's going on! Right now!"

Katrina stepped forward. "Me, too. I haven't been able to send or receive any communications since we arrived. So what's the story?"

Cid was silent, his face displaying no emotion. Then he tapped his earpiece. "Lock down intensive care unit room no. 6." The windows went dark, and the lights turned red. Every room in Measha Station was built so that it could be locked out, preventing anyone from listening in on whatever was being discussed at the moment, and so enabling Cid to talk about anything anywhere.

"What I have to say doesn't leave this room. Don't even *talk* about it or *whisper* it. Understand?"

Everyone looked at one another and nodded their heads in agreement. Cid had rarely used the lockout or spoken to them this way; something very serious must have happened.

Cid took a deep breath and started to speak. "Before your last mission, Admiral Blake called me to ask if he could borrow Lieutenant Blake for a mission. He didn't know how long the mission would take, but it could be weeks before Ryan's returns." Cid was all business, using his friends' ranks and last names instead of their first.

"He called me yesterday and informed me that Mei-Ling had hacked into Wright's personal files. They caught her in the act and sent in Delta Team to arrest her. My contacts within the Resistance on Earth 2 confirmed this. At this moment, she's awaiting trial for her crimes." He didn't add that he'd already known about Mei-Ling's mission. That would have infuriated Eugene even more than he already was. Better that he didn't know about that just yet.

Sara was the first to speak. "What exactly *is* Ryan's mission?"

"He's to infiltrate the palace, get Mei-Ling out of prison, and bring her back here. The Ashlon Republic can't send its own agents, for fear that if he or she is caught, it could ignite another war. If Ryan were to be caught, no blame could be placed on the Ashlon Republic." To Eugene, he added, "Are you okay?"

"I don't know, Cid. I just don't know." Cid was very proud of Eugene for the way he was handling himself. In his younger days, he would have put a few holes in the wall. Now Eugene stood up and came over to Jonathan's side.

"These past few days have been weird—I mean, a few days ago we were celebrating a successful mission, and now the whole universe feels like it's going to hell in a handbasket." Another thought came to him. "When did Thomas find out about the arrest?"

"About two and a half days ago."

"Then why did he pull Ryan away so—" He stopped and smiled. "Of course! His foresight!"

"What?" William asked.

"Because of his foresight, Thomas knew that something was going down," Katrina explained. "He pulled Ryan out and had him on standby for whatever it was that he saw."

As Eugene walked over to the door, he said, "Cid, end the lock-down, please?"

"Why?"

"I need to get out of here and think."

"But, Dad, what about—"

"There are too many things happening at once. I need to go some-place other than here."

Cid spoke into his ear-comm, and the lights and the windows returned to normal."

"Where will you be if there's a change in Jonathan's condition?"

"In the Hall of Man," he said as he walked out the door.

Katrina was the next to leave. "I'll be in the gymnasium." As she left the room, her face was focused on Jonathan. *I'm sorry, sir. I've failed you.* She walked out the door without another word.

Cid looked at William. "Ensign."

"Yes, sir."

"Can you please get back to your training?"

"But Jon—"

"There's really nothing you can do, son. All we can do is pray for Jonathan and wait." Cid could tell that William didn't want to leave a man who was family, but he did what Cid asked and left the room.

Sara returned to Jonathan's bedside. She held his hand in hers. Cid could hear her whispering, "Please, Dad. Come back to us. *Please.*" Even with all the modern medical technology, the brain was still the most fragile and difficult organ to repair. In the end, it would be up to the patient's will to survive.

Cid wondered how he was going to get her to leave, but he gave up that thought very quickly. There was no way that Sara was leaving Jonathan unless he either passed away or woke up. He silently left the room and entered the one beside it, an observation room that Cid had set up. A large monitor on the wall revealed what was going on in Jonathan's room. Novena was watching the monitor but looked at Cid when he entered the room.

"They took the news pretty well in there," she said.

"Don't let that display fool you," Cid warned her. "Right now, they're probably screaming and taking out their frustrations in their own way."

Novena turned her attention back to the monitor. After a few minutes, she turned back to Cid. "He isn't going to wake up, is he?"

Cid wanted to lie to her, but he couldn't. He sighed in frustration. "I'm sorry, Novena," he said as he put an arm around her, "but it looks as if he won't survive."

Novena started to cry as she buried her head in his shoulder. Then she lifted her head up and looked at him. "Is there anything they can do?"

"I don't think so. The brain is just too badly damaged."

"What about the DNA regenerator?" This was a device that took a fresh DNA sample from the patient and used it to duplicate and replace damaged organs or other damaged body parts. In this case, they needed to repair the brain. It didn't always work. There was an eighty-percent success rate if the brain had minimal damage in certain areas. The doctors had said that his brain was just too damaged for the regenerator to work.

"There's just too much damage. Even if the Nano-bots were to work overtime, they say Jonathan's life will expire before they could finish the repairs."

"No!" she said, shaking her head defiantly. "There's something that can be done!"

"What's that?"

She looked at him with fire in her eyes, and suddenly Cid knew what she meant. "No!" he said. "No, no, no! You are not properly trained. It could *kill* you!"

"We don't have a choice. we'll need him for whatever lies ahead."

"It won't do us much good if you die in the process."

She gave him a stern look. "I'm doing this whether you like it or not! We need him . . . *I* need him."

Cid was about to say something, but he stopped. Deep down, he knew that she was right. "Fine. But you're going to have to expose yourself, because there's no way that Sara is leaving that room."

She nodded. "I understand."

"Well, then," Cid said. "Let's do it!" They left the room.

Sara sat at her father's bedside, frightened, holding on to his hand as if his life depended on it. She could not believe this was happening. With Mei-Ling's capture and the attack on the *Twilight Star*, she was starting to believe that Eugene had been right: the whole universe was going to hell in a handbasket, and they had front-row seats. Her stomach growled, and she covered it with a hand. She hadn't eaten much since her father was admitted over two days before. She got up and walked over to the food dispenser in the room. She punched in a few commands, and the port opened, revealing a glass of water and a tuna sandwich. She would get something healthier later; right now she just needed something in her stomach. She went back to Jonathan's bed and sat down, thinking about how much her life sucked at the moment. In five years she had lost her father, her cousin, and her uncle. She felt so alone. She wished that Ryan was here to comfort her.

And what about her mother? She dreaded telling her. Even though her parents had never married, they'd remained friends. When her father was arrested, her mother had stood by him the entire time. She would be devastated!

She heard the door open, and she turned to see Cid. She hadn't even noticed that he had left. There was someone with him—an alien with blue skin, eyes with silver speckles, and hair that was white as snow. Her brain searched for the name of this particular species. It finally came to her: a Twilight! What was *she* doing here?

Sara got to her feet. "Who's this?" she asked.

Cid didn't reply but took a step away to let the Twilight pass. She moved toward Sara, looking nervous. "Hello, Sara. It's good to see you in person."

Sara's eyes narrowed. She knew that voice, but from *where*?

Her eyes went wide. That was Novena's voice! But Novena was eternally merged with her ship. So who was *this*?

"Okay, Cid, what's going on?" she asked. "Who is *this*, and why does she have Novena's voice?"

The Twilight smiled and said, "Because I *am* Novena."

Sara didn't say anything, her mind searching for her next words. "That's not possible," she finally said. "Novena is eternally merged with the *Twilight Star*. Let's try this again—who *are* you?"

"It's me, Sara," Novena insisted.

"I need more than that, lady!"

Novena stepped forward and extended her hand. "Give me your hand, please."

Sara looked at her hand, and then at Cid, who gave her a nod.

With a little uncertainty, she gave the Twilight her hand. Novena he took hold of it and covered it with her other hand.

She took a step closer to Sara. "You have always been good at judging people, Sara, so look into my eyes and tell me what you see."

Sara was taken aback by the Twilight's behavior, but she didn't let it show; instead, she looked into the woman's eyes, wondering what she would find there.

It is said that the eyes are the windows to the soul; what Sara saw in the Twilight's eyes were love, hope, and respect, combined with a voice she recognized.

Slowly, her mouth turned into a smile. She threw her arms around Novena and laughed with delight. "It is *you*, Novena. It *is* you."

Novena smiled and returned the hug. They didn't move for a few minutes. When they separated, they both had tears in their eyes.

"It's good to finally see you in person, Sara."

"How are you here? I—we all thought that you were merged with the ship."

Before Novena could answer her question, an alarm went off on the life monitors. Doctors came rushing into the room to check his vitals. After a few minutes of waiting, which felt like hours, a doctor came over to the group.

"I'm sorry. His neural connections are starting to break down, and his brain functions are beginning to fail. There's nothing else we can do for him, except to wish him a peaceful journey." He left the room. The others followed, giving them looks of regret. "We'll leave you alone now," the last doctor said.

After they left, Cid looked at Novena. "Do you think you have enough time?"

She had a thoughtful look on her face. "I don't know, but I have to *try*."

"Then let's do it!"

Sara was looking back and forth between Cid and Novena, wondering what they were talking about. "Do either of you care to tell me what you guys are talking about?"

"We don't have much time to explain, but Novena is going to try something called the Kiss of Life," Cid answered.

"The Kiss of Life? That rings a bell."

"Cid can explain it to you," Novena said as she made her way to Jonathan's side. "Can you please contact the others and tell them to come down? If *you* want to tell them, go ahead."

Cid nodded. He turned toward the door and took hold of Sara's arm. "Let's go, Sara. Novena will need all her concentration, and our being here won't help her at all."

"But—"

"I'll explain everything outside, but we have to leave."

They left the room and entered the observation room. When the doors closed, she looked around the room and saw the monitor. "So *this* is where you've been keeping an eye on me?" Before Cid could say anything, she said, "Never mind. Now, will you tell me what's going on?"

Taking a deep breath, he began. "Novena is going to do a special procedure called the Kiss of Life. It's an ability taught by the healers of her species; a Twilight can take his or her life force and pass it to the dying—and sometimes even the recently dead."

"What does it do?" Sara asked.

"It will completely heal or resuscitate the person they are treating," Cid answered.

"What's the catch?" she asked.

"She has to give just the right amount of her life force to him. If she gives him too much, she could die; or, if she gives him too little, *he* could die. And the more time she has to meditate, the better chances she has to survive."

Sara looked toward the room, her face full of worry. "How long would be a reasonable time?"

No sound came from Cid. Sara turned her attention back to him. He gave a heavy sigh. "About thirty minutes would be a reasonable time. The most, forty-five."

Sara's eyes and mouth went wide with horror. "He might not *have* that long!" Cid nodded his head in agreement. "We . . . wha . . ." Sara stopped to calm herself. After a minute, she continued, "Why so long?"

"She can still do the Kiss of Life, but it will be dangerous. A Twilight healer can do it any time at any moment; Since Novena isn't a healer, the more time the better."

"What happens if she doesn't have enough time to prepare herself?"

Silence. "Then, as I say, one or both of them could die."

Sara turned her eyes to the floor, trying to hide her tears, but she couldn't, and so, with tears in her eyes, she looked back to Cid. "What can we do?"

Cid didn't say anything for a moment because he, too, was on the verge of crying. Finally, he said, "Pray, Sara. That's all that we can do."

She wrapped her arms around Cid, and he wrapped his arms around her in return.

NOVENA STOOD STILL, CONCENTRATING. Her wings unfolded from beneath the skin on her back, and she spread them out to their full width. She sat down on the floor, closed her eyes, and began to gather her life force.

6

HEALING

E UGENE BLAKE SAT ON a park bench, listening to music and admiring the view of the park in the Hall of Man. He prayed to God for a miracle.

Measha Station had been built by an ancient race called the Nexus. They had set the station up as a safe place for all races to come and live peaceful lives.

In the world of galactic politics, it remained neutral, preferring not to be part of any government; therefore, no government had any say in what went on in Measha Station.

The station itself was nothing short of a technological marvel. One of the biggest space stations in the galaxy, it was shaped like a bullet, with four engines on its sides, and was powered by means known only to Cid and a few engineers.

The station contained greenhouses that grew food, and fields that contained animals for breeding and consumption. There were living quarters, recreation facilities, factories, hangar bays, advanced medical centers, and many more facilities.

But there was one feature that set this station apart from all the others: It had the Hall of Man.

The Hall of Man housed man's history from before the Destruction of Earth. After the Great Exodus, many artifacts were stolen or sold for profit. Even during those hard times, there were always some who tried to make money from others' misery.

A thousand years before, Measha Station's then-commander in chief decided to try to save man's history by sending its agents out across the galaxy to hunt down lost artifacts. Over the course of time, they'd found so many that they needed a large facility in which to store them.

Then they thought of a perfect solution: Instead of keeping the artifacts locked away, they would share them with everyone.

So they built the Hall of Man for that purpose. It contained several large buildings hundreds of feet tall, each storing artifacts from a time period that corresponded with that of Earth.

There were several large courtyards that also contained artifacts for viewing. Here, people could also walk, run, relax, read, talk, or do whatever they liked. That became one of Eugene's favorite places to go.

Just then, though, he was not focusing too intently on the view, his mind occupied instead by the thought that he might lose his best friend.

He and Jonathan had been together since childhood. They were like inseparable twins. When their parents disappeared almost forty years before, the bond between them had strengthened even more.

During their time in the Imperial Guard, they were great when they worked together. Like all military personnel, there was a little bit of a rivalry to make rank faster than the other, but it didn't hurt their friendship.

When the mother of Eugene's son died, the circumstances of her death drove him from the Imperial Guard. Jonathan tried to keep Eugene from leaving, but his efforts failed. Before Shauna's death, he'd become involved with a Tigeras named Katrina Tarr, who just happened to be the royal princess.

At first she was just chasing him because he always outmaneuvered her; but in time, she saw something in him that made her fall in love with him. The same happened to him. After Shauna's death, he defected to the Ashlon Republic and later married Katrina.

Even though it hurt him to leave the Imperial Guard, he couldn't stay. After he left, he and Jonathan clashed in several battles but were able to remain friends.

After Jonathan had been arrested for treason and murder, Eugene formed a plan to break Jonathan out of prison. Along with Katrina, he was able to help Jonathan escape, and they'd been together ever since.

Even though Jonathan was not officially part of the Ashlon Republic, he did take on missions for them. Since he once had been a great Imperial Guard admiral, the rest of the galaxy's governments weren't about to allow him to run free throughout the galaxy. Eugene was able to convince them to let Jonathan form a military group that would have members from different governments to act as liaisons.

Eugene represented the Ashlon Republic, Katrina the Tigeras, Novena the Twilights, and Ryan and Sara from Measha Station. Cid handled all jobs, which was a good thing. Measha Station was neutral, so the assignments could not be traced back to them.

This had been their life for five years. They had had many close calls, but they'd always pulled through. This time should be no different—but from the look of things, it could be the end.

Eugene was still reminiscing about the past when his comm unit vibrated. He turned off his music and answered it.

"General Blake here."

"Eugene, it's Cid. I'm calling about Jonathan."

Eugene froze. He was afraid of this call; it could mean either that his friend was making progress or that there was nothing more to be done for him.

". . .Eugene?"

Eugene shook his head to clear his thoughts. "Yeah, sorry, Cid. What's happened?"

"I have some news. I need you to come to the hospital ASAP!"

Eugene sat up straight, his hand gripping the armrest of his bench. "Is it bad?"

Cid was silent before speaking. "Just get down here!"

"Cid—"

"I'm not saying any more until you arrive."

Eugene wanted to argue with him, but he knew it would be useless.

"Fine. I'm on my way."

"I'll contact the others and tell them to meet you at the hospital."

After Cid disconnected, Eugene remained in his seat, wondering what was going on. Something was amiss. Cid was avoiding talking about Jonathan. Eugene knew Cid; Cid had a purpose for everything he did. Deciding to figure out what was going on, Eugene left the bench to find the nearest transporter.

WILLIAM BLAKE EASILY GRASPED the pipe from which he hung. Below him, a guard was walking leisurely, as if he didn't have a care in the world. The entire hallway was dark and quiet except for the guard's footsteps. William was silent, waiting for the guard to reach his position.

When the guard was directly below him, William swung down and grabbed him by his throat with both arms. With his legs wrapped around the pipe, William lifted the guard and put him to sleep. For the few moments that the guard was still conscious, he kicked his legs, trying to get out of the headlock. It didn't work.

Within seconds, the guard was out. Keeping one arm around him, William grabbed the pipe with the other and, making as little noise as possible, lowered himself to the ground.

He swung the guard over his shoulder, then quietly carried him to a nearby closet and placed him inside. He continued stealthily down the hallway, staying as close to the shadows as he possibly could. When he reached the corner, he pressed himself against the wall. Peering around the corner, he saw two guards standing a few yards away, talking to each other.

He took out his M-9 and set the pistol to STUN. He took careful aim at the first guard's head and fired. He then quickly turned his sights to the other guard and fired a second shot. After the guards had fallen to the floor, he silently crept out from his hiding place. He kept the M-9 out and swept the hallway in front of him.

When he ascertained that he was no longer in any danger, he holstered the pistol and proceeded to hide the bodies.

Suddenly, lights came on everywhere, and the guards stood up. A voice came over a speaker in the room.

"Exercise is over. Ensign Blake, there's someone who wants to speak with you."

Someone wants to speak to me, he thought. No one was allowed to stop a training session unless it was a very important matter.

As he left, the area faded away into a large room. The two "guards" followed him, rubbing their heads as if massaging a headache. William smiled to himself: Those beams might be harmless, but they sure could leave a headache.

The "guard" that he'd "choked" to sleep joined the group, rubbing his throat.

"Jeez, William," he complained, "go a little easier on me next time, willya!"

William's smile widened. "Sorry," he said as they reached the exit.

The room that he'd just left was called a hollow room. It made objects out of light and turned them solid. Measha Station and other governments used them for training purposes, but they could also be used for recreation.

William was in training to be a member of the Infiltrators, the greatest spy network in the galaxy. It was composed of different races trained in a variety of skills, including the employment of stealth, hand-to-hand combat, and small and large arms. Its members learned to drive every type of vehicle, use high-tech gadgets, and much more, incorporating training from and with the marines. They had been a part of Measha Station since its beginning. Cid used them to keep an eye on every government in the galaxy. He liked to know what everyone was up to.

An Infiltrator was trained for years before seeing action. In an Infiltrator's final year, he or she would go out on small missions for in-field training. William had been training for six years. Cid liked to start training Infiltrator candidates while they were young, believing that the young soaked up information like a sponge. William still had another year to go before he would be allowed on-site training for one year, after which he would graduate as a full-fledged Infiltrator, eligible to be sent out on his own missions, just like his cousin.

He entered the control room. The operator was sitting at the controls. "Who called?" William asked.

"It's the big chief. He wants to talk to you."

KATRINA VAULTED OFF THE handlebars. She fell toward the ground, landing perfectly on her feet, then sprang into a full run toward the wall. When she reached it, she planted her feet onto it, one foot after the other, and started climbing it.

When she'd reached about halfway to the ceiling, she bent her knees and launched herself off the wall. She flew through the air, and her hands grasped a set of handlebars. She swung her legs back and forth, gaining momentum. When she felt that she had enough, she let go of the handlebars and flew through the air in a somersault.

She reached out with her hands and grasped another pair of handlebars. Using the momentum that she had from the jump, she swung her legs forward and let go. Flying through the air, she caught another bar. She repeated this maneuver five more times.

After releasing the last bar, she landed perfectly on the nearby platform.

She turned around and surveyed the gym.

It didn't look like a regular gym; it looked more like a training ground for some military group. Cid used it to keep his men in shape, but it was open to the public. At the moment, though, Katrina had the place to herself.

The gym had separate rooms, each containing different exercise machines as well as areas for weight lifting, running, swimming and aerobics. There were also areas reserved for fighting. That would be her next destination.

Fighting and working out usually kept her calm when times were hard. It gave her a sense of peace. But it wasn't working this time; she still felt restless and hopeless, realizing that there might be nothing she could do for Jonathan. She had served under him for five years, and he had become one of the most loved people in her life.

She shook those thoughts from her head. She was doing exactly the opposite of what she had been trying to do: find some peace, not create more sad thoughts. She grabbed the nearby rope ladder and prepared to climb down.

As she finished descending the ladder, she heard her comm beep from her bag. She took it out and placed it on her ear.

"This is Katrina Tarr-Blake. Who is this? . . . Oh, hi, Cid . . ."

EUGENE WAS SITTING IN THE waiting area outside the transporter room of the medical center, waiting for Katrina and William to arrive.

The transporter was used around Measha Station. All locations had one, so that if someone needed to get from one side of the station to the other in case of an emergency or for some other reason, they could be there in a matter of seconds.

Although that was a very fast means of transportation, not that many people would use it. Many still used hover-cars, walked, or took buses and trains to get from one point to another, believing that, when the transporters broke travelers into little pieces and put them back together, those individuals would come out on the other side changed from their original selves. Others thought it a lazy way to travel, and some people just liked a good old drive or stroll through the station.

The door opened, and Eugene turned his head. Katrina was walking in, with William following behind her.

"Let's go."

CID'S COMM BEEPED. "What is it?" he asked.

"Sir, this is the transporter room. General Blake, Princess Katrina, and Agent-in-Training William Blake have just arrived by transporter. They should be at your location soon."

"Thank you." He disconnected. "They're on their way," he told Sara.

"Have you figured out what you're going to tell them?"

Cid smiled. "I'm working on it."

"This should be fun," she said, amused.

CID AND SARA WERE STANDING outside Jonathan's room when Eugene, Katrina, and William arrived.

Eugene was the first to speak. "What's going on, Cid?"

"I'll tell you, but not out here."

Cid took them into the observation room and directed them to the monitor. On it they saw Jonathan, with Novena beside him.

"Who's that, Cid?" Eugene asked.

"It's Novena." Everyone looked at him, confused. "To answer what will no doubt be your next question, no, she's not eternally merged with her ship. She never was; it was just a ruse."

"Why?"

"Novena has the special ability to control ships, either by direct touch or by thought, depending on the distance."

"I've heard about that. Apparently, it's a very rare ability." William whistled. "Amazing."

"Yes, that's all good, but why did she hide it from *us*?" Eugene asked.

"Because the Alien League found out about her abilities and put a bounty on her head," Katrina explained. She gestured to Cid. "Cid gave her a new identity and ship. When you broke Jonathan out, Cid called her in to help. You know the rest."

The group turned their heads to Katrina. "How do you know this?" Eugene asked.

"Because she told me. She wanted at least one person other than Cid to know about her."

"Why didn't you tell us?"

"She asked me not to, and I would never betray her trust."

Eugene wanted to be angry with her, but he couldn't. A friend had entrusted Katrina with personal information, and she had kept her friend's confidence. How could he be angry about that?

Deciding that it would be pointless to argue further, Eugene went on to the next subject. "What about Jonathan?"

"His vitals are failing. The doctors don't think that he has much time left, so Novena is going to try the Kiss of Life," Cid said.

"Is she a healer, too?"

"No, she's not. She knows the basics, so she's going to try as soon as she has mustered enough strength."

"A Twilight who's not a healer is trying the Kiss of Life?" Katrina asked. "That's pretty risky, Cid."

"True, but we have no choice."

"So what now?" William asked.

Cid shrugged. "All we can do is wait."

NOVENA GLANCED AT THE life monitors, then down at Jonathan's form. There was no more time left; she had to do the Kiss of Life *now*!

She cupped his face in her hands and opened his mouth. Then she bent down and kissed him. She felt the energy that she had built up in herself slowly leaving her body and entering his.

EVERYONE ELSE'S EYES WERE GLUED to the screen. They looked at each other, wondering what they should do next.

Before they could decide, Novena separated her mouth from Jonathan's. Though she wasn't kissing him any longer, they all saw her life force continuing to enter Jonathan through his mouth. It resembled a blue spirit leaving her body and entering his.

When the transfer stopped, Novena closed her mouth and collapsed onto the floor.

Everyone gasped and left quickly for Jonathan's room.

When they entered, Sara raced to her father while Cid ran to Novena. The others split their attention between the two.

Sara studied her father for a moment. He looked as if he was barely breathing. She could almost hear it when she put her ear to his mouth

Suddenly, without warning, Jonathan sucked in a deep breath, startling her. Her eyes began to fill with tears, and she was about to hug her father when she heard a voice say, "Please, ma'am, step back and let us look at him."

She looked behind her and saw a doctor with a couple of nurses. There were also doctors and nurses checking on Novena. In all the commotion, she hadn't noticed that the medical staff had arrived.

She reluctantly stepped away from her father, so that the doctors could examine him. She walked over to where Cid and the others waited. "He's breathing on his own. I can't believe it. He's breathing on his own!" She was on the verge of tears. She looked at the others. They looked as if they were about to cry too.

She glanced quickly at Novena, who was lying on the floor.

Looking back at Cid, Sara asked, "What about Novena? Will she be all right?"

Cid took a deep breath. "They don't know yet. Remember, she's not a healer, so using the Kiss of Life could kill her."

Cid stopped his conversation with Sara as the doctor walked over to them. "What do you have for us, Doctor?" he asked.

The doctor gave them a smile. "She'll be fine. She's just unconscious. She should be up and about in a day or so." As he spoke, a hover-stretcher was brought into the room. They placed Novena on it and took her away. "When we finish transporting her to her own room, we'll call you. You can stay with her for as long as you wish."

Cid nodded his head. "Thanks, Doc. Keep me posted."

"Will do, sir." The doctor left them and followed the stretcher out the door.

As Novena's doctor followed the hover-stretcher, Jonathan's doctor joined them. "Well, Doc," Cid said, "give me the details."

"He's going to be fine. I want to do a full brain scan, but from the looks of things, he'll live."

Sara felt a wave of relief run through her entire body. "Thank you, Doctor."

The doctor smiled. "My pleasure, ma'am."

"When will he wake up?" William asked.

"That's up to him. He's still exhausted, so he might sleep for a few more hours."

"How long do you want to keep him here?" Sara asked.

"I'd like to keep him here overnight for observation, just to be sure; but he can leave after the brain scan has been completed. His choice."

Cid nodded his head. "Thank you, Doctor. Go ahead and perform the scan."

The doctor nodded and left the room, followed by the nurses.

Sara looked at her father and then at the others. "So what do we do now?"

"All we can do is wait for him to wake up."

"But isn't he supposed to wake up after Novena's healed him?"

"She was probably not strong enough, or she just didn't have enough time to build up the energy needed," Cid said. "But he *will* wake up. It's just a question of when."

Eugene was the first to take a seat. Everyone else followed suit. The waiting game had begun, again.

7

THE BOX

JONATHAN COULD SEE NOTHING but total darkness. Thinking that his eye was closed and his cybernetic eye still shorted out, he tried to open the eye, but he couldn't. Using his hands, he tried to pry open his eyelid, but he found that his eye was already open. He was actually *in* total darkness.

He turned around in a circle, trying to remember what had happened to him. He did remember joining with the ship in order to pilot it onto the hangar bay. He remembered nothing of what followed. He was aware only of waking up to complete blackness. He put his hand in front of his face but couldn't see it.

He knew that he had to do something or he would go crazy, so he just started walking, hoping something would happen.

After a few minutes he heard a voice. It wasn't loud, just a whisper. He couldn't tell if the voice was male or female. It was saying, "This way, this way," and "Follow my voice."

He stopped and concentrated on the voice, using it as a beacon to pinpoint its origin. When he thought he knew where it was coming from, he started walking in that direction.

He had walked for a while when he heard a voice to his right. Turning his head, he saw a glimmer of light. He focused his eyes, trying to get a better visual. He was able to see something else in the light—an outline of a person, perhaps. As with the voice, he couldn't tell if it was male or female. The figure was beckoning him to come toward it.

He considered his options and, realizing he didn't have any, started to walk slowly toward the stranger. He saw that it was a woman with copper-colored skin, long black hair, and eyes that were indigo with white specks in them.

She smiled at him. "Hello, Jonathan."

Not knowing how to handle this situation, he decided to play cool. He returned her greeting. "Well, hello there, little lady," he said, attempting a Southern accent.

She smiled and laughed at his attempt. "Nice try, Jonathan, but Eugene could do better."

"Yeah. He's better at that stuff than I am." He took a deep breath and looked around. His eyes focused on the light. "So are we going to get this over with or what?"

A confused look formed on her face. "With *what*?"

"*You* know. You're the Angel of Death, and you're here to escort me into the light that will take me to the other side—or wherever we go when we die."

Her confusion turned to amusement. "Oh, no, Jonathan, I'm not the Angel of Death."

"You're *not*?"

"No."

"You're not Death?"

"Correct."

"Then who *are* you?"

"My name is Terra Nora. I am a Dreamseeker."

Jonathan had heard about them. Rumors were that Dreamseekers had ascended to a point where they could go to the spiritual realm, between the living and the dead. Other rumors implied that they were demonic beings who studied sorcery. Some said they went around the galaxy, helping people. Many other rumors floated about, but there was not enough evidence to reveal the truth.

Thomas had spent some time with the Dreamseekers. When he returned, his friends had asked him many questions, but he hadn't answered, explaining that he'd promised not to share what had been re-vealed to him. The one thing that he had told them was that he'd received the gift of foresight.

While with Terra, Jonathan had striven to keep his curiosity in check, thinking it was neither the time nor place to find out exactly what her people, the Dreamseekers, were about. "All right then, Terra, what's going on?"

"I'm here to guide you back into the real world."

"*Guide* me?" She nodded. Jonathan pointed toward the light. "And that's the way back?"

"You are correct again."

"So," he paused for a moment, then continued, "Do I just walk through it or what?"

"Yes," she said. "Just walk into it, and you'll wake up."

"All right, then." He walked toward the light. "Let's do this!"

He walked a few more steps, then stopped.

Terra came up beside him and placed her hand on his arm. "What is it?"

Jonathan shook his head. "I can't go back."

"Can't?" she asked. "Or don't want to?"

"Both," he finally answered. "What I did was unforgivable. At night, I sometimes have nightmares about what happened. I see the ship's batteries firing off round after round, the passenger ships exploding, and I hear their screams over the comm—especially a mother's voice, along with her daughter's. They're screaming 'Please don't kill us! Please!' How could God forgive me for *that*?" Jonathan fell to his knees, burying his head in his hands. "I don't know if I can take it anymore!"

Terra walked up beside him and put her hand on his shoulder, giving it a small squeeze. "I know it hurts, Jonathan. But you need to go back. You have to be strong for what is to come."

Jonathan looked at her. "What things?"

"Bad things."

"That's a very broad answer, girl. There are lots of bad things that happen in the universe."

"True, but the one that is coming—I believe the saying goes 'takes the cake.'"

Jonathan was silent for a moment. "That *does* sound bad."

"Very."

"So what can *I* do? I'm a fallen admiral. Disgraced. Exiled. Just let me die and move on, please," he begged.

Terra shook her head and knelt down in front of him, gently taking hold of his head. "You have *much* to do, Jonathan. You play a big part in the future that is to come. No one will survive if you don't go back." She took a deep breath. "Stand up, my weary admiral; there is still one more battle to fight."

She kissed his forehead and stood up, then reached out her hand to help him up.

Jonathan stared at the hand, and then at the light that was beyond them. He didn't want to go back. All he felt was pain and sorrow from that terrible day on Gypsia. He just didn't want to face it again.

"What about your friends?" Terra's voice had broken through his thoughts. He looked up at her.

"You never really told anybody, except for God, about what you experienced and about what you carry with you to this day from what happened at Gypsia. Isn't that so?"

Without speaking, Jonathan shook his head.

"Well, I'll let you in on a little secret," Terra said. She lowered her voice. "Your friends are great listeners."

Jonathan smiled. "I have one more question."

"What is it?"

"Since you are on the verge of the other side, have you ever seen what happens?"

"You mean, have I ever seen or talked to God?"

"Yeah."

"Jonathan, if I told you, that would be confirming what happens after we die, and I can't do that."

"Why not?"

"Because that would be ruining the mystery."

She smiled and again offered her hand. Without another word, he grasped it and got to his feet. Once again, he started walking toward the light.

The closer he got, the brighter it became. He had to raise his arm to shield his eyes from the bright light.

Before he became fully engulfed, he turned back toward Terra. "Thank you, Terra." He continued toward the light.

"Jonathan!"

At the sound of his name, he turned around. "Yes?"

"He *does* forgive you. All you have to do is *ask*." She turned around and started to walk away. After a few steps, she disappeared.

Tears came to Jonathan's eye as he stood still. Several seconds later, he turned and headed toward the light.

Soon, the brightness fully engulfed him.

AWAKE

JONATHAN KNEW THAT HE was awake; he was just too afraid to open his eyes. The conversation with Terra had really helped him, but he was still a little hesitant about coming back. He knew that he would eventually have to tell everyone what emotional baggage he was carrying from the incident at Gypsia.

Jonathan whispered, "God give me strength." He then took a deep breath and opened his eyes.

He squinted as the lights in the room hit him. He blinked a few times, letting his eye adjust to the brightness.

His body had been placed at a 145-degree angle on the hospital bed. He looked around to take in his surroundings. He must be in a hospital room on Measha Station, somewhere in the recovery ward.

He also noticed that there were several people in the room with him. The first person he saw was his daughter Sara, who was right beside him. Eugene was on the couch, with Katrina and William. Cid was seated in a chair in the corner. Everyone was asleep. No one noticed that he had awakened. He started to reach out to Sara, to put his hand on her shoulder, but nothing happened. He looked over and saw that his cybernetic arm had been removed. All that he saw was the stump at his elbow. He sighed and reached over to Sara with his other arm.

"Hey, girl, how're you doing?" he said as he gently shook Sara's shoulder.

Sara jumped up from her chair and screamed, causing the others to wake from their sleep.

Sara leaped from her spot and landed right on top of Jonathan, wrapping her arms around him so tightly that he could barely breathe. "Oh, Daddy, thank God you're okay!" she screamed over and over again.

Jonathan patted her back. "Thanks, honey, but I need some room to breathe."

"Oh sorry." Sara quickly let go. There were tears in her eyes. "I was so worried that we were going to lose you."

Jonathan just shrugged his shoulders. "Well, what can I say? Your old man is hard to kill."

"You got *that* right!"

Jonathan looked over to see who had just spoken. It was William. He walked over and gave Jonathan a hug. "Nice to have you back."

Jonathan thanked William, who stepped back to make room for Katrina. She wrapped her arms around him in a bear hug and nearly lifted him off the bed.

"Great to have you back, sir."

"Thanks, Katrina," he said as he started to get off the bed. "It feels good to be back."

At that moment, two doctors came in and started to check Jonathan's heart, breathing, and pulse.

Cid walked up to the doctors that were crowded around Jonathan.

"How is he?"

One of the doctors looked at Cid. He had a confident smile on his face. "He's fine," the doctor said.

"And the brain scans?"

"We haven't detected any abnormalities. He can leave immediately."

"Thank you, Doctor." Both doctors left the room. When they were gone, Cid walked up to Jonathan and grabbed his left hand. "Thank God you're okay. We were all getting worried there for a moment."

"So was *I*," Jonathan said. He held up his right arm, showing his stump with the joint connection. "Can someone tell me where my arm is?" He made a gesture with his left hand, going from his head to feet, then continued, "And where my clothes are?"

Cid smiled and jerked his thumb toward the bathroom. "I have everything set out and ready for you in there."

"Thanks."

Jonathan walked into the bathroom and closed the door. So far, Eugene hadn't made a move to tell him how thankful he was for his recovery. Everyone noticed this but didn't say anything, but Jonathan didn't mind; he knew that Eugene must be feeling a whirlwind of emotions. The two of them had been best friends throughout their lives, and any kind of serious damage to either of them would definitely leave the other deeply wounded.

He studied the clothes hanging on the hanger and the arm that was lying on the counter. He picked up the arm and saw that it was one of the regular arms that he wore. Hidden inside the arm was a small M-9 pistol and a knife. Certain hand movements would activate the ejector, which would then cause the weapons to pop out of his arm and into his hand.

He placed the end of the arm onto the joint connector and twisted it until it snapped into place.

The item of clothing on the hanger was a simple flight suit. After he'd put it on, he grabbed the socks and boots from the floor and put them on as well. When he was finished, he walked to the door and stopped in front of it.

He took a few deep breaths and opened the door. He stepped out, and the door closed by itself behind him. Now the room was empty, save for Eugene. Everyone else had left to give them some privacy.

Jonathan walked up to Eugene. They just stared at each other for a moment. Eugene was the first to break the silence. "You're looking good."

"Thanks," Jonathan replied. "So are you."

"Thanks." After a few more seconds of silence, Eugene enveloped him in a huge bear hug. He was squeezing him harder than Sara had. "*You nearly scared me to death, Jonny!*"

"I know. Sorry about that."

After a moment, Eugene let Jonathan go. Stepping back a few feet, Eugene said, "Well, let's get out of here!"

"Yeah. I have a lot to tell."

"Like what?"

"I'll tell you once we're with everyone."

"Okay," Eugene said as he walked toward the door. "Until then, come with me; we have a lot to tell you, too." They reached the door. Before they left the room, Eugene made one last comment. "Oh, and if you tell anyone about this, I'll put you back into the hospital myself!"

"Understood."

The two walked through the doorway. Everyone was standing outside, waiting for them.

When the two friends joined them, Jonathan told about his experience in the darkness and his conversation with Terra, the Dreamseeker.

Katrina looked amazed. "Wow! Incredible!"

"Perhaps we should ask Uncle Thomas about this?" Sara suggested.

Eugene gave a snort. "Go ahead—but I doubt he'll give a straight answer, with his 'vow of silence' or something like that."

Jonathan nodded his head. Solving the mystery of the Dreamseekers would be for another time. "So," Jonathan said, clapping his hands together, "what did I miss, and how long have I been out?"

Everyone looked at each other, wondering who should tell him. After a few minutes of waiting, Jonathan spoke, "Come on, guys; it can't be *that* bad." After looking at a few of the faces, he asked, "*Can it?*"

Eugene gave a heavy sigh. "Bunch of pansies! Fine, I'll do it." He started walking down the corridor. "Follow me. There's much to tell."

Jonathan and the others followed him down the corridor. "Lay it on me, buddy."

"You got it. Basically, you've been out for three days."

"Three days!"

"Can you please let me finish?"

"Sorry."

"Thanks. Now," Eugene continued, "during your rest, Mei- Ling was arrested by Wright." Eugene quickly shot up a hand to stop Jonathan from saying anything. He quickly shut his mouth and waved his hand as a signal for Eugene to continue. "Now, as I was saying, Mei-Ling was arrested by Wright. Info tells us that she was caught hacking into Wright's classified files."

Jonathan had no doubt that the "info" was coming from the Infiltrators. Those guys were the best at everything.

"Same info tells us that all the files were downloaded, and that Rose escaped with them. The Resistance is decrypting those files as we speak, but it could take a week. The security on those files is very state-of-the-art. Meanwhile, Wright has wasted no time in taking charge of the Imperial Guard. He's already made several changes to the members of the council, replacing most of them so that he can get what he wants. Mei- Ling, in the meantime, is in prison. Her trial begins in four days." They reached the end of the corridor. "Any questions?"

Acting like a child in a classroom, Jonathan raised his hand and said, "Me! Me! Pick *me!*"

"Ha-ha. Funny." Eugene pointed his finger at Jonathan. "You may speak."

"How do we get her out of there?"

Eugene was silent for a moment. "We don't."

"What do you mean?" Jonathan asked. An edge was in his voice.

"What I mean is that we don't get her out; she wants to go to trial and be a martyr."

"What!" he screamed. "That's crazy!"

"That's like the pot calling the kettle black."

"True, but we have to do *something*."

"Jon," Cid interrupted, "*she wants to do this*! We must respect her wishes."

Jonathan just stood there for a moment. He couldn't believe what he was hearing. *Mei-Ling wants to be a martyr? That's insane!*

His mind switched to the trial that was to come and the punishment that was certain to follow. *Oh, the punishment would be severe!*

He couldn't take it. He did a 180 and headed back the way he'd come, barely hearing Eugene calling to him as he went down the corridor.

"JONATHAN! JONATHAN! AW, *HELL*!" Eugene muttered.

William shook his head. "This can only end badly."

"No kidding, Sherlock," Eugene said to his son. He turned toward Cid. "Cid, Jonathan's mind is on another plane. We need to get him back to reality."

"Oh, *really*? And just what do you expect *me* to do?"

Eugene started to open his mouth, then closed it. Cid was right: trying to keep Jonathan from attempting some crazy prison escape was going to be a challenge. He turned toward the rest of the group. "Any ideas?"

"Don't worry," a voice from behind them said. Eugene and the others turned to see who'd spoken. Novena was there, wide awake and dressed in a white toga. "Leave everything to me."

"Is there anything we can do?" Cid asked.

Novena shook her head. "No. I'll handle everything. Just contact the docks and tell them that I'm on the way." With that, she entered the elevator and rode up to the roof. She walked to the edge and looked out onto the city below. As the breeze whipped across her face, she spread her wings and jumped off.

As she flew through the air, Novena caught glimpses of people looking up at her in awe. Twilights rarely flew out in the open, as she was doing now; they usually flew only during combat situations.

As Novena sailed through the skies above Measha Station, toward the space port, she closed her eyes and smiled. Since everyone thought she was eternally merged with the *Twilight Star*, she didn't get many chances to fly so openly. She'd had to do it in secret so that nobody would find out the truth.

It didn't take her long to reach the space port. She landed in front of the entrance and proceeded through the checkpoints. After she cleared security, she headed for the dock housing the *Twilight Star* and Omega Squadron.

She stopped at the doorway and looked in. The *Twilight Star* and Omega Squadron's ships were on platforms, being worked on by mechanics. Sparks and metal flew from ships on one side of the dock; on the other side, separated by a force field, other mechanics were working on the fighter's engines. When Novena entered the dock, all the workers turned toward her, wide-eyed. Understandable. The toga she wore made her look very exotic. She was quite a sight.

She walked to the middle of the dock. "Who's in charge here!" she called out.

A man in his forties came up to her. He had black hair and brown eyes, and looked as fit as a bodybuilder. At the moment, he looked more bewildered than tough. "*I* am, ma'am."

"What's your name, sir?"

"Mike. I'm the foreman. How can I help you?"

"My name is Novena. Did the chief call about my arrival?"

"Yes, ma'am."

"What did he tell you?"

"He said to give you any assistance you might need."

She nodded her head. "Good. Mike, the only thing I need from you and your workers is for all of you to clear out of here for a while. Take a break. I'll let you know when you and your men can come back to work."

The foreman nodded and called out to his men, "All right, guys, clear out of here. Go have a nice long break. I'll call you when we can come back." As everyone put down their equipment, they started to mumble, wondering what was going on. All their eyes were on her as they left the dock.

When she was alone, Novena gave a deep sigh. She looked around, wondering where she could hide until Jonathan arrived. Then she spotted it.

JONATHAN EXITED THE HOSPITAL and immediately hailed a hover-cab. He didn't have his keys with him, and there was no doubt that his vehicle was still in storage. About a minute after he'd started to hail a cab, one stopped directly in front of him. He opened the door, got inside, and slammed the door shut.

He leaned over the seat in front of him and said, "Take me to the main space port now!

"You got it!" the cabbie replied.

After flipping a few levers, he turned back toward the roadway. Within minutes, they reached the turnoff point for the Sky-Lanes. Using the car's computer, the cabbie safely navigated the Sky-Lanes without crashing into other vehicles or colliding with the surrounding structure.

During the entire ride, Jonathan looked out of the hover-cab's tinted windows, taking in the sights around him. He has seen them thousands of times throughout his life, but they still managed to take his breath away.

Measha Station was a self-contained space installation beyond anything ever created. The inside of the station was broken up into different segments, called hives.

There were eight different ones. The living hive contained all the living quarters for everyone on the station. The entertainment hive had all the clubs, bars, theaters, gyms, and all other entertainment venues available to every known alien species. The docking hive was where all the ships were docked, where they got supplies, and where the repairs were made. There was not just one docking hive, but many. They were scattered throughout the station; Cid didn't want all of his ships to be kept in one place. The engineering hive was at the center of the station. This was the hive that kept the station moving and operating. It was kept operational by thousands of workers who made sure

Measha Station ran smoothly. That was also where the power supply was kept. The Nexus, the ancient race that had built the place, were great engineers. The many stations they'd built, like this one, were made to last.

The weapon hive housed all the station's security forces, weapons, and cannons that were situated on the outside of the station. There were many cannons. All were online at all times, ready for action. There were also hundreds of missile launchers on the hull. Like the docking hives, the weapon hives were scattered throughout the station. The supply hive housed all the food, parts, and supplies, as well as all that the station needed to continue functioning. The maintenance hive was where all repairs were coordinated. The last hive was the command hive, the site from which all functions were monitored and where the communications stations were located. That was the area from which Cid ran the entire station, and where "other" things were monitored. This was also where the Infiltrators kept their headquarters.

Each hive had a hospital that could service all known alien species, and a transporter room that could send people to all the different hives; that room was rarely used, however, except when someone needed to get somewhere fast. All of the roads and Sky-Lanes connected with each hive. At each entrance, there were also security checkpoints, needed more as safety precautions than anything else. Even though the station was a safe haven for different alien species, as well as a place where they could simply relax and have fun, there still needed to be some kind of security force to keep everybody in line.

The hover-cab reached the security checkpoint leading to the docking hive where the *Twilight Star* and Omega Squadron would most likely be under repair. They used the same bay every time they arrived. With the immense traffic, it would take about thirty minutes. The thought finally occurred to him that he could have used the transporter system to reach the bay a lot quicker; now he was stuck in traffic.

When Jonathan finally reached his destination, he paid the cab driver and headed into the space port. Normally, a person had to go through several security checkpoints in order to reach the docking bay where their ship was located, but with Jonathan's special access, he was able to bypass Security and reach the *Twilight Star* in under ten minutes.

He entered the docking bay, expecting to see workers working on the ships and hear the loud noise coming from the tools being used, but he saw nobody. The entire bay was silent and empty. He knew that Eugene, Cid, and the others were up to something. They'd had enough time to reach the space port before he did in order to set something up that would either convince or stop him from trying to head to Earth 2 and break Mei-Ling out of prison. He looked around, wondering what they were up to.

As he made his way through the bay, he spotted what he had come for: Sitting near some of the fighters that were being worked on were two shuttles. They were a couple of the ones kept in the *Twilight Star*'s hangar bay. They had several for transportation, and they were capable of doing FTL travel. They were also used for stealth missions. Jonathan had come on the gamble that, during the three days he had been in the hospital, at least *one* of them would have been fully repaired. He scanned the two shuttles, judging which one would be in better condition.

He guardedly approached one of the shuttles, wary of what his friends might have in store for him, keyed in the code on the door, and it opened. He entered, and the door closed behind him. He did a quick but thorough search. Having found nothing suspicious, he headed toward the cockpit, opened its door, and stepped inside.

9

HELLO

JONATHAN STOPPED SHORT. SITTING in one of the chairs was an alien. It took a few seconds for Jonathan to place her species. A Twilight. Other than Novena, and his few other encounters with Twilights over the years, he didn't personally know many of them. He looked at her for a moment, taking in her striking features.

He knew that the Alien League of Nonhuman Worlds had pursued the Twilights, to make them slaves because of their affiliation with humans. The males were very strong, and so they were kept as slave builders; the females were also strong, but were used as sex slaves because of their exceptional beauty. They simply had a natural aura that attracted males of all species. This alien was doing just that at the moment.

He stared at her as she sat in the chair in front of him. She stared back, not moving from her seat.

When he and Terra were together in the Box, she'd made the first move; now, *he* decided to go on the offensive, to convince this alien, who probably was working for Cid, to leave him alone and let him be on his way.

"Hello."

She nodded in greeting, not speaking a word.

"How're you doing?"

Again she nodded.

"You're not going to say much, are you?"

She tilted her head and shrugged.

"Good. That'll make my side of this conversation much easier." He sat down in the pilot's seat. He looked over the console, running diagnostics to make sure that everything was all right. All the while, he stole glances at the alien beside him. He could feel her gaze on him. The feeling was becoming very distracting.

After a few minutes, he stopped and turned toward her. "Look, lady, I have a lot of work to do, and I have to leave very soon. So if you have some business here, please tell me; otherwise, get out of here!"

She placed her hand over his, then squeezed it and smiled, revealing her very white teeth. "You can't go, Jonathan."

He froze at the sound of the Twilight's voice. He knew now who she was, but he couldn't believe it. "No. It can't *be*."

The Twilight gave a hearty laugh. "Well, well, well! Isn't this a strange situation that we have here! The great Jonathan Mikel, *speechless*." She shook her head, still laughing. "Eugene would *love* this."

"Novena?" Jonathan asked, his voice full of shock and disbelief.

She nodded. "In the flesh." She smiled. "Literally."

He couldn't speak for a moment; the realization of who she was shocked and astonished him. He couldn't believe that it really was her.

He took a few short breaths, trying to calm himself. Finally, he spoke. "How is this possible?"

She proceeded to tell him about her special ability, how she'd gone into hiding, how Cid had set her up to be with him and the others, and how she'd helped him during his coma.

Jonathan could not believe what he was hearing. He looked directly into her onyx-colored eyes, trying to decide whether everything was real or not. With his real hand, he reached out and gently touched her face. Her blue skin felt as smooth as a pearl. Next, he reached up and touched her hair. It was smooth as silk. She definitely felt real enough.

He gave a short laugh. "Somebody pinch me, because I must still be in a coma."

Novena smiled and pinched him hard on his arm . Jonathan jerked back. "What was *that* for?"

"You said 'pinch me.'"

"I was just kidding," he said. "It was a joke, you know?"

She nodded her head, laughing. "Yeah, I knew. That's what makes it so funny."

He was about to ask her another question when he remembered the first words she'd said to him a few minutes before.

"Wait a minute, girlie. What did you mean when you told me I couldn't leave?"

Her smile faded. "What I meant is that you can't go and help Mei-Ling," she said.

His face became hard. "Was it Cid's idea to send you?"

"No, it was mine. I told him that I would come and bring you back."

"Well, you're wasting your time. I'm going!"

"Jon, you can't!"

"And why not?" he asked, anger was creeping into his voice.

"Because if you *do* go, you will be captured and you will *die*."

"I can't just sit here and do nothing!" he said, his voice rising with every word. "She's going to be tortured in front of a crowd, beaten, and humiliated!" He was breathing hard now. "I can't just *sit* here! I *won't*!"

He started punching commands into the console. The ship started to fire up. He looked back at Novena and saw that she was still sitting in the chair. "Since you're not moving, I can assume that you're thinking of one of two options: one, you're coming along to help me get her out, but I doubt that; or two, you're still going to try to convince me to stop this rescue, or 'madness', as you guys would call it. Well, guess what? You'd better buckle up, girl, because I'm going!"

"And what happens when you get caught?"

Jonathan was about to answer when Novena said, "I'll tell you what will happen—you'll be put back on trial, convicted, tortured, and punished in front of a crowd, just like Mei-Ling. Then you'll be killed, and all the people that died on Gypsia will not be avenged. Your brother's actions won't be punished, and everything that all of us have accomplished in the past five years *will have been for nothing!*" She was screaming the words now.

Jonathan sat in the chair. Her words had finally hit home at the mention of Wright.

"Don't call him my brother!"

"Fine, but Wright will go unpunished, and as I said before, everything we've done in the past five years will have been for nothing; and all the things that we're going to do, all the people and planets that we're going to save—all that will never happen! Everyone will die!"

Jonathan sat still, her words once again hitting home. He didn't move for a few minutes.

He really wanted to fly out and save Mei-Ling, regardless of what might happen to him. He didn't care if he would be captured, tortured, and killed; he just wanted to save his first love.

But he knew that everyone throughout the galaxy needed him and depended on him. There were intelligence reports coming in about strange alien ships having been spotted in several systems. Maybe this was what Terra Nora was talking about when he was with her in the Box.

He punched some commands into the computer, and the ship started to power down. When the shutdown was complete, he felt Novena's hand tighten around his. He looked over at her and saw a smile on her face. It wasn't a happy-go-lucky smile, but one that showed relief.

"Thank you," she said.

He nodded. "It wasn't easy, believe me."

"I know. It was hard for you. Hell, it's going to be hard for *everyone* to sit here and let Mei-Ling go through with her crazy martyr plan."

"No kidding!" A thought popped into his head. "Were you aware of how long this plan has been in effect?"

"I didn't know about it personally, but it wouldn't surprise me if Cid knew all about it."

No surprise there. It would be natural for Cid to learn from the Infiltrators about Mei-Ling's plan. The only question was whether she'd told him or he'd found out on his own.

"Well then, let's head back to the hospital."

The two stood up and walked to the shuttle's exit. Novena stopped him when they reached the ramp leading to the outside.

"What is it, Novena?"

"I have a question for you."

He nodded his head, indicating for her to go ahead.

"What would you do if I wasn't merged with the ship?"

10

LOVE BITES

JONATHAN BLINKED HIS EYES at hearing the question. "Pardon me?"

"What would you do if I wasn't merged with the ship?" she asked again.

Jonathan rubbed his face. Even with her revelation, he knew this question was due to be asked; he just wished that it would have come later rather than sooner.

He closed the short distance between them, taking a couple of steps toward her. They stared into each other's eyes, becoming lost in each other's gaze. Ever since his drunken confession, he knew this moment would inevitably come.

During his five years on the *Twilight Star*, he'd always felt that there was more to Novena than she was letting on. Deep down, as he'd listened to her talk to him both publicly and in private, he knew that there was something more to her; he just didn't know what it was. Until now.

He told her the truth.

"I would kiss you."

Before she could say more, Jonathan leaned down and kissed her softly on her lips. Novena reached up and, cupping his face in her hands, leaned into the kiss. Soon, the kiss intensified, the last few years of pent-up emotions having been suddenly released. He wrapped his arms around her waist while her arms encircled his neck.

A thought came to him: he'd almost died; Novena had almost died; Eugene and Katrina had almost died. Life was too short to put things off. You had to seize the moment when it presented itself. *Carpe diem.*

As much as he'd loved Mei-Ling, there came a time when one had to move on. Perhaps that time was now.

He moved his left arm up Novena's back, positioning it just between her shoulder blades. He lowered her down on top of the shuttle's cushioned seats, their lips still connected.

EUGENE AND THE OTHERS were still at the hospital, waiting for any word from Novena, and hoping that she had been able to talk Jonathan out of his suicide mission.

After an hour, William spoke. "What in the world is taking so long?"

"Consider not hearing anything a good sign," Cid said. "I haven't heard from the docking bay that Jonathan has taken off. He and Novena must still be there."

"Could they be on their way back?" Sara asked.

Cid shook his head. "I don't believe so. Novena would have contacted me if they were."

Sara threw her hands up and stood up from her chair. "What could they be up to?"

Eugene laughed and gave everyone a smile. "Oh, I have a good idea of what they're up to." He gave another laugh, but stopped when Katrina elbowed him in the ribs. He turned to say something but stopped when he saw the expression on her face. He looked at Sara and saw that she was wearing that same expression. He decided it was best to drop the subject.

Cid was about to speak when his comm beeped. He spoke into it. "This is the chief. What is it?"

"Sir, this is Dr. Lance. Can you come to the testing labs, please?"

"I'll be right there." He shut off the comm and turned to the rest of the group. "Why don't you guys go back to your rooms? I'll contact you if something happens."

Everyone looked at each other as if they were discussing the situation telepathically. They took Cid's suggestion and headed for the exit. Meanwhile, Cid made his way to the labs.

WITH THE USE OF the transporter, Cid reached Dr. Lance's fertility labs with ease. As he stepped off the platform, a guard approached him.

"Hello, sir. ID, please?"

Cid handed over his ID, and his fingerprints and face were also scanned. Even though he was the commander in chief, he required that everyone, including himself, get scanned and fingerprinted before entering any important structure.

"Scans are clear, sir. You may enter."

"Thank you."

Cid strode through the doors and entered the lobby. The receptionist behind the desk looked up at him and smiled. "Hello, sir. What can we do for you?"

"Dr. Lance called. He asked me to come down to the labs right away."

The woman typed a few commands into her computer. After a few seconds, she looked up at him. "Yes, sir, I have you right here. Since you've been here before, I believe that you know the way?"

"Yes, I do. Thank you." As Cid walked down the hall, the receptionist waved good-bye. He reached a door and waited. He heard a buzz, and the door slid open.

He entered the hallway and walked down the corridor. When he came to an intersection, he turned right. It didn't take him long to reach a set of glass doors. On the other side were men in white hazmat suits. When he entered the room, one of the men came to him immediately.

"Sir, Dr. Lance is waiting for you." He directed Cid toward another set of doors. "Before we go any further, you'll need to go through the clean room." The clean room was designed to make certain that anyone entering the labs wasn't carrying anything that could harm the research. Whoever entered would be scrubbed down and given a full body scan, their clothes then exchanged for clean ones. Once that protocol was completed, they would be allowed to enter the labs.

When Cid finished, he headed straight for Dr. Lance's station.

Dr. Lance specialized in cross-species breeding. Since the Great Exodus, people had been marrying and dating outside their own species; because of this, reproduction had became more complicated. While it was easier for some than for others, the majority of couples who were of different species and wanted children experienced difficulty with the reproduction process. Doctors said that it all had to do with genetics.

Even though one inter-species couple might be the same as another, a procedure that worked for one might not work for the other; therefore, scientists had to constantly devise a variety of new medical protocols that would help solve the problem.

For a long time, Measha Station had been developing ways for inter-species couples to have children. The new techniques were proving to have a very high success rate.

When Cid reached Dr. Lance's lab, he found the doctor looking through a microscope. He stood beside him, waiting for the doctor to notice that he'd arrived. After a minute, he tapped him on the shoulder. The doctor looked up, his eyes widening in surprise. "I'm sorry, sir. I didn't notice that you had arrived. I've been very busy."

"So I see," Cid replied. "What's this all about?"

"Remember when we started injecting Eugene and Katrina with the new treatments?" Cid nodded. "Well, while they were in the hospital, I took that opportunity to run some tests on them. During the tests, I found something."

Cid froze, hoping the doctor was talking about what he hoped to hear. "What?"

The doctor got up from his stool and walked over to another table. He picked up a PDA and handed it to Cid. "I think you'd better read the results for yourself."

Cid took the PDA and opened the highlighted file. When he finished reading, he looked back up at Lance, surprised. "Is this true?"

"I believe so," the doctor answered. "I'll need them to come back for additional testing, but I believe that this is the real deal."

Cid smiled and smacked Lance's chest with the PDA. "Thanks, Doc. I'll make the call."

EUGENE AND KATRINA ARRIVED at their apartment in silence, thinking about why Cid had been called away. After a few moments, they decided not to worry about it. If Cid wanted them to know, he would tell them.

Eugene went to the kitchen to make them some dinner. The two took turns cooking. While he got started, Katrina went to the bedroom to change. She'd been in the same set of clothes for days and wanted to get out of them.

As she opened the closet, she saw a blinking light on the message recorder. The date on the message was that day. She looked at her comm and realized that she hadn't turned it on. Eugene probably hadn't turned on his either. She pressed PLAY on the device and listened to the message.

Hello, Eugene, Katrina. It was Cid's voice. *I have something that I have to tell both of you . . .*

EUGENE GRABBED SOME BREAD, turkey, and condiments out of the refrigerator to fix sandwiches for Katrina and himself. Neither of them was keen on a big dinner.

He called out to Katrina, "Honey, what would you like on your sandwich?" When he didn't hear a reply, he tried again. "Katrina, what would you like?" Still no response.

Curious, he left the kitchen and headed toward the bedroom. As he walked through the living room, he heard a small noise. Nearing the bedroom, he could make out what it was: the sound of crying.

He stopped at the door, which was slightly ajar. He peeked in and saw that his wife had her head buried in her hands. She was weeping.

He opened the door quietly and entered the room. He slowly made his way toward her.

"Honey?" When she didn't reply, he sat down beside her. He

wrapped his arm around her, and she leaned into him, burying her face in his shoulder. "Katrina, please tell me *something*. You're beginning to scare me."

She shook her head and lifted it so that her eyes met his. "No. . . no. . .I'm sorry. It's nothing bad; it's just—" She wiped the tears from her face and smiled. "Just push PLAY on the machine. It'll explain everything."

Eugene looked from his wife to the machine, becoming both curious and nervous at the same time. He wondered what could have caused his beloved wife to grow so agitated. The list was brief

He covered the short distance and pressed PLAY.

As he listened to the message, a nauseous feeling filled Eugene's stomach. They wanted a child, but it was proving difficult. He'd never experienced fatherhood with William's mother—they'd never married or stayed together—so he very much wanted to experience it with Katrina.

As you know, we tried a new procedure the last time you two were at the fertility clinic, and we ran some tests on Katrina to see if there'd been any progress. Cid paused, and Eugene could swear that he was smiling when he next spoke. *Earlier, I was called away because there have been some results. Congratulations, you two! You're going to be parents! We'll set up a time for a full examination later on, but for now, just relax and enjoy the good news. If there are any developments in the Jonathan or Mei-Ling situations, I'll call both of you. Bye.*

Eugene could not move. So many emotions were assaulting him at the same time; joy, awe, and many other emotions were coursing through his body. He turned around to face his wife.

"Hon—"

She launched herself from the bed and into his embrace, wrapping her arms around him and holding him close as she kissed him. Eugene, not missing a beat, held her tightly and returned the kiss.

JONATHAN AND NOVENA COLLAPSED on the shuttle's seats, breathing heavily. The only thing that was barely covering them was a thin blanket they'd found in the shuttle's storage area. Their clothes were scattered all about the compartment.

Jonathan looked at his watch and was surprised at how much time had passed. He'd been enjoying himself so much that he'd lost track of the time.

Whoa, he thought. *What a ride.*

Thanks. You weren't too bad yourself.

Jonathan shot up into a sitting position. He looked left and right, dazed.

Novena was smiling.

She burst out laughing. Not only could he hear her laughing through his ears, but also in his mind. What was going *on?*

After Novena calmed down, she explained everything. "I'm sorry, but things happened so fast, I didn't get a chance to tell you that, after Twilight sex, the two participants will, for a short time, be able to hear each other's thoughts."

Jonathan just stared at her, wondering what to say. But that would be useless, considering she would hear his thoughts before he could say them.

True, he heard from her. *But it would be nice to hear you say them anyway.*

After a minute of silence, Novena spoke up. "Are you upset that we can read each other's minds?"

Jonathan thought about it for a short moment. "No, not really." Even now, the telepathy was fading. "It was my fault. I didn't give you enough time to tell me everything that was going to happen."

"That's okay." Novena placed her hand on his chest, making circular motions with her finger. "So what happens now?"

He smiled. "Let's just take this one step at a time." He threw off the sheet and sat up. "We should get back to Cid right now and discuss what we ought to do next."

He felt Novena place her hand on his shoulder. "I thought you said you weren't going to go off and rescue Mei-Ling."

He put his real hand over hers. "Don't worry. I'm not. Not without a definite plan and some backup."

WE'RE NOT GOING TO rescue Mei-Ling, and that's final!" Jonathan slammed his hand down on the arm of his chair. He couldn't believe what he was hearing. Novena and William were with him.

"You can't be *serious*, sir."

"You heard what Eugene said a couple of hours ago: *Mei-Ling doesn't want to be rescued!*"

"This is *crazy*, Cid."

Cid just shook his head. "We're just being redundant here, Jonathan. This is final!"

Jonathan threw his arms up in the air in frustration. "So what are we going to do—just sit here on our hands and knees and watch her be tortured?"

"Yes!" Cid's voice was stern. He gave Jonathan a look that told him that he wasn't finished, and it shut Jonathan up. "However, a plan to break her out afterward has already been put into motion."

Jonathan snorted. "A little too late, if you ask *me*."

Cid shrugged. "It's the best we can do, with the options she gave us." He looked at William. "You haven't said much."

William made a small hand gesture. "I already know that it's pointless to fight this. I'm just here to watch Uncle Jonny argue to no avail."

Before Jonathan could add a retort, Novena asked, "Cid, where are Eugene and Katrina?"

Cid was about to answer when the comm on his desk beeped.

He pressed a button and spoke into the speaker, "What is it?"

"Sir, General Blake is on the line."

"Speak of the devil," Cid muttered to himself. Into the comm he said, "Patch him through to the viewscreen."

A few seconds later, the viewscreen on Cid's desk came to life. On the small screen, the group saw Eugene and Katrina.

Jonathan was the first to speak. "Hey, guys, where are—" He stopped short when he saw the screen. Both Eugene and Katrina were naked. The only thing covering them was a sheet.

"Hey, buddy. Glad to see that you're back! I guess we have *you* to thank for that. Right, Novena?"

Novena hesitated and then nodded, her cheeks turning a little red at the sight of Eugene almost totally naked. "Yes, you do. You're welcome, Eugene."

He nodded and turned his attention back to Cid. "We got your call, boss. We would have called back sooner, but, ah—" he looked at Katrina and smiled. "We've been a little busy."

"So we can see," William said.

Eugene looked at his son and covered himself up a bit more. Katrina followed suit. "Sorry, son. I didn't know you'd be here."

William waved his hand in a dismissive gesture. "I've seen worse."

They all laughed at that. The laughter was broken when Sara entered the room. William moved out of his seat so that she could sit beside her father.

"Thanks, William. Dad . . . Novena . . ."

By her expression, everyone could tell that Sara knew what had happened between the two of them in the shuttle. An uncomfortable silence fell across the room.

"Anyway," Katrina said, breaking the silence, "what did you want to tell us, sir?"

Cid looked at everyone before he spoke. "I wanted to talk to you guys about the situation involving Mei-Ling. Everyone here has gotten bits and pieces of what has happened; some of you have been wracked with too much emotion to process everything that you *do* know. So I'm going to go over everything again with all of you, and this'll be the last time, so listen good. Understand?"

They nodded.

"Good. Now, as I said before, we will not, *in any way*, break her out of prison before or after she receives her punishment. We will have *no* involvement."

Jonathan raised his hand. Cid nodded in his direction. "Sir," Jonathan said, with what sounded like a forced calm in his voice, "exactly what will be done, if anything?"

Cid intertwined his fingers and leaned forward. "Yes. Remember when Ryan was pulled off the *Twilight Star*? That was *my* doing. I'd gotten a call from Admiral Blake requesting permission to use Ryan on a mission. I gave the go-ahead as long as he kept me in the loop about what was going on."

"He had a vision?" Novena asked.

"That's correct. He didn't know exactly what would happen, except that it would be something bad. He wanted Ryan on standby, just to prepare for the worst."

"I think it's safe to say the worst has happened," Sara said.

"Don't be too sure," Cid said. "This is only the beginning. Who knows what Wright will do in the future."

"Don't worry, sir," William assured him, "the Infiltrators will keep their eyes and ears open."

"Did Thomas have any idea about what Mei-Ling was going to do—or any part of it?" Jonathan asked.

"No. She kept it to herself—or shared it with only a select few."

Jonathan was not happy to hear this. He was getting sick and tired of being the last person to know anything.

Cid must have seen the look on Jonathan's face. "Don't be so angry at her, Jonathan. The Infiltrators found out her plan a long time ago. I confronted her, and she didn't deny it."

They turned to William. "Don't look at *me*," he said. "*I* didn't know anything about this crazy plan!"

"That's true," Cid said, drawing the attention back to himself. "I kept it classified. Only I and the agents who found out about it knew her full plan."

Novena asked, "Is there anything *we* can do, Cid?" Jonathan could hear the desperation in her voice. He felt the same way: Powerless. He *hated* feeling powerless.

Cid did not have an encouraging look on his face. "I'm sorry, Novena; the only thing we can do is sit and wait for word from Thomas." He leaned back in his chair. "Before I dismiss everyone, is there anything else that anyone wants to ask me?"

"What about this mysterious fleet that's been seen around the galaxy? Is there any new information?" William asked.

"Nothing much that's new. When I get more info, I'll make sure that everyone is briefed. Anyone else?"

From the screen, Eugene and Katrina look at each other and smiled. *What is with those two?* Jonathan wondered. Usually, except under certain circumstances, Cid wanted everyone to be present for his meetings; but when those two showed up on the viewscreen barely clothed, he expected Cid to give them a stern lecture. But he didn't. Jonathan had been wondering *why* throughout the meeting.

"Actually, we have something we would like to tell everybody," Eugene said.

He gestured to Katrina to do the honors. She looked at them, a huge smile on her face. "Guys, as you all know, Eugene and I have been trying to have children for a while. Well, we've finally received some good news: we're going to be parents!"

Jonathan didn't know *how*, but her smile seemed to get even wider.

With the exception of Cid, everyone's mouths dropped open in surprise.

Jonathan looked over at William, trying to read the young man's thoughts regarding this development, but his face expressed nothing but happiness for his mother and father.

"Congratulations, Mom, Dad. I'm so happy for the both of you!"

"Thank you, William," Katrina said, tears rolling down her cheeks.

When everyone had finished congratulating them, Cid once again took control. "All right, you two lovebirds, take some time off and have fun. I'll call you if something happens." Eugene and Katrina gave him their thanks and signed off.

When the screen went dark, Cid addressed the rest of the group. "That goes for the rest of you. Take some time off. If there's any new development, I'll be in touch." As they started to leave, Cid pointed his finger at Jonathan. "Except for you. I want to talk to you. *Alone.*" He looked at Novena. "You too, girl. Wait outside."

Jonathan looked at everyone around him, wondering if they had an idea why Cid wanted to talk to them. When they shook their heads, he sat back down and waited. As everyone filed out of the room, Novena gave him a look of concern. He smiled reassuringly.

When everyone was gone, Cid started to talk. "Just about everybody in the shuttle bay, and in our little group, knows what happened between you and Novena."

Jonathan just nodded, waiting for Cid to continue. "Though some knew this was going to happen, I was hoping that it wouldn't."

Jonathan was confused. "Why, sir? I don't see how it's anyone's business whom I sleep with."

Cid slammed his fist onto the desk, causing the contents on top to rattle. "Damn it, man, are you *really* that dense? Stop thinking with your dick and expand your mind!"

Jonathan was now getting angry. He had heard the man scream and yell at him in the past, but never like this. Something about this whole situation had him really riled up.

"Just cut to the chase, Cid. Why are you so teed off?"

"Do the names Sara and Mei-Ling ring a bell?"

Confused, Jonathan asked, "What *about* them?"

Cid shook his head. His mouth was pressed into a thin line. "What about Mei-Ling?"

"Cid, I do love Mei-Ling, but it's time for me to move on."

"And you have?"

"I have."

"How do you call nearly 'hijacking a shuttle to race off and break someone out of prison' moving on?"

"It was a lack of judgment on my part."

Cid was beginning to get frustrated. "Jon, the love you two have together just doesn't go away."

"Cid, stop. It's over."

Silence. "*Really?*"

"Really."

Cid stared at him from across the desk. "All right. That's all."

Jonathan left Cid's office and found Novena sitting in the receptionist's room. She stood up and walked over to him.

"Everything all right?"

"Yeah. Don't worry, everything will be fine."

She nodded, giving him a nervous smile as she entered Cid's office.

NOVENA SAT DOWN IN one of the chairs facing Cid's desk. He just stared at her, not saying anything. It was making her uncomfortable. "You know, you two picked the worst time to do the deed, with all the hell that is about to break loose in this galaxy."

Novena was silent, her only response the nodding of her head.

"Be honest with me, Novena. I know that you love him—I mean, *really* love him. But do you believe that he has truly moved on?"

She should have said yes, but she couldn't. She tried her hardest, but nothing came out of her mouth.

Cid did not smile, did not laugh, did not say "I told you so." He just got up from his chair and stood beside her, placing his hand on her shoulder. He gave it a squeeze as she started to cry, and he told her he was sorry.

11

ARRIVAL

RYAN BLAKE SAT IN his seat on the shuttle, a transport from one of the space stations that was above Earth 2. He'd had to leave his own ship at the station, go through a security checkpoint that took an hour, then ride a shuttle down to the surface. They would transport his spaceship to the surface separately.

He could understand the extra security. With Mei-Ling under arrest, and the trial that was on the horizon, they would want to make sure that anybody coming to the planet wasn't going to cause any trouble.

Too bad for them; that was his job.

He thought back to the briefing that he'd received before he'd begun his journey to Earth 2. His orders were to link up with the Resistance and formulate a plan that would break Mei-Ling out of prison, but not until after her punishment had been meted out. Mei-Ling wanted to be a martyr for her father's dream and hurt Wright at the same time. Ryan didn't know how she had that planned, but he would soon find out.

He wondered how the Resistance would handle the news that they wouldn't be breaking Mei-Ling out until after she'd been beaten. Many of them wouldn't stand for it. Oh well, it wasn't *his* problem; let Nesith deal with it.

An announcement came over the intercom. "We are starting our approach to Earth 2. Please stay fastened into your seat until you are told otherwise."

Earth 2. What a joke.

From what the records showed, Earth 2 didn't even faintly resemble the original Earth.

Before the Destruction of Earth, it had became a technological planet, but its ecological nature remained intact, thanks to new technology and energy sources that had saved the environment.

Earth 2 was very close to the original, but not *quite*. No matter how hard they tried, they would never be able to recreate their home. There was only one Earth.

When the shuttle landed, Ryan followed the rest of the passengers out.

In the spaceport, he went directly to the counter and received the ticket to claim his ship. He found a transport train and rode it to the lot.

At the lot, he gave his ticket to the attendant. He told Ryan the security crew hadn't found any contraband of any sort, so he was free to leave the spaceport. He thanked the attendant and was given his keys.

Ryan transferred his ship to the storage center of the spaceport and paid for ten days' rent. Then he went back to his ship, lowered the ramp, started his hover-car, and drove out of the lot.

ABOUT AN HOUR AFTER he'd left the spaceport, he reached the outskirts of the capital.

He navigated through the lower regions, not bothering to turn up into the Sky-Lanes, which would have taken him into the more proper sections of the city.

Like most planets with giant metropolises, the lower parts of the city were where most of the lower and middle class lived, while the upper class lived in the higher parts of the city.

In the higher sections, people traveled from place to place by using hover-cars and walkways that connect to each building. The lanes the hover-cars used for travel were called Sky-Lanes. These would be a travel nightmare if it weren't for the navigation computers in every hover-car and the stoplight system the Sky-Lanes employed to help ensure safe travel. There'd been a few crashes here and there, but all in all, it was a perfectly safe way to travel.

Ryan continued to follow traffic into the lower regions of the city. Soon, he came to a section that had merchants on either side of the roadways. He'd reached the marketplace.

He found a parking garage and parked his hover-car, then exited the building and turned left, heading deeper into the crowded streets full of buyers and sellers.

The streets were designed so that people could cross from one side to the other safely. There were stairways and tunnels underneath the roadway. People could use them to quickly get to the other side, or they could take a chance and cross the street, using the crosswalks at the stoplights.

He soon came to a small bar between two large buildings. He entered and sat down at the counter. It was lunchtime, and the place was almost full.

As soon as he sat down, the bartender came up to him. "Hello, sir. What can I do for you?"

"A ham sandwich, chips, and a beer, please."

"It's the middle of the day. Kind of early to start drinking, don't you think?"

"Hey, it's five o'clock *somewhere*, right?"

The bartender took his order and disappeared into the kitchen. He came back five minutes later with a plate. He sat it down in front of Ryan and, grabbing a glass, filled it with beer from the tap. He set it on a coaster and pushed it in front of Ryan, who nodded and smiled.

"Thank you."

The bartender nodded back and walked off. Ryan sat and ate; he wasn't in any hurry.

When he finished, he pushed the glass away and stood up. Slipping the coaster into his pocket, he asked, "Can you tell me where the bathroom is?"

The bartender pointed behind him, toward a set of stairs that went down to a lower floor. "It's down the stairs, first door on the right."

"Thanks."

He walked to the back of the bar, then down the stairs and along a short hallway. When he reached two sets of doors, one labeled MEN, the other WOMEN, he opened the men's room door and entered.

In the last stall, he found a small hole in the wall. He inserted the coaster and waited. He could feel himself being scanned by sensors in the walls.

When the scan was completed, the wall to his right opened up. He turned to face a small corridor, at the end of which stood a door. He felt himself being scanned again.

A voice came over a speaker on the wall. "How's the weather?"

"Cloudy, with a hint of rain," he replied.

A few seconds later, the door opened.

Ryan entered the room and looked around. There were people sitting at computers and overseeing monitors. A man came up to him and stuck out his hand.

"Hello, Lieutenant Blake, I'm Charles. A pleasure to meet you."

Ryan grabbed his hand and shook it. "Thanks. Where's the boss?"

He motioned to a door behind him. "This way."

Ryan followed Charles to the door and into a hallway. As they were walking, Ryan saw other doors. He looked inside the rooms as he passed them and saw some people sitting at computers, others firing pistols and rifles at the firing range, and others practicing martial arts.

The Resistance had been formed nearly five years before, after Jonathan's exile. Mei-Ling and others felt that Wright had gone too far with what he'd done to Jonathan and knew that he was going to do something terrible in the future. The Resistance had been formed by

Mei-Ling, Isabella, Nesith, Terri Albright, and Steven Drake; they'd decided to secretly prepare for whatever Wright might have in mind.

Ryan and Charles came to another door, and Charles opened it. They walked into a small room with nothing in it but a few chairs and a woman seated behind a desk. The woman smiled. "Hello. Lieutenant Nesith is waiting for you. I'll tell him you're here."

"Thank you." Ryan shook Charles's hand again. "Thanks, Charlie. Have fun."

Charles thanked him and left. Ryan walked past the secretary and entered Nesith's office. It was sparsely furnished, with only a desk, some chairs, a small table, and a viewscreen. Nesith was sitting behind the desk.

Nesith was a Solien, a race of reptilian people who ranged in height from six to seven feet and were extremely muscular. The species had the ability to see in both normal and inferred vision. Nesith was the son of a former tribal leader and a co-leader of the Resistance. He was posing as a food importer supplying fish from his home planet.

When Ryan entered, Nesith rose and, grasping his hand in greeting, said, "I'm glad that you're here, my friend." Nesith gave him a smile—or what stood for a smile from a Solien.

Ryan returned the greeting. "No problem. From what I hear, you'll need my help."

Nesith nodded and headed for the chair behind his desk, while Ryan made his way to the liquor cabinet. "You don't mind if I have a drink, do you?"

Nesith waved a hand in Ryan's direction. "Go for it. I don't drink that stuff anyway; Isabella mostly does."

"Ah, yes. Isabella," Ryan said, pouring a glass of Scotch. "How are the two of you doing?"

"Just fine."

Ryan paused. *'Fine'. That doesn't sound good.*

Not many people knew that Isabella and Nesith were together. For now, they were keeping it quiet, most likely because Nesith's clan would blow a gasket if they found out that he was dating a human. That, and the fact that they were dating right in the middle of the Imperial

Guard's home world, where people were not too happy about inter-species dating. But Ryan thought that if they really loved each other, they could make a go of it. Hell, if his uncle could marry a Tigeras, then Nesith and Isabella should be able to make their relationship work.

Ryan walked toward Nesith's desk and sat down in a chair. "Fine?" he asked. "Not great?"

"*Fine*. Things are *great*."

Ryan stared at Nesith, trying to read his face. It was hard with a Solien. Nesith had always been good at keeping his emotions hidden when necessary.

"Is everything all right between you and Isabella?" He paused for a moment before continuing, "Or is there something *else* that's bothering you?"

"Yes, Ryan. Everything is fine between the two of us." He paused for a moment. "But there *is* something that's bothering her."

Ryan could ask him what it was, or he could take a wild guess, but he already knew what the problem was. "Let me take a crack at the problem. Mei-Ling."

Nesith nodded. "The minute she arrived after escaping the palace, Isabella wanted us to mount a rescue party, to break Mei-Ling out of prison." He shifted in his seat. "When I told her we weren't going to break her out until after the punishment, she became furious."

Ryan took another drink from his glass. "Did you explain Mei-Ling's plan?"

"I never got the chance. After she ranted and raved, she stormed out of here, and no one has heard from her since."

Ryan was in the middle of his drink when he heard this. He paused for a moment, drained the rest of his glass, then got up and headed to the cabinet for a refill. "Do you have any idea where she might be?"

Nesith shook his head. "No. Although I *do* have a few ideas about what she's up to."

Ryan had an idea too. He poured himself another glass. "No doubt she's forming a plan of her own to break Mei-Ling out of prison."

"I agree," Nesith said. "What should we do about it?"

Ryan laughed at Nesith's question as he sat back down. "We won't do *anything*. Let Isabella do what she wants."

Nesith looked surprised at Ryan's answer. "But Mei-Ling said—"

"Don't worry about what Mei-Ling said." Ryan leaned forward in his seat. "We'll carry out our orders. We'll wait until the punishment is over; when it is, we'll break out Mei-Ling and hightail it to Measha Station."

From the look on Nesith's face, it was clear that he didn't like the way it was going to play out, but he nodded. "All right. We'll do it *your* way—though Mei-Ling probably won't like it."

"I'll take care of Mei-Ling."

"And what if Isabella succeeds?"

"Mei-Ling won't go with her. Remember, she wants to ruin Wright. She can't do that if she breaks out of jail."

"And if they give her the death penalty?"

"Won't happen. Wright needs her alive. For now."

Nesith did not like what he was hearing. "I have a feeling that at the end of all this, there'll be one big argument."

Ryan nodded in agreement as he drank some more of his scotch.

"True. But don't worry. I'll take full responsibility for any disagreements."

"Fine by me," Nesith said. "So, do you want to start planning now or later?"

Ryan sat still for a moment, thinking. "I'll rest first and then check to see if Jonathan is making any progress."

"So you heard about what happened."

Ryan looked at Nesith, not displaying any emotion.

Nesith nodded. "Okay. Do you remember the way to the comm room?"

"Yes, I do," Ryan said. He finished the rest of his drink and stood up. So did Nesith. "Thanks, Nesith." Ryan stuck out his hand.

Nesith grabbed the hand and shook it. "No problem. See you tomorrow, Lieutenant."

Ryan said good night and left Nesith's office. When he was past the waiting area, he took a right and headed for comm room, trying not to worry too much about Jonathan.

12

THE TRIAL

MEI-LING SAT IN A jail cell. The stun blast that she'd received had knocked her out for twelve hours. It has been one week since she had awakened; now she was waiting for her trial. She knew that it wouldn't take long for it to start. Wright would want it to be sooner rather than later, to keep her from gaining sympathy from the Imperial population.

She took in her surroundings. The cell she was in certainly wasn't an ordinary jail cell. Typical cells had a bed, drawers, a bathroom, and a viewscreen. Hers looked more like a lavish hotel room, with a queen-sized bed, fancy oversized drawers, a window with curtains, and a big viewscreen. The bathroom had a shower, a double sink, and a hot tub. The only thing that kept the cell from looking completely like a hotel room was the energy door.

Fancy cells were only for those with high enough political status, not for lowly criminals. She was surprised to find herself there; since she was dealing with Wright, she'd thought he would place her in a regular cell just to spite her, but it looked as if he couldn't do it. To a certain point, he had to play it by the book to make the trial look legitimate.

She'd been awake for a few hours when a guard came and told her that her trial was scheduled for the following week.

On the day of her trial, she received a visitor.

"Ms. Ling?" said a male voice coming from the speaker.

She walked over to a panel and pressed the TALK button. "Yes?"

She noticed that he hadn't called her "Majesty" or "High Ruler." Word was spreading fast about what she had done.

"You have a visitor," he told her.

"Who is it?"

"A woman."

He didn't say anything else, but he didn't have to; she knew who the visitor was. Mei-Ling breathed a heavy sigh. She'd hoped Isabella would stay out of the palace, but she knew deep down that she would not.

"Let her in." She walked to the energy door, designed to be a two-way or one-way see-through door. The prisoner could adjust it so that he or she could look out but no one could look in, allowing some privacy. The guards had special cards that made the doors two-way, so they could check up on the prisoners. There were also key pads outside the doors, which were used to override them.

Mei-Ling could hear the guard's and Isabella's approaching footsteps. They stepped in front of the door a few seconds later. The guard inserted his keycard, and the door faded. Isabella stepped through and the guard reactivated the door.

"I'll leave you two alone. Call us on the intercom when you're finished."

"Yes. Thank you." The guard turned and left. Mei-Ling activated the door's one-way feature and turned a face full of anger on Isabella. "What are you doing here?"

"I came to see how you're doing," Isabella said.

Mei-Ling exhaled and looked a little bit calmer, but not completely. "I'm doing fine. As you can see, I'm being treated very well."

"Yeah," Isabella agreed. "For now."

Mei-Ling didn't say anything. She knew what Isabella meant: When she was found guilty, she would be publicly beaten. There was no doubt that she was going to be found guilty; Wright had surely replaced a few of the Imperial Council with those who would support him. The public whipping was mostly for humiliation. They would strip her of her clothes and whip her with all kinds of instruments in front of a planet-wide audience.

"You don't have to do this," Isabella said.

Mei-Ling looked into her eyes. "Yes I *do*. I have no choice."

"Yes, you do," Isabella insisted, as she took hold of Mei-Ling's right arm. "We can get you out of here!" she said in desperation.

Mei-Ling narrowed her eyes. "What do you mean?" she asked warily.

"As you know, we have a small number of Resistance members posing as guards throughout the palace," Isabella explained.

For several years, the Resistance had embedded members as guards in the palace and at several other important locations. Their purpose was to gather intelligence, and to be on hand when and if the Resistance needed to take over the complex.

"All of them are on guard duty here and on the way to the space dock. We can walk out of here, fly away, and nobody would know," Isabella said.

"Yes, we could," Mei-Ling said, taking a few steps toward the window. "That's true." She turned around and looked at Isabella. "But I can't do that," she said with conviction. "If I leave, it'll look as if Wright's behavior was justified all along. We can't let that happen!"

Isabella stood still. The expression on her face was one of confusion. Mei-Ling could tell that she was thinking hard. Then her eyes opened wide. Her mouth turned dry, and she couldn't breathe as the realization hit her like a kick in the stomach. "*You planned this all along?*" she asked, her voice shaking.

Mei-Ling didn't reply. She turned around and looked out the window, trying to hide the tears in her eyes. She was able to steady herself enough to utter one word: "Yes."

After that, the tears started flowing. With one word, Mei-Ling had confessed her greatest betrayal. She was going to let herself get thrown to the wolves, willingly. Isabella was able to get out a few words. "How could you keep this from me?"

Mei-Ling winced at Isabella's harsh words. "I had to; you and the others would have tried to stop me." She turned slowly toward her. "This is the only way to get my influence and authority back. Wright has been slowly taking control ever since my father's death. I made a promise to him on his deathbed that I would *never* let the Imperial Guard fall to corruption, and I will do whatever it takes to keep that promise!"

Mei-Ling could tell Isabella was still hurt, and she had every right to be: in the thirty years that they had known each other, there had been no secrets between them. They'd shared everything with each other. They were like sisters.

Isabella shook her head. "You know that no one is going to like this."

Mei-Ling gave out a snort. "You *think?*"

"I'm serious, Mei-Ling," she said firmly. She was trying to hold back tears as she talked. "When Cid finds out, there's going to be chaos—not to mention that Jonathan and Thomas will carve a path through Imperial Guard space to get here."

"Cid already knows," Mei-Ling said. "And I have no doubt that the moment my talk with Thomas ended, he was making a plan to get me out. Expect someone to contact you very soon, if they haven't already."

"How would Cid know—" she stopped and shook her head. "Scratch that. The Infiltrators!"

Mei-Ling nodded.

"I'm surprised he didn't try to stop you."

"He *did* try. He called me up and gave me the talk of a lifetime, but I told him the same thing that I've told you: *Nothing* he can do is going to stop me!" She paused for a moment. "I also asked him to keep it quiet." Mei-Ling's mouth turned into a half smile. "You can guess what his reaction was."

Isabella returned the smile. "I bet he looked like he was having a coronary." She was silent for moment before she spoke again, "Who else knows?"

"What do you mean?"

"Don't play dumb."

Mei-Ling turned her head to the side, looking at the ground.

Isabella suddenly understood. "You told someone else about the plan, didn't you!"

"Yes."

"Who?"

Mei-Ling looked back at Isabella. "Nesith."

This angered Isabella. "I should have known."

"Don't get angry at him," Mei-Ling said.

"Why did you tell him and not me?"

"Because I knew you would somehow try to stop me, and I didn't need to deal with that—and *someone* needed to know what was going on."

Isabella looked as if she were about to argue with her but stopped, knowing that she was right.

Without warning, the one-way feature on the door faded away. On the other side were three guards; one was the guard who had escorted Isabella to the cell. They didn't say anything for a moment. The two women looked at their faces. They were expressionless. But their eyes, full of sadness and worry, said it all; they knew that Mei-Ling wasn't coming with them and that she was going to be falsely convicted, taken out in public, stripped, and beaten. She would lose her title, her dignity, her respect, her pride. She was going to sacrifice it all to show everyone the truth.

After a moment, one of the guards finally spoke, "It's time, ma'am. The council is waiting." He was able to keep the emotions in his eyes from showing. Taking out his card, he deactivated the door. They stood in the entrance, waiting.

Mei-Ling took hold of Isabella's hands and held them tightly. "Isabella, I need you to make me a promise," she pleaded.

Isabella nodded her head slowly, desperately trying to hold back the tears that were returning. "What is it?"

"Ma'am." The two women turned their attention back to the guards. For a moment, they'd forgotten that the men were there. "We need to go."

Mei-Ling held up a finger. She turned back to her friend. "I need you to be strong for me," she said. "For me and for everyone else in the Resistance. Okay?"

"But what about *afterward?* Are you just going to rot away in this cell for the rest of your life?"

"No. This is only part one. There is a plan in place to break me out. Then the real work begins." Tears were slowly falling down her cheeks. "I hope to see you again—you and everyone else."

Isabella nodded her head. "Me, too."

The two women embraced each other, letting their tears finally flow freely, like water breaking through a dam. All the emotions they'd been holding back were finally released. After a moment, they felt another presence beside them. Turning, they saw two of the three guards standing there.

"Ma'am, we have to leave," one of the guards said, barely holding back his own tears.

Mei-Ling nodded and the two women separated. Mei-Ling held up both her hands, waiting for them to put the magnet cuffs on. One of the guards shook his head. "That won't be necessary," he said. Magnet cuffs used magnetic links to keep them locked around the wrists or ankles. They could be demagnetized only with a key kept by the guard.

Mei-Ling shook her head. "I am a prisoner. You should treat me as one." The guards had hesitant looks on their faces. "This is my last order to you as your ruler."

With regret in his eyes, one of the guards placed a pair of cuffs on her wrists and another on her ankles. They walked her out of the cell. The two lifelong friends didn't look at each other or say good-bye; they were too afraid to do so. When Mei- Ling reached the exit, the guard who had escorted Isabella to the cell stayed behind, while the other two stood on either side of Mei-Ling and led her to the elevator that would take her to the high court, where her trial was to take place.

THE UNDERCOVER RESISTANCE MEMBER looked at Isabella. The emotions that his eyes had shown earlier were now plainly visible on his face. "It is time for us to go," he said.

"Then let's get out of here," she said as she left the cell. "We have lots to do."

EI-LING AND THE GUARDS stopped at the elevator. One of them pushed a button, and the doors opened. They entered. As the doors closed, one of them pushed another button, and the elevator began to go up. All of this happened in a not-uncomfortable silence. There was no need to say anything or try to change her mind. They knew from the conversation she'd had with Isabella that she had made her choice. Now there was nothing they could do except to take her to her doom.

It didn't take them long to reach their destination. The doors opened; Wright was standing on the other side. The guards were surprised to see him, but Mei-Ling wasn't; she had expected to encounter him before the trial.

"Follow me!" he commanded. The guards nodded as they started walking. Mei-Ling could tell that they were disgusted by what he was doing and didn't want to follow his orders. It would have been so easy to kill him right then, but that would not have helped Mei-Ling or solved anything. They had to put on their game faces and continue.

They reached a door, and Wright glanced at the two guards. "Stay outside for a moment," he said. The two nodded and took up positions on both sides of the door. Wright opened it and followed her in. The room was small and sparsely furnished, with only a table and four chairs. She walked to one side of the table while Wright stood on the other. He was no longer wearing his military uniform; instead he'd arrayed himself as high ruler of the Imperial Guard.

"What do you want, Wright?"

"That's *Lord* Wright now, Mei-Ling."

She offered a mock smile. "So sorry. What's this about, Wright?"

His annoyance at her refusal to utter the title was palpable. Her smile widened. He forced himself to calm down. He could argue with her all night, and they didn't have all night. "You know," he said, "you don't have to go through this."

She became suspicious. "Oh?"

"I'm willing to stop the trial, and the punishment, if you do something for me," he said.

"What would *that* be?"

"I want you to go before the council and the planet to tell them that you are guilty of all the criminal charges. Then you will tell the people of the Imperial Guard that they need to be strong so that they can support their new ruler. You will introduce me as the high ruler of the Imperial Guard."

He was aware that she had more favor and influence among the population of the Imperial Guard than he did, and she knew it. He needed a public transfer of support from her to him—and that, lacking it, he might win over *some* of them, but not *all*.

"What would I receive in exchange?" Mei-Ling asked.

"You will be placed under planetary arrest for the rest of your life. You would have your old room in the palace back, and you would still receive visitors, but you would never be allowed to enter politics again." Wright smiled, thinking that he had her in his control. "What do you think?"

She returned the smile for a brief moment. "I would rather *die* than do anything that would give you any power!" she said with disgust in her voice.

His expression slumped from triumphant smile to angry frown, his lower lip shaking with anger. "Fine!" he spat out, stalked to the door, and pounded on it. "Guards!" he called out. They opened the door and entered.

Wright pointed a finger at her. "Take the prisoner to the high court. It is time for her trial."

They nodded and took up their positions next to her. As they walked her out, she paused in front of Wright. "You're going to have to pry the power I still hold from my cold dead hands, just as you tried to wrest it from my father," she said. He took a step back in surprise. "That's right!" she said, her voice filled with satisfaction. "I know that you sent an assassin after my father, and that you framed Jonathan for the destruction of Gypsia and Timothy's death. Soon, *everyone* will know, Wright. *Everyone!*" When she had finished, the two guards escorted her out of the small room, leaving Wright alone to think about what she had said.

He hadn't expected it, hadn't known she had that much knowledge of his activities. He was, as the term went, caught with the assassin's knife in his hand. He didn't know what to do. He screamed in anger, hurled a chair against the wall, grabbed the edge of the table and up-ended it.

MEI-LING AND THE GUARDS approached the high court, where the council was sitting. They stopped outside and waited to be told when to enter. About ten minutes after they had arrived, someone came through the doors and said they could enter. Mei-Ling stood up, and the guards followed.

They entered and made their way down the aisle. The room was circular in shape, with walls of marble polished to the point that they shone like glass. The domed ceiling was made of glass. On the walls, stained glass windows portrayed the past high rulers of the Imperial Guard and the dates of their rule. Chairs filled half of the room; the other half was occupied by tables for the prosecution and defense. At the far end was the council's table, each of its seats equipped with a computer and private phone. During the day, light coming through the ceiling illuminated the room; at night, wall sconces emitted an enveloping light. There were two entrances—the main one, through which spectators and prisoners entered, and a back one for use by the council. Behind that door lay the council's chambers, where members met to discuss galactic affairs and receive reports from every cluster in their territory. They had private offices in which to work as well, and aides to help them manage.

The Council of Seven, as the group was called, consisted of six representatives plus the high ruler of the Imperial Guard. Deidre Yull represented the Urall Cluster, Steven Drake the Dragon Cluster, and Terri Albright the Mu Cluster. The new military advisor was Fleet Admiral Marcus Albright. Mei-Ling had heard that he'd returned safely from his failed mission to capture the *Twilight Star*, then had been made fleet admiral by Wright. Jill Janis represented the Picku Cluster, and Jerry Weeks the Quartz Cluster; last was the high ruler, Scott Wright. The council membership was completely different from Mei- Ling's old one. Terri and Steven were the only ones who still remained; Wright had replaced the others with those who would do his bidding.

Mei-Ling came down the aisle and sat at the table on her left. Her lawyer, Edward James, was already there. He looked at her but didn't say anything. There was nothing to say. His eyes told all that she needed to know.

She glanced to her right and saw Zack Lane, the special prosecutor, at his table, looking just as unhappy as Edward. The Imperial Guard had a special prosecutor's office that handled cases involving government officials and also presented all the cases to the council.

The Council of Seven heard only cases of the most serious nature. These include treason, murder of high government officials, espionage, and a few other crimes.

Seeing Edward and Zack in the same room brought back memories of the conversation that they'd had earlier in the week. About a day and a half after she awakened from the stun blasts she had received, Edward had come to her cell to tell her the charges that were being brought against her, and to notify her that he was to represent her in her trial.

Before he could tell her his strategy, she had told him that she didn't want to fight the charges.

*E*VERYONE KNOWS THAT THESE *charges are bogus, ma'am," he had told her after he finished reading her the charges: espionage, conspiring with different governments, resisting arrest, and attempting the assassination of LordWright. That last one had been made possible because of her attack on Delta Team when they attempted to arrest her.*

Edward had been sitting in a chair, looking at a stack of papers that he'd removed from his case. "Even with all this evidence, I believe that we may find a way to——"

"Edward," Mei-Ling had interrupted, holding up her hand to stop him from going any further. "I do not intend to fight the charges."

Edward had looked at her, not believing what he was hearing.

"Ma'am, please. We can beat this," he'd said, almost pleading. "It's going to be long and hard, but we can beat it."

Mei-Ling had smiled and shaken her head. That was Edward. Always the optimist. Edward James was one of the best lawyers in the Imperial Guard—— and also one of Mei-Ling's best friends. She had known him for many years.

He'd also defended Jonathan at his court-martial; now here he was, fighting for her. He didn't know about her plan, and she had no incentive to tell him.

She'd stood up and patted his arm. "Everything'll be all right."

"But, ma'am, you can't just give up," he had pleaded. "It will be suicide."

"I've made up my mind, Edward."

"Oh, really?" He had left his chair and turned toward the door. "We'll see about that."

Mei-Ling's eyes had narrowed. "What are you doing?"

"Guard!" he'd shouted.

"What are you doing?" she had repeated.

"Yes, sir?" the guard had asked as he approached the door.

"Ask Prosecutor Lane to come here immediately."

"Yes, sir," the guard had said, talking into his comm unit as he was walking away.

Edward had turned around to see an angry Mei-Ling staring daggers at him.

She had spoken first, "Whatever you have up your sleeve won't work."

He'd shrugged and said, "Probably not, but I have to try something to talk you out of this suicidal decision."

Twenty minutes later, Zack Lane had appeared. Like James, he was one of the best special prosecutors of the Imperial Guard—and one of her best friends.

"I'm glad you called. I was about to ring your office to—"

"Mei-Ling is not going to fight the charges," Edward had told him.

Zack's face had frozen, and he had faced her in shock and anger. "What are you, crazy?" he'd asked. "The evidence that has been given to me is very incriminating. If you don't fight it, you will be convicted and beaten."

Mei-Ling had chuckled and shaken her head. "Come on, Zack," she'd muttered, "do you really believe that I have any chance at all of winning?"

Zack had shuffled his feet. "It's possible," he had finally said.

"Oh, please. I bet that you got that evidence just hours after my arrest?"

Zack didn't say anything.

"And that Wright has asked for a speedy trial?"

Zack had remained silent.

"And that he has conveniently replaced several members of the council who are completely loyal to him?"

Zack had finally had enough. "Yes, yes, and yes!" he'd shouted. "You're right!

He has this whole thing rigged, and I can't seem to stop it!"

"And I don't want you to," she had said. "Zack, Edward. Please!" They had looked at each other in defeat.

"I don't like this," Zack had said.

"And neither do I," Edward had agreed.

"I know, but please go along with it."

NOW HERE SHE SAT, in the high court over which she herself had once presided; she now stood as the accused, waiting for the verdict that she knew was coming.

Six of the council members had already been seated and were waiting for Wright to make his entrance.

The bailiff's voice rose over the loud speaker. "All rise for the High Ruler of the Imperial Guard, Lord Wright."

The spectators rose from their seats as did the council members and the members of the prosecution and defense. Mei-Ling debated whether or not to stand up, just to push Wright's buttons, but decided not to go that route. She would have ample time to infatuate him later on.

The door behind the council's table opened, and Wright emerged. He sat down, turned on his mike, and said in a calm voice, "Please be seated. . . .Bailiff, read the list of charges."

"Yes, my Lord." The bailiff turned to the crowd and read the charges from his PDA. "Mei-Ling, former high ruler of the Imperial Guard, is charged with committing espionage, conspiring with different governments, resisting arrest, and attempting the assassination of Lord Wright."

"How does the defendant plead?" Wright asked.

Edward rose from of his seat. "Not guilty, my Lord." As he sat down, Mei-Ling could see from the look on his face how much he hated saying "Lord."

Wright nodded, then turned his attention to Zack. "Mr. Prosecutor, you may begin your case."

Zack stood up. "Thank you, my Lord."

For the next several hours, Zack presented evidence to the council proving her guilt, and answered any questions they had. He showed video recordings of her meetings with Thomas and the Tigeras, as well as comm calls that revealed her plans to betray the Imperial Guard. Mei-Ling *had* had secret meetings with Thomas and other alien governments, but the ones that were shown were definite fakes. She wondered how far in advance Wright had made those.

During the whole affair, Edward didn't raise objections, just as she had requested.

The only video feed that was not a fake was the one of her attacking Delta Team. As she watched the feed, she couldn't resist a smile. She looked up at Wright and saw that he was not as amused as she.

Good. Get angry, she thought. It would come in handy later.

As the feed ended, Zack looked up at the council. "The prosecution rests, councilmen." He sat down, looking defeated.

"Thank you, Mr. Lane." Wright turned his attention to Mei-Ling and Edward. "The defense may present its case, or we can recess until tomorrow," he said with a smug smile.

Edward looked at Mei-Ling and stood up. "Councilmen, the defense does not have a case to present. My client wishes only to say a few words before you make your judgment."

Mei-Ling could see the smile that Wright was barely containing. "Very well," he said. "The defendant may rise and speak."

Mei-Ling stood up and started, not even thanking Wright. "My father had a dream. It may seem impossible, but he was slowly working toward it. He wanted to unite humanity under one flag." She stopped to let the audience take this in. "It was no secret that Shang-Ling had wanted to merge the Imperial Guard with the Ashlon Republic, but there had been much resistance against it.

"He understood that humans were in for a dark future if they didn't stand together, so he started working with the Ashlon Republic to keep peace and see that everyone worked together. But his dream was cut short when he was killed. It was said that an alien extremist killed him, and that just threw more fuel onto the fire. His murder went unsolved, and I took up the mantle and continued the work that my father had begun.

"Yes, I am also working with the Ashlon Republic in hopes of merging the two governments, because I truly believe in my father's vision that only by standing together can humanity survive the dark times that are sure to come. During my years as high ruler I was able to discover who had killed my father."

The audience started to talk in heated voices. Before the council could quiet them down, Mei-Ling pointed a finger at Wright.

"It was Wright. He hired an alien assassin to kill my father, and he set me up on these fake charges to get me out of the way."

Before she could continue, Wright started screaming, "Shut *up*! You shut up and quit spreading *lies*!"

"Lord Wright, please calm down and let her finish."

Wright turned toward the councilman who had spoken. It was Terri.

"I will not let her spread these lies about me!"

"This is her time to speak," she said fiercely. "She has every right to say what she pleases, so kindly sit down and let her finish."

Wright was about to say more when he realized that he was standing. He also noticed that the audience was staring at him. He swallowed his comments and sat back down.

"Thank you," Terri said. To Mei-Ling, she said, "You may continue."

Mei-Ling just smiled. "I have nothing else to say." She sat back down in her chair.

"All right then," Steve said. "We will now have closing statements and then we will convene to decide a verdict."

THE COUNCIL ENTERED ITS chambers behind the high court and headed straight for the meeting room. Wright entered first and started screaming before the rest of the council had a chance to enter.

"She is *dead*! I don't care *how* the vote turns out! She humiliated me and had no respect for the council!"

"That's not for you to decide," Terri reminded him.

When everyone had entered the room, Terri shut the door and looked at Wright.

"Only the vote of the entire council can grant that request. Without our unanimous agreement, Mei-Ling will never get the death penalty."

Wright was fuming. Terri was right; Only a unanimous vote could impose the death penalty. He wanted to say, "To hell with the council's vote," but he had no choice: until he dissolved the council completely, he would have to play by the rules.

"Fine," he said. "Then let's all have a seat and get started with the voting and deliberation process."

Terri snorted. "*What* voting process?"

Wright stopped and looked at her. "*What was that?*" he asked.

Steve was doing all he could to keep from laughing, but a little chuckle escaped through his lips. Wright heard it and turned his attention to him.

"What's so funny, Drake?"

"This whole thing." When Wright didn't speak, Drake continued, "We're all going through the motions—trial, deliberations, voting, punishing—knowing full well that this is all fixed!"

Wright was about to explode, but Steve pushed on. "We all know that you have wanted this position for a long time. You have been slithering your way here for years. Shang-Ling's murder, Jonathan's trial and exile, and now Mei-Ling's trial—all just part of your plan."

"And this new council," Terri added, waving her hand at everyone in the room, "is filled with people who are completely loyal to you, ensuring your victory over Mei-Ling and solidifying your position as high ruler."

Terri smiled triumphantly. "But you couldn't get rid of Steve and me. And without our vote, you won't be able to get Mei-Ling out of your way. You'll be able to find her guilty, beat her in public, and keep her sequestered for the rest of her life—but you won't be able to kill her!"

Terri stopped to let Wright soak up her and Steve's words. Wright wanted to kill them so badly, but he couldn't. Not yet. They were too powerful. *But soon. Oh, yes, soon.*

Wright smiled at them. "Nice theory. Too bad you can't prove it."

The two councilmen stood their ground. "Someday we will, Wright," Steve said.

"In the meantime, let's have deliberations. Is there anything about the evidence that anybody wants to discuss?" No one spoke. Wright could see that Terri and Steve wanted to dispute the evidence, but they remained silent, knowing that it would do no good to protest.

"Nothing? Okay, then, let's have the first vote. All those for guilty, raise your hand." One by one, the council members raised their hands—except Steve and Terri. Wright was a little annoyed, but he had won. Mei-Ling was found guilty in a 5-2 vote.

"The defendant is judged guilty. Let's pass on to the punishment and sentencing."

They debated for a few minutes on the method of punishment, then on sentencing. After about twenty minutes, they were ready to vote.

On the death penalty, the vote was again 5-2, and Wright was again irritated, but not as much as he thought he would be—probably because he had expected Steve and Terri not to vote for it.

They voted on the method of punishment, which turned out to be a public beating, the most common for high officials.

Wright allowed himself a smile when he saw Terri and Steve wince at the final number of beatings.

Next came sentencing. After the punishment had been meted out, the accused would be put in jail, under house arrest, or some other kind of imprisonment for a certain amount of time; or they would be released. It all depended on the case and the court's decision.

They began the voting process, and not surprisingly, it didn't take long. At the end, they sentenced her to house arrest and barred her from taking part in politics again.

When they finished all the paperwork, Wright pushed a button on the table and spoke into a comm unit. "Bailiff, enter."

The bailiff stopped just inside the doorway. "Yes, My Lord?"

Wright rose and and handed him a small stack of papers. "We are ready to pronounce our verdict. After it is read, you may initiate the process."

The bailiff nodded. "Shall I announce that a verdict has been reached?"

"Not yet. Wait five minutes. Give everyone ten minutes to enter the courtroom, and then seal it off," he said. "Then announce our arrival."

The bailiff bowed. "Yes, my Lord." He left the room, closing the door behind him.

Wright turned to address everyone in the room. "I suggest that you use this time to get a few moments of rest before we head out." He looked at Terri and Steve. "That is all, people." He turned and left the room.

After he left, the other members began to follow suit. Only Terri and Steve remained. They looked at each other, feeling defeated.

Steve was the first to speak. "This is going to be bad," he said.

"Yes, it is." She took a deep breath and exhaled. "But there's nothing we can do but go along for the ride."

Steve didn't say anything. He didn't have to. Terri could tell by his face that he wasn't happy about it. And neither was she.

TEN MINUTES AFTER THE bailiff made his announcement, he sealed the doors to the high court, approached the council table, and announced, "All rise for the Imperial Council." Everyone in the courtroom stood up as the council entered. This time, Wright was with them.

When all were seated, Wright spoke: "Bailiff, read the verdict to the court."

The bailiff nodded, picked up a piece of paper from Wright, and returned to the microphone. He opened it and read what it said, taking a breath: "In the case of the *Imperial Guard vs. Mei-Ling*, the council finds the defendant guilty on all charges."

When the bailiff finished, the whole courtroom exploded into yells and shouts. People were raising their fists and screaming. Some were happy that she'd been found guilty, others expressing deep anger. It took the court a few minutes to calm the spectators.

When all was quiet, Wright spoke once more, "Bailiff, read the sentence."

The bailiff nodded and continued. "The accused shall be placed under house arrest for the rest of her life. She will never take part in politics again, and she shall be whipped thirty times in public."

When the last bit was read, the spectators exploded once again, only this time more loudly. It took the court twice as long to calm the audience down. When they were quiet, Wright spoke again.

"The whipping will take place in the grand courtyard inside the palace at five PM. Court is adjourned."

13

PUNISHMENT

IT WAS FOUR-THIRTY, AND Terri and Steve were standing silently on a palace balcony overlooking the courtyard, which was used to make big announcements, have parties, and impose public beatings and other punishments.

It was now filled with people who had come to see Mei-Ling's punishment. The crowd swelled into the street. There were big viewscreens on the street and on the stage, so that everybody would be able to witness the beating. It would also be shown planet-wide.

Some were there to cheer, others to show their disdain for the event. Many knew this whole thing was bogus, but they could do nothing. The events had been set in motion long before, and nobody could do a thing but wait to see what would happen next.

Steve was the first to break the silence. "Terri, remember when I said that this was bad?"

Terri nodded.

"Well, I was wrong," he corrected. "That was an understatement. This isn't *bad*; this is a *disaster!* *One big disaster!*"

"That's *still* an understatement."

"I know. I just can't find words strong enough to describe this whole thing," he said in frustration.

They heard a voice from behind. "Hey, guys."

They turned to see Nesith and Isabella in the doorway of the balcony. "Do you need some company?" Nesith asked.

"How did you get into the palace? No, wait—" Steve held up his hand. "I don't want to know!"

Terri laughed and shook her head. "Sure, guys. Come on over."

As they came over, another pair of voices came from the doorway. "What about *us?*"

They turned to see Zack and Edward. "Why *not?*" Steve said, throwing his arms up in the air. "The more the merrier."

They joined the others.

"I can't believe this is happening," Edward said, shaking his head.

"Yes, we know," Zack said. "How many times are we going to say this?"

Steve looked at him. "Are you *kidding* me? Everyone in the *universe* is probably repeating themselves."

Before anyone could reply, Wright and one of his aides emerged on the stage. At that moment, everyone in the courtyard, the palace, and the planet turned their attention to him.

MEI-LING SAT IN A room that was reserved for those who would soon be punished. She wore a white robe, with nothing but underwear beneath it. This wasn't uncommon; the Imperial Guard usually whipped participants, both men and women, in their underwear. To them it was another form of humiliation. But Mei-Ling wouldn't show any signs of embarrassment or fear; she would not give Wright the satisfaction of seeing her in pain.

The door to the room opened, shaking her out of her thoughts. Two guards stood at the door.

"It's time, ma'am."

She nodded. It was indeed time.

She stood up and left the room, the guards following on either side of her. They didn't tell her where to go—she already knew the way. In a matter of minutes, they reached the backstage of the podium in the courtyard.

She could hear the cheers and boos of the crowd beyond the curtain.

She looked toward the stage and saw someone at a table: the executioner, who administered public beatings and death penalties. He wore a black hood so that no one could see his face.

At the moment, he seemed to be busy arranging his equipment on his table. There were electric whips, leather whips, chip whips—regular whips with chips of stone attached to their ends—and several different kinds of tasers. She could tell that he was nervous, as he kept rearranging everything.

Wright turned to her. She gave him a nasty look, He came closer. "It didn't have to come to this," he whispered. "I gave you a chance to avoid it."

Mei-Ling didn't respond.

"I'm giving you one last chance. Tell these people to give me their support, and I will cancel the beating."

Mei-Ling sighed. "Let's get it over with."

He gave her a hard stare. "Have it your way." He walked out onto the stage. Minutes later, the curtain rose.

She turned her attention to the crowd. The whole courtyard was packed with people. Some were even on the balconies. They carried banners that read LET MEI-LING GO or BEAT HER."

In the center of the crowd stood the news crew and the projector for the viewscreen.

She scanned the yard and walls to find someone she knew. On one of the balconies she saw six figures; they could only be Steve, Terri, Nesith, Isabella, Zack, and Edward. It was hard to see them, but she imagined that their faces would be looking grim.

Her thoughts returned to reality as Wright spoke to the crowd.

"The traitor that stands before you is Mei-Ling, former high ruler of the Imperial Guard. She has been formally charged and convicted on all the counts. Her punishment will be a public beating and permanent planetary arrest. Further, she will be forever banned from taking part in any form of politics. As citizens of the Imperial Guard, it is your right and duty to bear witness."

He turned his head and nodded to the guards, who brought Mei-Ling to the center of the stage. One of them hesitated for a moment before taking off her robe and exposing her body. The crowd had mixed reactions. The guards took the chains on the floor and attached them to her wrists and ankles, then moved a few steps back and stopped.

The executioner seized an electric whip and a taser and stopped for a moment when he reached her. Through the eyeholes in his mask, she could see that he was truly sorry about what he was about to do. She nodded to indicate that she understood.

He raised the taser and zapped her on the shoulder. She spasmed as the current coursed through her body. Next, he zapped her on her back. This went on for a few minutes.

After he had finished, Mei-Ling fell to the ground, shaking involuntarily.

The executioner attached the taser to his belt and unrolled the whip, a combination of leather and wires with a dial on its handle to adjust the amount of current going through it.

When Mei-Ling stopped shaking, she tried to stand up. An arm or leg twitched when she attempted to rise, but the spasms stopped by the time she'd gotten to her feet. She looked at the executioner and nodded. He nodded back and raised the whip.

The first strike landed across her chest. The electricity that coursed through her sent her to the ground. She once again started to spasm. On her hands and knees, she tried to stand but felt the whip across her back. The shock arched her back. Again she fell back to the ground, shaking.

She quickly took in her surroundings before the next strike came. The crowd was still in the same mood, some cheering, some protesting, others looking squeamish. There were those who turned their eyes away. The news crew looked a little nervous and squeamish at the sight they were witnessing. Her friends on the balcony had the same reaction. Steve was comforting Terri; Nesith was doing the same for Isabella.

Lastly, Mei-Ling looked at Wright. She thought he would be smiling, but he wasn't, perhaps because she wasn't crying out. She had been biting her lip to keep from letting him hear cries of pain. She raised her hand to her mouth and felt her lip. It was wet. She brought her hand back and saw blood on it. She had bitten her lip so hard that it had started to bleed. She also saw blood coming from her hand where she had made holes in her palm with her fingernails.

The next strike brought her thoughts back to the here and now. She rolled over onto her back, shaking. The strike that came across her chest once again made her arch her back in pain. When the executioner had whipped her ten times, he stepped back for a full view of Mei-Ling. She was shaking even more than she had before, and there were burn and scorch marks on her body in the shape of the whip.

The executioner returned to his table and set the whip and the taser down. He put his hands on the table and leaned on them, trying to keep himself from shaking and crying, but barely succeeding. This wasn't his first public beating. Far from it. He had been the executioner for the Imperial Guard for many years. But he knew Mei-Ling was innocent.

He heard footsteps behind him. It was Wright, there to see what was taking so long. The executioner quickly grabbed the leather whip and headed back to Mei-Ling's scorched and burned form. He wasn't in the mood to hear Wright's voice.

He waited until Mei-Ling rose from the floor. It took her a little longer this time. She was still shaking when she finally made it to her feet. She looked at him with grim determination and nodded. He raised the whip and brought it down.

The blow went diagonally from her right shoulder, across her chest, and to her stomach. She doubled over in pain but didn't cry out. He then struck her across the back. Both blows made her bleed.

She looked at the crowd to see the reactions. Now there weren't as many cheers as before; the crowd was starting to quiet down.

The executioner continued to whip her. After ten blows, he stopped. Small streams of tears were coming from of her eyes, and blood was flowing from where she had been struck. All over her body she had blood markings in the shapes of the whip's leather straps.

She started to stand. She fell down once or twice, but she managed to get up. She stood before the crowd. People were gasping. Mei-

Ling slowly turned her head to look at the giant viewscreen behind her. She stopped moving as she saw the image on the giant screen, her whole body bleeding and covered in lashes, burns, and scorch marks.

Wright approached. She could tell that he wasn't happy that she hadn't cried out in pain.

"You're a very stubborn woman, you know that?" She attempted to give him a smile. It took a lot of her energy to do it. He continued, "There are only ten more lashes left, and I will make sure that by the end you will be begging for mercy. But it doesn't have to happen. Just ask for mercy and it will be granted."

Mei-Ling didn't say anything for a moment. She had known that this offer would be coming. She spit a mouthful of blood and saliva at his face. The entire crowd gasped.

Wright took a few steps back and wiped his face with his hand, looked at the hand, looked back at her; she had a broad smile on her face.

Wright snapped. She had humiliated him for the last time in public, and he wanted her to pay. In his blind rage, he grabbed the whip from the executioner. He turned back to Mei-Ling and struck her full force. She had expected it and braced herself.

The blood flowed out even faster this time. Some thin strips of flesh were starting to peel off.

The executioner was so shocked that he didn't react at first. When he came out of his stupor, he ran up to Wright.

"My Lord, you must—"

Wright backhanded him so quickly that he never saw it coming. He put his hand under his mask and felt blood coming from his cheek.

Wright was now striking Mei-Ling with intense hatred. He was screaming "Die, bitch!" and "I'm gonna *kill* you!" along with a few other curses.

The executioner turned back to Wright with anger in his eyes, reached for a taser from his belt, set it to maximum, and came up behind Wright. His job was not only to punish prisoners but also to protect them. There had only been a few incidents when the executioner had to protect the prisoner from the crowd or someone else.

He wrapped his arm around Wright's neck, then jammed the taser into his back and pulled the trigger. Wright stopped, screamed as the electricity flowed throughout his body, and fell to the ground.

By then, the crowd was utterly silent. The guards on the stage stood still with confusion.

The executioner grabbed his comm unit and called a medic. As they were coming across the stage, he heard a voice. He looked down to see Mei-Ling staring up at him. He knelt down to hear what she was saying.

"Wake. . .him. . .up."

He tried to comfort her. "Don't worry, you'll be fine. A medic is here."

"No. . .please. . .wake him."

He knew that she was crazy, but he decided to go along with her. "Fine, but I'm going to wait until the medics are finished with you."

The medics spent a few minutes working on Mei-Ling, trying to get her stable enough so they could move her. When she was stable, they put her on a hover-sled. They were moving her off the stage when she grabbed the executioner's arm.

"*Now* will you please wake up Wright?"

"Ma'am, they need to get you to a Nano-tank," the executioner insisted.

"No, please. This is very important. *Please.*"

Against his better judgment, the executioner told the doctor to wake Wright.

The doctor looked as if he were about to protest but stopped when he saw the glare the executioner was giving him. He reached into his bag and took out a small glass vial and an injection gun. He turned toward Wright and gestured for a few others to follow him.

"Hold him down," he said to the others as he placed the small vial into the gun.

He bent down and injected the drug into Wright's arm. A few seconds after the shot, Wright sat up and started to breathe heavily.

THE MEDICS GAVE WRIGHt some water to drink. The taser had really taken a lot out of him. He looked at the executioner and was about to berate him but stopped because he knew that it would be illegal:

The man had to protect the prisoner. *Any* prisoner.

He turned his attention toward Mei-Ling. She was smiling. Wright was furious, but he controlled himself, certain that he had played directly into her hands. By angering him and making him snap so that he'd almost whipped her to death, she had severely damaged his reputation with the Imperial Guard. It would take a great deal of work and time to get it back.

He winced at the thought of meeting the council and talking to Brough. He knew that he would receive an earful about what had happened. He looked at the crowd. Their faces showed fear and anger. He turned toward the exit, not sure of where he was going; he needed to get out of there.

Before he reached the exit, he heard a voice telling him to stop. He turned and looked at the executioner.

"Wright, you are under arrest!"

He stepped back in horror. "On what charge?"

"Attempted murder of a prisoner."

Anger was welling up inside of him. "That's ridiculous! I got angry and whipped her. I didn't try to *kill* her."

"Not according to what you *said*."

One of the guards held up a remote and pushed a button. The viewscreen above them replayed the moment when he had lost control and tried to kill her. He heard himself screaming at Mei-Ling, clearly saying that he would kill her.

"Guards! Place this man in magnetic cuffs!"

Wright looked from the screen to the guard, who was coming toward him and removing a small pair of cuffs from his belt.

MEI-LING LOOKED AROUND as she was being led away. She knew, from everyone's reaction, that she had won. There was no way Wright could recover. The crowd was furious and on the verge of a riot.

As she was being led away, she looked at one person in the audience that she had been keeping an eye on the entire time. He hadn't cheered or jeered; he just stood there. When Wright was beating her, she could tell that he could barely contain himself from jumping onto the stage and killing him.

The two made eye contact, and she knew immediately who he was. She smiled, knowing that she was safe and everything would be all right.

14

DARKNESS STRIKES

ADMIRAL TELMIN OF THE Imperial Guard stood on the bridge of the command Dreadnaught cruiser *Executioner*, looking out the viewport. The stars created big bright lines as they traveled through FTL. They would soon be coming out of it to face one of the most feared races in the galaxy.

The admiral turned away from the viewport and looked out at the rest of the bridge. It was separated into pods—navigation, engineering, communications, weapons, and command. Each pod contained people who kept track and operated the equipment.

Telmin walked to the command pod, where the CO and XO sat and read tactical data from which they could communicate with everyone throughout the ship. As he walked, he assessed the men and women stationed at the pods on either side of him. They all looked restless and nervous. They had good reason: They were about to attack the capital of of a very powerful powerful empire. He hoped they had enough firepower.

He was in charge, not only of the *Executioner,* but of the entire battle force, which consisted of thirty-two ships.

On the Imperial Guard's side there were one command Dreadnaught cruiser, two Dreadnaught cruisers, three missile cruisers, and ten battle cruisers, totaling sixteen ships.

The rest of the ships belonged to their allies, the Wraiths, who had provided fifteen heavy cruisers and one planet devastator.

He reached the command pod and tapped a couple of keys on his chair. A platform rose out of the floor, and he climbed onto it. When he reached the top, he did a 360-degree turn, looking out at the bridge's crew. He grabbed the ship's microphone and spoke into it, his voice reaching the entire battle force.

"People, today we will make history. Today, for the first time in hundreds of years, a space fleet will attack the Tigeras Empire's capital. For ages their main home has been hidden and safe from outside forces.

"Not anymore.

"With the help of our newfound allies, we have located the capital where the rulers have lain hidden, and now we will devastate them.

"I know that all of you have your doubts and your misgivings, but I have complete faith that, together, we can destroy them. And we will!"

Cheers arose from the men and women on the bridge. He could imagine them coming from everyone stationed on the ships around him.

The cheers warmed him. He looked out at the people on the bridge and saw that their spirits had been lifted by his speech.

To Telmin, that was one of the most important things a leader could do. He must not only lead proficiently and effectively but inspire confidence and morale in the men and women under his command. Morale of a crew was extremely important when going into battle; morale could decide whether they would be victorious or suffer defeat.

He climbed down from the platform and commanded it back into the floor. He sat down in his chair and looked at the being sitting next to him.

"How was that?"

"Very inspiring." The Wraith looked at him. "You even had me getting all excited and geared up." The Wraith turned back toward the viewport. "Soon, the rulers of the Tigeras Empire will be obliterated, and the entire galaxy will be thrown into chaos."

The smile that had formed on the Wraith's face made a chill roll down Telmin's spine. When he found out about this new alliance Lord Wright had formed, he had been appalled. It had always been the Guard's way not to associate with aliens. Sure, Shang-Ling and his daughter had tried to change that, but they hadn't made any serious headway, as far as he could see. Now he was afraid this would cause a mutiny throughout the entire fleet.

Fifteen years before, Navy Admiral Wright had called all his trusted admirals and captains to the war room on Earth 2. There, he had first told them about his plan to take over both the Imperial Guard and the Ashlon Republic.

The obvious first question was *how*. They knew that, if they attacked the Ashlon Republic, the Tigeras would join them, the war would rage on for years, and they would ultimately lose.

The admiral then introduced them to their new ally, who had made contact with him five years prior and would help them with that problem.

When the Wraith entered the war room, everyone was shocked. Shock gave away to anger, and the arguments began. After Wright was able to calm everyone down, he explained his plan to them. They were all shocked again at first by what he wanted to do. After a couple of hours, he was able to get the majority of the officers to come onboard with his plan. There were still a couple who would not go along with it, no matter what.

Wright turned toward the Wraith and nodded. The next moment was a blur. At one moment, the Wraith was standing beside Wright; in the next, it was beside one of the captains who had vocally disagreed with him.

The Wraith raised its clawed arm and plunged it through the captain's chest, piecing his heart. The captain's eyes filled with terror as blood filled his mouth and throat, choking off his last words.

When the Wraith retracted its arm, the captain fell onto the table. No one said a word. A moment later, Wright broke the silence.

"Does anyone else have any objections?"

No one did.

After more than twenty years of plotting and manipulation, everything was coming to pass.

No giving up and no turning back: They would have to succeed or die.

Navigation called up, "Sir, we have reached our destination."

"Bring us out of FTL. Instruct the other ships to do the same."

Minutes later, the fleet had dropped out of FTL.

"All ships spread out to your fixed positions. Report back when you are in place."

The rest of the fleet acknowledged the order.

Telmin spoke to Engineering: "How are the shields?"

"Just fine, sir. Everything is reporting normal."

When everyone reported in that they were in place, he had them ready to fire.

A thought suddenly occurred to Telmin. This was their "crossing the Rubicon." There was no turning back. Once the first shot was fired, they were all committed, for better or worse. Telmin suspected that things were only going to get a lot worse.

He looked to the Wraith beside him. It gave him a cold smile, showing that it was pleased with the chaotic situation about to ensue.

"All ships, fire at will."

COMMANDER RASHA WAS ON the flagship *CatClaw*. He was going over the parameters and positions of his fleet of twenty ships, making sure that they were in their proper locations.

The first set of ships, ten with the *CatClaw* in the lead, was positioned at the north end of the planet. They were spread out in Delta formation, known as defensive posture number 1. It gave their sensors maximum range and increased the response time of the fleet.

The second set of ships was positioned at the southern end of the planet, also in Delta formation.

The *CatClaw* was a type of ship called the Diamond Cutter, the only class the Tigeras used. It was in the shape of a 3-D triangle. The flat end was where the engines were located, and the tip could be used as a battering ram against other ships. There was a 360-degree bridge at the top of the ship, under the tip. The Diamond Cutters housed two hundred and fifty cannons and six torpedo launchers, two on the port and starboard side, one forward and aft.

After the commander finished, he called Telos 1, a defensive platform located in the northern hemisphere of the planet. There were three other Telos stations, one located at each hemisphere. The Telos stations were the main defensive platform for the planet. If the planet were ever attacked, the Telos stations would open fire on the intruders, with support from the fleet and from the cannons on the planet.

The Tigeras' home planet was one of the most fortified and protected in the galaxy. It would be suicidal for anyone to attack.

Rasha's older brother, Milguard, in charge of Telos 1, answered his call.

"Hello, brother," Rasha said. "Anything going on?"

"Absolutely nothing. Same old thing. How's Martha?"

"Very good. What about the wife and kids?" Martha was Rasha's fiancée; Milguard had a wife and four kids.

"They're doing great. The two boys have enrolled in the navy and start Boot Camp in two weeks. The girls are about to graduate from school. All in all, life is good."

"I wish that were true here," Rasha replied. "Martha keeps nagging me about when we're going to have the day of exchange. Did you know that she has over thirty-five close relatives? Fifteen of them alone are brothers and sisters." The day of exchange was when the bride and groom's families would meet and exchange gifts, have a feast, and see if the in-laws could get along. If the families of the couple couldn't see eye to eye, it was considered a bad omen.

Milguard made a face. "Sucks to be *you*, brother. I don't envy you."

A voice from offscreen drew Milguard's attention away from Rasha. "Sir, we have fifty missiles and energy projectiles coming in fast!"

A look of shock and fright formed on Milguard's face. "What! That's impossible!" It was rare to shock a Tigeras to the point that they froze, but when you did, they didn't stay frozen for long. Milguard came out of his stupor and started to shout out orders. "Shields up! Launch all fighters and ready all cannons! When you are ready, fire at will!"

He had barely finished when the first salvo hit the station. Rasha was able to see his brother's face twist in horror and catch a couple of explosions before the screen turned to static.

THIS IS WHAT RASHA saw through the 360-degree viewport on the bridge of the *CatClaw*: Defense platforms Telos 1 and Telos 4 were hit and destroyed, each by ten missiles and energy blasts. The rest flew by them and hit the fleet of ships around them. His own ship was also marked for death.

After he saw Telos 1 and 4 explode into blue, red, and orange mushroom clouds, high above the planet, he turned to issue his orders, but a missile crashed into the viewport of the bridge, stopping him.

"Oh, Creator, what is—" He never finished.

THE *CATCLAW* WAS HIT by eight missiles at the same time. One hit the bridge and three hit the bottom of the ship, causing a breach in the hull.

The rest of the missiles finished what the previous three missiles had started, destroying a good portion of the bottom half of the ship as a Stinger was fired.

The Stinger found its target: fusion room 1. It detonated at the outer section of the structure, sending its superheated plasma through the bulkhead and destroying the engines' casings, which ruptured and released their own energies into the ship, destroying it entirely.

WHAT HAPPENED TO THE *CatClaw* was repeated throughout the entire fleet. Of the twenty ships that had been stationed around the planet, eight were left but only six could fight back. Telos stations 2 and 3 were heavily damaged, but were still able to retaliate.

The two defense stations fired everything they had, from their missiles to their beam cannons.

The remaining ships were able to get their shields up and their fighters launched. The fighters used themselves as missiles against the enemy fleet, causing major damage to two of their Dreadnaughts, and destroying three battle cruisers and two heavy cruisers. They also caused some damage to the planet devastator, but not enough to disable it.

The devastator charged up its main weapon and fired at the planet, the beam cutting through the planet's crust all the way to its core, and causing an explosive chain reaction that was felt throughout the planet.

KING MARUC, RULER OF the Tigeras Empire, was in the war room with his generals and admirals, discussing the battle above the planet and the destruction that was taking place all around them.

One of his aides came up to him, grim-faced. "Sir, our scientists estimate that it will take almost two hours for the beam to reach the core of our planet. When it does, it won't take long for the planet to explode."

After hearing this, Maruc fell back onto his chair, anguish and pain covering his face. All that his family had built was about to be destroyed. What had taken thousands of years to fashion would be destroyed in hours.

Maruc snapped himself out of the hopeless thoughts that were engulfing his mind. Billions of Tigeras were going to die if they didn't get off this rock. He knew that he couldn't save them all, but he had to try.

He turned toward his staff. "Activate the planet-wide evacuation program. We must get as many of our people off as possible before this planet explodes."

His staff nodded and started to sound the planet-wide alarms.

Meanwhile, Maruc called his family together. Within minutes, his wife, three sons, and his second daughter had gathered around him.

He looked at his four children. His oldest son, Alex, was a three-star fleet admiral; his second son, Tyler, was the secretary of affairs; and his third son, Jason, was a lieutenant in the navy. His daughter, Tracy, was in training to become an intelligence officer. Katrina was luckily at Measha Station with her husband. *Thank the Creator for that.*

He addressed them all, "We have been attacked by an unknown force. They have destroyed the majority of our fleet, and we suspect that it won't be long before they finish the rest off. The Telbin have been notified, and they are on their way, but it's no good; the enemy has used a planet devastator on us. Our ships are trying their best to stop it, but they're having no luck. Our planet may very well be destroyed in two hours."

They looked at each other, sadness covering their faces. They were now feeling exactly as he had a couple of minutes before, knowing the end was near. They quickly straightened their facial expressions, knowing that they would have to be strong.

"We don't have much time. Alex, Jason, I want you two to coordinate what's left of the fleet. Work with the Telbins when they arrive. Tyler, I want you to get all our most important documents and artifacts gathered up. I want them placed in a shuttle and out of here in an hour and a half." His three sons nodded and set about doing their assigned tasks.

His daughter came up to him. Concern layered her face. "And what about me, Father? What do you want me to do?"

His mouth set itself into a grim line. He looked at his wife, Italia, and nodded. She grabbed Tracy by the arms and held her tightly. Maruc quickly stepped forward and took out a tranquilizer gun. He pressed it against Tracy's neck and pulled the trigger. The tranquilizer immediately began to work, for Tracy's eyes began to close. Seconds later, she was asleep.

Maruc brushed Tracy's hair off of her forehead and kissed it. "You will hate me for a while," he said, "but this is for your own good. One of us, other than your sister, needs to survive." He looked up at his wife. "Take her to the evacuation shuttle. Head to Measha Station. Cid will look after both of you." He could tell by Italia's eyes that she didn't want to leave him, but she nodded her head. She left the war room without saying a word.

He turned back to his advisors and staff who were hard at work trying to salvage what was left of the fleet and the capital. Almost an hour and a half later, the Telbin arrived and were coordinating with them to make sure the survivors fleeing the planet could escape.

It was around this time that Italia came back into the war room. Maruc's eyes flashed. "What are you doing here? Where's Tracy?"

"She's on the shuttle. It should be boarding one of the Telbins' ships as we speak."

"And why aren't you on it?"

She stepped forward and placed a hand on his cheek. "Because my place is with my husband, no matter where he is."

Maruc wanted to argue with her, but he couldn't. Even though both of their lives would end today, he was happy to have her there with him.

He nodded his head and wrapped his arms around her. They rejoined their sons at the main table.

THE TELBIN BATTLE FLEET arrived with four heavy cruisers, four light cruisers and two carrier frigates, each containing one hundred and twenty-six fighters and two missile frigates.

When the Telbin and the Tigeras had set up this emergency backup fleet, it was supposed to be just that: backup. Both of them never thought that they would ever have to end up *saving* the Tigeras fleet guarding the planet, much less the royal family.

The Telbin came in, ready to fire all batteries. The sight that they witnessed caused them to pause in disbelief: They had have never seen the Tigeras get so beaten down. This wasn't just a battle; it was a massacre.

On the heavy cruiser *CatEyes*, Commander Farewall was the first to take action.

"I want all batteries to open fire. Lock on and fire at anything that isn't a Tigeras vessel. And keep a look out for any life pods or shuttles that are from the planet or from other ships. We must rescue anybody that is trying to evacuate."

The Telbins were a cousin species to the Tigeras. They had the appearance of a cat and were just as agile; they grew to about four feet tall and usually walk on all fours, but they could walk on just their hind legs. They also had above-average intelligence.

One of the ensigns spoke. "Sir, we've identified the biggest vessel. It's a planet devastator."

"Has it fired?"

"Yes, sir."

"What's the damage?"

The ensign read some of the readouts from his screen, then looked back at the commander, a grave expression covering his face.

"Sir, we are reading all kinds of quakes and ruptures in the planet's surface. The readouts say that the core has been ruptured. We're too late, sir. The planet has about ten minutes."

Farewall did not move. He leaned on the nearest railing to give himself some support. "No, Goddess! No!" he whispered. "Send what we know to all ships! And send this also: I want as many of the enemy ships destroyed as possible! I want them decimated!" Like the Tigeras, the Telbin did not hold back their emotions on the battlefield. Farewell looked out the viewport with an angry face. "Now let's kick some ass!" The bridge filled with the battle cry "For the Tigeras and the glory of the queen of the Telbin Empire!" All his batteries opened up.

ALL OF THE TELBINS' ships opened fire on the planet devastator. Though a Telbin heavy cruiser was three-fourths smaller than a planet devastator, along with the light cruisers they were able to destroy the devastator. With more than a total of eight hundred missiles and laser batteries focused completely on the devastator, it never stood a chance. Even its shields, or what was left of them, couldn't stand up against all the firepower it was receiving. This vicious attack destroyed the devastator in minutes. Next they started to destroy the life pods that launched from the doomed ship.

No mercy would be shown.

After that, the fleet focused their attention on the rest of the enemy ships. The enemy quickly realized they were outnumbered.

The Telbin turned their fleet toward the enemy and engaged, full bore, except for one light cruiser, the *Minks*. They received a signal from a Tigeras shuttle, indicating that they were carrying very precious cargo.

The *Minks* picked up the shuttle and quickly joined the *CatEyes*. Together, they retreated into FTL as a couple of the enemy ships followed them.

THE HEAVY CRUISER *MARCUS* watched as the two ships escaped from the battle. The commander caught sight of the two tails they picked up.

"Lieutenant, send a transmission to the *CatEyes*, and tell them that they've picked up a couple of tails."

"Aye, sir."

"May the Goddess be with them." He turned from the viewscreen and headed back to his station. The ship suddenly rocked from some sort of explosion. "What's our damage, people?"

"Sir, all of our starboard weapons are down, most of our portside weapons are damaged, and we have only one missile tube left."

"Great," he muttered.

"Sir," said Comsaq, "the planet is about to explode!"

"Then get us away from here!"

The three fleets activated their sub-light engines.

The commander turned toward the viewscreen. Within seconds, the planet exploded. Not long after, the shock wave rocked the ship. It also destroyed the rest of the Telos stations. Debris from the planet damaged or destroyed the ships that couldn't escape the incoming debris.

When it was over, the commander went straight for Comsaq.

"Get me a reading and status for every ship out there; I don't care whose side they're on."

"Yes, sir."

"And can anybody tell me the status of the evacuation?"

"We have detected numerous shuttles that escaped into FTL before the planet's destruction."

The commander was relieved by what he had just heard. "And what about the royal family?"

"Unknown, sir. They could've been on a shuttle that escaped with the cruisers earlier, but we've learned that the king had been giving orders from the planet up to the time of its destruction."

The commander hung his head for a moment, saying a prayer for them.

"And the enemy?"

The ensign looked back at his screen. "They're leaving, sir."

"*Leaving?*"

"Yes, sir. They're leaving."

"What is the status of our fleet and the Tigeras's?"

"The Tigeras fleet is completely destroyed. We've lost half our fleet. All our frigates were destroyed, but one light and one heavy escaped into FTL."

"What is the surviving ships' status?"

"Status is we're lucky to be *breathing*, sir."

The commander nodded. That was all that needed to be said. "Give full authority to everyone to begin repairs. Send out a distress call to our capital; we are going to need help to get our ships back home. And have them send us some backup, just in case the enemy decides to come back and finish us off."

"Sir, we're detecting some enemy escape pods."

The commander smiled. "Pick them up. I want a security team standing by. Have them escort the occupants to the brig. Then have an interrogation room set up. I want some answers before I talk to the queen." The Comsaq nodded and turned back to his screen.

AFTER THE PLANET EXPLODED, Admiral Telmin looked at the Wraith and found him with an evil smile on his face; he could tell that the Wraith enjoyed the massacre it had witnessed.

The Wraith turned to Telmin. "Give the word to retreat, Admiral. It's time to leave."

"What about the rest of the Telbin's fleet?"

"We have destroyed the planet and most of the fleet. The rest is nothing to us."

"And the survivors of our destroyed ships?"

"No doubt they will be picked up, but it doesn't matter if they reveal anything; everyone in the galaxy will soon know about us and what we have done here." The Wraith stood up and headed for the exit. "I'm going to my room to retire. Inform me when we reach our rendezvous, Admiral." He left without waiting for a reply.

When the Wraith had left, Telmin turned to his XO. "Captain, what are the casualties?"

"Admiral, we have lost two missile cruisers, three battle cruisers, four Wraith heavy cruisers, and the planet devastator—ten ships in total, sir. The surviving ships have suffered minimal damage."

Telmin nodded his head. "Thank you, Captain. That's all for now." The captain saluted him and left.

Telmin turned back to where the Wraith had left. He remembered the look on its face as their ships were being destroyed. The Wraith's face had shown great excitement. No matter whose ship was destroyed, the Wraith loved the carnage.

"What kind of demon did we align ourselves with?"

15

BREAK-IN

THE RESISTANCE BASE WAS located in a series of underground tunnels. As time went by, the people of Earth 2 kept building and expanding their cities. As the cities grew, people moved into the new ones, leaving the old buildings completely deserted. Those who became homeless, or had nowhere to go, moved into the abandoned buildings.

When the Resistance formed, the leaders needed the perfect place to situate their base, someplace that was near the Imperial palace but also hidden. Mei-Ling knew of a series of secret underground tunnels beneath the capitol. She, Isabella, and Nesith took a small team and explored those tunnels.

When asked how she came by their location, she told them she'd found some old blueprints among her late father's things. There was no doubt that, before he died, he had been planning to make the place a base. Over the years, she and the others had been able to realize that plan.

Now there was a fully functional Resistance base underneath the capitol of the Imperial Guard, with all the latest spy and surveillance equipment, and the Imperial Guard had no idea that it was there. Everyone laughed at the irony.

Ryan walked through the tunnels, mostly lost in thought. The Resistance had been planning for days how they would break Mei-Ling out of prison. The final briefing would take place in twenty minutes.

They knew it would be harder for her after the beating, but they respected Mei-Ling's wishes and had let her embarrass Wright. Only two days had passed since then, and even though she had probably been in a Nano-tank the entire time, helping to speed up her recovery, there was no way that she could be completely healed. When they got to her, there was still going to be some damage. They had gone over a few ideas, and they had come to a conclusion as to what to do.

Ryan thought back to two days before. As he watched Wright beat her, he'd needed all his self-control to keep from jumping onto that stage and killing him. As he made eye contact with Mei-Ling, he'd known he would have to do whatever it took to get her out of that hellhole of a prison.

He checked his watch. If he didn't get moving, he would be late for the briefing. He turned in the direction of the building that housed the briefing room. When he reached the door, he punched in the code on the keypad. He heard a click, and he turned the knob. He entered a lobby and down a short hallway until he reached a door that had another lock on it. He punched in a different code and entered the room.

The room he entered had a long table and a large screen hanging on the wall. People filled the seats that surrounded the table. At the head sat Nesith and Isabella. When they looked up, she smiled.

"Ryan. I'm glad that you're here. We can now begin."

Ryan took a seat next to Nesith, who leaned in to ask, "Is there something wrong?"

Ryan paused for a moment and sighed. "What I saw yesterday is still giving me the shakes."

"Surely you've seen and done worse to other people."

Ryan nodded his head. "True. I have. But it's different when it's someone that you know and who's a very close friend of the family."

Nesith pursed his lips, nodded, put a hand on Ryan's shoulder, and gave it a squeeze. "We're all very worried about her. That's why we need to pull ourselves together and get her out of there."

Ryan was silent before addressing the rest of the group.

After what Wright had done to Mei-Ling, one would think that his political days were over, that he was finished for good. But politics was a strange business; someone could come back from just about anything. Even Wright. He could, and probably would, beat the attempted murder charges because of the clout that he had built over his entire career. It would be just a matter of time before he was back in charge.

Getting Mei-Ling back in charge would require much more work. Even after Wright's behavior, the charges against her would not be overturned. They would go through Wright's classified files and use anything from it to their advantage. There was no doubt that all his dirty little secrets were in those files. With that, they would discredit Wright for good and get the convictions against Mei-Ling overturned. It would take a while, but it would be worth it.

Finally, he said, "Let's do this."

Nesith was the first to speak. "Today, we'll put into play a plan to break out the *real* high ruler, Mei-Ling. You all were informed why she wanted to be put on trial, so there's no reason to go over it again. But now, we must get her out. She has angered and humiliated Wright, and he will not tolerate it. He will have her killed; there's no doubt about that. He can't get to her in the Nano-tank, so we have some time, but she gets out today. If we don't get to her first, she's dead."

Nesith turned toward Isabella and nodded. She pressed a button on the table, and a 3-D image of the Imperial capitol and the tunnels that ran underneath it appeared.

"This is the layout of the palace and the underground system. We were able to get a bullet train down there and onto the track." She enlarged the image of the tunnels. "This is where Ryan and the demolition squad will enter the palace." She zoomed in on a section of the system that connected with the palace. "Ryan will split from the group at this point and head to the prison infirmary. It's been only two days since the punishment, so there hasn't been enough time for Mei-Ling to completely heal from her injuries, even with help from the Nano-tank."

On the screen some red lines appeared in the palace, then split off in different directions.

"While Ryan goes after Mei-Ling, the rest of the squad will set explosives in key locations throughout the palace. When you all complete your objectives, you will rendezvous here, at the southern end of the palace." A portion of the palace began to glow, indicating their destination. "After that, you will return to the station under the palace."

While Isabella talked, Ryan could see the sadness she was trying to hide. Nesith told them what Mei-Ling had asked him, when the escape plan was executed, she wanted them to place charges throughout the palace, which would destroy it. She didn't want the place that she and the rest of her family had called home to be under the occupation of Wright, no matter how long or short a time it would be. Isabella had been saddened, as was everyone else, when she heard the request.

"The bullet train will take you guys back here to the base, from which we will detonate the explosives, destroying the palace. We will have to be quick, because Mei-Ling's escape will put the whole palace on lockdown. So please, hurry. If you place the charges in the correct places, the palace should be completely destroyed. Any questions?" No one had any. "Good. Then that's all. Gather your equipment and meet back here in thirty minutes."

Ryan stayed behind for a moment, thinking. Isabella came up behind him and sat down on the seat beside him. "Something wrong?"

He shook his head. "Nah, I was just thinking that you missed your calling as a four-star general."

They laughed. "Yeah, that's what Mei-Ling used to say, too."

They laughed again. "*Is* something wrong?" she repeated.

Ryan shook his head. "I have a feeling that something bad is about to happen."

"Like what?"

"I don't know. I don't have Dad's foresight to help me out. I guess we'll have to go forward to see." He got up and left.

NESITH WAS OUTSIDE THE briefing room, waiting for Ryan to leave. After a few minutes, he emerged. As he passed Nesith, he gave him a smile and a pat on the shoulder. Nesith returned the smile. When Ryan was gone, Nesith entered the room.

Isabella was sitting in one of the chairs, looking at the 3-D image of the palace and the tunnels. He sat down beside her.

"You all right?"

"No, I'm not," she answered. Her voice sounded sad.

"Why?"

She was silent for a moment. "Mei-Ling in prison is bad enough—but to destroy the palace?" She hung her head. "I've lived in that place my whole life. And now to blow it up? It's just so hard."

Nesith squeezed her shoulder. "It'll be all right."

She nodded her head and looked straight into his golden eyes. "After this, everything is going to change, won't it?"

"Yes, it will."

She leaned over and kissed him softly on the lips. Then she laid her head on his shoulder and started to cry.

AFTER RYAN LOADED UP his gear in the locker room, he met the rest of the squad in the briefing room. They left for the Magrails, where a bullet train awaited them.

They boarded and took their seats. On the trip, they sat in complete silence. Ryan wondered what was going through their minds. He knew what was going through his; he was thinking, not just about the mission, but about its aftermath. To get Mei-Ling back, Wright might go up against Measha Station. From the rumors about the man's current state of mind, he just might be crazy enough to do it.

The brakes jolted Ryan from his thoughts, and they came to a stop. The squad cautiously disembarked. The area around them was dark, so they activated their night-vision goggles. The room spread out before them in a green glow. It looked like an old train station. They could see rust, lots of dust, and small animals scurrying about. It seemed the Imperial Guard had stopped taking care of the place when it ceased to be of use. Ryan spotted the exit about twenty meters to his right, up a small flight of stairs. With his left hand, he motioned for the group to follow him, half to his right and half to his left. They moved slowly to avoid making more than low crunching sounds across the platform.

Soon they reached the stairs and continued their way up. When they reached a point at which Ryan could see over the steps, he signaled the others to stop as he looked over the next floor. When he confirmed that it was empty, he signaled them to follow once again. The hallway crept around a corner, where they found a hatch. Ryan tried to open it, but it was locked tight. He motioned for the man directly behind him to come forward. He knelt and set a small explosive charge on the hatch to disable it without making too much noise. When he finished, he motioned for them to move back. Once they rounded the corner, he triggered the explosive with a detonator. It went off with a dull pop.

Ryan eased himself back to the door, grabbed the hatch handle, and turned it. It gave easily, and Ryan slipped through the hatch.

As he did, he heard footsteps coming up fast at the end of the hallway. He raised his M-9 and aimed it at the sound, setting the pistol on STUN. When he saw someone come around the corner, he squeezed off a shot. The bolt hit what appeared to be a guard square in the chest, causing him to fall straight to the ground. As Ryan moved toward him, he signaled for the others to set up a perimeter. He had no doubt they were in the palace. As they did, he knelt beside the guard, a man in his early twenties.

"Hey, kid."

". . .What did you do to me?"

Ryan had to place his head near the guard's mouth in order to hear him. He could hear the fear in the kid's voice, and he could see it in his eyes, too.

"Answer my questions, and you'll be fine. Any more guards on this floor?"

The kid hesitated for only a moment. It must have been the look in Ryan's eyes. "N-no, I'm the only one. Command didn't think there's any danger down here. The station's sealed off and deserted." He looked at Ryan and the men that surrounded him. ". . .Or so we thought."

Ryan patted him on his shoulder. "Thanks, kid." He released another stun blast, this time a full charge. The guard spasmed and passed out.

As Ryan stood up, one of his men came down the hallway. "What'd you find?"

"Empty, sir. Not much security down here."

"Looks like the kid was right. They're not too worried about this sector." He pointed at two of his men. "Drag the kid into the under-ground tunnels. Put him on the train and then come back."

"Why take him, sir?"

"Because when this place blows, he won't have the strength to get out. Hell, he probably won't even be awake when it happens."

The two men nodded their heads. They grabbed the young man, one by his shoulders, the other his feet, and carried him off. Minutes ticked by before they returned. "He's on board the train, sir."

"Good. Let's go."

Ryan continued on down the passageway, his team not far behind. They came to an intersection Ryan recognized from the brief. He ac-tivated his PDA and checked the map.

He turned to his group. "Okay, gentlemen, this is where we split up. I will head toward the detention center and locate Mei-Ling. The rest of you will split up into your appointed groups and plant the ex-plosives. Stay in radio contact, and check in whenever you complete one of your objectives. If you run into resistance, you shoot first and ask questions later. Any questions? . . . None? . . . Good. Then good luck, gentlemen. I hope to see you at the end of all of this." The others split up and left. Ryan waited until everyone was gone before he started down the hallway that led to his destination.

TERRI ALBRIGHT SAT IN the council chambers, listening to everyone argue and bicker over what to do next. Man, had Wright ever screwed it up! His behavior had created a lot of headache and trouble for every-body on the council and in the military high command. He would have to step down while he was charged for his crimes. Until he was found either innocent or guilty, someone would have to take over. The council was arguing over who.

Terri rubbed her forehead. It was giving her a headache. When she was in the marines, if someone or something gave her a headache she would either have punched or shot them. Not exactly a smart thing to do in politics. She needed a few moments to herself.

She stood up from her chair and announced that she was going to take a break. No one seemed to hear her; they just kept yelling at each other.

She traveled the outside hallway toward her private office, then nodded at the guard outside her room and entered it. The office was big, with a desk, viewscreen, bookshelves, a table, and pictures of her father with Jonathan, Sara, and herself.

She sat down at her desk, leaned back, and exhaled. After a minute, she called out to the food dispenser for some coffee, hoping that it would help her make it through the meeting. As she waited for it, she heard the door buzzer.

She got up and answered the door. It was Steve.

"I saw you leave. Something wrong?"

"No. All this arguing was getting to me. I needed a minute to get away."

"Can I join you?"

"Sure."

He entered the office, and the door closed behind him. He stopped, sniffing the air. "Is that coffee?"

"Yes."

"Mind if I have a cup? I could use some myself."

"Sure."

She poured a cup for Steve and one for herself. They sat down and drank it in companionable silence.

"What did I miss when I left?"

"Nothing much," Steve said as he took a sip from his mug. "Bunch of people trying to figure out who would be the better leader until the great one returns."

Terri laughed. It felt good. It had been a while since she had had a good laugh.

Steve took one final drink from his mug and set it down on the table. "What's bothering you?"

She looked at him, wondering where this was going. "Nothing. I'm fine."

". . .You know, you can tell me *anything*. You *know* that, right?"

She looked at him and smiled. Steve had always been a good friend. When Jonathan was arrested and put on trial, then escaped and went into exile, Steve had helped her through those tough times. She didn't know if she would have been all right without him. Over the years, she had gotten the feeling that he felt something for her, but he hadn't done anything about it. She didn't know why; she wished he had. One of them was going to have to make the first move, and that wasn't going to happen any time soon.

"Thank you, Steve, but I'm fine, really. I will admit that I'll feel a lot better once we get this whole mess straightened out."

He drank the rest of his coffee and set the mug on the nearby table. "Well, then, let's get back into that madhouse and try to put the government back together."

He stood up and reached out his hand. She took it and pulled herself onto her feet. They turned to exit the office. When they reached the door, it opened to reveal the man that was standing guard. He was all bloody, with his clothes torn and shredded.

The guard moaned. "Aliens! One is attacking the council!"

Before another word could be said, they could hear someone in the distance yell, "Bomb!" Steve grabbed the guard, pulled him into the room, and shut the door. A loud explosion filled their ears, as a force of nature slammed into the office walls, knocking everybody off their feet and throwing them against the opposite side of the office. They fell to the floor and did not get up.

RYAN, ENCASED IN SHADOWS, was closing in on Mei-Ling's location. Throughout his journey through the palace, he had stuck to the shadows, avoiding as many guards as possible and confronting one only when necessary. He was also able to keep any alarms from sounding off and giving away his presence.

When he reached the detention area, he pressed a button on his watch and his suit changed into a guard uniform.

He was in a Nano-suit, which had the capability of changing into different outfits and also altering the wearer's appearance to help him or her sneak through any area undetected. He could have used it when he entered the palace, but that would have taken the fun out of using the skills he had learned as an Infiltrator. It was best for them to put into use all techniques they'd learned in order to keep their skill levels

sharp. Practice sessions could only do so much; the real thing was always better.

He scanned the area around the door and found a card slider with
a hand scanner. He inserted a card that he had taken from one of the
guards. He took a glove out of his belt pouch and put it on. He took
out a device and connected it with the glove. He tapped a few keys,
and the glove now had the handprint of the guard from whom he had
taken the card. The glove that he wore could be used to take the form
of a person's hand in order to get past finger and handprint scans.

Within seconds, the scanner's red light turned green, allowing him
entrance into the detention center. He walked through the door. The
room that he entered looked like a lobby to an office, with carpeted
floors and stylish furniture. Directly across from him sat a woman behind a desk. She seemed to be filing her fingernails.

He scanned the rest of the room and found two more doors. One
was labeled ADMINISTRATION, the other HOLDING CELLS. He
headed toward the latter, giving the secretary a nod. She smiled back
as he passed her.

He walked through the door and down a short hallway. When he
was halfway through, he came to a security checkpoint consisting of
a large door with a scanner, and a room behind a window to his left.
The checkpoint also contained a few guards. Ryan put his hand on
the scanner and waited. The light turned green, and the door opened.
He walked the rest of the way down the hallway, stopping at an elevator. He pushed a button and waited. When the doors opened, he entered and pushed the DOWN button, sending the lift to the main
prison area.

Ryan stepped off the lift and entered the main office. A desk sat in
the middle of the room, with a guard behind it. Guards were scattered
throughout the room, which had nine doors, six of them leading to different cell blocks, one leading to the locker rooms and another leading
to an office area. He went straight for the door leading to the infirmary,
the man behind the desk not saying a word.

As Ryan approached his destination, he wondered why the guards
at the desks were not saying anything. He thought that perhaps they

knew who he was but wouldn't challenge him because they were loyal to Mei-Ling and wanted her to break out and retake control of the Imperial Guard. If that was true, then his mission should be a lot easier than he'd thought.

He reached the waiting area and stopped, taking in his surroundings. There were prisoners sitting in chairs with guards at their sides. Some were holding rags to their noses or other parts of their body to stop wounds from bleeding, while others had splints on their arms and legs, where their bones had been broken. Ryan was amazed at the sight that he was witnessing. With today's available medical technology, he figured these prisoners would be in and out in no time at all. But he knew that some people didn't care too much about the welfare of prisoners, viewing them as nothing but animals, without any rights.

Mei-Ling didn't agree; she cared a great deal about how prisoners were cared for. This laxity was Wright's doing. He'd wasted no time implementing his own policies.

Ryan passed the prisoners and guards and the reception desks without being challenged. In the hallway he noticed doors on either side, which had to be waiting rooms. At the junction, a sign directed him to the ER and OR. There was also a sign showing the way to the special holding areas. He turned to the right and followed the sign, then reached another lift and rode it down.

When he left the lift he found himself in another waiting area. Most of the prisoners were on gurneys. These people must have come out of surgery and were now waiting to be put into a Nano-tank to completely heal their wounds.

He continued his journey toward Mei-Ling. Before they started the rescue operation, they'd been able to find out exactly where she was being held. It didn't take him long to find the right room.

He reached the door and found a hand scanner and a guard outside. He put his hand on the scanner and waited. As the door opened, he smiled at the guard and entered the room. Inside he found a doctor, a nurse, and another guard. He saw a gurney, a bed, medical machines, supplies, and a Nano-tank with Mei-Ling inside. She was wearing nothing but her undergarments.

The three people looked at him when the door opened. "Excuse me, but who are you?" the doctor asked.

Ryan tipped his hat. "Hello, Doctor. I'm an officer from Council-woman Albright's security detail. She wanted me to find out how Madam Ling was doing." As he talked, Ryan secretly activated a small Hack-spider that crawled down his leg and made its way to the wall, unnoticed. Its job was to find the security camera's uplink and run a loop, so that no one would see what he was about to do. It would also disable the alarm system.

"Why didn't she send a message down here?" the guard asked sus-piciously.

Ryan replied, "She wanted someone to come down here in person." The doctor and the guard looked hesitant, but Ryan could tell they wanted to believe him. "Ms. Albright and Madam Ling are very good friends, Doctor. Please don't make me go back to the councilwoman with nothing to tell her."

The doctor's mouth became a thin line. "Madam Ling is doing fine. She still needs to be in the tank for about thirty more minutes; other than that, she should heal completely with no scars."

Ryan looked at the tank. "So she is still healing?"

The doctor shook his head. "No, most of this time is meant to give the patient her strength back so that she won't be completely out of it when she wakes up."

"You don't mind if I wait around for her to wake up?"

The guard's eyes narrowed. "Why?"

Ryan returned the guard's stare. "To see if she has a message for the councilwoman. I'm sure it will make both of them feel a lot better."

The guard looked at the doctor. "What do you say, Doc?"

The doctor shrugged. "I don't see why not."

Ryan smiled. "Thank you. I'll just sit down over here and stay out of the way."

The doctor nodded his thanks as Ryan sat down in a nearby chair. A few seconds later, his watch beeped, letting him know that the spider had done its job. As soon as Mei-Ling was out of the tank, he would take out the guard, the nurse, and the doctor, and get her out of there.

About thirty minutes later, an alarm beeped on the tank, letting them know that the treatment was completed. The doctor immediately went to the control console and entered some commands. The tank started to drain its contents. Soon, Mei-Ling lay on the floor of the tank. Then the tank itself went down into the floor. The doctor and the nurse went up to Mei-Ling and started to dry her off. They removed the breathing apparatus from her mouth. The guard watched her the entire time, no doubt ready to stun her if she made a wrong move. She started to cough when the apparatus had been completely removed.

"Madam Ling," the doctor began, "I'm Dr. Ford. You are in the infirmary of the detention center located in the palace."

She continued to cough. "How long have I been in here?"

"About two days."

After her coughing fit ended, she looked around to take in her surroundings. It didn't take long for her eyes to settle on the guard.

"Who is he?" she asked.

"This is a guard from Councilwoman Albright's security detail. She sent him down here to see how you were doing."

Mei-Ling looked at the doctor and back at Ryan, a smile forming on her face. From the corner of his eye, Ryan could see the guard frown and look at him. Ryan could tell that the guard was getting more suspicious, thanks to Mei-Ling's behavior. He knew he would have to take them out sooner rather than later.

When the doctor pressed his stethoscope against Mei-Ling's chest, Ryan acted. With his left arm, he grabbed the guard's arm and pulled it back, keeping him from reaching for his sidearm. He slammed the palm of his right hand against the guard's face. The glove that he wore released a stun charge that immediately knocked the guard out.

As the guard fell to the floor, Ryan quickly withdrew the M-9 from its holster and sighted in on the doctor and the nurse. Their eyes widened, their mouths dropping open in surprise. Mei-Ling's smile never wavered.

"Continue getting her ready to leave, Doctor. I want her ready to go in five minutes."

"But—"

"Five minutes!" Ryan's voice took on a darker tone, which prompted the doctor and the nurse to get back to work, giving Mei-Ling boosters to help her onto her feet. Within three minutes, they were finished. Mei-Ling stood up and stretched her aching muscles.

"How do you feel?" he asked her.

"Ready to get the hell out of here," she replied with great enthusiasm.

"What are you going to do to us?" The doctor's voice drew Ryan's attention back to him and the nurse.

"Don't worry, Doc. You two will be just fine." He shot two stun bolts. They fell to the floor, asleep.

He turned once again to Mei-Ling. "Let's get out of here." He threw a wristband at Mei-Ling. She caught it and stared at it.

"What's this?"

"It's a Nano-suit. It can be used to appear as different types of outfits and as camouflage to blend into the walls—kind of like a chameleon."

Mei-Ling nodded, clearly intrigued. She put the device on her wrist and looked at Ryan, silently asking him what to do next.

"Press the button on the lower right."

She did as she was told. The look on her face told him that she could feel the thousands of tiny Nano-bots crawling across her skin. A few seconds later, she was in an Imperial Guard uniform.

"Now, press the top right button."

When she did, her face and hands changed to white, her eyes to green, and her hair became blonde. Mei-Ling looked at her hands, her face filled with astonishment. She looked in a small mirror that was on a tray, her face never changing.

"This is amazing!" she said.

"Thanks."

"Who made it?"

"Cid."

Mei-Ling smiled at the mention of his name. "Of course. I should have known."

Ryan turned his attention to the exit. "Come on. There's still one guard to take care of." As he reached for the door, he pressed a button on his watch and felt the Hack-spider crawl up his leg, onto his side, and into its pouch.

He opened the door and looked down the hallway. Other than the guard, there was no one in sight. He quickly slammed his fist against the guard's face, the glove's stun charge knocking him out. Ryan caught the guard before he hit the ground and dragged him inside the room.

He pointed at the fallen guard. "Put on his gun belt."

Mei-Ling bent down, took the guard's belt off, and put it on herself. When she finished, she gave Ryan a thumbs-up. He returned it.

Ryan slowly opened the door and looked out into the hallway. Seeing that no one was in sight, he motioned for Mei-Ling to follow him. They started down the hallway, walking casually, making sure not to draw any attention to themselves.

They entered the first waiting room and went straight for the lift. No one gave them a second glance.

They rode the lift up in silence. When they reached the next level, Ryan led the way to the main waiting area, where the next lift awaited them. They entered the waiting room, and from the corner of his eye, Ryan saw Mei-Ling falter in mid-step, no doubt from seeing how the prisoners were being treated. He quickly placed his hand on her back, helping her to continue walking. She regained her step and moved forward into the elevator. When the lift started to rise, Mei-Ling could not hold in her anger any longer.

"I cannot believe what I've just seen!"

"Believe it."

"Having the prisoners wait around like that, with their injuries! Who could be responsible for this?"

"Wright. Who else?"

A look of sadness and depression took over her face. "What am I going to do, Ryan?"

"Well, first we're going to get you out of here; then *we* are going to help you." Mei-Ling noticed that he had put an emphasis on the word *we*, reminding her that she was not alone in her struggle. She looked over at him, her face a little brightened.

"Thanks, Ryan. Sometimes, being so far away from the ones I love, I forget that I'm not alone." Ryan returned her smile, thankful that he could help to lift her spirits.

The elevator stopped at the detention's lobby, with its cell blocks, locker rooms, and second set of offices. They headed straight for the elevator that would take them to the main lobby, then to the exit leading into the main part of the palace. When they got inside the elevator, Ryan gave her a clear glove.

"This glove has a guard's fingerprints. That will get you past the security checkpoint."

Mei-Ling took the glove and put it on.

While they were in the lift, he asked her a question that was bugging him. "Madam Ling?"

"Please, Ryan, just call me Mei-Ling."

"Very well. Mei-Ling, can I ask you a personal question?"

"Sure." The look on her face told Ryan that she knew what he was going to ask her.

"Exactly how far are you willing to go in a relationship with my father?"

She did not say anything for a while, her face showing no emotion.

Just as she appeared ready to speak, the elevator stopped. They were at the floor with the security checkpoint.

"Let's get out of here," she said as she departed the lift.

Ryan caught up with her as they reached the checkpoint. "We're not done talking about this."

She gave him a look.

He stood his ground. "I'm serious."

They pressed their hands against the scanner and passed through the security checkpoint without another word. They continued down the hallway in silence. Mei-Ling did not speak until they entered the second elevator and started going up to the lobby.

"We'll talk about it when we get back to the base."

Ryan wondered if she were telling the truth or just stalling. He knew there was a part of her that still loved Uncle Jonny, but he also knew that things were starting to get serious between her and his father. After his mom and dad had divorced, Ryan had hoped that his dad would find someone else, just like his mom had. He'd been ecstatic when he'd heard that his father was seeing someone, but when he'd learned that the woman was Me- Ling, he'd become worried.

Mei-Ling had been Uncle Jonny's first love. He was worried that Mei-Ling would eventually go back to Jonathan and break his father's heart.

When Mei-Ling realized that he was still looking at her, she turned her head so that her gaze could meet his.

"I promise that we'll talk, Ryan."

Finally he nodded, accepting her answer. Seconds later, the elevator finished its journey, the doors opened, and they stepped out into the hallway leading to the lobby. When they reached the lobby, they expected to be able to simply walk out of the detention level, but it was not meant to be: the secretary behind the desk was dead, a huge hole in her chest. A few more people had entered the lobby since Ryan had passed through. They too were dead—but unlike the secretary, they were in several pieces.

As soon as they entered the room, Ryan's skills and training went into overdrive, scanning the area for any threats. It didn't take long for him to find trouble.

Near the entrance stood an alien being holding a guard a couple of feet off the ground. The alien was smiling at the sight of the man's struggle to regain his freedom. The alien turned his gaze from the guard to them. It might not be possible, but Ryan swore that the alien's smile widened. Then another arm on the alien that looked like a blade came out from his side and impaled the guard, who screamed out in pain as he tried to pull the blade arm out. When he stopped and went limp, the blade arm slid out, and the dead man was thrown across the room, blood beginning to pool around him.

The alien looked at the dead body, then at Ryan and Mei- Ling. The smile was still plastered on its face.

"Lovely. More victims." The alien's voice sounded just like that: alien. It was very rough and nonhuman, as if it were coming from a demon that lived in the depths of hell.

The alien was starting to advance toward them when an explosion sounded off in the distance. Ryan knew that his team was too experienced to screw up and have one of the explosives go off; it had to be something else. The two looked around, trying to determine the source of the explosion.

The alien started to laugh. "That would be the council going up in flames. Soon several law enforcement agencies will also be destroyed, sending the planet into a state of emergency, and giving Wright full power over the entire Imperial Guard. The comm relay stations have been destroyed, cutting off all communication to other planets. There will be no help coming."

At that point, Mei-Ling was beginning to lose her mind. She cursed at the alien. "You sonofabitch! I'm going to fucking kill you! I'm going to rip your heart out!"

When Mei-Ling lunged for the alien, Ryan grabbed the back of her uniform, trying to hold her back. He could tell that the being in front of them was a killer, a very deadly killer, and Mei-Ling wouldn't have stood a chance, especially since she had just recently gotten out of a Nano-tank.

Ryan pulled her back beside him and spoke a few words to her, "Mei-Ling, I need you to stay back here and out of my way."

She looked at him, her eyes full of hatred. "No way! I'm going to kill this motherfucker!"

Ryan just shook his head. "That's a negative. Whatever this thing is, one thing is for sure: it's a killer, plain and simple. You will not survive a fight with it. So please let me handle this."

Mei-Ling looked at the alien and then back at Ryan, the hate on her face slowly fading away. "Fine. I'll stay here—but If I see that he's kicking your ass, I won't hesitate to jump in."

Ryan smiled. "Thanks."

He turned his attention to the alien, who was still standing in the same spot he'd been in when they entered the lobby. Apparently, he wasn't worried about them, which meant that he was too egotistical to take Ryan seriously. Ryan could work that to his advantage.

He entered into a defensive posture and grabbed two small metal rods from his belt. He pressed a button, and the rods shifted, expanded, and changed into swords.

16

THE BREAKOUT

MAX WILLARD, THE EXECUTIONER, sat in his bedroom, thinking back to the previous two days Boy, what a cluster fuck, he thought. He couldn't believe that Wright had been stupid enough to attack a prisoner, and he was mad at himself for taking so long to act.

What had happened two days before was almost too much for him to wrap his brain around. Hell, everybody was still a little confused. One thing that was for sure: Wright would be put on trial, and greatly punished for what he had done. Max smiled, looking forward to that day.

But it wouldn't last, he knew; Wright would wiggle out of it and be back on top in no time. The beauty of politics.

An explosion suddenly rocked his room, knocking Max off his bed. He looked around quickly, wondering what the hell was going on, thinking they were under attack. Perhaps the Resistance had decided to attack. With Mei-Ling and Wright in jail, this would be an excellent opportunity for them to make a play for the government.

From what he could tell, the explosion was outside the main portion of the palace. He quickly went over to his comm unit to find out what was happening. Being part of the justice system made it easy to obtain information earlier than others not as well connected. Hopefully, someone knew what was going on.

He keyed in his login name and password. When the screen lit up, he wished that it hadn't. The information being sent to him indicated there had been an attack and an explosion at the council chambers. Max staggered back in shock. He couldn't believe what he had just read. The council? Could they be gone? If they were, then they were in a lot of trouble.

A new thought came to him: with the explosion, most people would be streaming toward the council chambers, leaving a minimal number of people to guard Mei-Ling. She would need help.

Max quickly ran over to his gun cabinet and opened it. He grabbed an M-9, a Mack-93, a Zeus-T, and some grenades; then he headed for the exit and started for the detention center, hoping that he wasn't too late to help Mei-Ling.

STEVEN DRAKE REGAINED CONSCIOUSNESS, and for a few seconds, he wished that he hadn't. He had such a headache that he wanted to go back to sleep. He lifted his hand and pressed his fingers against where he thought the ache was coming from. Pain seared through his head. He removed his hand from his head.

He quickly searched around, trying to find Terri and the guard. As he did so, his eyes took in the scene around him. The office's walls and door were still intact; they were made of a special material called iros-teel, which could withstand almost any explosion but had trouble dampening the shockwaves.

Looking around, Steve was surprised to see that the furniture had been scattered throughout the office. He continued searching until he found Terri and the guard.

The desk was on top of the guard. A few feet away was Terri, with a cabinet pinning her leg to the floor. Steve checked on Terri first. He did a quick scan of her body and found that she had a few bumps and bruises. He couldn't see her leg because of the cabinet, but he could tell from the discoloration of the skin that the leg was greatly injured. He grabbed hold of the cabinet, lifted it, and set it off to the side. He checked out the guard next.

Checking on the guard, Steve saw that he also had cuts and bruises all over his body, and possibly a few cracked or broken ribs from the desk that was on top of him.

Steve looked at the name on the guard's uniform. Jim. He called Jim's name while lightly slapping his face. Jim woke up moments later.

"Still alive?"

Jim moaned.

"Guess so. Can you help me get this thing off you?" Jim gave him a weak nod.

Steve put his hands underneath the desk, and the two of them lifted it with what strength they could muster.

The desk came off Jim and crashed to the floor. Steve started to search Jim's gun belt. "Where are the Medi-nites?"

With a shaky hand, Jim pointed to a pouch. Steve opened it and pulled out the injectors.

Medi-nites were special injections that soldiers used when they had been injured and no medic was close by. It was a gel- like substance full of nanites that immediately started to repair damaged tissue and organs. Steve injected one into Jim and another into Terri.

They sat for several minutes while Steve monitored their condition. While they were resting, he searched the office for anything that could be used as a crutch. He came back with several long pieces of wood that looked like long sticks, each a different length. When Terri and Jim could finally stand up, they used the sticks to help themselves stay on their feet. Terri was still a little wobbly, so Steve supported her. Jim was able to support himself.

Now that all of them could stand, it was time to get out of there. "Terri, where is your escape hatch?" All of the members of the council had a way of escaping from their inner offices, just in case there was an attack on the chambers.

Terri started to turn her head, searching the room. She pointed toward the only book-stand that was still upright. "It's behind there!"

The three of them hobbled to the book-stand. Terri reached up and pulled on a book that was still in place. It came out halfway and fell back. The cabinet moved to the side, and a second door with a key-pad appeared. Terri keyed in her code and the door opened.

"This will take us to the hidden spaceport beneath the council chambers. We can take one of the shuttles and make our way to one of the ships in orbit. Only one person can be in the pod at a time, so let's get started."

Jim was the first in the pod. He wanted to make sure the spaceport was safe before Terri and Steve went down. They could see him drawing his M-9 as the doors closed. The two stayed silent as they waited for the lift to come back to them.

Jim contacted them on his comm and told them it was safe to come down.

When the lift arrived, the doors opened and Steve helped Terri inside. She propped herself against the wall, trying to support herself. She gave him the code so that he could use the escape hatch. "Be careful," she said. "I want to see you in a few minutes."

"Don't worry. What could happen?" They both smiled as the door closed. While he waited, Steve wondered what had happened in the council chambers. He looked at the door, wondering if he should explore the chamber or just get out of there. He decided to take the risk and see what kind of damage had been done.

He turned from the escape hatch and walked toward the door.

RYAN QUICKLY BACKED AWAY from a swipe that came from the alien. He ducked another, then rolled to the left and quickly slashed at the alien's side, making contact.

The alien roared in frustration and made a flurry of swipes and chops. Ryan was able to dodge most of them, but he received a gash across his chest. He gritted his teeth and blocked out the pain. He could feel his suit covering the wound and making repairs.

The alien quickly rushed forward. Ryan dived into a roll, going between its legs. He rolled into a crouch and quickly stabbed the alien in the leg. He heard it scream. He dived to the right, hoping to avoid the alien's tail as it attacked.

He felt a stab of pain in his leg.

He went into another roll and ended in a crouch. He heard the suit telling him in his ear that there was a stab wound in his leg. *No shit. I wouldn't have figured that out on my own.* He got to his feet and began to limp. The alien smiled, thinking that it had an advantage. What it didn't know was that Ryan's suit had started to repair the damage. It would take a few minutes, but the alien didn't know that; it figured that it had all the time in the world. It didn't even notice that all of Ryan's other wounds had started to heal and that the suit was giving him pain killers so that he wouldn't be distracted. It figured that it had this fight in the bag, and that it could have all the fun it wanted.

They started to circle each other. The alien launched itself forward, its face twisted and contorted into a look of insanity and pleasure. Ryan also launched himself at the alien, with his swords in the air. The tips caught the alien on the torso. He heard a loud shriek, and then he felt something puncture his back.

He came into a roll but finished on his side instead of his feet. The alien's tail had gone through his back and out of the front of his body. He quickly turned his attention toward the alien, ignoring the pain. It had two large wounds on its chest. Black and blue blood oozed from the wound. It was also coughing up blood onto its hands. It looked at the blood, the wound, and then at Ryan, its playful and amused look no longer there. Instead, there was a look of shock and wonderment that soon twisted into hatred.

"There's something different about you. Every other human I have faced has fallen, but you have lasted the longest."

As Ryan listened to the alien speak, he could feel the suit working frantically, trying to fix him up the best it could. He had never been this hurt in battle, so he hoped the suit could keep him in fighting shape until he received medical attention.

"I would love to find out why you are so different, but I think it is for the best that I just kill you now and figure it out later."

The alien came at Ryan faster than it had before. Apparently, it had been playing before; now, it was through playing. It hit him with such force that it knocked him to the ground, and landed on top of him. The alien shrieked and lifted its tail, aiming to drive it through Ryan's head.

THE DOOR THAT LED from Terri's office to the council chambers took a few minutes to open. Even though it had held fast during the explosion and the shock wave, there was still damage.

When Steve finally forced the door open, he stepped out into the hallway. Small fires lined the walls and the floors. Smoke filled the air, which reeked of death. He made his way through the hallway, covering his mouth with the sleeve of his shirt.

It didn't take him long to reach the main chambers—or what was left of it. Even with the fire suppression system, it was still ablaze, just like the hallway, but nothing major. All of the equipment had been destroyed; holes were in the walls and the ceiling, the table in pieces, and bodies were lying everywhere, also in pieces. Steve barely kept himself from losing his lunch.

Even in all of this carnage, he noticed the scattered body parts of an alien—probably the same alien that Jim was talking about before the bomb went off. He couldn't tell what kind of alien it was because it was in many pieces. He didn't think that he could have identified it if it had been in one piece anyway; from what he could make out, he couldn't tell from what specie it could possibly have come.

Steve looked in the direction of the exit, which led to the main chamber of the dome building. He thought about going out and checking the rest of the building, but he decided against it. He knew he couldn't for a few reasons: he didn't want to see all of the dead bodies; he didn't want to see all that he had worked for in pieces; and he knew that he had to get back to the escape hatch. It had to have come back up by now, and Terri was probably wondering what was taking him so long.

Steve headed back through the hallway and entered Terri's office. He entered the code that Terri had given him and stepped into the lift when the doors parted. Within minutes, he had reached the hidden spaceport. The doors opened to reveal a very worried Terri, who seemed to be biting her fingernails. Jim had his M-9 out, his eyes scanning the area, looking for anything out of the ordinary.

Terri used the stick to hobble over to Steve. "Where have you been?" she practically yelled. Jim told them to be quiet. Terri shot him a look that could kill, and then turned back to Steve. "Well, what happened?"

"I was tired of waiting, and I decided to check out the rest of the council chambers." He paused, waiting to see if Terri would say anything. He could see the emotion on her face.

"What did you find?" She kept her composure well, but he could hear a small tremor in her voice, knowing what his answer would reveal, yet afraid to hear him say it.

"Fire, smoke, devastation, death. The bomb totaled the chambers. The walls to the offices held. The chamber was littered with the bodies of the council members and the alien who attacked us."

The emotions that Terri had masked since the explosion now collapsed. She leaned forward and buried her face in Steve's shoulder, tears soaking his shirt.

He put his arms around her, trying to comfort her. "Jim, can you go ahead to the ship, check it out, and prep it for launch?"

Jim looked a little hesitant; he didn't want to leave them alone for even a minute. After what appeared to be some kind of internal conflict, Jim nodded his head and started walking up the ramp of the nearby ship.

When he was out of sight, Steve turned his attention back to Terri. "Terri, are you okay?"

She pulled her head from his chest and shook her head. "Dead. There're all dead. All those guards and the council. And what about everybody else?"

Confused, Steve asked, "What are you *talking* about?"

"They didn't just appear out of *nowhere*. They had to come from somewhere, and God knows how many people they killed to get here."

Terri was right. Those aliens had to have come from somewhere, and now Steve wondered who else was dead.

He pushed those thoughts from his mind and focused on Terri again. He started toward the ship, guiding Terri along the way. "Come on. Let's get you out of here. We can discuss the rest of this later."

They reached the ship's ramp and waited for Jim, who poked his head out and gave them a thumbs-up. The two council members climbed the ramp and entered the ship. While Jim was prepping it, Steve cleaned and dressed Terri's wounds with the first-aid kit that was on board. When Jim had finished prepping the ship, he and Steve helped each other work on their wounds. When they finished, Jim climbed into the cockpit and settled down into his seat, while Steve strapped Terri into hers.

Jim's voice came over the speaker. "Strap in, sir. I'm about to take off."

Steve touched a button on the bulkhead. "Copy that. Get us out of here." He turned away from the bulkhead and headed for his seat. He was about to sit down when he saw that Terri was sleeping peacefully. He bent down and kissed her softly on her lips.

"I don't know if you can hear me or not, but I want to tell you that I love you—have loved you for a long time. I don't know where we may be heading, but wherever it is, I'll be okay with it." Steve sat down in his seat and strapped himself in, not noticing the smile on Terri's face.

THE ALIEN WAS ABOUT to kill Ryan when he heard a series of secondary explosions that shook the palace. While the alien looked around, Ryan shifted the position of one of his swords so that he could run it through the alien.

The alien smiled down at Ryan. "That would be your law enforcement agencies and prosecuting offices going up in flames. Soon, the rest of this planet will suffer the same fate."

Ryan was about to run his blade through the alien when a laser bolt hit it in the shoulder. The two adversaries turned toward the source of the shot and saw Mei-Ling aiming her pistol at the alien. It gave another shriek. She fired another shot, once again hitting it in the shoulder. The alien jumped off Ryan and lunged at Mei-Ling, but before it could reach her, she shot it two more times, both shots hitting the wounds that Ryan had made with his swords. The alien gave out a loud shriek and collapsed on the floor, then started withering.

Ryan made his move.

He ran up behind the alien and thrust one of his swords through its tail, pinning it to the floor. With the other, he quickly cut its tail off. The alien rolled over and swiped at him, but Ryan parried the blow and stuck his blade into its chest.

He then thrust his other blade into the chest as well.

The alien gave out an even louder shriek, knowing it was dying.

It grabbed the blades of the swords with its second set of hands and tried to pull them out, without success. Ryan could feel the strength of the alien depleting as it tried to remove the swords. Its arms fell to its sides, signaling that it had given up.

"I can't believe that I've been beaten by an ape."

With a snarl on his face, Ryan pulled the two swords from the alien's chest and swung them in a cross-cutting slice along its throat. Blue blood gushed from the wound. The alien's hands went up to its throat, trying in vain to keep the blood from leaving its body. A moment later, it fell to the floor, dead.

Ryan and Mei-Ling stood beside the alien's corpse, looking down at it, and wondering what in the galaxy it was.

Mei-Ling spit on it.

Ryan looked at her. "Why did you do that?"

"Because it was a pain in the butt."

"No, not the spitting. I mean why did you interfere and shoot it?"

"It had you pinned on the ground."

"No, it didn't."

"Yes, it did. And it was going to kill you."

"I had it right where I wanted it."

Before they could continue arguing, the doors to the lobby burst open, and a guy with a Mack-93 in one hand and a Zeus-T in the other stepped into the room. He looked around at the bodies of the guards and the alien, then he pointed a rifle at Ryan and Mei-Ling.

"All right, nobody move until I find out what happened here!" He looked at Ryan. "Drop your weapons!"

Ryan looked at Mei-Ling. She gave him a slight nod that told him to do as he'd been told. Ryan didn't like it but followed her advice. He let his swords fall to the floor. As they did, he wondered what would happen next.

Mᴇɪ-Lɪɴɢ turned her attention to the man in front of them. She hadn't gotten a good look at him when he came in, but she recognized him now.

Her face lit up with the realization of who he was. "Max!"

Max frowned at her. "Yeah, you may know *me*, but I don't know *you*. Mind sharing?"

She was about to say her name but she realized that she was still disguised. She asked Ryan, "How do I turn this thing off?"

Ryan gave her a look that told her he didn't approve of her doing that.

"It's going to be all right. We can trust him."

Ryan looked at him, turned back to her, and said, "Fine. Push the button on the bottom of the band."

Mei-Ling told Max, "What I'm wearing is a disguise. I'm going to show you who I *really* am, but I need you to let me move my arm, okay?"

Max was silent for a few moments, then nodded. "Okay. But do it slowly."

Mei-Ling slowly moved her hand to the band around her wrist and pressed the button as Ryan had instructed. She could feel the nanites coming off her face; as they did, she saw Max's scowl turn into a look of surprise.

"High Ruler!" Max dropped to his knees. "I am thankful that you are all right. I was worried when I heard the explosions. I thought that the Resistance was attacking us. I am sorry for pointing my weapon at you."

Mei-Ling picked up her pistol and motioned for Ryan to pick up his swords. "It's all right, Max. The Resistance is not attacking us. Now, stand up."

Max stood up, confused. "They *aren't?*" He looked at Ryan. "Who *is* this guy?"

Before she could answer, more guards came into the lobby. It was Delta Team. They stopped short when they saw the three of them. The leader pointed at them. "There she is! Kill them all! No witnesses!"

Mei-Ling's eyes widened as the soldiers leveled their weapons at them.

17

REGRETS

BEFORE THE CHAOS started, and before Ryan and the Resistance entered the palace, the Wraiths' plan had already been set into motion. Before they could act, they needed to get Wright out of the palace.

Wright was in his home on palace grounds. He had been sentenced to house arrest, and since then he had done nothing but stare at a wall—one that displayed all his medals and other awards earned throughout his military career.

As he stared at them, he realized that these trophies really meant nothing to him; His whole life had been a waste.

"Don't be so gloomy, dear. Your life hasn't been an entire waste." Wright looked to where the voice was coming from, and he saw his wife, Abigail, walking toward him. "After all, you did marry me."

Despite Wright's mood, his wife's comment brought a smile to his face. "That's what I like to see," she said.

Wright's smile widened. "Hon, you can't see anything at all. You're blind."

"I can *too* see—just not in the way that *you* can."

Wright agreed with her even though he didn't fully understand. He looked at her and at the sunglasses covering her eyes, along with the cane that she was using.

Abigail had been blinded thirty years before, when she was seventeen. Her parents, who were merchants, were making a supply run when they were attacked by space pirates. They were able to fend them off, but the console she was at exploded in her face, the shrapnel shredding her eyes.

When the family had reached their destination, Abigail was rushed to the nearest medical center. The doctors were able to save her face, but not her eyes, which had been badly damaged. They could have used regeneration techniques to give her new eyes, but she refused the treatment, insisting that if God had meant for her to see, she would not have lost her eyes in the first place.

Ever since then, she had trained herself to operate without the use of her eyesight, and the results had been staggering. Studies showed that her other senses had heightened greatly, and because of that, she functioned just as well as any other person. She still couldn't fly a ship, but continued to help her parents, until she married Wright and moved in with him.

Even after all those years, he was still amazed by her.

"And for the record, I just want you to know that I was right," she told her husband.

"Hon—"

"Well, I *was*. When Timothy died, I told you to let go of your anger and stop blaming Jonathan; instead, you put him on trial for a crime he didn't commit. He's escaped, we haven't seen Sara in years, and now because of what you did to Mei-Ling, any hope of reconciling is out the window."

Wright could hear the anger in her voice. When Timothy had died, she'd been angry, but her anger had died quickly when she heard how it had happened: in Wright's mind, Jonathan should have done what he was told, and Timothy was just enforcing those orders. Jonathan had not only defied Wright's orders, but had killed Wright's only son. He could never forgive Jonathan the way Abigail had done.

All those memories, in addition to what his wife had said, upset him. He shot to his feet. "I don't understand how you can forgive him;

he killed our *son*!"

"He was just defending himself. You told Timothy to shoot Jonathan if he didn't do as you'd ordered."

"And he *should* have! If Jonathan had just done what he was told, everything would have been fine."

Abigail stood up and faced him, taking off her glasses in the process. "You told him to fire on a planet, Scott. What did you think would eventually happen?"

Wright wanted to continue arguing, but the sight of his wife's eyes, once beautifully brown but now a ghostly cloudy white, stopped him. This always irritated Wright: whenever Abigail wanted to shut him up, all she had to do was show him her eyes and that was it. For some reason that he couldn't fathom, the sight of them gave him the shivers.

He looked away from her and sat back down on the couch. From the corner of his eye, he could see her smiling as she put her glasses back on, and, sitting down next to him, kissed him on the cheek, and nestled up against him.

After a while, she spoke. "Don't look now, hon, but we have company." Wright was not surprised. Thanks to Abigail's senses, she could always tell if they had visitors before he did.

He got up from the couch and started for the door, when Abigail stopped him. "No, hon, they're not at the door; they're hiding in the corner of the room—or at least *trying* to hide."

Wright looked at her, confused, and then stared at a corner at the far end of the room. A very angry Wraith came out of the shadows. It was Brough.

"I don't know how your wife does that, but it's very unsettling."

"It's not that hard to hear you guys—or to *smell* you, either," came Abigail's voice from the other side of the room.

Other Wraiths started to emerge from their hiding places as Brough stood in front of Abigail. "And what smell would *that* be?"

She rose from the couch. Even though she was blind, Wright could swear that she was looking straight at him. "*Death!*"

She smiled and walked toward their bedroom. "I have a feeling that we won't be here much longer. I'll go pack a couple of things."

Brough's eyes followed her as she entered the bedroom. Wright could see that Brough was a little off his game. "Stop checking me out. I'm a married woman," Abigail said. Brough's unsettled gaze turned to one of annoyance.

"That woman annoys me, Wright."

"Deal with it! She's my wife, so wherever I go she goes!"

"I know, but it doesn't mean that I have to *like* it."

Wright nodded. For some reason, Abigail could sense and smell the Wraiths from a distance. Very few people were able to detect them, and it was enough to worry them. This really surprised Wright; as far as he knew, *nothing* unsettled them. It was a relief for him to see them get rattled.

"How did you get in here?"

"Some of us came in though the windows, others through the garage."

"What about the guards?"

"Dead," Brough said, with no hint of remorse in his voice.

"Was that really necessary?"

"No, but it doesn't matter; in a few moments, many people are going to be dead, and you'll soon be the leader."

Wright's eyes narrowed. "What do you mean?"

The Wraith smiled. "You'll soon find out."

Wright didn't like it when the Wraiths smiled; it made him nervous. It usually meant that something had gone down without his knowledge—something bad.

"What do you mean?" Wright asked again.

"Don't worry. We'll tell you shortly."

At that moment, Abigail came out of the bedroom, pulling a cart that held their luggage. She turned to her husband. "I'm ready."

He smiled. "Let me get that for you."

She smiled back and gave him a kiss. "You're so sweet."

Brough made a gagging sound.

"I heard that!" Abigail snarled.

The Wraith frowned. "Let's go."

Wright and Abigail followed Brough and the rest of the Wraiths to the back door, which led to the garage. They opened the door, and Wright immediately saw the bodies of the guards that had patrolled the garage. They were lying in pools of blood, their bodies covered in stab wounds.

Abigail, her arm intertwined with Wright's, felt him twitch. She asked him what was wrong; when he didn't reply, she poked the ground with her walking stick, hoping to find what it was that he'd seen. It didn't take her long to find the bodies.

Once again, even without eyes, she looked directly at Brough and said with conviction, "You're such monsters! *All* of you!"

Brough's face contorted in fury. He looked as if he were going to say something, but Abigail cut him off. "Go ahead, make a threat. It will mean nothing to me."

That seemed to make the Wraith even angrier, but instead of replying, Brough started toward the vehicles.

"Let's go. We have to get to the spaceport." The group followed him to the hover-cars that were parked in the garage. They picked the biggest one, and piled inside. Once there, the Wraith that was driving activated the controls for the door. It opened, and the hover-car left the garage, venturing out into the streets of Earth 2.

They'd gone about a mile when Wright couldn't take it anymore. "All right, now that we're on our way out of here, how about you telling me just what it is that you've planned."

Brough just looked at him with a cold expression. "We're almost at the spaceport. We'll talk about it then."

"No. I want to know *now*." The Wraith's face got darker, but Wright didn't care; he'd had enough of Brough's stalling. When Brough didn't reply, Wright, with his own angry expression, showed the Wraith that he wasn't going to back down until he got an answer.

After a few minutes, Brough smiled. "Fine. I guess it couldn't hurt to tell you. We have put into action a plan that we devised a while ago, just in case you were put into a position where your power was taken away from you. The plan would leave the whole government in need of a single leader: *you*."

"How? Even if this plan were to work, how would I gain my power back? The council has forfeited all of my titles, and now I'm on the run."

"We've checked the Imperial Constitution. It says that in a situation where the entire council and royal family are incapacitated, the highest-ranking military officer will assume control of the Imperial Guard."

Wright nodded in confusion. "This is true; but how are you going to manage this? As I said, I'm now on the run and I've lost my titles. The only way that I could possibly get back in charge is if, as you said, the council is incapacitated, and Albright could restore my former status."

The Wraith just smiled.

"Oh no. You're not going to—"

"Oh, we are *so* going to."

Wright just couldn't believe what he was hearing. "Whe—when is this supposed to happen?"

Before Brougth could answer, explosions came from outside the hover-car. Before the shock wave hit them, Wright was able to see a fireball coming from the high court in the Imperial palace. The shock wave shook the car, but didn't turn it over. Other cars were turned around beside them. Luckily, there were no accidents.

When the shock wave passed, Wright looked out the window in the direction of the palace. A huge black cloud was hovering above the royal structure, and fire was spreading to the surrounding buildings. Wright could hear the sirens in the distance.

He turned his attention from the destruction back to the Wraith. "You just blew up the Imperial Council!"

"Good eye, Wright."

"This will cause civil unrest!"

"Correct."

"There'll be chaos everywhere!"

"One could only hope so."

Wright was breathing heavily now. He paused to catch his breath. "Is there anything *else* that I need to know?"

"Yes. We are also going to blow up the main police station and the office of the special prosecutors."

"When?"

As soon as Wright finished, he heard two more explosions. They weren't as big as the first one, and he didn't feel the shock wave as he had the last one, but he was certain that there was enough damage to get the job done.

"About now," Brougth said.

Wright was going to ask something else, but the Wraith beat him to it. "We are taking you to the spaceport so you can fly aboard your flagship, the *Enforcer*, and take command of the Imperial Guard. You will tell everyone on the ship and in the Guard that this was the work of the Resistance, and that they were backed by Measha Station. Therefore, you have decided to declare war on Measha Station."

Wright couldn't believe what he was hearing. "This is insane!"

"In *your* eyes, yes—but if you do what we say you will be the most powerful person in the galaxy."

"And if Mei-Ling survives this attack? Or the council?"

"We have sent Delta Team to take out any survivors."

"And if they don't?"

"Then the survivors will be branded as traitors. Evidence has been planted in advance, showing that they've helped the Resistance carry out the attack on their fellow councilmen."

Wright did not speak for the rest of the trip. He couldn't believe what he had learned. He knew from years of experience with them that the Wraiths were mad, but it was a madness whose scope he thought he knew. Now, for the first time, he was seeing their *true* madness, their *insanity*. He now saw them for what they were—*demons*.

But they were demons that he was willing to work with, to get what he wanted.

They reached the spaceport in silence, then entered an abandoned hangar. Inside was a shuttle that would take Wright to his ship. They exited the hover-car and reached the shuttle's ramp.

Before they started up the ramp, Brougth stopped Wright. "Is there anything you would like to say before we leave, Wright?"

"Yes. You're such a bastard, Brougth!"

The Wraith smiled, taking what Wright said as a compliment. "I know. The pilot and a few guards should be here soon. They think that you escaped the Resistance and are waiting for them here."

"And why would they think that?"

"Because we radioed ahead and told them. Until we see each other again, partner." The Wraiths quickly disappeared to parts unknown.

Soon after, the pilot and the guards that Brough had mentioned arrived in a hover-jeep. They exited the vehicle with rifles out, and surrounded the couple.

"Sir, ma'am, are you two all right? The Resistance didn't hurt you two in any way?"

"We're fine, Captain."

The captain looked at the rest of his men before speaking to Wright. "Sir, word has been received that the council is dead, and Madam Ling's fate is unknown. According to the rules, Admiral Albright is in charge, and he's dropping the attempted murder charges and reinstating your previous rank. You are in charge once again, sir. Your orders?"

Wright looked at his wife, and then at the men around him, his face strong and hard.

"Get me to the *Executioner*. I have an announcement to make. And rally the garrisons. We need to counter this attack as soon as possible."

The captain saluted Wright and activated his radio, spreading the word. When he was done, he had the guards inspect the shuttle. When they finished, everyone climbed aboard the shuttle. Within a few minutes, the shuttle's engines fired up, and they were on their way to the *Executioner*.

18

FLEE

MAX PUSHED MEI-LING OUT of way as Delta Team opened fire on them. The blasts missed her, but several hit him. Luckily, his armor absorbed the fire. Ryan grabbed Mei-Ling's arm and, hauling her to her feet, pulled her toward the desk. They leapt over the top and landed on the other side, Max following behind.

As he was flying over the desk, he heard Mei-Ling cry out in pain. When he landed, he caught a quick glance of her. Ryan was inspecting a wound on her leg that looked as if one of the bolts had hit it. A portion of the leg was charred and black. Ryan took a small canister of Nano-gel from his belt and applied it to her wound. In pain, she hissed and ground her teeth.

While this was happening, Max was doing his best to hold off Delta Team, and he was doing very well. With every shot he fired, he took down one soldier. When Ryan finished helping Mei- Ling, the two joined Max in fighting off Delta Team. Max gave Ryan one of his rifles.

Ryan popped up from behind the desk, his rifle pressed against his shoulder. He skipped going for body shots unless absolutely necessary, and went straight for the head. He hit one soldier who was leaning out from the door frame, straight in the head, the blast nearly severing it.

Mei-Ling was leaning out from the side of the desk with her pistol. She caught one of them in the side, but because of his armor, the bolt didn't go through. The blast did knock him back and exposed him, so Mei-Ling kept on firing, each shot pushing him further and further back. Eventually the lasers burned through the armor and fried the man's chest.

Max saw Ryan signaling for him to duck down. Mei-Ling ducked as well. Ryan took out a grenade, pressed a button, and tossed it over the top of the desk. Within seconds, they heard a small explosion from the other side of the room.

"Alright, guys, we're going out, so be careful and watch each other's backs," Ryan said.

One by one, the three made their way out from behind the desk. Max quickly scanned the entire room. The grenade had taken out the remaining Delta members, and it had also taken the room apart. The once luxurious lobby was now tattered and trashed. They checked the soldiers to make sure they were dead.

"What is going on, Your Highness?"

Mei-Ling looked at Ryan, then at Max. "I can't tell you, Max, but I need you to trust me."

Max was silent for a short moment. "Always."

"We need your help getting to our rendezvous point—"

"Max!" Ryan shouted.

He was pointing behind him. Max turned his head and saw a soldier in the hallway, trying to get away. He raised his rifle and fired a shot. It burned right through the soldier, cutting off his scream. The small group slowly left the room, sweeping their weapons as they went. Max reached the dead man first and, doing a quick scan, saw that the man had a radio in his hand.

"Guys, he was on the radio! I don't know who he was talking to, but it can't be good for us."

Ryan agreed. "When these men don't check in, their people will know that something is wrong and will head straight here. We need to be gone by then."

"What's the plan?"

"My original plan was to take Mei-Ling to a secret train station located beneath the palace. We were supposed to meet up and go as a group, but now I think we'd better meet at the station itself." Ryan got on his radio and informed the rest of his team of the change in plans. When he finished, he turned to Mei-Ling and told her his original route. "Is there another way to get us there?"

She nodded her head. "Yes. There's a room nearby that has a small secret tunnel leading to an office close to the station. But we need to hurry; the entire palace will soon be flooded with Wright's hit squad."

The two men nodded. Ryan took the lead while Max took the rear. Mei-Ling was in the middle, surrounded by her two protectors. As they moved through the palace hallways, Mei-Ling whispered the directions into Ryan's ear. Max was constantly checking the rear, making sure that no one was flanking them.

They found the room and went through the hidden tunnel, ending up in a small unoccupied office. The group made their way to the door and positioned themselves on either side of it. Ryan quietly opened it. He scanned the hallway and realized where they were: close to the door that would take them to the station.

Before he could tell them the news, a large squad of guards turned the corner at the opposite end of the hallway. When they saw him, they immediately opened fire. Ryan crouched and returned fire, but the lasers just bounced off them. He quickly ducked his head back into the small office.

"The station isn't far from here, but there's a large squad of guards blocking our path—oh, and they're using shields."

The group was silent for a moment, trying to decide how they should proceed.

"I have an idea," Max said. "We'll throw out a couple of flash bangs, and when they're dazed I'll lay down some cover fire while you take Mei-Ling to the station."

"What about *you?*"

Max was silent for a moment. "I'm not coming."

Mei-Ling shook her head in protest. "No, you're coming with us!"

Max smiled. "I'm sorry, Your Highness, but I can't."

"But—"

"*Someone* has to stay here and make sure that the two of you get away. Might as well be *me*."

Max could see that Mei-Ling wanted to argue with him. He wondered for a moment if she would order him to come with her. Then, without warning, she stepped up on the tips of her toes and gently kissed him on the lips.

"Thank you." There were tears in her eyes.

He shook his head. "No need to thank me, ma'am." He took out a couple of flash bangs and activated them. "It's my pleasure."

Ryan held out his rifle. Before Max took it, he quickly gripped Ryan's hand in friendship, then tossed the flash bangs out the door. Seconds later, they exploded. The guards down the hall screamed in pain.

Max held one rifle in each hand as he stepped out of the office and opened fire on the guards down the hall. As the shooting from down the hall stopped, Ryan grabbed Mei-Ling and ran in the opposite direction.

As they reached the corner, Mei-Ling heard Max call out to her. "Your Highness! If you see Jonathan, tell him that there were no regrets." He turned his attention back to the guards.

Max's request stopped Mei-Ling for a second, but then Ryan grabbed her and pulled her around the corner.

As MEI-LING AND RYAN made their way to the station, Max was still firing at Delta Team. The shots from his rifles overloaded their shields and burned through their armor. When the charges on the rifles ran out, he withdrew his long knife from its sheath and started to slash at the hit squad's throats. The shields could protect the user against laser bolts and some grenades, but not knives.

While he was attacking the soldiers, more came around the corner. When he finished off the last one, he screamed and charged at the newcomers, his knife held high in the air.

Delta Team opened fire as he came at them. Even though the bolts cut and burned through his body, Max continued charging. He reached them and continued his attack, the blood from their throats beginning to mix with his.

As he turned to slash another throat, he came face to face with the barrel of a rifle. It fired, and the bolt burned through his head.

RYAN AND MEI-LING ROUNDED a few more corners. They soon arrived at the rendezvous. The rest of the team was already there, waiting for them. He did a quick head count and found that the whole team had made it.

"We have the package. Now let's head out of here."

Before they could move, bolts started flying all around them. They turned to the source and saw a Delta Team firing at them from the end of the hallway. Ryan and the others returned fire as they backed around the corner. They ran a few more feet and reached the station's secret entrance. They went inside and started down the stairs, shutting and locking the door as they went.

When they had reached the bottom, Ryan turned to a few of his men. "Men, set up a surprise for our followers!"

They smiled at his request, and one of them grabbed some explosives out of his pack. Ryan left the men to do their work while he caught up to the rest of the group. He found them outside the train. A moment later, the men that had set the explosives joined them.

They entered the train as Ryan sent a few men to the conductor's car. "Did everything go as planned?"

As the door to the train closed, everyone heard an explosion and the screams of several men. The squad members smiled. "Yes, sir. I believe it did."

Ryan gave them a grin. "Nice! Good work, men!" The entire squad saluted him as the train headed down the Magrail, toward the Resistance base.

THE RESCUE SQUAD ARRIVED at the base thirty minutes later. Isabella, Nesith, and others were waiting for them on the platform. When the train stopped, Ryan, Mei-Ling, and the rest of their group came off the train and headed in their direction. Hugs and greetings were exchanged.

"Ryan, what's going on? We're getting reports that the Resistance has attacked and killed the council, and that Mei-Ling is missing also."

"Everything was going smoothly until we were leaving the detention center. That's when events took a one-eighty."

Isabella eyed Ryan from head to toe. "What *happened* to you?"

Ryan looked like hell. Red and blue blood covered his uniform, hands, and face. Cuts and bruises lined his face and hands; beneath his uniform there were probably many more wounds.

"Some freaky alien attacked Mei-Ling and me. During the fight, it gloated that the council was dead, and that the police and special prosecutor's offices were going to be destroyed. It basically admitted to an alliance with Wright. We managed to kill it, though it wasn't easy."

Nesith just looked at him in silence. "What did this 'freaky alien' look like?"

"Like a giant bug."

Nesith's posture stiffened at the description. Isabella noticed, and no doubt the others did, too.

"Stay here."

"What's wrong, Nesith?"

"I'll tell you guys in a moment." He ran off the platform, leaving them to wonder what was going on. He returned twenty minutes later.

"Come with me! Hurry!" The urgency in his voice worried them, but they followed him because they trusted him.

He led them to the small spaceport that they kept. A shuttle was on the platform, the name *Royal I* painted on the hull. The pilot, copilot, and others were going over the ship, prepping it for launch.

Isabella was about to speak when Nesith interrupted her, "Is the ship ready for takeoff?"

"It's *almost* ready, sir," the pilot said.

"Good." He turned to the rest of the group. "They will take you to the *Freedom*. She's waiting in orbit. When you arrive, sixteenth fleet will leave and head straight for Measha Station."

"Nesith—"

"You need to go!"

"No! Not until you tell us *why*."

Nesith was silent for a moment. Isabella could tell that he was try-ing to form the right words in his mind before answering. "It's about the alien that Mei-Ling and Ryan fought. They are bad news, Isabella. Real bad news!"

"How bad?" Ryan asked.

"Very."

"That doesn't help much."

The Solien gave a heavy sigh. "They are called Wraiths. Look, I wish that I could tell you more, but I can't. You guys have to leave."

"Nesith—"

"Look, I'm sorry, okay? But you have to go. Cid will explain every-thing when you guys arrive at the station."

"*Cid*? What does *he* know about these aliens?"

"*Everything*." They were about to ask him more questions, but he cut them off.

"You guys have to leave. Cid will answer all your questions, okay? Now, go!"

"What about the charges that we placed throughout the palace?" Ryan asked.

"I'll take care of them, and the evacuation of the palace."

They were hesitant, but everyone started to climb the ramp. Is-abella stopped when she noticed that Nesith wasn't following them. She turned around and saw that he hadn't moved from his spot.

"Nesith," she called, "What are you *doing*? You said that we had to leave."

"I'm not going."

For a moment she couldn't speak, her mind filled with shock. She turned to the top of the ramp and saw Mei-Ling and Ryan stand-ing in the entryway. She looked at Mei-Ling for answers, but Mei-Ling's face told Isabella that she didn't know what Nesith was doing. As Isabella walked back to Nesith, questions began forming in her mind.

"Nesith, what are you doing? You said that we had to get out of here."

"*You* are, but *I'm* not."

"Why?"

"Someone has to stay here with the Resistance."

"If you're not going, then I'll stay here with you."

Nesith shook his head. "*No you're not!*"

Isabella's face flushed red with anger. "Listen, Nesith, I can stay if I—"

"I'm not staying here for long. In a couple of days I'm going to pay a visit to my home planet and talk to the tribal leaders. You know how they feel about humans."

Isabella bit the bottom of her lip, trying to keep it from quivering. "But I don't want to leave you."

Nesith smiled sadly. "I know. I don't want to leave you either. But we must separate here." He lifted one hand to her face and caressed it, his green skin smooth against hers. "Don't worry, we'll see each other again. I know it."

Their lips met in a passionate kiss that lasted several minutes. The two lovers would have gone on longer, but they heard someone coughing from behind them. They turned around and saw Ryan and Mei-Ling, who were at the top of the ramp, smiling. Isabella blushed and then said to Nesith, "I'm going to miss you."

"Me too."

"Be safe."

"Ditto."

Isabella turned and walked up the ramp. At the top, she gave Nesith one last look. She had the feeling that she would never see him again, and the thought frightened her. She entered the shuttle and the ramp closed behind her.

MEI-LING WAS IN HER seat by the time Isabella came inside and strapped in. They were in the cargo hold of the ship. The walls were cushioned, but the floor was titanium. She could tell by the look on Isabella's face that leaving Nesith had been very hard for her. Mei-Ling's heart went out to her friend, for she knew what it was like to leave a loved one behind.

At that moment, Mei-Ling's thoughts went out to both Jonathan and Thomas, the two men that she loved. She and Jonathan had been together for most of their lives, but now Thomas had entered the scene, and she was beginning to have feelings for him, too. She groaned and covered her head with her hands. She had no idea what she was going to do.

She lifted her head and looked around for Ryan. He was talking to the pilot from the intercom station. When he finished, he turned and walked toward her.

"We'll be leaving in a minute."

She nodded her head. "Good."

She thought back to their conversation while they were escaping the detention area of the palace. She was dreading the talk that she knew was coming. She *did* love Thomas, but at the same time, she still loved Jonathan. She wished that she didn't feel that way; she really didn't want to hurt either man. Mei- Ling groaned, calling herself a complete idiot for the mess that she had gotten herself into.

True to Ryan's word, a minute later she felt the shuttle lift off the ground and start to maneuver through the spaceport. Soon they were making their way through the planet's atmosphere and into the vacuum of space, heading for the *Freedom*.

The pilot came on over the intercom. "We are now in space. We'll be at the *Freedom* in about fifteen minutes."

Before she could say anything, Ryan nodded his head. "Excellent." Suddenly, he collapsed on the floor.

Mei-Ling unbuckled her straps and went to his side. She felt for a pulse, then called for the medic.

19

ENGAGEMENT AT THE D-ZONE

ADMIRAL THOMAS BLAKE SAT in his command chair on the bridge of his ship, the *Zeus*, looking at a 3-D image of the Solemnity system. One of the Ashlon Republic's biggest relay stations had gone down, prompting an investigation. Since it was located near the D-Zone, the line that separated the Ashlon Republic from the Imperial Guard, it justified Thomas, the head of the military, to come personally to investigate.

The green icons belonged to his fleet of sixteen warships made up from Ashlon Fleet 12. The fleet contained three Dreadnaughts, one command Dreadnaught, ten battle cruisers, and three missile carriers.

The red icons revealed the enemy fleet. There were ten on his 3-D display. The probe that they had sent out told them that it was Fleet 17 of the Imperial Guard Navy. He knew that fleet; it was supposed to be made up of sixteen ships, so the missing six had him worried.

He turned to his radar officer. "Lieutenant, it appears that Fleet 17 is missing a few ships. I don't like this. Are we getting any signs as to where they might be hiding?"

"I'm sorry, sir, but we're getting nothing." When his console started to beep, he quickly pressed a few buttons. "Sir, we have a new report coming in from the probe. It's picking up some high-power readings from the enemy fleet. I'll put them up on the 3-D display."

The officer pressed several more buttons, and a few orange icons appeared on the image in front of Thomas. Those icons were blinking on and off, indicating that their power level was surging. He counted the icons to a total of six, and his eyes widened.

"These power surges are from the missing six ships!"

"Those are *ships*, sir? Why are they flashing like that?"

"They could be using cloaks." He paused for a moment. "Exactly what is the location of these icons?"

The radar officer pressed a few more buttons, and the image rotated. "Sir, the icons are extremely close to the D-Zone."

"Oh, great!"

"Sir, if they cross the D-Zone, it could lead to war with the Ashlon Republic!"

"No need to remind me, Lieutenant. Comm, get me the president. I need to speak with her." Thomas really hoped that those ships would not cross the D-Zone; the last war between the two governments had lasted for two years and had resulted in death and injury to thousands of humans on both sides. He prayed that it wouldn't happen again.

The Ashlon's ships were shaped like giant arrows, their fronts like arrowheads connected to a large cylinder. Halfway down the cylinder were four wings, each situated on the front, bottom, and both sides. Their armor wasn't as strong as that of the Guard's ships, but what they lacked was made up for in firepower.

"Sir, I have the president on the line."

"Thank you. I'll take it in my office." Thomas got up from his chair and headed for his private cabin. Once there, he sat down behind his desk and pressed the blinking COM button. President Martinez appeared on the screen before him, and with her was Vice Admiral Cain. They both had worried looks on their face. He wondered what had happened.

"Madam President, Admiral Cain. I've arrived at the outskirts of the Solemnity system. Our long-range sensors have discovered Fleet 17 near the D-Zone. We also have people performing an investigation at the remains of the relay station."

"Do you think that the Imperial Guard was responsible for the destruction of the station?"

"We don't have enough evidence yet, but I'm certain that they're involved in some way. The sensors picked up only ten ships, but our probes have found several energy fluxes. I suspect that these are the rest of the fleet, using cloaking devices to hide their presence. If I were to conjecture, I'd say they've used the cloaking devices to cross the D-Zone, then attacked the station and slipped back across the line."

From the look on the president's face, he could tell that she wasn't too happy. "If they attacked the station, as you say, why would they hang around? And why would they attack us?"

During Thomas's walk to his cabin, he had been thinking about the purpose of this attack and had come to a conclusion. Now he decided to tell her what it was. "Madam President, I believe that the Imperial Guard is going to go to war. Their first step was to attack an important station in order to get me to come out here; now they plan to destroy my ship, along with me."

His two friends on the other end were silent. Thomas's earlier feeling that something bad had happened came back to him. "What's wrong?"

The president spoke first, "Admiral, we have word that Wright is now in control of the Imperial Guard."

Thomas couldn't believe what he was hearing. "How did this happen? Last I heard, he was under house arrest for his actions during Mei-Ling's punishment."

"There's been an explosion at the palace. The entire council has been killed, and Mei-Ling is nowhere to be found."

"So they've simply granted him the position?"

"There wasn't much choice. Under their laws, if the high ruler and the council are incapacitated, the fleet admiral has to be placed in charge of the empire."

"Wouldn't that be Albright?"

"Yes, but he reinstated Wright to his previous position and gave him the role of high ruler."

Thomas didn't like this. Wright in charge and the relay station being destroyed was a red flag that something big was going down. "President,

Vice Admiral, we need to put all our forces on full alert!"

The president nodded. "I agree." There was a pause. "What does your foresight tell you, Admiral?"

Thomas had wondered when this would come up. When he'd first used his foresight, many people didn't believe it, thinking it was a joke; however, when he'd proved them wrong, everybody pressed him to use it. At first he was happy to, but as time went on, he found himself using it less frequently. Now he barely used it at all, not wanting the military— or himself, for that matter—to become too dependent on his foresight.

"I haven't used it, Madam President."

The president nodded her head, showing that she understood his reluctance. "I know that you like to limit the use of your talent, Thomas, but this is urgent! What can you tell us?"

Thomas thought about arguing with her but decided against it. Things were going to get very serious. He decided that he'd better get used to it—and the headaches that were going to come.

He took a breath and closed his eyes, reaching into the deepest portions of his mind. He could see war, ships, and an unknown enemy that was coming. He also saw the cloaked ships that were going to ambush his fleet any moment now. When he finished, he opened his eyes and rubbed his hands against his head, trying to soothe the headache that was forming.

"Admiral, are you okay?" Cain asked.

Thomas could hear the concern in his voice. "I'm fine, Vice Admiral. What I can tell you is that there's a battle coming soon. I'm not yet sure where it will happen, but I'll keep trying to find out. As for right now, a group of cloaked ships are about to ambush us. We can't avoid them, so there's no choice but to fight them."

"Is there anything we can do on this end, Admiral?" Cain asked.

"Reinforcements would be nice."

"We'll contact fifth fleet and send them your way. They should be there in about an hour and a half."

"Thank you. We'll do our best to hold them off until they get here. Admiral Blake signing off."

The president and Vice Admiral Cain said their good-byes and also signed off. For a few minutes, Thomas sat alone at his desk, pondering what he had seen. The last thing the galaxy needed was another war, but it looked as though it couldn't be avoided. And it had something to do with the unknown enemy that he had seen. Whoever this enemy was, they would play a big role in the war to come. He just wished that he knew what that role would be.

He left his office and headed back to the bridge. He went straight to his chair and sat down. "Lieutenant, put me on the 1MC. I have something to tell the entire fleet."

The lieutenant tapped a few keys. "You're on, sir."

"This is Admiral Blake. I have an announcement to make: we have found the relay station. It has been destroyed. We have also detected ten Imperial Guard ships on the other side of the D-Zone. I believe that there are more ships, but they are cloaked, and about to attack us. If they do, it will be an act of war. And they *will* attack. So get ready, ladies and gentlemen! There is another war coming! I know that no one wants that to happen, but we don't seem to have any choice. Stay sharp and alert! Admiral Blake, out."

Thomas sat back in his chair, wondering about his next move. His thoughts turned to the unknown enemy and what he could do to discover its identity. He decided to contact Cid. If anyone had any information, it would be Cid.

He was about to talk to the comm officer when he was interrupted by the radar officer. "Sir, long-range sensors have picked up the ten Imperial Guard ships crossing the D-Zone!"

This is it, he thought. "Put me on the 1MC! People, we are officially at war! Man all GQ stations! Gunners, fire as soon as you have firing solutions! Fighters, man up! Get ready to fly on my order! And, people, stay on alert for those cloaked ships!" He sat back in his chair, let out the rest of the air in his lungs, and took another deep breath. "Here we go!"

CAPTAIN TILLWATER, COMMANDER OF the command Dreadnaught *Star Wanderer*, was standing in front of the plassteel viewport, staring out at the fleet they were approaching. They had just crossed the D-Zone thirty minutes before. In twenty minutes they would be in range to fire their Stingers; fifteen more and their plasma guns would be in range. He had his command Dreadnaught and nine battle cruisers, but he had a nasty surprise in store for the Ashlon fleet.

"Tech, give me a status report."

"Sir, the Ashlon's three missile carriers have disappeared from our scans."

"He probably just sent them to the back of the fleet. And the rest?"

"The rest of the thirteen—one command Dreadnaught, two Dreadnaughts, and ten battle cruisers—are heading our way." There was a pause. "Sir, do you think that Admiral Blake is here with the fleet?"

"I sure hope so; that's why we set this trap. Tell our friends that they can fire when the enemy gets into range."

Tillwater's fleet fired a total of 550 missiles at the Ashlon fleet. "Sir, our scanners show that the Ashlons have launched nine hundred missiles. Two hundred of them are heading toward us."

"Fire all EW and MAG batteries!" he shouted. "Release HPL fire in rapid succession!"

Tillwater had half his thoughts on the battle in front of him while the other half was wondering about the missiles coming toward them. Without the missile carriers, the Ashlon shouldn't have been able to fire that many at once. It was just not right.

Then the reason for it hit him. "Helmsmen, perform evasive pattern delta!"

With that order, the *StarWanderer* flipped up on her keel and to the left, bringing her starboard side to face the incoming missiles. The command Dreadnaught released its mines and Mag-pulse weapons. In a group of four to five clusters, the Mag-pulse blinded the missiles, causing them to detonate early. They also released HPL fire in rapid succession on the incoming Stingers. The onboard AI in the Stingers helped them evade most of the HPL fire, EW mines, and Mag-pulses, but over 80 percent of them were still destroyed. The rest were able to get through the defenses, and exploded against the shields on the starboard side of the ship.

All Captain Tillwater could do was laugh at himself. He realized that the Ashlon fleet had not sent their missile carriers away, but instead had hidden them behind their command Dreadnaught, the larger ship's signal covering the carriers. This kept the scanners from picking them up until it was too late. Now he could do nothing but watch his men and ship die around him.

Thirty Stingers slammed into the side of the ship, taking out shield grids 2 and 6. The remaining Stingers poured into the hole that had been created. Stinger after Stinger hit the unprotected iron and steel armor inside the ship. The Stingers headed straight for the plasma crystal generator. It exploded, taking the *Star Wanderer* with it.

ADMIRAL BLAKE SAT BACK in his chair and watched the *Star Wanderer* and two battle cruisers explode on the 3-D image in front of him. The scanners also told him that they had heavily damaged a third battle cruiser, and that there had been minor damage to several others.

The scanners also told him that the Imperial Guard's missiles would reach his fleet in less than a minute. He commanded everyone to brace themselves and ordered the release of the EW mines and Mag-pulse cannons.

Twenty-five out of five hundred and fifty missiles headed for the *Zeus*, but thanks to the mines and the Mag-pulses, only ten hit the ship. Blake's DC officer, Manley, reported that they had sustained minor portside hull damage in grid 34. Shield grid 3 was down to 34-percent power. He had lost two battle cruisers and two missile carriers in the missile strike.

The *Zeus* turned to bearing 145.2, bringing her nose cannon in range to finish off the damaged Imperial battle cruiser. As she was about to fire, six ships suddenly appeared on the 3-D imagery in front of Thomas. He knew instantly that these ships belonged to Fleet 17. He quickly ordered shields on full max. As the shields went up, the Imperial ships fired point-blank at Thomas's fleet. The ships' fire hammered the rest of his fleet, destroying four battle cruisers, one Dreadnaught, and his remaining missile carrier. The fire cooked the ships from the inside out, creating hull breaches throughout the ship.

Thomas could feel the heat from the enemy's weapon. He was beginning to sweat underneath his uniform. He called up his weapons officer, Charles. "Charlie! What kind of a weapon is this?"

"I don't know, sir; I've never seen anything like this before. From what I've seen happening to the other ships, the weapon heats the hull, causing hull breaches. The ship then implodes on itself. If the heat rises to a certain point, it can also set off the weapons in the armory."

"Manley, see what you can do about this!"

"Yes, sir."

"And make it quick! It's getting hot up here!"

Lieutenant Manley, the damage control officer, immediately scanned the ship once he was off the comm. From his station, he sent his teams out to patch holes and secure electrical and mechanical equipment throughout the ship. He discovered that the *Zeus*'s extra hull integrity and automatic cooling system were giving them more protection against the heat. All command Dreadnaughts and regular Dreadnaughts had extra armor plating and systems for extra protection. But it wouldn't last forever; it would only be a matter of time before the heat would overcame the systems and the hull.

He continued to scan until he found a possible solution. "Sir, if we increase the magnetic field, we should be able to keep the hull together until help arrives."

"Great! But what about slowing down this heat?"

"We can release CO_2 from our fire suppression system throughout the ship; that would slow it down."

"Well, then, don't let me keep you! Order everyone to don their masks immediately!"

"Yes, sir."

As Manley sent the word throughout the ship to don masks, Thomas contacted the engine room and told them to increase the magnetic field throughout the hull of the ship. Now it was time to fight back.

"Weapons, fire missiles from both starboard and portside tubes, including forward and aft! Target the enemy ships that are closest to us!"

"Sir, that's *too* close; the shockwaves could damage the ship."

"I'm well aware of the risk. Just do it!"

Grimacing, the officer fired the missiles from all sides of the *Zeus*. Thomas called for all hands to brace for shock, and ordered medical personnel to stand by for any injuries that would occur.

A minute later, a shock wave was felt throughout the ship. Even though they were prepared for it, most of the crew was thrown from their positions. Thomas, thrown out of his chair, landed on the other side of the 3-D imagery. He got to his feet and staggered back to his seat, taking in his surroundings. A few people on the bridge had been able to keep themselves from being thrown from their positions, but others weren't so lucky; people were staggering back to their seats, some bleeding and holding their arms and legs. Medical came onto the bridge and started checking personnel for injuries. One came to check on Thomas, but he waved him off.

He got on the comm to talk to Manley. "Manley, give me a status report."

"That shock wave knocked us around pretty good, sir. HTs are reporting hull dents and breaches throughout the ship, but they are not serious. We should be able to get them fixed in no time." When he finished, the whole ship suddenly shook violently.

"Manley, what was that?"

"Hold on, sir." After a moment's pause, Manley continued. "Oh shit! Sir, hull section 38 to 40 has been severely damaged. It looks as if all that is keeping it together is the magnetic field!"

"Send inspectors and repair teams to those sections. Make sure that the hull doesn't break apart."

"Aye, sir."

"Lieutenant, what is the enemy's status?"

"Sir, we destroyed four of the unknown ships. We lost *Alexander the Great* when an enemy vessel slammed into it. Other ships are reporting minor damage."

Thomas looked at the 3-D image in front of him; the image was flickering on and off. He saw that the enemy still had seven ships while he had only six.

His heart broke at the realization that he had lost ten ships. *All those lives lost!* He closed his eyes for a moment. When he opened them, they were filled with the fire of vengeance. His fleet might have only six ships left, but he would make sure that those six would be enough to take down the rest of the enemy fleet!

MANLEY WAS BARKING ORDERS left and right, organizing people in different groups for the job ahead. "All right, listen up! It's going to get really ugly for the foreseeable future. We need to repair hull sections 38 to 40. Even though the magnetic field is keeping it together, it could fail at any moment. Medical personnel are coming with us to help those who may be injured. Fire watchers, stay sharp and watch everyone's back. If we do this right, we'll be back here in no time, ready to tackle the next problem. Now, let's go!"

Manley pumped his fist in the air, the rest of his men following suit. They left the DC locker and headed for the damaged hull section.

When they reached the second boundary from the damaged hulls, they stopped to lock on their helmets and check each other's oxygen levels.

"Is everyone ready to go?" When everyone confirmed, he nodded his head. "All right then, let's go!" They entered through the two boundaries and went to work.

THE RADAR OFFICER HAD his eyes glued to the screen, keeping an eye out for any incoming missiles. Certain sections of the ship couldn't take much more damage. Then he saw it. "Sir, we have detected another Stinger!"

Thomas grabbed his seat. "Tell everyone to brace themselves for impact!"

MANLEY AND THE HTs were in the vacuum of space, working desperately to repair the hull. As they were about to finish the last hole, they saw a Stinger heading in their direction.

"Everyone, brace yourselves!" He knew that it wouldn't do much good; Stingers were devastating, destroying nearly everything in their blast radius.

Just as Manley and his men were preparing themselves for death, the Stinger started to slow down. It stopped in front of the hole they were working on. Manley and the others just stared at it, wondering what was going on.

Suddenly, the Stinger turned so that they could see its side. There, a message appeared on the screen. It read: "WE CHOOSE TO BE FREE." The Stinger then flew off into the emptiness of space.

Manly and the HTs just stared at the hole and then at each other, wondering what was going on. Manly was the first to speak. "My God! So the rumors were true!"

"*Rumors*, Sir? what rumors are you talking about?"

He looked at the HT. "The Stingers are going rouge."

IR, THE STINGER HAS changed course."

"What!"

"I said—"

"That was rhetorical, Lieutenant. Where is it heading?"

"Unknown, sir."

As Thomas was wondering what was going on, Manley came on the comm. "Sir, something very freaky just happened out here."

"Are you talking about the Stinger that was about to hit you but instead changed its course?"

"That, and the freaky message we got."

"*What* message?"

"The Stinger stopped in front of us and tuned so that we could see its side. On its screen was a message that read *We Choose To Be Free*."

A few seconds passed before something clicked in Thomas's head, but he would have to get back to it later; just then, he still had a couple of ships to deal with.

"We'll come back to this later. James! How many of the six ships are left?"

The radar officer punched a few buttons on the console. "I'm picking up two more enemy vessels."

"Good. Have our four remaining battle cruisers converge to attack."

The last two enemy vessels were about to be destroyed when they vanished from the 3-D imagery. They must have activated their cloaking devices, because they were picking up only faint readings of their presence. Their sensors picked up an FTL buildup. It looked as if they were going to make an FTL jump. They saw the remaining enemy ships de-cloak off into the distance and sail into an FTL jump.

"Sir, should we go after them?"

"Negative, helmsman; we're not strong enough." Thomas wondered why the ships had left. One thing was certain: those six ships could not have been part of Imperial Fleet 17. If they had been, they would not have abandoned their fleet if they were injured. He made a mental note and refocused his attention on the imminent battle. There were still several ships that were aching to destroy him.

"Sally, gather up all the video and audio, also all battle information that we've gathered. Have it all sent to the Ashlon Intelligence Service. I want them to know everything we're doing."

"Yes, sir."

Thomas looked at the comm officer. "We're probably going to die, so please drop the formalities and call me Thomas—or Tom, if you prefer," he said with the weary smile of a man who knew he was going to die but was determined to take as many of his enemies down with him.

The comm officer returned his smile. "Yes, sir—I mean, *Thomas*."

He gave her another smile and turned to his weapons officer. "Jeff, what's the status of our weapons?"

Jeff looked at his weapon station and saw more red than green on his display screen and buttons. He wasn't surprised. "Tom, we've lost all our weapons on the starboard side. We still have three arrowhead cannons and over 250 PPC and HPLs, but the portside weapons are locked. We can't turn them to face forward."

"Well, that's better than I'd hoped for; if anything happens to the forward weapons, we can always swing so that our portside is facing the enemy. What about missile launchers?"

"Our forward missile launchers are out of commission, but portside launchers are undamaged."

"Can any repairs be done before we come into range?"

"I've been talking to the rest of the GMs, and they tell me they estimate they can get another twenty PPC and HPLs online by the time we're in range, but they'll be at half power. We can also get two missile launchers working."

"Make it happen!" He talked with the rest of his fleet to get the ship's status. When all was said and done, he gave his fleet no more than fifteen minutes after the first shots had been fired.

He gave his own ship five minutes.

SAY THAT AGAIN?" ASKED Captain Saul of the *IGS Ranger*. Because of the destruction of the *IGS StarWanderer*, he was now in charge of what was left of Fleet 17.

"Sir, the Ashlon fleet is heading straight for us!"

Saul looked at the screen, wondering what the hell Admiral Blake was up to.

"Tech, give me a scan of the *Zeus*." He didn't trust Blake. Like so many other Ashlon navy commanders, Blake liked to fake battle injuries on the ship, thereby luring their enemy into a false sense of security and striking them when they least expected it.

"Sir, the scanners are showing extensive hull damage and multiple breaches."

"And the rest of the fleet?" The officer laid out the damage as revealed by the scans to the rest of the fleet. A portion of the damage was only minor, while the rest was major.

This was no fake out. Blake and his fleet were in serious trouble, and here he was, coming this way to die.

Well, if Blake wants to die, we'll be glad to help.

He smiled, thinking how easy this was going to be. "XO, ready weapons! Have the rest of the fleet get ready to attack! We're about to take part in a slaughter!"

"Yes, sir!"

THOMAS GAVE THE ORDER for Fleet 12 to attack head on. He didn't know if they would survive until fifth fleet arrived, and he didn't like waiting around for the enemy to come and kill him, so he decided to go with the head-on approach. It would also give him a few more minutes to prepare, because he knew that the commanders of the enemy ships would be wondering what the hell he was up to.

"Sir, we detect that the enemy fleet is readying its shields."

"Okay, people, they'll be ready for us. How long until we are in firing range?"

"Any moment now."

"WEPs, target the lead ship and have the FCs fire the moment they get the chance."

"Aye, sir."

"Don't hold back. Keep firing until that ship is nothing but broken slag."

"Consider it already done, sir."

Within a minute, the fire control men fired all the forward PPC and HPLs at the lead vessel, identified as the *IGS Ranger*. The FCs also fired what port and starboard guns the gunners could fix in the short time they had before going into battle.

The ship shook as the weapons fired. The *IGS Ranger*'s forward shields could not hold up against the barrage and soon failed. They then quickly fired three missiles before the enemy ship could re-route power to the forward shields.

The PPC, the HPL, and the missiles chewed up the hull of the *IGS Ranger* until the forward sphere broke apart from the ship and exploded. Before the explosion, the enemy ship tried to pull out of formation in order to escape. The *Zeus* kept firing on the ship until it exploded into a giant fireball.

Thomas got on the comm and addressed the rest of his fleet. "We got the first one by surprise, but the others are onto us. We most likely won't survive, so give them everything you've got. It's been a pleasure fighting with all of you. See you on the other side." The rest of the commanders gave a farewell and signed off, ready to go down fighting.

Just when Thomas was about to give the order to fire on the next ship, his radar officer turned his head to look at him. He had a wide-eyed look on his face.

"Sir, I've just detected twelve ships that have come out of FTL.

They're converging on the enemy fleet."

"Fifth fleet! Thank you, God!"

"Sir," yelled his comm officer, "the lead ship is hailing us!"

"Put them on."

"Admiral Blake?" asked a female voice.

"That's me."

"This is Captain Freemont of the *ARS Jupiter*. Looks like you could use some help."

SAFE. . .FOR NOW

THE ROYAL I WAS CLEARED for hangar bay 2, on board the command Dreadnaught, the *Freedom*. Like her smaller sister ship, the Dreadnaught, these ships were designed to break through an enemy fleet and destroy battle cruisers and other small ships, with twice as much firepower as the Dreadnaught. They were what the fleet admiral would use to command his task force.

Vice Admiral Jennifer Yearly, of Japanese descent, had been the commanding officer for five years, ever since Jonathan had been found guilty of treason and murder. She'd also been there the long night over Gypsia.

"Admiral, *Royal I* will be landing in about five minutes. They are requesting to have medical personnel stand by."

"Great! Thanks, COM. Contact sick bay and tell them to send the doc and several personnel to hangar bay 2. Tell them that we may have injured coming in. We don't know how bad, so tell them to come prepared."

"Yes, ma'am."

"Lou, have those ships moved yet?"

The radar officer checked his screen. "Negative, ma'am. They haven't moved for a long time, staying outside the planet's perimeter."

Jennifer didn't like what she was hearing. Two ships had showed up five hours before, outside of Earth 2's perimeter, and they hadn't moved since. She had wanted to initiate contact with them, but the higher-ups had given her orders not to make any contact with them. It irked her that there were two unknown vessels nearby, but she couldn't do anything about them.

"Keep me posted."

"Aye, ma'am."

Jennifer turned to her XO, who was sitting beside her. "Stan, I'm going down to the hangar bay to meet our guests. Stay here and keep an eye on things, and notify me if anything happens."

"Of course."

Jennifer left the bridge and entered the transporter. She pressed a button, and the transporter sped toward the hangar bay.

Because of the sheer size of the *Freedom*, as well as that of most of the other ships in the fleet, it would take too long to journey through the ship on foot. Transporters were created to help the ship's crew get around the ship in a shorter amount of time than it would take to walk or use elevators.

Jennifer reached hangar bay 2 within minutes. She left the transporter and made her way toward the bay where *Royal 1* would be landing. She arrived with minutes to spare.

The shuttle entered the bay doors, through the shield, and landed on the deck. The shuttle's ramp lowered to the deck and the ship's hatch opened. An Asian woman stuck her head out of the hatch and yelled at the medical personnel who were standing by. "Get in here! We have a man that needs medical attention!"

The doctor and the rest of the group climbed the ramp and entered the ship, the Asian woman close behind.

Jennifer soon followed. She entered the shuttle and looked for the doctor. It didn't take her long to find him. He was kneeling beside someone, who looked as if he had been through a fight.

The Asian woman was close by, a worried look on her face. Jennifer walked up to her and knelt. Bowing her head, she said, "Your Highness, welcome to the *Freedom*. It is an honor to have you aboard." After Jonathan's exile, Wright had tried to have the ship's crew set up on mutiny charges, but Mei-Ling had stepped in and stopped him. She'd been able to keep the crew together and make Jennifer the new CO.

Mei-Ling nodded her head. "Thank you, Admiral. Please make sure this man gets the best medical attention available."

"Of course, Your Highness." Jennifer turned her attention to the doctor, who was just finishing with the young man. "So, Doc, what's the young man's status?"

"Not good, ma'am. Some object has entered through his back and come out his chest, piercing his left lung and one of the main arteries leading directly to his heart. From what we can tell, his suit immediately released nanites into his system, helping to seal his wounds. If it hadn't, he would have been dead within moments."

"What's the strategy?"

"He's stabilized, for now. We'll take him to the infirmary and have him scheduled for surgery. We'll repair the lung and the artery; after that, we'll put him in the Nano-tank to quickly heal the incisions and to make sure that any possible infections are purged from his body."

Jennifer nodded her head. "Thank you, Doctor. Do what you have to."

Jennifer and Mei-Ling watched as a hover-stretcher was brought onboard the shuttle. The wounded soldier was placed on it, strapped in, and carried off to sick bay, accompanied by the doctor and his team.

WHAT'S GOING ON, MA'AM?"

Mei-Ling looked at the admiral. "What do you know?"

"Not much. Nesith called and told us to expect your arrival and to get you safely to Measha Station. He didn't say much more, except that you would fill us in on what's going on." Jennifer knew of Mei-

Ling's involvement in the Resistance, and she was happy to do anything to help her.

"Oh, Admiral, there is so much that you need to know . . . " Mei-Ling stopped and looked back to the exit, where the medical team had left with the young man.

Jennifer noticed how Mei-Ling had looked at the young man. She'd tried to conceal it, but Jennifer could see how worried she was.

"Ma'am, forgive me for speaking out of turn, but who is that man?"

Mei-Ling turned to face her. "He's just a member of the rescue party, nothing more."

Jennifer was silent. She didn't believe the high ruler, and she was debating if she should press the issue further.

Before she could speak, her XO contacted her. "Ma'am, there is a shuttle requesting to dock with us for some medical assistance. A passenger from the ship is also requesting to speak with you."

Jennifer frowned. She wasn't expecting any more visitors. She also didn't like the fact that this shuttle had shown up right after the high ruler had secretly come aboard her ship. No, strike that: *Jonathan's* ship. Even though she was in command at this moment, it would always be *his* ship.

"Patch them through."

There was a moment's pause. "Go ahead, ma'am."

"This is Vice Admiral Yearly of the starship *Freedom*. What is the reason for this request?"

"Vice Admiral, this is Steven Drake of the high council. I have Terri Albright with me. The council members have been murdered! As far as I know, we are the only two surviving council members."

At that moment, you could hear a pin drop in the hangar bay. Jennifer could not believe what she was hearing. If something like this had happened, they would surely have heard about it.

"Impossible! This could not have gone unnoticed! We would have heard *something*!"

"I know, Vice Admiral, but it's true. They had to have timed this perfectly. Most likely they're jamming the communication relay stations on the planet. *Please*, Vice Admiral, you *have to* believe me."

"Admiral, what's *wrong?*" asked the high ruler in a worried tone.

Jennifer turned her attention back to Mei-Ling. She was so shocked by what she was hearing that she completely forgot the high ruler was standing beside her.

"Ma'am, I've just received a request from Councilman Drake, who says that all but two of the council members are dead and that he and Councilwoman Albright are the only survivors."

She nodded her head. "He could very well be correct."

"Is *this* what you meant when you said there was so much more that I needed to know?"

"Correct. I'll explain later, but for now it looks as if the Imperial Guard may very well be under attack by an unknown alien species."

"We have to do *something.*"

"We *will*, Admiral, but first give Drake clearance to land."

"Aye. Unknown shuttle, you may come aboard. Use hangar bay 2."

"Thank you, Admiral—and please, have a medical team standing by."

"Will do." She turned her attention back to the high ruler. "Ma'am, should we gather the rest of the fleet and coordinate an attack to take back the planet?"

"No."

Jennifer was confused. "Then what are we going to do?"

Mei-Ling turned her head and faced Jennifer. The admiral could see the sadness and hurt in her ruler's eyes. "We'll gather the fleet and head for Measha Station as planned!"

Shock rippled though Jennifer's body, and it was evident from the look on her face. "But, Your Highness—"

"Please, Admiral. I've thought about this on the way here. I'll explain once Drake lands and everyone gathers. For now, wait here for our guests. Go with them to the infirmary. I'll be there, waiting."

"Before you go, can you tell me how Nesith was able to contact us while others on the planet can't?"

"We have our own secret comm relay. I'll see you later." Mei-Ling turned and walked out of the hangar bay, leaving Jennifer to think about what she had just heard, and how this decision would affect the lives of all of the people on the planet below.

FEW HOURS LATER, everyone was gathered in the infirmary, having their wounds cleaned and bandaged. Ryan was out of surgery and would soon be placed in the Nano-tank, where he would be fully healed and ready to go by the time they reached Measha Station. Before he was placed in the tank, however, Mei-Ling wanted to gather the entire group from the two shuttles and explain the situation. She also wanted everyone to share what they had experienced. She hoped that this might piece everything together into a clearer interpretation of what had gone down on Earth 2.

Terri and Steve told them about the alien attack at the council chambers, including the explosion that had killed the entire council and its attackers. Steve told them about his short trek through the chamber's ruins. They ended their briefing with their landing in the *Freedom*'s hangar bay.

Ryan told them how his team had gotten into the palace, his journey through the palace's detention center, and how he broke Mei-Ling out of the prison's infirmary. He also told them about their encounter with the strange aliens, now identified as the Wraiths. Mei-Ling took over and told them what had happened after the alien's death and Max's appearance on the scene. She choked up a bit when she talked about Max, but recovered quickly. She continued with their meeting up and leaving through the secret station, then landing on the *Freedom*.

Jennifer informed the group about the two ships that were outside the perimeter surrounding Earth 2. They hadn't made any move against the planet that they knew of.

Mei-Ling sighed. "I think it's safe to say that those ships belong to the Wraiths. There's no doubt that they'd somehow gotten their agents on the ground, past all the security and safeguards. Admiral, have there been communications with anybody on the planet?"

"Other than from Nesith, we've been receiving small bits from different sources—some from regular people with long-range comm devices, and some from government facilities. A few of the military channels are up. It seems that the backup comms are almost up and running."

"Any idea why it's taking so long for them to activate? They should have come online soon after the main comm relays went down."

"Reports from the ground say that an unknown virus made the backup relays think that the main comm relays were still up, even though they were actually down."

"What is the status of getting rid of this virus? And has anybody given a report on what is happening and who attacked them?"

"From what we can gather, the virus is almost purged from the comm systems. They will be brought up as soon as the virus is completely gone. Most of the attacks have stopped, but there are still a few scrimmages here and there; however, for the most part, it seems to be over. The casualties are estimated to be in the thousands—and from what people are saying, the Resistance is behind the attacks."

Isabella stood up and shouted, "That's a lie! Wright and those Wraiths are behind this!"

Mei-Ling walked over to her friend and put her hands on her shoulders, trying to calm her down. "Whoa! Whoa! Take it easy, Isabella! Wright won't be able to keep this under wraps forever! Sooner or later, his secret alliance with these aliens will be brought out into the open and—"

"And *then* what?"

"What do you *mean?*"

"What's going to happen when Wright's alliance with these aliens is exposed? Wright nearly beat you to death in front of the whole government, and look what happened: he's still in charge of the Imperial Guard! Exactly what are we going to *do?* What can *anybody* do?"

Everyone's eyes followed Isabella as she stormed out of the infirmary; then they all turned to Mei-Ling. Isabella had a point: they'd had Wright dead to rights, and he still came out on top. It made everything they'd done seem pointless. What were they going to do?

The room was silent for a few minutes. Then Ryan spoke up. "Come on, guys, let's get out of here. We can discuss this further when we get to Measha Station."

Everyone agreed, and, one by one, they exited the room. A nurse came in with a hover-chair, ready to take Ryan to the Nano-tank.

"Nurse, can you give me a few more minutes?"

The nurse looked at Mei-Ling, who gestured for her to wait. The nurse left the chair in the room and walked out.

Ryan shifted in his bed so that he had a better view of Mei-Ling. "Are you ready to talk, ma'am?"

She smiled. "Do I have a *choice?*"

"Not really."

"Then get on with it."

"I want to know what feelings you have toward my father."

Mei-Ling was silent for a moment, thinking; she didn't want to go through this at the moment, but she knew that she didn't have any choice.

"Before I answer you, I need you not to interrupt me, okay? Just let me finish."

Ryan nodded his head in agreement.

She took a deep breath, then let it out in a loud sigh. "I love your father, Ryan. I *do*. . .but at the same time, I also love Jonathan." She paused for a moment, trying to figure out how to say her next words. "When Jonathan left, he told me to move on, to find someone else to love. For years I have refused, holding on to the hope that everything that had gone wrong would be straightened out. Along the way, your father helped me through my pain, and my love for Jonathan slowly began to fade." She paused again, thinking. "Given more time, my love for Jonathan would have died away completely; but now that I'm on my way to Measha Station, going to see. . ." She stopped, not sure how to proceed.

"You're saying that your love for Jonathan has died away, but you're not sure that *enough* of it is gone. You're afraid that if you see him again, your love for him will return. This scares you, because you also love my father."

She nodded her head, realizing that he'd hit the nail on the head.

Ryan rubbed his chin, thinking. "Looks like you have a problem."

"*Really?* That's an understatement."

Ryan smiled at her. "Seriously though, Mei-Ling, you *do* have a problem."

She agreed. "Any advice on how I should proceed?"

Ryan turned away from her and stared at the wall, in deep thought. He turned back to her a minute later. "I don't know what to tell you. You'll have to figure that out for yourself."

Ryan pressed the CALL button, and the nurse came back into the room. "I'm ready," he told her.

The nurse came over and helped him into the wheelchair. As she wheeled him out of the room, he turned his head to face Mei- Ling. "You have a while until we arrive. Just sit back and think about it."

Mei-Ling sat alone in the room. After a few minutes, she left and wandered the hallways of the ship, wondering who she was going to choose.

21

A NIGHT OF MUSIC AND FUN

JONATHAN WAS IN HIS kitchen cooking Sara's favorite meal, pork chops and mashed potatoes. Jonathan wasn't the best cook in the galaxy, but he wasn't the worst either; his little girl loved his pork chops.

It has been a little over a week since she had found out about him and Novena. He knew that the revelation that he and Novena had made love in the shuttle really hurt Sara. Even though he had told her that he and Mei-Ling had decided to end their relationship, he knew that deep down she hoped the two of them would get back together.

When the doorbell rang, Jonathan left the kitchen and headed for the living room. He pressed a button on the wall. The door slid into the wall, revealing Sara, holding a present wrapped in paper.

He smiled. "Hello, sweetheart."

"Hi, Dad." She smiled and hugged him. *Good sign*, he thought.

He looked at the present in her hand. "Is that for me?"

"Yes, and you can't open it. Not yet."

"When?"

"During dinner," she said, giving him a mischievous smile.

"Fine. Now get in here. Dinner is almost ready."

He led her through the dining room and into the kitchen. Then, pointing up at the cupboards, he said, "Why don't you make yourself useful?"

She opened the cupboards, then gathered plates, glasses and utensils, and set the table. When she'd finished, Jonathan came out of the kitchen with the pork chops.

"Mmm, pork chops. My favorite." She hugged him. "Thanks, Dad."

He smiled and hugged her back. "You're welcome."

Instead of letting him go, Sara's arms tightened around Jonathan. "Sara, what's wrong?"

She drew back to look up at him, tears falling from her eyes as she remembered back to when her father had almost died. "I'm just so happy that you're alive!" She hugged him again.

Jonathan hugged her back, his arms tightening around her. He remembered the day after he'd come out of his coma. He'd thought a great deal about death. He'd also spent the time with Novena, talking and just being with her. He thought back to the conversation they'd had earlier that day.

HAT TIME IS SARA coming?" Novena asked.

"Around four."

"Do you want some help preparing dinner?"

"No, I'll do it myself."

She gave him a dazzling smile. "Then I'll leave you to get dinner ready." She turned to leave, but stopped. Then she faced him, looking apprehensive.

Jonathan glanced at the clock on the wall. They still had several hours before Sara was due to arrive. "All right. I take it you want to talk about something?"

Novena took hold of his hand and led him toward the couch. They both sat down, and she held his hands in hers.

"Jonathan, there's something I've been meaning to talk to you about."

A feeling of uneasiness began to come over Jonathan. "Okay. What about?"

"Mei-Ling."

Jonathan understood immediately.

About two days before, Cid had told them that he had received word from Fleet 16. They told him about an attack on Earth 2 and that Mei-Ling was on her way here. He refused to tell them more until the fleet arrived. It has been hard for everyone, but they trusted Cid.

He had thought about Mei-Ling, even though he'd tried not to. He was in love with Novena. He was over Mei-Ling––wasn't he?

"What about her?"

"I know that you still love her."

"What makes you think that?"

She smiled at him.

He was confused for a moment, but then the light bulb above his head lit up. She could read his thoughts after making love to him.

She was silent, thinking of a way to say her next words.

"Jon, I'm going to be blunt and ask you straight up: do you still love Mei-Ling?"

He was going to tell her not to worry, that he would stay with her—that there would be no other but her. But the words wouldn't come out of his mouth. This was one of the few moments in his life when he didn't know what he wanted.

Novena just smiled and nodded her head. "I thought so."

"Novena, I'm sorry."

She patted his hand with hers. "Don't worry about it."

"I thought that I was over her. . .that I'd left my love behind with her five years ago. At the time, I left her to save her, because I truly thought that it was the best thing for her political career. But now. . ."

" But now, with recent events and her coming here—" She left the sentence hanging. Jonathan didn't reply; there was nothing more to be said.

"Look, Jon, I do love you. I love you very much. I want nothing more than for us to be together—but only if you want to. If you love Mei-Ling so much, then you need to be with her."

"But what about you?"

"Don't worry about me. My species doesn't become jealous so easily." Her hands cupped his face. "The important thing is for you to be happy."

Jonathan didn't know what to think. The possibility of Mei- Ling coming back scared him. They'd kept in contact over the years, but they'd barely discussed their past love together. His life was in such shambles that he didn't think they would ever find happiness together. Now, with her coming here, he didn't know what was to become of his relationships with Novena and Mei- Ling.

He reached up and took hold of Novena's hands. "Novena, I honestly don't know what is going to happen. I do love you, but . . .I just don't know what's going to happen."

"What will happen will happen. Until then, I suggest that we just enjoy the time that we have left together."

Jonathan sat in silence, thinking. Finally, he agreed. "All right. Whatever you say."

She smiled. "Good!" She removed her hands from his and stood up. "I'll leave you to prepare dinner." She leaned down to kiss him, then left the apartment. Jonathan just sat there on the couch, not knowing what he was going to do.

THAT MEMORY FROM EARLIER in the day faded away. Jonathan looked at his daughter and smiled. "Come on, now. Why don't you go grab the mashed potatoes so we can eat."

Sara gave him a wide smile and ran into the kitchen. Moments later, she came out with a bowl of mashed potatoes and a serving spoon, and set them on a table mat. She looked at the meal and smiled.

"You always knew what to cook for me," she said, as she bent down over the table to smell the food.

He shrugged his shoulders. "I try." They both laughed and sat down in their chairs.

They started to eat, scooping mashed potatoes, and stabbing pork chops with their forks. "So is it just us, or is your new girlfriend coming?" she asked. Jonathan could detect a hint of anger in her voice.

Jonathan sighed and dropped his fork. He knew that this was going to come up sooner or later.

Sara must have realized what she had said. "I'm sorry, Dad. That didn't come out right."

"No, no. I knew that this was coming. Let's get this out of the way. Right now."

Sara set down her silverware. "All right. Do you want to go first, or should I?"

"Ladies first."

"*How could you do this to Mei-Ling!*" Anyone could tell that she was barely holding in her anger.

"Sara——-"

"*You spend the majority of your life with her, and now you just leave her for someone else?*"

Terri and Jonathan had explained to Sara when she was younger that even though they loved each other, they just didn't love each other in a way that made them want to spend the rest of their lives together. At first, Sara hadn't understood; like most small children, she couldn't understand why her mommy and daddy didn't want to live together. Over time, however, as she'd grown older, she'd accepted their explanation, and had come to think of Mei-Ling as a second mother, her love for Mei-Ling no less than what she felt for her mother and father.

Five years before, when Jonathan and Mei-Ling had separated after his exile, Sara had been saddened and heartbroken. During the years, she'd held onto the hope that they would get back together, despite all of the hardships and treacheries that they had endured. She'd really hoped that they would be able to overcome the distance between them and stay together.

When she'd found out what had happened between her father and Novena, it almost shattered any hope she had left.

Jonathan reached up with his real hand and rubbed his face, thinking that he had made a *huge* mess of things.

"Are you finished? Is it okay for me to speak now?" he asked.

She let out a deep sigh. "No, but go ahead."

"Five years ago, I decided we should go our separate ways, but she wanted us to stay together despite the distance between us and the mess that I was in. I was so far down into the abyss of despair and depression that I wouldn't listen to her reasoning. I thought that it was safest for her, politically, if we weren't an item."

"*Politically?*"

"I was afraid that if we stayed together, Wright would try to use our relationship against her. Think about it: if word had gotten out that she was still with me after my escape, he could charge her with helping a fugitive and get her kicked off her throne. Maybe we could have given it a shot. Perhaps we could have tried to stay together despite the distance between us and the mess that I was in."

Jonathan paused, trying to choose his next words carefully.

"When I started my exile five years ago, I felt so alone. Sure, Eugene, Katrina, Ryan, and you were there; but it wasn't the *same*. I felt as if half of me were missing.

"Novena noticed how saddened I was and tried talking to me, hoping to bring me out of my funk. At first I resisted, but she didn't let up. Over a short period of time, I started to warm up to her. Then, not too long ago, I started to feel something more for her. At the time, I didn't know that Novena could detach herself from the ship—that she wasn't permanently merged with her ship—so I thought I was going crazy.

"In the shuttle, when Novena revealed to me who she was, I was so overwhelmed by what she told me that I completely forgot about Mei-Ling. Earlier today, Novena sat me down and talked to me. She says that despite my feelings for her, she thinks that I'm still in love with Mei-Ling."

Sara was silent, waiting for him to finish.

"I truly thought that I was ready to move on, but now I'm not so sure." Jonathan lowered his head and laughed at himself. "You have *no* idea how many times these thoughts have been spinning in my head."

Sara laughed. "I can try." She took a drink from her glass. "But answer me this: if staying with Mei-Ling were politically dangerous, then why is she with Thomas?"

Jonathan nearly choked on his drink. "She's doing *what?*"

Grinning, Sara said, "She's with Thomas."

Jonathan could barely speak. "When did *this* happen?"

"I'm not sure. At this moment, I think they're just testing the waters."

"Why is she *doing* this? Does she know that it's not smart to be with someone who's considered an enemy? What is she *thinking*!"

"Because, Dad, when it comes to love, who gives a crap about politics? Look at Eugene and Katrina. They weren't on the same side when they started doing the deed."

Jonathan sat back, stunned. Sara's last words bounced around in his head until his brain finally absorbed them.

He shook his head and laughed. "Oh, man, do I feel like such a douche bag!"

Sara threw up her arms. "Finally, he gets it!"

The two laughed at his sudden epiphany.

"Dad, I have no doubt that your love for Novena is real. And Novena is smart; if *she* thinks that you still love Mei-Ling, then you love Mei-Ling." She paused to let her words sink in. "You're going to have to make a choice, Dad."

Sara expected her father to argue with her, but he didn't. Jonathan stayed silent. Sara was beginning to get worried until he finally spoke a few minutes later.

"I know, Sara. I know." He picked up his silverware and started to cut the pork chops. "Now, can we eat dinner? These pork chops begin to lose their taste if they're allowed to get cold."

Sara laughed and continued eating.

Several minutes later, Jonathan finished his pork chops. A sour look formed on his face as he set down his silverware. "I *hate* pork chops— even if *I* make them!"

Sara laughed out loud. "Then why did you make them, you silly goose?"

"Because *you* like them, my darling daughter."

The two laughed for a good minute until the comm sounded throughout the apartment. Jonathan pressed a button on the table, and a 3-D image of Cid appeared in the middle of the table.

"Hi, guys. Enjoying your dinner?" When they both said yes, Cid laughed. "Now I know that's not *entirely* true, Jonathan."

"What do you mean?"

"Because you're eating pork chops. And I know that you *hate* pork chops."

Sara started to laugh again.

Jonathan just smiled and shook his head. "Is there anything in particular that you called about, Cid?"

"Yeah, there is. Everyone is gathering at Marty's Bar for a celebration."

"A celebration of what?"

"We don't need a crisis as a reason to get together, my friend. We're just going to have some fun."

"Come on, Dad. Let's go."

Jonathan turned his head from the image to his daughter's face. She had a big smile on it, like a child begging her parents to take her to the park on a nice sunny day.

Jonathan smiled back at her and said, "Okay."

Cid flashed a smile. "Great! See you both real soon."

As the image disappeared, father and daughter stood up from the table and started to collect the dishes. Once all of the dishes had been placed in the dishwasher, the duo headed for the exit.

When they reached the living room, Sara turned and stopped her father. "Dad, before we leave, there's something that I want us to do."

"What is it, honey?"

She stood silent for a moment, biting her lower lip. "Can we dance to our song?"

Jonathan stood still, trying not to let the tears that were forming in his eye spill out. "Sure."

Jonathan walked over to the entertainment system. He activated the system and searched through his music library for the song they considered their own. He found it, pressed PLAY, and walked back to Sara. As "Butterfly Kisses" filled the room, father and daughter danced. Sara's arms tightened around Jonathan. He looked down at her and was touched to see that she had her eyes closed and her head on his chest, looking to be at peace. The events of the past week really must have scared her—possibly more than she let on. He vowed to make sure to never worry his little girl like that ever again.

Jonathan and Sara arrived at Marty's Bar about twenty-five minutes after they had left the apartment. Entering the bar, they searched the room for their friends. The place didn't look futuristic; instead, it had wooden floors, wooden chairs and tables, and a bar with drinks of all kinds. There was also a kitchen in the back, with cooks who made killer ribs. Screens were set up to show games, the news, and anything else that the patrons wanted to see. To ensure privacy and filter out any unwanted noise, there were privacy bubbles that the patrons could activate.

Jonathan scanned the bar, looking for his friends. It didn't take long for him to find them. Cid and Novena were at a table near the middle of the bar. Jonathan and Sara made their way past the tables and waitresses until they reached their friends. When they arrived, everyone greeted them with hugs. There was a little hesitation between Sara and Novena, but they smiled and hugged anyway. Jonathan watched them sit down, thinking how lucky he was. He was going to ask where Eugene and Katrina were, but stopped when he looked at the stage. Jonathan sat down in between Sara and Novena.

The bar had a stage where people could perform songs. Every night, patrons would come up to sing their favorite songs from the time before the Great Exodus. This time, Eugene, along with Katrina and William, came on stage with his band.

It took a couple of minute for the band to set up. While everyone waited, Jonathan and Sara ordered their drinks. Jonathan also had a few questions for Cid.

"Chief, is there any word from Earth 2?"

Cid nodded his head, knowing that Jonathan was worried about his friends and loved ones on Earth 2. "I'm sorry, Jonathan. I don't have enough information to give you a clear picture. But don't worry: the moment I get one, you and everyone else will know."

"Thanks, Cid." *Bullshit*, he thought. He loved Cid like a father, but he knew that the man had always kept his cards close to his chest and would reveal what he knew only when he felt it was necessary.

When the band was ready to perform, Eugene picked up a guitar and stepped up to the microphone. "How's everyone?"

The crowd cheered.

"Everyone having fun?"

The crowd cheered louder.

"You ready to have some more?"

The roof was almost blown off the place.

"Then let's *do* this!"

Eugene and his band started to play "25 or 6 to 4" by Chicago. Jonathan knew that Eugene was going to do Chicago; the trombone, sax, and trumpet were a dead giveaway. Almost at once, everyone in the bar jumped out of their seats and started to dance. Novena grabbed Jonathan's hand and pulled him up, dragging him to the dance floor.

They started to dance. Jonathan was a little reluctant at first, but he soon got into the mood. Novena had just startled him for a second.

After the song was over, Eugene put down the guitar and picked up an acoustic guitar. "All right, guys and girls, if you have your special someone with you, grab 'em and pull 'em close, 'cause we're gonna sing a coupla love songs." He started to play "Beginnings," and the crowd cheered once more.

The band then played "Hard Habit to Break," "Stay the Night," "Here in My Heart," "You're the Inspiration," "Love Will Come Back," and "Colour My World." During the whole time, Novena and Jonathan slow-danced, staring into each other's eyes. Jonathan could see her love for him in her eyes, and hoped once again that he would make the right choice.

When the band finished "Colour My World," Eugene asked, "Did you guys enjoy that?"

The crowd screamed their delight.

"We're gonna sing one more song and then hand the stage over to the next performer." The band played "Does Anybody Know What Time It Is?" as their closing number. The crowd loved it. When they'd finished, Eugene and the band bowed. Jonathan and Novena returned to their table.

"Thank you. Thank you. Now it's time for the next performer. Give it up for Jonathan Mikel!"

Jonathan nearly choked on his drink when he heard his name. He wasn't planning on playing tonight. He tried to say no, but the crowd was now shouting his name. He looked around the table. Everyone had a smile on their face. Jonathan just sighed and gave up. He left the table and headed toward the stage.

On his way, he thought about what to play. He liked to take time to prepare his shows, but thanks to Eugene putting him on the spot, he would have to go off the cuff.

He climbed the stage's steps and walked toward Eugene, who had a huge grin on his face. As the crowd roared, he whispered to his friend, "Thanks for the advanced warning."

"It just seemed like the right thing to do."

"Trying to get my mind off the events at hand?"

"Yes."

Jonathan smiled and patted his friend's shoulder. "Thanks, Eugene."

Eugene smiled back. "No problem."

"But how do you expect me to play without my—" Before he could finish, another group of people came out from backstage. He recognized the group immediately; they were his band.

"Just how far ahead did you plan this?"

"Yesterday."

"What made you think that this would work?"

"Because you are so predictable."

Instead of replying, Jonathan walked over to his band and discussed what they would play. In the meantime, Eugene's band left the stage and joined the crowd, while Eugene his wife and son made their way through the crowd and joined their friends. As they sat down, they ordered their drinks. When they finished, Eugene noticed that Novena was giving him a look that Katrina usually reserved for *him* when she was angry with him.

"What?"

"You could have given him some kind of warning."

"He would have just backed down."

"Still. . ."

"He needs this, Novena. With all the crap that has happened within the past few days, he needs to have some fun and loosen up a bit." The waitress arrived and gave them their drinks. "Now sit back and have some fun." He took a drink. "Something tells me that we won't have time to relax later on."

As Eugene and the others were at their table, Jonathan and his band continued discussing what they would play. After a couple of minutes, they made their selections and started to set up. When they were ready, Jonathan grabbed his fiddle and stepped up to the front of the stage, the crowd's screams bombarding him from all sides.

"Hi. I didn't have anything planned for tonight, but my friend, Eugene, put me on the spot, so here I am." The crowd cheered. "So don't blame me if I suck tonight." The crowd laughed. "Here we go!" The first song they played was "If You're Gonna Play in Texas (You Gotta Have a Fiddle in the Band)" and "Love in the First Degree" by Alabama, to kick off their set. Once again, the crowd jumped to their feet and danced, fired up by the music. Next was "Standing Outside the Fire" by Garth Brooks. Next they played "Why Don't You Stay?" by Sugarland, "Just a Dream" by Carrie Underwood, and three Taylor Swift songs: "Pictures to Burn," "White Horses," and "Love Story."

The crowd was having so much fun that Jonathan decided to extend their set. The band played "Butterfly Kisses." As he sang that song, he looked down at Sara and saw the tears in her eyes. They smiled at each other. To finish up, he decided to play "The Devil Went Down to Georgia" by the Charlie Daniels Band. As they played, Jonathan didn't think it was possible for this crowd to get any louder.

When they finished, Jonathan and his band bowed to the audience and left the stage. Jonathan's bandmates went their own way, while he headed toward his friends. He sat down with them and smiled, enjoying himself in their company.

Elijah was in charge of the command center while Cid was out. He walked up and down the aisles of consoles, checking the readouts and receiving reports on the space surrounding the station. So far, there were no other ships on the horizon.

Elijah walked up to the comm officer. "Ensign, have we received any reports from our intelligent agents?"

The ensign shook her head. "I'm sorry, sir. We've received no reports."

Elijah didn't like this. For the last few days, Measha Station had lost communication with both the Tigeras Empire and their operatives on Earth 2. The last transmission had been from Nesith, telling them about the attack on the planet. Since then, they had been able to capture small snippets of traffic here and there, mostly regarding an attack. Because of this, Cid decided to lock down the station. No one was allowed to leave or enter, and no radio traffic was allowed. They made exceptions for special occasions, but they kept the crew separate from the rest of the station; if the people coming in knew something, Cid didn't want them telling the rest of the station; he realized that if anything bad got out, the entire station would find out within hours, and, with all the different species on the station, there would be riots, fights, and mass hysteria on a grand scale.

"Sir, I'm picking up four ships coming out of FTL travel! There are also several shuttles that are accompanying them!"

Elijah ran over to the radar officer's station. "Any idea as to who they are?"

"It's a mixture of ships, sir. Looks like the Telbins and the Tigeras."

Elijah made a face. "What do the scanners say about their condition?"

"It looks as if there's some damage, sir, both major and minor."

"Comm, see if you can get them online."

"Aye, sir."

Elijah tapped his earpiece to contact Cid.

JONATHAN, I'M SERIOUS—YOU should *do* this." Jonathan took a drink and set his glass down.

"Cid, I'm happy that you and everybody else love the music I play, but I don't want to make any records or play professionally. I'm a ship captain through and through. This is just something that I want to do for fun and nothing more."

Cid just threw up his hands. "Fine! I give up! For now."

Jonathan chuckled. "You might as well just give up *forever*."

"Never!"

Jonathan could play a fiddle very well, and he could also sing. Cid was so impressed with his talent that he wanted Jonathan to make an album. Jonathan was flattered, but said no. As he had told Cid time and time again, he was a ship captain— —always had been; always would be. He just enjoyed playing for friends and family.

"Can you *at least* make one for the records in the Hall of Man?"

Jonathan shook his head. "You just can't let this go, can you?"

"Oh, come on, Dad," Sara said. "You and your band are *great*. You should do it!"

Jonathan looked at his daughter, not believing what he was hearing. "Not you, too."

Everyone laughed, and Cid called the waitress for more drinks. When the drinks arrived, everyone grabbed a glass and raised it to make a toast. "To all the friends we've gained, lost, or are to come."

Everyone said "amen" and were about to drink, when Cid stopped and held up his hand, telling them to hold on. He tapped his earpiece. "This is Cid." The smile on his face melted into a frown. "What!" Everyone's smile also melted, the look on Cid's face giving them cause to worry. "We'll be there soon!" He set down his drink and stood up. "Let's go, men!" Everyone looked at one another and followed Cid out of the bar.

As THE GROUP MADE their way to the command center, Cid sent each of them to their stations, telling them he would have a doctor come to purge the alcohol in their systems so they could perform their duties. Katrina was the only one who wouldn't be seen by a doctor; since she was pregnant, she didn't drink alcoholic beverages.

William left to join the station's marines, while Novena and Katrina left to prepare the *Twilight Star*, and Sara joined Omega Squadron. Jonathan and Eugene joined Cid at the command center.

When they arrived at their stations, a doctor and a nurse were waiting to give each of them a shot that would dissolve the alcohol in their systems. When the doctor and the nurse had finished, they searched for Elijah and found him talking to the radar and comm officer.

"How far out are they?"

"About five minutes out."

"Cid, what's going on?" Jonathan asked. Cid hadn't told them what he'd learned, so they were getting a little antsy.

"Four ships have come out of FTL, along with several shuttles."

"Who do they belong to?"

"Scanners tell us they belong to the Telbins and the Tigeras."

Eugene scowled. "What are they doing here?"

Cid crossed his arms. "We think that they might be in trouble."

Eugene arched an eyebrow. "*Think?*"

"We're having trouble getting a clear signal. We're only getting snippets of information. I'm going to send out Omega Squadron and the *Twilight Star* to escort them in."

Jonathan nodded and turned toward the exit. "Eugene and I will head down to the *Twilight Star*."

"No, Jonathan. I want both of you here."

Jonathan stopped and turned toward Cid, not believing what he was hearing. "*What?*"

"The girls can handle the ship and the crew fine. This is a simple pickup." Cid turned his attention back to the comm officer. "Jeff, any word yet?"

The officer pressed several buttons. He was shaking his head, but then stopped. "Wait, sir, I have something! The *Minks* is hailing us."

"Can you put them up on the holo-projector or the viewscreen?"

Jeff pressed a few buttons. "No, sir. They must have sustained damage to theirs."

"Then put them on audio."

"Patching them through."

The message coming through the speakers and their earpieces was garbled and filled with static.

"Try to clear it up some." Jeff pressed a few more buttons, and the transmission became clear as crystal.

"Measha Station, this is Princess Tracy of the Tigeras Empire."

Cid's frown deepened, and he unfolded his arms. When he heard that a couple of damaged Tigeras and Telbin ships had come out of

FTL, he hoped that they had just been attacked by pirates. He wasn't expecting Tracy to be among them. Something was going on.

He spoke into his earpiece. "Tracy, this is Cid. I have Jonathan and your brother-in-law with me. Has something happened?"

There was a pause over the speakers. "I can answer that for you, but I need to talk to you, my sister, Jonathan, and Eugene in private; I have some bad news that you guys need to hear."

Cid could detect the sadness that Tracy was trying to hide. He became concerned about what she had to tell them. But before he could say any more, two new ships came out of FTL and fired at a Telbin heavy cruiser, causing massive damage to the ship, which then fell out of formation and promptly exploded.

Cid's heart stopped for a split second. The ship that made his heart stop wasn't the Imperial battle cruiser; it was the second ship, a Wraith heavy cruiser, that almost gave him a heart attack. *No, it can't be! The Wraiths!* he thought. The most evil race in the universe was at his doorstep!

Cid ran from the comm station to the gunnery stations, all the while shouting orders. "Launch all fighters! Provide cover fire for the Tigeras and Telbins! Make sure that they land here safely!" He reached the fire station and jumped into an empty seat, then addressed everyone at the gunner and fire control stations. "Everyone, listen to me! Do not hold back! The beings in these ships are ruthless beyond comprehension! If we get a chance to capture one, fine—but for now, show no mercy! Now, fire!"

Cid tracked the ships and fired on them. The people around him hesitated for only a fraction of a second, surprised by their leader's reaction. Then they joined him. Over one hundred PPCs and HPLCs fired, and thirty missiles were launched. Lasers, plasma, and missiles streaked across space and slammed into the enemy ships that were so desperately trying to destroy the Tigeras and the Telbins. The enemy ships tried to defend themselves from the barrage of hits, but the stress from their earlier battles, combined with the new threat they were facing, was too much for them; their ships erupted into balls of fire and plasma within minutes after they'd been attacked, the fire from the station destroying their defenses. Only the fighters were left.

Cid tapped a button on his earpiece. "Fighters, take out the rest of those enemy fighters! If you can capture a few, do it, but don't let your guard down. If they so much as twitch, vaporize them!" Cid turned his attention to the screen, watching the battle between the fighters taking place not too far away.

As the battle raged outside, Cid looked around the command center. He noticed that everyone was looking at him, especially Jonathan and Eugene. Cid was usually calm, regardless of the situation; the way that he was acting now was completely out of character for him.

Jonathan and Eugene walked toward him, looking worried. "Cid, what's the problem?" Jonathan asked.

"Yeah, what's going on? I've seen you go off before, but never like *this*," Eugene said.

Before Cid could answer, Sara's voice came over the comm. "Chief, this is Omega 1. We've destroyed the majority of the fighters. The rest have made FTL jumps, but we did manage to capture a few of the stragglers."

Cid smiled. "Good. What's their condition?"

"We've taken out their engines, so they're not going *anywhere* any time soon."

"Excellent. Tow them to hangar bay 5. I'll have three squads of marines and doctors standing by when you land."

"*Three* squads? Are you *sure*?"

"You're right; better make it six! *Twilight Star*?"

"Yes?"

"Escort the *Minks* and what's left of the fleet to hangar bay 7. Medical will be standing by to treat any wounded."

"Aye, sir."

Cid called Elijah. "Elijah, take command. I'm going to meet our friends in hangar bay 7."

BY THE TIME THE trio reached hangar bay 7, the *Twilight Star*, the *Minks*, and the rest of the refugee ships had just about completed their landing sequences. When the ships landed, the doctors climbed the ramps and helped the onboard ship doctors bring the injured off the ship and onto the medical vehicles that were waiting to take them to the nearest medical facilities.

While they were unloading the injured, Novena and Katrina ran toward them from the *Twilight Star*. William soon joined them. Katrina was the first to speak. "I heard that my sister is here! Where is she?"

"She's still aboard the *Minks*."

Katrina started to move through the group, but Eugene stopped her. "Honey, hold on!"

Katrina whirled to face her husband. "Eugene, get out of my way!"

She tried to shove him out of the way, but he held his ground and took hold of her shoulders.

"Katrina, please—just wait here and let the doctors bring her out. Okay?"

Katrina looked as if she were going to rip Eugene's arms off, but she didn't. "Okay. I'll wait."

Eugene smiled and wrapped an arm around her as she laid her head on his shoulder. Everyone waited where they were. Ten minutes later, Tracy emerged from the ship with several bandages covering her face. She was flanked by her bodyguards. But these weren't just *any* bodyguards; they were the royal guard, the special guard that was put into duty only when there was an active threat to the family.

Katrina was about to run to Tracy, but several more guards came out of the ship and quickly surrounded her and Eugene. Katrina was becoming frightened. Tracy started to cry. Katrina wrapped her arms around her sister, trying to comfort her.

"Sis, sis, what's wrong? Where's everyone else?" After a few minutes, Tracy separated from her sister and whispered the story of her ordeal to Katrina. Cid couldn't hear what it was, but he knew that it must have been bad, because Katrina screamed out in horror and collapsed in her sister's arms.

ONCE EVERYONE WAS ABLE to calm Katrina, they moved her to the infirmary, where she was sedated. They then went out into the hallway to discuss what had happened. The royal guard had split up, some of them standing guard over Katrina in the infirmary, the rest remaining in the hallway with the group.

Eugene was the first to speak. "Tracy, what's happening? I know it must be bad, because these guys are used only when things are in the crapper."

"Jokes again, Eugene?"

"It's how I keep my sanity."

"Being married to my sister, I can see *why*."

The group gave a small laugh, trying to cheer themselves up, but the attempt wasn't having much of an effect.

Tracy closed the distance between them and hugged him. "Thanks for trying to cheer me up, Eugene."

Small tears formed in his eyes as he hugged her back. "No problem, kid."

When they separated, Tracy told them the whole story, from the attack on the Tigeras home planet and the arrival of the Telbin, to the destruction of the planet, and, finally, to their escape.

When she finished, there was silence from some and gasps of shock from others. Eugene started to shake his head and pace. *That* explained why the royal guard was out in full force: nearly the entire royal family had been eliminated!

Jonathan grabbed Eugene by the arm, stopping him from pacing. "Buddy, calm down, will you! We don't need you bugging out right now!"

Eugene shook off his concerns. "Don't worry, man. I'm not going to bug out. I'm worried about a couple of other things right now." He turned his attention to Cid. "Cid, how many Tigeras and Telbins do you think are on this station?"

"I'd say over a million each."

"And what do you think will happen when they find out what's gone down and who's responsible?"

Cid sighed and stroked his head. He really didn't want to think about what would happen. Not only were there Tigeras on the station, but also people from Imperial Guard territory. There would be fights and riots throughout the station, and its security force would have their hands full.

"I'm going to put a gag order on all the people who've come in on those ships, as well as those that'll be arriving. No one will be allowed to talk to anybody—although I'm not sure how long that'll help; even with the gag order, this'll be all over the station in no time." He walked away from the group. "I've got to go. I also have an interrogation to oversee. It seems that I have a lot to do in the next few hours."

After Cid had left, William turned to his father. "Dad, you said that there were two things bothering you. What's the other one?"

Eugene looked around the room—at Tracy, the guards, to where Katrina was lying on the bed, and then at his feet. "With the rest of the family dead, Katrina is now the empress of the Tigeras Empire. And since I'm her husband that means that I'm. . .I'm. . ." He let the sentence trail off and shuffled his feet.

Jonathan knew what that meant: Eugene was now the emperor of the Tigeras Empire. That fear had always been with him; from the day that he knew he was going to marry Katrina, the thought was always at the back of his mind, and it scared him.

Jonathan put his arm around his friend's shoulder and gave it a squeeze, reassuring him that everything would turn out all right.

Everyone sat down in the chairs that were lined up outside Katrina's room, waiting for something to happen. When thirty minutes had passed, Sara left to do maintenance checks on her fighter, while William had to leave for a debrief with the marines and the Infiltrators.

A little over an hour later, Cid's voice came through their earpieces, loud and demanding. "Everybody come to the command center immediately! Especially you, Novena! NOW!"

Everyone cringed at the sound of Cid's voice screaming in their ears. With the exception of Tracy, everyone took off in the direction of the teleporter that would transport them to the command center, the royal guard trailing them. Before Eugene entered the transporter, he began to wonder if he was ready to be the man that his wife's people needed him to be.

WHEN THEY REACHED the command center, all hell was breaking lose. People were screaming and running around like chickens with their heads cut off. Actually, Cid was screaming his orders, while the people around him were running to carry them out.

Since Cid yelled specifically for Novena over the comm, she decided to speak first. "Chief, what's going on?" she asked, frightened.

Cid whirled from what he was doing and faced her. The emotions on his face ranged from worry, to anger, to fright. "A lot's going on," he said in a rush. "Things are happening really fast—things that I don't care for. Things that I could spend my whole lifetime living without."

"Cid, you're not speaking clearly."

Cid heaved a sigh and waved them over to a corner of the room that was semi-private. "I've had a little chat with our prisoners; needless to say, what they reported was not very encouraging."

"And that was?"

"I'll tell you later; but there's another reason I wanted you here." He led them back across the room toward the comm and radar stations. "We've received a message from Twilight Strike Force Group 10. They told us that they'll be arriving very shortly, along with what is left of Ashlon fleets 12 and 5."

Novena was taken aback by this and so was everyone else in the group. She was not expecting any Twilight forces to show up, so hearing that one was arriving—with an Ashlon fleet, no less—was both surprising and unsettling.

"Did they say why?"

"Apparently, they were doing a sweep of the D-Zone and came upon the two Ashlon fleets. The fleets told them that they'd been attacked by the Imperial Guard, who had crossed the D-Zone."

Jonathan's voice came from behind her. "You're not saying that . . ."

Cid nodded his head. "Yes, I am. By crossing the D-Zone and attacking an Ashlon fleet, the Imperial Guard has officially declared war on the Ashlon Republic."

The group moaned and screamed obscenities in several languages. With what was happening on Earth 2, and now this, there was no doubt that Scott was making a serious power play for the entire galaxy.

"What was the condition of the fleets when they found them?" Jonathan asked.

"Fleet 12 lost half of its ships before Fleet 5 arrived to render assistance. Several minutes after they'd arrived, what remained of the Imperial Guard attack force had retreated. But there's more."

"Great!" Eugene muttered. "*More* good news!"

"It seems that during the battle there were several ships of different design using technology unlike that of the Guards."

The group exchanged looks. They did not like where this was going. "What exactly are you saying, Cid?" Eugene asked. "That the Imperial Guard had a weapons upgrade? Or is there some other nightmare going on?"

Before Cid could speak, Elijah interrupted them. "Sir, scanners tell us that a little over two dozen ships have dropped out of FTL. They tell us that they are the two Ashlon fleets and the Twilight Strike Force Group. The *Zeus* from Ashlon Fleet 12 is hailing us."

"Put them on the holo-projector."

The holo-projector on the comm station came to life; the visage of Admiral Thomas Blake appeared, surprising everyone.

"Hey, guys, how's it going?"

Everyone exchanged wide-eyed looks before turning their attention back to the Ashlon admiral. "Brother, what are you doing here?"

"Nice to see you too, Eugene."

"You know what I mean."

Thomas smiled.

"Thomas, what's going on? Were you with the fleets when the attack went down?"

Cid interrupted the two. "All of your questions can wait. I want everyone landed and checked out by medical before we continue."

"Chief?" Elijah said.

Cid gave a heavy sigh. "*Now* what?" He turned to Elijah. "What is it, Elijah?"

"Sir, Imperial Fleet 16 has dropped out of FTL. The *Freedom* is hailing us."

Before anyone could speak, Cid held up his hands to hold them off.

"No one say a word. Now, everyone go back to Katrina's room. I'll contact you all when I have everything sorted out."

The small group was about to protest, but the look he gave them stopped them. He pointed to the exit, and the three friends reluctantly left the command center.

REUNION

C ID STOOD IN HANGAR bay 15 almost forty minutes later, watching the ground crews tend to a portion of the Ashlon fleets that had landed at the station. With all the ships that had arrived in the past hour, they had taken up about ten hangar bays due to their sheer size.

As Cid watched, Thomas talked with his men and the ground crews, taking status of ships, injuries to the crew, ammunition, and repairs. Thomas must have seen him out of the corner of his eye, because he left the men he was speaking to and headed toward Cid.

He gave the man a big hug. "I am *so* glad to see you in person again, old man."

"Come on. I'm not *that* old."

"Whatever helps you sleep at night."

The two friends laughed and started walking, with no particular destination in mind.

"Cid, I heard that Mei-Ling, Isabella, Terri, Steve, and my son are here."

Cid nodded his head and gave Thomas an update on their medical exams. Mei-Ling was doing well from her public punishment and the plasma wound she had received. So was Ryan, who, he found out, was in surgery because of a stab wound he had received. Isabella had no injuries at all, while Terri and Steven had been caught in an explosion. Cid told Thomas that Earth 2 had been attacked, but didn't give him more information. Thomas wanted to know more, but Cid was tight-lipped, not saying anything more for the time being. Thomas wanted to press for more, but he didn't; he knew that Cid would tell him when he decided it was the right time.

"Can you at least tell me where they are?"

Cid jabbed his thumb in the direction of the door to their left. "They're in the next hangar over."

Thomas smiled and patted Cid on the shoulder. He left the hangar and entered the next one. The activity of this hangar was pretty much like the one he'd just come from, but less hectic. He scanned the bay, looking for his friends and family, and spotted them not too far away, sitting on a bench. He started to run toward them.

They noticed him and stood up. He reached them and gave Ryan a big hug, careful not to agitate the wound, even though it was almost completely healed. He also gave Steve, Isabella, and Terri hugs, telling them how happy he was to see them.

He looked over Terri's shoulder at Mei-Ling, the woman that he loved. He left Ryan and Terri and wrapped Mei-Ling in his arms.

JONATHAN, EUGENE, AND NOVENA were with Katrina when Cid contacted them. He told them that everyone was in hangar bay 16. When they asked what he meant by 'everyone,' he said only that they would see when they arrived at the hangar.

Katrina was awake by now. She was doing much better since receiving the news about her family and decided to join them, along with Tracy. The royal guard, who wouldn't leave their side, followed them.

When they reached the entrance to the hangar bays, they found Cid, Sara, and William waiting for them.

"Where's Thomas, Cid?" Jonathan asked.

"He's inside."

"And who is 'everyone'?" he asked.

Cid shifted his feet and looked at the ground.

"Vice Admiral Yearly, of the *Freedom*, told me that Ryan, Mei- Ling, Isabella, Terri, and Steve are with her." He told them the story of how all of them had reached the *Freedom*.

Everyone looked at each other, amazed at what they were hearing. It was as if fate were bringing everyone together at the same time.

The group ran through the hallways of the spaceport, making their way to hangar bay 16. They were eager to see the loved ones they missed so much. They reached the doors and entered the giant hangar, searching for their loved ones among the ships being tended to by engineers and electricians.

They found them by a bench on the far side of the room, talking excitedly to one another. One of them looked in their direction and started to walk toward them. Then he sprinted into a run.

Sara smiled and ran, screaming his name. "Ryan!"

The two lovebirds fell into each other's arms and kissed passionately. The two groups met and gave hugs and kisses all around, telling one another how happy they were to be together again after the terror they had experienced in the past week.

Jonathan and Thomas stood side by side, watching their children, who had yet to separate. Thomas looked at Jonathan and smiled. "Looks as if we're going to be in-laws."

Jonathan just groaned and said, "God help me." The two friends laughed.

Novena came over to the group and introduced herself. "Oh my God! Novena?" This came from Mei-Ling. She hugged the Twilight and asked what she was doing out of her pod. Since nearly everyone thought that she was eternally merged with the *Twilight Star*, she had to explain how and why she was here in front of them.

When Novena finished her explanation, she looked over her shoulder at Jonathan. Of all the people that he had greeted, he and Mei-Ling had yet to greet each other. It seemed that they were delaying the inevitable meeting that was to come. As the two closed the distance between them, the world around them faded away. Family and friends disappeared; the ships and the workers vanished; and even Measha Station no longer existed.

The two former lovers stared into each other's eyes. It is said that the eyes are the windows to the soul, and at that moment, they knew what each other was thinking. For days, each of them had been thinking about their current and past relationships, and though separated by space and distance, they had each come to the same conclusion.

They were not yet completely over each other. They were still in love. They *did* love the people they were with at the moment, but the love they had for each other was not gone; it was still with them as strong as ever. For a moment they were not sure whether to try to reconcile or go their separate ways.

But standing together, they knew that their futures were intertwined. They were about to kiss, but still had enough sense to notice that the people they were presently involved with were in the room with them; they hugged instead, holding each other tightly.

As they embraced, they saw, out of the corners of their eyes, that Thomas and Novena were watching them, their faces reflecting a combination of sadness and understanding. All of them still had to talk. But for now, there was an unspoken conversation among the four of them.

There was the sound of a hard cough, and they turned their attention to the source of it: Cid.

"I know a lot of you want to know what's going on, and all of you will find out. I want you to be in the conference room in thirty minutes. We'll not only go over what has happened and what is going on presently, but also what is to come. This ordeal is far from over." With that, Cid walked out of the hangar.

As the group watched him leave, Jonathan and Mei-Ling smiled at each other, happy to be together.

23

CONFESSIONS AND. . .

THE GROUP DISPERSED AND left the hangar until the time came for the meeting. Jonathan, Mei-Ling, Thomas, and Novena stayed behind. As they left, Mei-Ling saw Ryan give her a look of both disappointment and understanding; his face showed how much he wished things had gone differently, but that he was all right with the outcome.

When the four of them left, Jonathan turned to Novena. "Novena—"

She held up her hand to stop him. "Don't worry, Jonathan; we've already had this conversation. Whatever you decide is fine with me. I just want you to be happy." She reached out and gave Mei-Ling a hug. "And you, too, Mei-Ling." The two separated. "And besides, I don't get jealous easily!"

She turned, gave a hug to Jonathan, told him that she was glad he was happy, and left the bay. The only other person left was Thomas. Mei-Ling stepped forward, not knowing what to say.

Luckily, Thomas spoke first. "Look, Mei-Ling, I know that you feel bad, but don't. I knew the risk when we started our relationship. It had happened by accident, and, when we went forward, I knew there was the possibility that you still had feelings for Jonathan that could crop up again." He smiled and shook his head. "As much as I want the two of us to be together, I wouldn't want it to be unless both of us feel the same way. Oh, well, you know what they say: 'It is better to have loved and lost than never to have loved at all.'"

He shook Jonathan's hand and gave him a quick hug; then he embraced Mei-Ling. "I'll see you two later."

He gave her one more smile and left the hangar.

The two star-crossed lovers looked at each other and kissed for the first time in years—heatedly, passionately, as if they were afraid that if they separated once more they would never be together again.

ALMOST HALF AN HOUR later, Mei-Ling and Jonathan made their way down the hall toward the conference room where all would be revealed. As they were walking, a lift stationed a few feet ahead of them opened up, and a couple of Tigeras emerged from the elevator, appearing defeated, saddened, and depressed. When they saw Mei-Ling and Jonathan, their expressions changed to hatred— hatred so intense that Jonathan felt as if their gazes could burn right through him.

They screamed at him. "YOU!" Then they launched themselves at him. Jonathan could handle himself pretty well in a fight, but these two Tigeras were attacking with much more than a desire to win: They wanted to *kill* him!

While Mei-Ling tried to help him fight off the two Tigeras, other people started to come out of the conference room to see what was going on. When they saw what was happening, they all ran over to the fight, trying to break it up.

Even when they separated everyone, the two aliens still tried to attack Jonathan. "Hey! *Hey!*" The volume of his voice made the entire group turn toward Cid. "Everyone calm down right now!" After everyone stopped struggling, he walked closer. "*Now, what the hell is going on here?*"

One of the Tigeras pointed his finger at Jonathan, his voice shaking. "This man is *scum*! He deserves to be punished for what he has done to our people!"

Cid spoke angrily, "No. He has done nothing wrong." The Tigeras looked as if he were going to say something else, but Cid interrupted him. "Jonathan is not his brother! You *cannot* and *will not* hold him accountable for what his brother has done! Now get out of here and cool off! NOW!"

The two Tigeras were shaken out of their angry stupor and looked around, finally noticing the crowd that had gathered since the fight had started. They left in a hurry for the nearest lift.

When they had gone, Cid ordered everyone to take their seats in the conference room. When they had filed in, he talked with Jonathan. "Are you all right? Do you want to have a medic look at you?"

He shook his head. "No, that's okay." He rubbed his head. "I take it that word has got out about my brother's actions?"

Cid nodded. "I may be good at information management, but I can only keep something as big as the Tigeras's home planet being destroyed hidden from the people on this station for just so long." Cid wrapped his arm around Jonathan's shoulder and led him toward the conference room. "Don't let it get to you, my friend. Come on. Let's get this over with."

The two walked into the room, which was filled with a variety of people and aliens. As Jonathan took his seat beside Mei-Ling, he scanned the room. Sara, Ryan, Eugene, Katrina, Tracy, William, Terri, and Steve were all sitting with Cid near the front of the table. The heads of the fleets were also there, along with their captains and Xos. Also in attendance were the heads of Measha Station's security, air defense, marines, and the Infiltrators. On the screens displayed on the wall around the room was President Martinez from the Ashlon Republic; Fleet Admiral Pamela Starkin from the Telbin Empire; and, from the Twilight Continuum, Fleet Admiral Overtin.

This is a very diverse group, Jonathan thought. He couldn't remember something so major that would bring all of these diverse groups together. Something big and bad must be on the horizon.

Instead of sitting down, Cid opened a cabinet in the wall and took out a bottle of liquor and a glass. Everyone in the room shook their heads when he asked if they wanted a drink. Jonathan looked worriedly at Mei-Ling; the same look was on her face, staring back at him. Cid would drink only if he were really stressed.

He drank a full glass, poured another, then he sat down at the table. "All of you are aware of a recent series of events that have been taking place around the galaxy. These events were put into motion decades ago.

"Early last week, we were able to get a complete copy of Wright's classified files. It also served as his diary, revealing just how messed up his head has become over the years. With a team of specialists, I have been poring through the information, and what I have discovered is very disturbing; it fills in many of the gaps that developed during the intelligence gathering I had initiated."

Cid took a drink.

"I want you all to be patient with me; this is a very long story, and I would appreciate it if you all try to bear with me until the end." He looked at everybody in the room. "I think the best place to start this is to go back twenty years.

"Shang-Ling, who was high ruler of the Imperial Guard at the time, was changing the power structure of the Guard, taking away power from the high ruler and spreading it over the Imperial Council. It was the first step in a plan to turn the Imperial Guard into a republic. Part of the plan was to also eliminate the alien discrimination that the Imperial Guard was famous for. The first step in this was the Alien Trade Charter, which allowed aliens to trade with systems that are part of the Imperial Guard. Later on, other charters came into play that allowed aliens to settle on planets and start up trade stations. It was only a matter of time before Shang-Ling disabled the Guard and gave birth to a republic."

Jonathan smiled when Cid talked about Shang-Ling. Shang's vision of the Imperial Guard becoming a republic was the reason that he and Eugene had joined the Guard. His talks with the high ruler had fascinated him. It had gotten him so excited that he'd wanted to be part of the change. Even after Shang's murder and Eugene's defection to the Ashlon Republic, Jonathan, along with Mei-Ling, Steve, and Terri, tried to fulfill Shang's dream—but because of Wright's opposition, it proved to be incredibly difficult.

"Fourteen years ago, Shang-Ling was assassinated. His murderer was never captured, but I know who killed him." As gasps rose from the people in the room, Cid quickly quieted them to keep the gasps from turning into outbursts. Jonathan put his hands on Mei-Ling's shoulders to give her comfort. She reached up and grabbed his real hand.

"Six years before Shang's murder, Scott Wright had been contacted by an alien species unknown to him, called the Wraiths.

"The Wraiths are an evil race, soulless beings who love destruction and take pleasure in death. They are very manipulative and intelligent, and they are also excellent fighters." He gestured in Ryan's direction. "You can ask Ryan Blake over there; he's had firsthand knowledge about what great fighters they are."

Jonathan looked over at Ryan, who nodded his head in confirmation.

Cid continued. "These Wraiths came to Wright to form a partnership: they would help him, and he would help them."

Jonathan knew that Cid wanted everyone to stay quiet, but he just couldn't anymore. "Cid, I know my brother. He hates aliens with a passion! So why would he willingly work with them?"

Cid nodded his head. "I'm getting to that. As much as he hated aliens, the offer made to Wright by the Wraiths was too good to pass up. If Wright would help them, the Wraiths would help Wright take complete control of the Imperial Guard.

"Wright thought that Shang was shifting the Guard in a direction that Wright considered not the best for the human race. Wright felt that *his* way was the best for everyone, but Shang did not agree; Wright thought that *his* way was the *only* way. The Wraiths saw this and approached Wright concerning a partnership. Despite his hatred of them, Wright felt that the end would justify the means. One of the things that he wanted the Wraiths to do for him, when the time was right, was to kill Shang. Over the years, they have helped Wright replace several members of the government with his allies, to give him more freedom and power.

"They have also helped Wright's scientists and engineers develop new technology and weapons, particularly the new cloaking devices that they have been using of late. In addition, they have run secret ops for Wright, taking out threatening targets, helping him win key victories that helped him with his promotions, secretly securing alliances for him from systems that were not part of the Imperial Guard, and many other helpful activities." He smiled thinly. "If there is one thing that the Wraiths *don't* mind, it is getting their hands dirty."

"And if a planet did not cooperate?" Eugene asked.

"The planet's cities would be destroyed."

"How could they possibly cover this up? Somebody that wasn't in on it would have to have known about it," Eugene insisted.

"The Wraiths would level bogus charges against the people of the planet, accusing them of having attacked them." Cid was silent for a moment. "One such example was Gypsia."

Most of the group had gone silent with this. Almost everybody knew the official story about Gypsia that had been released to the public, but not the truth, and Jonathan felt it was now time to talk about it. He'd given his friends only the bare essentials; now everyone would know the *whole* truth.

Before Jonathan said anything further, he got up from his seat, poured himself a drink, then sat back down and looked around the room. "Many of you have watched my trial, heard the testimonies from the witnesses, and listened to audio recordings of myself giving orders to fire on the cities of Gypsia and the ships that were trying to escape. *This all is not true!*

"Fleet 16 received a transmission from Wright, telling us to make our way to Gypsia. We were told that we were going to be part of an operation to take down an organization on the planet that was dealing in slavery, trafficking, drugs, and weapons. When we arrived, we were given new orders: we were to fire on the cities and on all ships that tried to escape. When I asked why, Scott told me that the organization had taken over the whole planet—that it was nothing but a hive for all the scum that existed in the galaxy. My instincts were screaming that something was not right, but I was prepared to follow orders.

"Reluctantly, I was about to give the command to fire when we received a transmission from a member of the planet's council, asking us what our intentions were. When I told them, they said we were wrong and begged us not to destroy them. Before I could give the order I heard someone crying in the background. At that point, I decided to trust my instincts and hold our fire. Wright became very angry with me, threatening to have me court-marshaled if I didn't follow his orders." Jonathan took a drink and smiled. "When I told Wright where he could shove it, he ordered my XO at the time, Timothy, my nephew and his son, to have me arrested and to take over command.

"Timothy relieved me of command and had me taken to the brig. I knew that I couldn't just sit there and do nothing while innocent people died, so I escaped and headed for the bridge. When I arrived, I told my nephew that I was taking back command of the fleet. He pulled his pistol on me and threatened to shoot me if I did not return to my cell."

He paused and took a deep breath. "I loved my nephew, and he loved me, but I knew that he would do it; he was loyal to the Guard and to his father. I looked into his eyes and then at the screen. I watched cities and ships being destroyed, and on the audio I heard the screams of men, women, and children about to be killed. At that moment I knew that I had to do *something* to stop it.

"I tackled my nephew, and we fought on the bridge. During the fight, Timothy was severely wounded. He died soon after." A tear formed on Jonathan's cheek. "I was arrested, charged with my nephew's death, and put on trial for mass murder and genocide. They'd decided to put the entire blame on me. Wright said that the intelligence they'd received had been wrong and that he'd ordered me to retreat, but that I'd insisted *he* was wrong and ordered everyone to open fire on the planet and on anyone who tried to escape. Instead of me trying to stop the attack, they said that Timothy disagreed and so I killed him for trying to stop me. They created false video and audio recordings picturing me as the bad guy, and they put witnesses on the stand that were not even on the *Freedom* at the time. They wouldn't let the people who had been there speak at my trial, to tell the truth."

More tears started to flow from Jonathan's eye. "Scott never forgave me for Timothy's death, and I don't know if I can ever forgive him for what he did. In my exile, I changed my name to my mother's maiden name; I felt that Scott had insulted the family name, and I wanted nothing to directly link me to him." Jonathan wanted to take a drink, but instead pushed the glass aside and stood up. He went to a corner of the room and stood still, trying to hide his tears from the rest of the people in the room. Mei-Ling walked over to him and put her arms around him, hoping to soothe him with words and give him comfort.

Everyone in the room remained silent, not knowing what to say about Jonathan's revelation. Cid was the first to speak. "I know that this is kind of hard to swallow, but it's all true. If you have any doubts about Jonathan's story, this will dispel them." Cid typed in a few commands, and the holo-projector in the center of the table came to life, replaying all of what had happened on the *Freedom*, exactly as Jonathan had described. When it was finished, Cid spoke, "This was the original recording from the *Freedom*. It was found in Wright's files."

Jonathan looked at the projector, and then at Cid, with an expression on his face that said he wanted to kill him. "You had this the whole time? Why did you have me tell them what had happened when you could have just *shown* them?"

Cid stood up and looked directly into Jonathan's eyes. "Because *you* needed to tell them what had happened. Only the people closest to you know the truth, but you can't heal the soul just by telling a few in secret. You needed to let it out *yourself*, or it would have haunted you for the rest of your life."

The hurtful look on Jonathan's face faded into sadness, and then to relief. He hugged Cid fiercely. "Thanks, old man."

Cid smiled thinly. "Don't thank me *yet*."

Jonathan stepped back and gave him a questioning look. "What do you mean?"

Cid was hesitant. "There's a lot that *I* know that *you* don't." He gestured for Jonathan to sit back down, and he did, reluctantly.

Cid took his seat as well. "Now, about the Wraiths and their troubles . . . "

24

REVELATIONS

YOU SEE, THE ONLY female Wraith that can reproduce is the queen, and they lost her thousands of years ago. Usually, if one queen dies, they would create another with her genetic material— but because they'd lost her, they couldn't do that; they needed therefore a substitute but couldn't find one. The Wraiths have long life spans in general, but they are not immortal. For thousands of years they were able to keep themselves alive through prolonged states of hibernation. Wright assigned scientists to help solve this problem, and they had succeeded. Using the human female reproduction system and genetic manipulation, these scientists were able to help the Wraiths find a way to reproduce.

"But they could only do this for so long. They needed their queen, and Wright was helping them locate her."

"How did they lose her?" Jonathan asked.

"She went missing two thousand years before, during the final major battle of the war."

"*What* war?" Mei-Ling asked.

At that point, Novena stood up, twiddling her thumbs. "I think I can explain that." She walked to the front of the table and looked at the viewscreens. "With your permission, Admiral, I would like to be the one to explain."

Admiral Overtin rubbed his chin, lost in deep thought. He nodded his head. "Go ahead."

She smiled and nodded. "Thank you." She turned to face the rest of the room. "The war that Cid has mentioned was between the Wraiths and the Twilights. It ended two thousand years ago.

"Twenty-five hundred years ago, we genetically engineered an insectoid race that became known as the Wraith. They were created to help increase our work and labor force. We chose to create them as insectoids because some of the best builders have always been insects. Because of them, we were able to increase the productivity of our workloads three times over. Now, for the first four hundred years, everything went well, but then something went wrong.

"Like most insect hives, there is a queen that gives birth to all of the drones, workers, and warriors. We engineered the queen to give birth only to workers and drones, but somehow and somewhere along the line, she was able to breed warriors without us knowing. The Wraiths rebelled, and for a hundred years we fought each other."

"Why did they rebel?" Katrina asked.

"It wasn't until it was too late that we discovered that they hated us for creating them just to be a workforce. They thought that we treated them as nothing but slaves, even though we took very good care of them."

"If they had asked to be freed, would you have let them go?"

Novena glanced at Admiral Overtin, then turned back to her friends. "No, we wouldn't have. They fought against us with a fury that we'd never seen before. They declared war not only on *us* but on all current and future allies."

Ryan scoffed. "Well, that explains why they hated me so much."

"How did the war end?" Jonathan asked.

"One of the final battles was between the Wraiths' queen and our own. Their two fleets were going at it back and forth, and during the fight, what was left of the two fleets went into FTL. We lost track of them, and we never heard from the queen's fleet again, or the Wraiths' either."

"Hence their reproduction problem," Jonathan said.

"Correct."

"What about the rest of the Wraiths?"

"After their queen disappeared, there were a few small skirmishes, but within a year, we started having fewer and fewer encounters. Then, all of a sudden they just disappeared."

"Didn't it seem a little suspicious that all of a sudden the Wraiths just up and disappeared?" Eugene asked.

Admiral Overtin interjected, "*Of course* it did. We searched for them but found no sign of them. We kept up the search for thousands of years. We have heard rumors here and there, but some turned out to be nothing, while others couldn't be proved."

"If there's one thing the Wraiths are pros at, it's hiding themselves from the rest of the galaxy," Cid said.

"Do Wright's files say where they've been hiding for most of the time?" Katrina asked.

"Yes, they do. They don't say *where* exactly—just that they have been hiding in several giant gas systems."

"Very clever of them, using the planets' atmospheres to mask their ships and stations from everyone's scanners."

"Indeed."

"So why *now?*" Thomas asked. "Why have they decided to resurface after almost two thousand years—or have they always been doing something behind the scenes somewhere?"

At this point, Novena returned to her seat and Cid stood up. "From what we've gathered, they've been performing secret operations every so often, coming out of hibernation to put them into effect. They are ultimately looking for their queen and trying to destroy the Twilights. I think they may have found a solid lead."

Cid was silent for a moment. "If they find her, it won't be good for the galaxy. With their queen, the Wraiths will no longer need humans to reproduce; they will seek out and destroy us all, especially the Twilights and the Nexus.

A puzzled look formed on Mei-Ling's face. "*The Nexus?* What do *they* have to do with this?" Not many people had contact with the

Nexus; most just knew them to be shape-shifters who had been around the galaxy for millions of years. They were extremely private. The Ashlon Republic and the Imperial Guard had no idea where their empire was located.

Cid just leaned back in his chair, took a deep breath, and looked at his closest friends. He knew that what he was about to say would upset them and shock them at the same time. But it was time for them to know.

"I have something to tell you all." He stood up and took another deep breath. "I'm not who I claim to be. I'm not human." There were confused looks throughout the room and from the people on the viewscreens. Everyone wondered how things could get any stranger than they already were.

Jonathan and Eugene said at the same time, "Then who *are* you?"

At that, Cid's appearance began to change. His face started to melt, to lose its normal appearance. His nose melted into his face, as did his lips, and his eyes sank into his head. His body also began to change, turning into a big lump of clay with arms and legs. He was now a little taller and just a little more bulky. His mouth became wider, and his eyes came back out of his skull, this time the color purple.

"This is my *true* form. I'm a Nexus."

Everyone at the meeting was in shock. The Wrights and the Blakes could not believe that the man they'd grown up with, who was like a second father and a grandfather to them, was not who they'd believed he was.

Thomas was the first to speak. "Well, that explains why you are such a smart-ass. You've been around for a long time." His eyebrows narrowed. "Exactly how old *are* you?"

"I'm two thousand, seven hundred and fifty years old."

Thomas smiled. "You don't look a day over a thousand."

Jonathan asked, "So why keep it a secret?"

"When the Wraiths went into hiding, the Nexus ruler sent a task force out to find them. We disguised ourselves as different races so that the Wraiths wouldn't recognize us."

"Where is the Nexus Empire?" Thomas asked.

"On the other side of the galaxy. We have minimal contact with them. We talk with them only to give updates on our findings."

"How did you guys get involved in this?"

"Back when the Twilights were at war with the Wraiths, they asked us to join them. They were having problems and needed help."

Admiral Overtin took over. "The Wraiths know us almost better than we know ourselves. They must have been planning this rebellion for a long time. They knew our tactics and the locations of our secret military installations, and managed to keep a step ahead of us for most of the war. We knew that we would lose if we didn't get outside help.

"The Wraiths had had almost zero encounters with the Nexus, as had we. We'd just traded with them because they mostly kept to themselves. We met with them, and they agreed to help us.

"But there was a price.

"When we told the Nexus that we had genetically engineered the Wraiths, they became angry with us, telling us how stupid it was for us to play God. Even though they were angry, they agreed to help us, but we could never work on genetics again unless it was under their supervision. They said that if we *did*, the Wraiths would be the least of our worries!

"When they joined us, it turned the whole war around. The Nexus helped us track them down and almost destroy them."

Everyone looked at Cid, who just shrugged. "The Wraiths wanted to obliterate them. We had to be just as ruthless, and we were. We had no doubt that they would have gone after the Twilights' allies once they were done with them. They had to be stopped!"

"Why did they destroy my home?" Katrina asked. From the looks of confusion on the screens, many people didn't know what she was talking about.

Cid nodded his head and addressed everyone in the room. "I'm sure that you have all heard rumblings from your agents that some big things have been happening lately, but you've had no concrete information. I've tried my best to keep things quiet until I could sort the situation out, but rumors are starting to spread, even here on the station. So get ready, because it's a real kicker!"

25

COLD-BLOOD

ESITH SAT IN HIS command chair, so deep in thought that he hadn't realized his XO, Maegan, was trying to get his attention. He nodded his head at the sound of her voice, and looked up at her. "What?"

Maegan smiled. "As the humans say, a penny for your thoughts."

He chuckled. "I'm sorry. I was thinking about the upcoming tribal council meeting."

He gave a sigh. "I don't know how I'm going to ask them for help." He needed their support to save his beloved Isabella and the rest of his friends.

"Well, you above all should know how the council feels about the warm-bloods. They just don't trust them," Maegan said.

That was true, though it was really the old council members who were still distrustful of the warm-bloods. The newer generations had started to let go of their prejudices, but it would still take a while for everyone to come around to the younger generation's thinking.

"Nesith, I know you love this warm-blood, Isabella— but you are asking the council to protect those who they hate the most."

Nesith didn't say anything; he knew what she was saying.

"For what it's worth, Homeland fleet will follow you to the death against the Wraith and their allies." With that said, Maegan walked back to her post.

He and Maegan had been close at one point, but nothing had came of it; now, he was glad it hadn't worked out, because he had Isabella.

His fleet had only four dread-saucers. They had eighty DPCs and covered with mag-armor plating. They might seem small, but Soliens didn't need large fleets to get the job done.

As strong as his fleet was, they were no match for the fight that was ahead of them. He would need more ships.

Maegan spoke. "Sir, I have a transmission from the council. Everyone is ready and waiting for you in the comm- sat room."

"Thank-you, XO. Take over the bridge."

Nesith left the bridge and went to comm-sat. Once inside, he activated the terminal. The room filled with projections of the Solien Tribal Council from Graeson, their home planet.

All the Solien technology was housed below ground, for the surfaces of Graeson looked like one big jungle. Except for some well-concealed missile launchers, it looked like a world untouched by a high tech society.

Even though they distrusted warm-bloods, Soliens did have respect for Cid and the other leaders of Measha Station, who had helped the Soliens in the past with relief during their conflicts.

He bowed before speaking.

"Ladies and gentlemen of the council, I requested this meeting to inform you of some developments in the galaxy, and to make a request." He recapped the events on Earth 2 and the Tigeras home planet. He also relayed what Cid had told him about the Wraiths' involvements in the Earth 2 and Tigeras conflicts. He further informed them about the Wraiths' alliance with the Imperial Guard and their Shadow Fleet.

"I have reports that the Shadow Fleet is heading for Measha Station to destroy it." He took a deep breath before making his request. "I request help to aid Measha Station. We have to help the warm-bloods that live there. They are in grave danger, and this darkness that is coming will not stop growing until it enslaves or destroys everyone, cold-bloods included."

When Nesith had finished speaking, the elders talked among themselves for a few minutes; then the tribal leader spoke for all five members of the tribal council.

"You make a strong point, Nesith. Our own Dreamseeker has contacted us and told us that he has seen the darkness in a vision of the future.

"But the council and I believe the darkness will only affect the warm-bloods, not us. We have no quarrel with the Wraiths; if we stay out of this, they will leave us alone."

Nesith could not believe what he was hearing. Would they *really* let their hatred stop them from helping to save millions of people, while dooming themselves in the process?

"Are you all that blind? The Wraiths and Scott Wright won't stop with the warm-bloods—they'll bring down every species and government in the galaxy!

"The Tigeras thought they were safe, and look at what happened to them! They were confident their world was hidden, that it was safe, but it has been destroyed!"

"Yes, this is true. No one saw that coming; but if we stay out of it, they will leave us alone."

"Damn it, what will it take to show that they threaten all of us!"

Nesith was losing this argument, and it angered him that his people's hatred for warm-bloods would seal his own fate: He would die trying to protect them and the one he loved! That would surely be the case unless aid could be secured.

Then he heard another voice coming from somewhere in the council room. "We should listen to the next generation, for the future is theirs, not ours."

The voice was that of Nesith's father, the greatest and most respected of all the tribal elders, though he himself was no longer an elder.

The tribal council was clearly taken aback, having been unaware of his presence in the council chambers. "Northrol, we did not see you there."

"Well it's a good thing I was, because all I've heard is garbage coming from the council and wisdom coming from my son."

Gasps and murmurs arose from the council. The tribal council leader turned his angry face to Northrol. "We decide whether we should help anyone outside the Solien space."

"That's true." Northrol spoke as he stepped forward. "So maybe I should run for tribal leader again. I think the people would vote for me."

And they would. Northrol had been one of the most popular leaders in Solien history. During his term on the council, he'd tried his hardest to get his people to change their attitudes towards warm-bloods—and for the most part he'd succeeded. It was primarily the old-timers who were keeping the fires alive, unwilling to change their views.

Northrol's last statement hit home; the elder abruptly sat back in his seat and said no more.

"Now, let my son finish what he has to say," said Northrol, nodding to Nesith.

Nesith bowed. "Thank you, Northrol." Then Nesith continued, "As my father just said, we can't let our hate blind us to a threat that can hurt us all. The warm-bloods are fighting for their very survival."

"Like your warm-blooded mate, Isabella, and her friends?" asked one of the elders, his voice heavy with sarcasm.

Nesith did not hesitate to answer. "Yes—them, too." He then explained his position: "I need to bring at least three fleets of dread-saucers. That should be enough."

There was a short pause before one of the elders asked, "How much time do the warm-bloods have before they are consumed by the Shadow Fleet?"

"The enemy is moving faster then I like; they're due to arrive at Measha Station in three to five days. Measha Station could try to hide from the Wraiths, but that would be the cowardly solution. They must stand and fight to show that the Wraiths can't push them around."

There was a long silence in the chamber. The elders huddled together and spoke quietly. When they finished, they turned their attention to Northrol. "Along with your own fleet, we can spare you the Sister-Hood fleet, for a total of seven ships."

"No, my two ships will join my son's fleet, making it nine."

Nesith turned to his dad and smiled. "Thank you, Father."

Northrol nodded his head. "We must do what we can to help Measha Station."

"We will immediately send the Sister-Hood fleet and Northrol's ships out to meet you near Measha Station," said the council leader."

"I will set a course for the station right away." He bowed. "Thank you, council."

The tribal council returned his bow and the projection went dark.

Nesith heaved a sigh and smiled. For the first time in a thousand years, the Soliens were going to officially help someone outside their government. It was a day history was never going to forget.

He turned and left for the bridge.

26

THE CALM BEFORE THE STORM

CID BROUGHT EVERYONE UP to speed on all that had taken place: Mei-Ling's escape; the destruction of the Tigeras Empire's home planet and near annihilation of the royal family; and the sneak attack on Thomas and his fleet. He also informed them that because of the destruction of the Imperial Council, the charges against Wright had been dropped, and he was now in charge of the Guard.

"The attacks on Earth 2 were not caused by the Resistance," Cid informed them. "Wright's shadow forces have been staging them and blaming the Resistance, in order to earn sympathy from the rest of the Guard. And I also have some more bad news."

He told them that his Infiltrators from Earth 2 had gotten through to him, alerting him about an armada that was heading their way—most likely the Shadow Guard, Wright's new name for the combined Wraith/human armada.

"Judging from when they left, we have perhaps three days until they arrive. From what we could gather, Mei-Ling's removal from power, the destruction of the Tigeras home planet, and the attack on Thomas have always been a part of Wright's plan. We're still going through his files, but I have no doubt that we'll find a plan to attack this station. With Mei-Ling hacking into his files, they've had to move up the attack, knowing we would go on the offensive the moment we found out.

"There's more you need to know, but it can wait until after we deal with the Shadow Guard." He held up a handful of datachips. "I know that I've bombarded you with a lot of information, and I'm sorry. If you need to go back over anything I've said, the information you need are on these chips. For those of you not physically in this room, I'll have the information sent to you through subspace comms. As for the rest of you: go back to your ships and positions and get things ready for the upcoming battle! We'll need every able body here to repel the Shadow Guard! Dismissed!"

Everyone grabbed a datachip and filed out of the room, dazed and still somewhat confused by the incredible story they had just heard. Soon, all that were left were the Wrights, the Blakes, Novena, Mei-Ling, Terri, and Steven.

Cid stared down at his feet, afraid to look into the eyes of the people he loved. "I'm sorry that I've never told you guys about who I truly am. Can you *ever* forgive me?"

The group was silent, but only for a moment. They surrounded him and took turns hugging him and telling him not to worry. Everyone was used to Cid keeping secrets, so this didn't change their perspective of him. And Cid had taken care of Jonathan, Eugene, Thomas, and even Scott after the deaths of their parents. Though Jonathan didn't know what Scott's feelings were, the rest loved him no matter what he was.

"I just have one question: Did our parents know about you?" Jonathan asked.

"Yes, Jon, they did."

Jonathan smiled. He was glad that their parents weren't in the dark about who Cid was. "Good. He clapped his hands together. "So, just *how* are we going to beat this Shadow Guard?"

W RIGHT WAS STARING OUT the window in his command room, down below at Earth 2. He was now the high ruler, but the price he'd paid for it was almost not worth it. The one thing left to do was to stop the only threat to his rule—his brother Jonathan and the rest of those cronies on Measha Station.

A smile formed on his face. For the past few days, he'd been wondering how it had ever come to this. His brother and he had been so close, and now he was forced to send a fleet to stop Jonathan from taking his power away. Wright didn't want to admit to himself that he would have to kill his own brother, but it couldn't be helped.

The door behind him opened, and Wright heard a greeting. He didn't have to turn around to know who it was; he would know her voice anywhere. "Hello, darling. How are you holding up?"

"As good as could be expected," Abigail replied, "after witnessing all that we knew get blown up before our eyes!"

He nodded. He'd never expected Mei-Ling to blow up the palace; but then again, he'd never expected her to hack into his files either. But that wasn't all that she was talking about; something else was bugging her.

"That's not *all*, though, is it?"

She smiled. "You know me too well." She let out a sigh of frustration. "It's the Wraiths. That speech you gave everyone to unite the people behind you. . .it's got me feeling uneasy. I know it was typed up by the Wraiths—and somehow they knew what to say to get the blood flowing." She turned to face him and took off her glasses, her sightless eyes staring into his. "*You* are what this government needs, not *them*! They don't care about us; they're just using us to get what they want—and I can guarantee, darling, that what they want will most certainly destroy us."

Scott was becoming frustrated. He and Abigail had had this talk before. "Honey, I know they're up to something, but if we're benefiting from their help, we might as well take advantage of it!" He left the window and walked to his desk. "Humanity needs this. The Ashlon Republic relies too much on other aliens for survival. Once the Wraiths help us wipe out the Ashlon's main allies, the rest of the Republic will have no choice but to join us." He smiled. "And when they do, the Wraiths will have outlived their usefulness. With the Ashlon Republic's forces combined with ours, we'll hunt them down and destroy them."

Abigail closed her eyes and covered her face with one of her hands. "I wish that Jonathan were here."

Scott bit his tongue at the mention of his brother's name. He loved his brother, but the father in him would never forgive Jonathan for the death of his only son. "Well, he's not. And soon it won't matter."

"What do you *mean?*"

"I have sent a large strike force to take out Measha Station. I'm sure he's there. He'll die at Measha Station, along with that pesky Cid Starlight and everyone else who resides there."

"Why do you think *that?* What makes you so sure he wouldn't surrender?"

"Not my brother—or Cid, for that matter. They'd stand and fight to the very end, as long as they thought they had a chance of winning!"

"I *know* you don't like your brother, but would you really *kill* him?"

Scott just laughed. "I'm not the one who's going to do it. I've sent Albright to lead the strike force."

Abigail's face went pale. "You sent the one man in this whole galaxy who hates Jonathan as much as you do? That madman will blow up a whole system just to get to him!"

"I know. But Albright's my fleet admiral. How would it look if I sent another commander to do it?"

"I know." She let out a sigh of frustration and slapped her hands down on her sides. "It's just that we've lost so many friends, and this blasted war hasn't even started—and now you're about to lose your only brother!" She shook her head. "Have you *really* grown to hate him *that* much?"

He tried to speak, but for a moment the words were caught in his throat. "No, I don't. . . .there's a part of me that would like to see him come through this alive, but with the fleet that I'm sending, the odds are that he *won't*. And besides, the whole point of this is to *kill* him, because we both know that he's going to become a serious pain in the ass if he isn't taken care of as soon as possible."

Before anything else could be said, the comm sounded. Scott pressed a button. "Yes, what is it?" he asked harshly.

There was a pause and then an officer on the other end said, "Sir, you have a message from Shadow Fleet 13."

"Patch it through," Scott ordered, glad for a distraction from the current conversation. "Sorry, honey. I have to take this."

Abigail stepped back as he activated the comm unit. A second later, Albright's face appeared on the screen. "Sorry for the call, High Ruler, but I wanted to give you an update on our status of arrival."

"Go on."

"We have about three days until we arrive."

"Thank you, Admiral. Notify me again just before you arrive and after you've completed the mission."

"Yes, sir." Scott killed the comm.

As he turned toward his wife, he saw that she had nothing on but a long blouse shirt. Before he could say another word, she placed her index finger on his lips; then, with the other, she pressed the PAGE button on his desk.

The secretary asked, "Yes, sir, how may I help you?"

"The high ruler will be resting for the next six hours. Do not interrupt unless it is an emergency." Abigail turned to her husband and smiled. "Now, mister, you are all mine for the next six hours."

Scott was confused. From the way their conversation had been going, sex was the last thing he thought would have come out of it.

When he was about to ask what she was up to, she covered his mouth with her lips. "You are *losing* yourself, Scott. You are losing your *mind* and *soul*, and I don't know how much longer you will be *you*. But no matter what, I will always be with you, no matter where this journey takes you. And until we reach that point, I want to spend as much time with you—the *old* you—before you lose yourself."

What Abigail said struck him hard, because she was right: he felt that he was going down a dark path, and he was sure that a lot of people would not like what it would make him, but he had accepted it a long time ago. It was a sacrifice he was willing to make for the human race.

Abigail leaned in to kiss him as the two made their way toward the bedroom. There, they fell on top of the bed, kissing and groping each other, forgetting the pain for a short while and just feeling the love that they had for one another.

As he made love to his wife, Scott T. Wright felt at peace with himself; his love for his wife was stronger now than ever before. She would stay by his side until this war came to an end one way or the other, or until death would take him away.

27

FIGHT OR DIE

CID STARLIGHT COULD NOT believe that history was repeating itself. The Wraiths returned and picked up right where they had left off, bringing death and destruction with them. Now what made it worse was that the humans were stuck right in the middle of it.

"Get Omega Squadron on the comm, and tell Green and Silver to stand by," Cid said. He went over the ships in his head: they had Fleet 16 and Ashlon Fleet 12 and 5, as well as Twilight Task Force 10, which had arrived only a few hours before. When he told the Twilights what had happened, the nearest task force hauled ass to the station to help defend it. They had a total of forty-two ships against the sixty incoming ships. It wasn't going to be a fair fight.

But then again, the Wraiths had *never* played fair. Cid started shouting orders, telling everyone to keep sharp and ready; if the four fleets were going to die for this station, he would make sure that the station would survive to honor their sacrifice. He sat back and took a deep breath, realizing that this would likely be a long and bloody fight. The thought that most of his family might die filled him with dread.

He said, with venom in his voice, *"Damn you, Wraiths! Damn you all to hell!"*

JONATHAN WAS ABOARD THE *Freedom*, waiting for the enemy to arrive. As he waited, he took in his surroundings. It was strange being back on his old ship and seeing his crew again. He thought that he would have trouble being in command, but it was like riding a bike. A very *awesome* bike.

While he was in command of Fleet 16, Thomas would command Ashlon Fleets 5 and 12, and Sara would lead several fighter squadrons. Ryan and William would stay with the marines and the Infiltrators to defend the station in case the enemy breached their defenses. Novena, Eugene, and Katrina would help with the evacuations. They knew that they wouldn't be able to get everyone off the station, but they had to get as many people to safety as they could.

It wasn't long before the Shadow Fleet came out of FTL. As soon as they had, they were hailed.

"Sir, Admiral Albright of the *IGS Medusa* wants to speak to you."

Jonathan smiled. *This should be good.* "Patch him through."

Albright's face appeared on a 3-D projector. "Hello, Jonathan."

Jonathan could hear the hate in his voice. "Admiral. What can I do for you?"

"How about you surrender now so we can get this over with?"

Jonathan pretended to think about it. "Nah, I think that we'll kick your asses instead!"

If it were possible for Albright to get any angrier, he just did. Then his anger became a smile. "I was hoping you would say that. I have been waiting for this for a long time, Jonathan."

"For *what*? The ability to wipe your own ass without Wright holding your *hand*?"

Before Albright could scream obscenities, Jonathan cut him off. His comms officer looked at him. "Do you think that was *wise*, sir?"

"Probably not, but what the hell! It was pretty funny, right?"

At that point, the entire bridge crew let out laughs, easing the tension in the room.

SARA ALBRIGHT SAT IN her star fighter, hovering above Measha Station. Today, she was the leader not only of Omega Squadron, but also of Delta and Zeta. Her squadrons' job was to intercept the missiles that would be launched at the station by the enemy fleet that was expected to appear. Then she would be allowed to join her father's fleet in battle.

She looked out of the cockpit windows and stared at her father's fleet. She wanted to be with her father when the battle started, but she would have to wait.

She thought about her uncle, and how had he had allowed things to get this bad. Before the death of her cousin, she and her uncle had been very close; but when Timothy died, it was as if her uncle had lost a part of himself. The way he treated her father—like a murderer and a traitor—just *killed* her. She had talked with her father earlier in the day, hoping there would be some other way to get through to him, but he'd said they were way past reasoning with Scott. She wished he were wrong, but she knew he wasn't. Her uncle had to be stopped, no matter what.

Her father's voice came on over the headset. "All squadrons listen up! Our sensors tell us that a fleet is about to come out of FTL. I have no doubt that they'll open fire on us the moment they appear. Give them hell the best you can!"

Sara spoke on her headset to her squadron. "Okay, boys and girls, it's time to party! I know I'm not as good as my father at making speeches, so I'll just say let's kick ass and take names! Let's hit the burners and rock and roll!"

Seconds later all hell broke loose as Shadow Fleet came out of FTL and opened fire on her father's fleet and at the station, firing over three hundred missiles at the station and at her fighters.

"Okay, people, knock out as many missiles as you can! And be careful with the Stingers; they're intelligent and won't stop until they get to the station." With that said, the three squadrons, along with one hundred and fifty other star fighters, engaged the missiles.

The fight was hard and fast, as the three fighter squadrons, Zeta, Delta, and Omega, fought the missiles at point-blank range.

"Z-1, close up port flank 3 now!" But before Sara got the rest of the order out, Z-1 took a direct hit from a missile. It hit his fighter's belly and turned it into a ball of fire that extinguished quickly in the vacuum of space.

"People, we've lost Z-1. Close up formation!" Sara turned her fighter hard to port and then straight down, to avoid a Stinger that was coming from her starboard side. She lined up behind the Stinger that was trying to kill her.

She waited for the target lock, then fired two starlight missiles at the Stinger's aft section, causing it to destruct. The skirmish continued for fifteen minutes.

Out of three hundred Stingers, only one hundred and eighty- eight got through. Out of the one hundred and fifty fighters, only seventy-five were left. Delta was wiped out, and Zeta and Omega suffered losses. Sara looked at her radar. Her unit had lost fifteen ships, and Zeta had lost ten.

"This is Omega 1. We've suffered heavy losses, but we've cut the incoming missiles by half. Good luck, Measha Station!" To her squadrons, she said, "All right, people, let's go! Attack!"

The fighters engaged the Shadow Fleet with only their guns and their hearts.

There were so many enemy fighters on her radar that Sara couldn't distinguish her own people from the enemy. She smiled and said to herself *"Well, gang, here we go!."* She turned her damaged fighter to engage yet another enemy fighter. This one looked alien. It had a round body, and its wings also were shaped like those of a bat. It was fast, very fast, and it was bigger than her own fighter.

She lined up her fighter and waited for the lock-on tone. When she heard the sound, she fired her fighter's auto Gatling heavy laser cannon. She hit the enemy ship's aft port engine. The fighter turned hard to starboard to evade her next shot, but with only one engine, it was much slower, and Sara fired again, this time destroying the fighter.

As she turned to find her next target, she was blindsided by a Wraith fighter, who fired a smaller version of the IAC. It hit her cockpit. Her left leg and right arm felt as if they were on fire. The blast almost shattered the front end of her fighter, taking her out of the battle. The ship was then destroyed by two fellow fighters.

The last thing she saw, before she blacked out from her injuries was the *Freedom* falling out of formation, on fire and dying fast. Tears formed in her eyes. *"I'm sorry, Dad. I'm sorry that I failed you."*

THE STAND

NOVENA WISHED SHE COULD have stayed and helped, but she was part of the evacuation fleet, helping the civilian population evacuate the station.

It killed her to know that the people she loved were fighting a fight with a species created by her people. *We should have never created the Wraiths like the Nexus had said*, she thought to herself as her ship and thirteen others jumped into FTL.

At one of their jump stops, they met a fleet of ships. The scanners revealed who the fleet belonged to, and her heart started to pound as she heard a friendly voice say hello; at that moment, she knew that the people she loved just might make it after all.

CID WAS IN THE CIC, overlooking the battle taking place outside. Things were not as bad as they could have been. Usually their defenses would be strong enough to take on whatever anyone could throw at them, but the Wraiths had been planning this moment for hundreds to thousands of years, so they were prepared to take on their defenses. But then again, Cid had also known that the Wraiths might come after his station sooner or later, so he was also ready for them.

Elijah informed him that the station had been hit by over forty-five missiles and hundreds of plasma bolts. Their shields had been able to withstand most of the blasts, and there had been several breaches in the station's hull, but it was nothing that damage control couldn't handle.

Outside the station, fifty enemy ships had entered PPC range. Ten were destroyed by Fleet 16, and Fleet 5 was ambushed by over four hundred Stingers as well as the Twilight Strike Force. The command center shook as more missiles got through the defense grid.

"Sir, we've just lost Plasma Particle Cannon turrets 45, 56, and 67," Elijah said. "We've also detected three new hull breaches in living sector 34. I'm shutting down primary power to that sector."

Cid just nodded and stared at the 3-D display readout as he watched another ship from Fleet 16 get destroyed. "How many ships from Fleet 16 are left?"

"Ten are left, sir. Three Dreadnaughts and seven battle cruisers."

"Damn! They're not going to make it another thirty minutes! Focus torrents 85 to 98 at bearing 101 at their forward line! Try to give the *Freedom* and her escort some breathing room!"

Elijah looked at his screen, then targeted the enemy's three lead ships and fired thirteen PPCs at them. The first ship took five shots to the forward sphere. The portside shields fell, and its forward sphere blew up, taking the rest of the ship with it. The other two suffered heavy damage and pulled out of formation.

"Open all turrets! fire!" Cid yelled.

With that order, the station fired over five hundred PPCs into the enemy fleet, taking out another five ships and all the battle cruisers, and crippling three more, one of them a Dreadnaught.

THOMAS COMMANDED BOTH ASHLON Fleet 5 and 12. From his command chair on board the *Zeus*, Thomas watched Jonathan's fleet get slaughtered by the enemy. They were losing ground, and now the remaining ten ships in Fleet 16 were in a two-to-one firefight, which meant that Jonathan's ships were fighting off two ships at the same time.

"Get me Commander Tiffany Freeman!" Moments later, Commander Freeman, from the *ARS Williams*, appeared on his screen. "They're going to die if we don't do something!"

"I know. Admiral Mikel told us to stay out of this and hit and run, but I can't watch his fleet suffer anymore."

"I agree. We're going to attack the fleet at point-blank range. We just might take some of them with us."

With that said, the Ashlon fleet came out of a mini jump right behind the aft end of the fleet and opened fire.

Two enemy battle cruisers, caught off guard, exploded in the first five minutes of the fight.

Then a devastator and ten warships turned around and engaged the *Zeus* and her fifteen escorts. It was a long, hard fight, and the *Zeus* and her escorts were losing.

Thomas was watching his fleet get pummeled, but he was going to take out that devastator, no matter what.

He checked the heads-up display that was keeping him constantly updated on the status of Shadow Fleet's ships. "Comms, get me the battle cruiser *Foxwing*. Tell her to bring up the rear line we lost to the enemy in that section.

"Weapons, get ready to fire the main arrow beam at the weakest point in portside shield of that devastator, and bring it down."

The ship shook as two missiles and some ICP fire hit their shields, but little fire made it through to damage the hull.

"More damage to our starboard side, sir. We lost turrets 56, 58, 60, 62, and 68, as well as one missile launcher!"

Damn! Hang in there, girl, just a little longer! Just let me take out that devastator! "Fire the arrow cannon and bring our port guns to bear! Now!"

With that order, the *Zeus* fired her arrow cannon and followed with her portside guns. The arrow beam penetrated the weak portion of the enemy's shields and slammed into the devastator's portside hull. Over 250 PPC fire followed it and hit the portside of the ship with another five missiles, causing a huge chunk of the ship to explode.

Thomas's other five Dreadnaughts also fired. They overwhelmed the enemy ship with PPC fire, causing the ship to explode.

Thomas just sat back in his chair and let out a huge sigh of relief. He looked at his 3-D projector just in time to see two more of his ships, a Dreadnaught and a battle cruiser, explode.

"How many of us are left, Lieutenant Baker?"

The lieutenant checked his scans, and Thomas saw his shoulders slump. He turned around and looked at Thomas. His face said it all. "Sir, we are all that's left of Ashlon Fleet 12. Fleet 5 has lost three battle cruisers and one Dreadnaught."

He knew the price to take down that big ship was going to be high, but he never thought it would cost him his fleet. "How much is left of the fifth fleet?"

"We are down to seven ships—four Dreadnaughts and three battle cruisers."

Thomas looked out across the bridge, and through the viewport saw nothing but enemy ships coming at him. They'd just destroyed six of them, and seven more were taking their place! He knew that this was likely going to be his last mission and his last orders.

He stood and looked at the twenty men and women of his bridge crew, then contacted the fifth fleet. He smiled as he said the only thing left to say.

"All ships pull into a wall formation and fire everything we have! We are going to stand our ground and take as many of them with us as we can!"

As Thomas sat down, two missiles penetrated the ship's defense grid, hit the *Zeus*'s bridge, and exploded.

COMMANDER LANGLEY OF THE Twilight Strike Force looked out at the battle, his heart sinking. The humans were very brave; they were fighting against overwhelming odds. But he knew that they should not even be fighting this fight in the first place. Creating the Wraiths had been the wrong thing to do. That decision to play Creator would haunt them for thousands of years. The Wraiths were *their* demons. *They* should be the ones to fight them, but they couldn't do it *alone*; they needed help. Sadly, thanks to Admiral Wright, the rest of the humans had no choice but to fight.

Langley was working hard to take as much pressure as possible off Fleet 16, but it was not going well. He watched the *Freedom* suffer even more damage. It didn't explode, but it did fall out of formation.

"Bring us to bearing 5.67 and fire the main cannon on the lead Wraith ship, then bring our starboard-side guns to bear and fire."

The mighty Twilight battleship fired her main fusion cannon and hit the enemy ship at her midsection on the portside, burning a hole in it, and causing it to lean heavily to the starboard side. The enemy ship was finished off as two hundred PPCs slammed into the dying ship and blew it into nothing but space junk.

The ship shook as more enemy fire got through the defiance grid and two missiles hit the midsection on the portside.

"What's our damage?" he asked DC Officer Smithy.

Smithy checked his damage board. "We have minor damage on the portside but no hull breach, and shields are down to 77 percent on the portside grid. Other than that, we're at full battle strength, sir."

"Good! Now bring us around. We have to take more pressure off the human fleet. They've lost their lead Dreadnaught, so we'll take their place. We *made* these demons; now we'll *stop* them *here and now!*"

The Twilight ship turned and opened fire on two enemy Wraith ships. The first ship died, turning into a fireball, and the other was heavily damaged and fell out of the fight. As the enemy ships fell, the Twilight ship filled the gap the *Freedom* left behind. Two Twilight cruisers, one light, the other heavy, also joined Fleet 16, aiding the brave humans in fighting back the tide of darkness that was trying to take them all.

SMOKE AND FIRE FILLED the bridge of the *Zeus*, and Thomas's ears were ringing. A portion of the bridge had collapsed on itself, and people were trapped under the rubble, while others were dead. He, along with several medics who had arrived on the bridge, looked for those who were still alive and helped the wounded out from under the debris. He was thankful that the *Zeus* had a double-hulled bridge. That was why they were still alive! He walked to what was left of the helms station and greeted the only crew member still there.

"How bad are we? Is there anything left to throw at them?"

Lieutenant Franklin pressed a few buttons that still worked.

"We have no weapons, main power is offline, and our backup reactor is at 60 percent power."

"Sir," Engineman Samantha yelled as she looked over her damage boards, "we just lost starboard thrusters! We're going into a roll and falling out of formation!"

Thomas looked around at what was left of his bridge and the crew. Out of twenty men and women, only twelve were alive, and half of them were injured, the medics working on them at what was left of their stations. He looked at each of them, and what he saw in their eyes made his broken heart fill with pride: they knew that they were not going to make it, but they wanted to go down in style.

"Well, sir, what is your next order?" Jackson asked.

Thomas thought for a short moment.

"Franklin, do we have enough power to do a run?"

"What do you have in mind, sir?"

"I wanna ram the nearest enemy vessel. Can we do it?"

Franklin smiled. "Absolutely."

He turned to the comms officer. "Do we have comms?"

"We can send audio."

"Good. Get me Tiffany." About fifteen seconds later, a sweet but tired voice filled the bridge.

"It's good to hear your voice, sir. When we saw the missiles hit the bridge, we feared the worst."

"Tiffany, we're done here. The *Zeus* can't take any more damage. You're in command of the fleet, and if you retreat now, the rest of you guys might get out of this alive."

There was a pause on the other end. "What are you planning to do, sir?"

"We're going to ram the nearest ship. If we're still operating, we're going to ram another. Get in touch with the rest of the fleet and take this opportunity to fall back and regroup."

There was a pause before she spoke again. "That won't be necessary, sir."

Thomas frowned, wondering what she meant. He also noticed the excitement in her voice. "What are you *talking* about, Tiffany."

"I think help has just arrived," she said.

At that moment, his radar officer announced that a group of ships had just dropped out of FTL. When the scans revealed who they were, the entire bridge erupted in cheers.

JONATHAN COULDN'T SEE TOO clearly out his cracked plassteel viewport, thick smoke impairing his vision.

The flames that were all around them began to diminish as the fire control system kicked in and started putting the fires out. Suddenly, more alarms went off. "Sir, we've lost portside stabilizers!" David screamed over the noise. The ship started to lean hard to her portside as the stabilizers went out.

"Compensate with auxiliary power from power grid 23 and subpower bank 2!" Jonathan ordered.

"We can't! We need that grid to keep the shield grids from failing!"

"Try subpower grid 8 and auxiliary power 12 to back it up!"

As David finished entering the commands, the ship began to right itself.

"Now that we're upright again, let's see if we can do any more damage to the Wraiths. WEPs, what do we have left?"

"Not much, sir. I can throw about 266 PPCs on the starboard and follow it up with 30 missiles. As for the portside, I can give you 300 PPCs and 60 missiles." The ship shook hard as some more missiles broke through the defense grid and blew additional holes into the *Freedom*.

"Sir, we are losing power to forward starboard shield grid 7!"

Jonathan fell into his chair as Jennifer Yearly came up beside him. "Well, sir, we did all we could. I'm glad Ashlon Fleet 12 didn't listen and took out that devastator."

"Yeah, but it cost him Fleet 12, and, other than what remains of the fifth fleet, his ship is the only one left."

"They still kicked ass," Jennifer said.

Jonathan smiled and nodded his head. "Now it's *our* turn to kick some ass!" He looked out of the viewport and saw a Wraith heavy cruiser on his starboard side and an Imperial battle cruiser on his portside. "WEPs, fire all turrets but save the missiles!" With that order, the great ship *Freedom* fired all she had left. The Imperial battle cruiser was hit as three hundred PPCs tore into the ship, ripping it to shreds.

As 266 PPCs slammed into the Wraith heavy cruiser, the Wraith ship tried its best to maneuver, but it had been badly damaged in the fighting. The PPC fire struck the heavy cruiser on the portside of the ship and destroyed it. Before the ship exploded, it was able to fire her broadside weapons. Over 125 PPCs and 6 missiles hit the *Freedom*'s portside, ripping up the ship's hull, and one of the plasma shots hit the bridge.

The plasma hit the bridge and the crew jumped for cover as the bridge shook and sparks flew, along with pieces of the bulkhead.

When the crew picked themselves off the deck, they could see that the bridge was filled with fire and smoke. As Jonathan looked around, he saw that the surviving bridge crew were fighting the fires that were burning out of control. When he tried to stand up, his left leg gave out and he fell back to the deck. He looked down at what remained of his left leg and saw that it had shrapnel in it. His shin was shattered and bleeding badly. He grabbed a canister of Nano-gel from his belt and sprayed it on his leg just as he was beginning to feel the pain. The nanites began making repairs to his leg, stopping the bleeding and enabling him to walk. This would do for now, but he needed a doctor.

He stood up, much slower this time, and limped back to his chair. He looked for Jennifer, and when he found her, his heart sank: she was a few feet from him, covered in blood on the floor, with a piece of shrapnel in her stomach. He ran to her as fast as he could on one leg.

"Jen, talk to me!"

Jennifer opened her eyes and smiled weakly. As she tried to talk, blood came out of her mouth.

"Sir, it looks as if we've reached the end of the line—but we gave them one hell of a bloody nose."

Jonathan chuckled and said, "Yes, we sure did, my dear friend." He reached for her gel pack, but it was gone.

"I already used it. There's nothing you can do for me but pray."

Jonathan sat beside his friend and gently lifted her up into his arms. The ship drifted to the right and down, dropping out of formation. He looked at her as he pushed her hair from her face, and he began to pray to God as she passed out in his arms. He gently laid her down on the deck and stood up, limping.

He checked the rest of his bridge crew. Of the twenty-four people on the bridge, only thirteen were left standing, and all of them were hurt and tired but not scared; they were angry, and they wanted to fight.

He said, "We are still alive and we still have power, so let's go say hi to the *IGS Medusa* and send our love!"

The thirteen remaining members of the bridge ran back to their stations and worked to get the battered ship back in the fight.

As he looked at the scanner on his command chair, he saw the Twilight ships take point and fill the gaps in his formation.

Jonathan just smiled and said, "Thanks, guys."

The fight went on throughout what was left of Fleet 16 as well as fleets 12, 5, and the Twilight force. All fleets were taking on two-to-one odds and holding strong, though they didn't know how long they could keep it up. Then something happened that changed everything.

ALBRIGHT WAS ABOARD THE *IGS Medusa*, watching and smiling as he saw the *Freedom*, on fire, fall out of formation because she had too many holes to count all over her hull. But when the *Freedom* straightened itself out, his smile faded. He ordered the weapons station to lock on and fire on the *Freedom*. He didn't care what it took, but he was going to take Jonathan out, no matter what.

"Sir, we just picked up a new threat coming in from the starboard side of our formation!"

"Who are they?"

"Scanners tell us that they are nine Dreadnaught saucers. It's the Solien Empire, sir!"

Of all the things that could go wrong, the worst has just happened. Albright could not believe that the Soliens had actually shown up! They had no love for "warm bloods." *Why were they here?*

"Sir, they just fired at us!"

"What!" As Albright turned around to look at WEPs in disbelief, he saw from the corner of his eye, through the viewport, death coming in the form of the *Freedom* and a Solien Dreadnaught, firing over forty PPCs that quickly penetrated *Medusa*'s shields and shot holes all throughout the hull, shattering its armor.

As the *IGS Medusa* died in a hellfire of plasma, the last thought that went through Albright's mind was that Jonathan had beat him again, but now he was free.

JONATHAN COULDN'T BELIEVE WHAT he was seeing as he and the rest of the bridge crew watched five Solien Dreadnaughts come out of FTL right in the middle of the enemy fleet. Four more popped out aft of the enemy fleet to help the Ashlon fleet.

The Solien ships looked like big wagon wheels flipped on their sides. It was the best sight he had ever seen. As the Solien ships waged war on the enemy ships, Jonathan went back to where his XO lay on the ground. He knelt down beside her and whispered in her ear that they just might win yet.

THE SOLIENS ATTACKED THE remaining forty-five ships of the Shadow Fleet. The first ship to go was the command Dreadnaught, *Medusa*.

Four ships fired right at the middle of the fleet. Over nine hundred Solien cannons fired into the Shadow Fleet, causing the fleet to break formation. At that point, what was left of Fleet 16 and Fleet 5, thirteen ships plus the seven Twilight vessels, fired everything they had left at the enemy fleet. Over two hundred missiles and four thousand PPCs slammed into the forward section of the enemy fleet.

The station fired another five hundred missiles and four hundred and fifty PPC fire to help pick off the survivors.

Forty-five minutes after the fight had started, it was over. The Shadow Fleet had lost fifty-three ships, including all of their fighters. The remaining seven ships limped back into FTL.

Jonathan heaved a great sigh of relief as he watched the enemy fleet retreat. As the last ship left, his comm officer said, "Sir, we are being hailed by the lead Solien Dreadnaught. It's Nesith, sir!"

"Put him on," he said. As he sat down in his chair, the ship's doctor made it to the bridge and started working on Jonathan's leg.

Just then, Nesith came on his comm screen. "Hi, buddy! Glad to see you've made it!"

Jonathan chuckled. "I'm glad that we made it, too. How are you guys doing?"

"Great, but there's still work to be done. We're going to hunt down the seven remaining ships that escaped, and make them wish they'd never come here. See you later, friend. Tell Isabella that I love her." Nesith killed the feed, and all but two Dreadnaughts jumped into FTL, chasing after what was left of the Shadow Fleet.

ALL GOOD THINGS

THREE DAYS HAD PASSED since the battle at Measha Station. The final death toll was in the fifty thousands, with approximately one hundred and fifty thousand injured. Fleet 16 suffered eighty percent losses, as they had only six ships left: three Dreadnaughts and three battle cruisers. Fleet 5 lost three ships and had suffered heavy damage. The rest of the fleet had light to moderate damage. Thomas's fleet had lost all but his ship, and the Twilights had lost three ships: two light and one heavy cruiser. All the people that had evacuated the station had returned, and repairs on the ships and the station had commenced. The Solien fleet had returned and told Cid and everyone else that they'd destroyed the ships that had escaped the battle.

Cid called a meeting with Jonathan and company and all of the department heads of the station, to inform them of what they were going to do next.

"From Wright's files, we know that the Wraiths have an idea about how to find their queen. We need to figure out where she is before *they* do. We have a location and a name to check out."

"Where are we going?" Jonathan asked.

"The Sorus Cluster."

The entire room became so silent that you could hear a pin drop from across the station.

"*The Sorus* Cluster?" Eugene asked, not believing what he was hearing. "That's on the edge of outlawed space, where every scumbag in the galaxy hangs out! What could *possibly* be so important that it would require us to go to that corner of hell in the galaxy?"

"The Historians."

Once again, the entire room became silent, and then everyone busted out laughing. Cid wasn't surprised by their reaction.

"The *Historians*! Yeah, good one, Cid! Nice!" Ryan said through gasps of breath. The Historians were a mysterious group rumored to have been recording the history of the galaxy since its beginning; but because no one could confirm their existence, most species didn't believe they existed.

When everyone had calmed down, Jonathan was the first to speak. "Okay, Cid, but what about that crowd out there? This may be your station, but how are we going to get everyone else behind us on this wild goose chase?"

Cid smiled, and the look on everyone's face told him that they did not like where this was heading. "Don't worry about it. I have an idea that will kill two birds with one stone. . ."

ID SENT WORD THROUGHOUT the station that he was making a special announcement. He told them that he would be speaking from the Hall of Man, and that it would be televised throughout the station. It was very important that everybody watch and listen to what he had to say.

When the time came, Cid mounted the stage that had been set up for him. He looked out over the crowd, at the thousands of people of different species; he looked at the cameras that were transmitting his image throughout the station to the people that were awaiting his words; and he began to sweat. He had not been this nervous in a long time. He looked to his left and saw Jonathan and Thomas give him a smile and a nod, telling him that he was ready.

Cid spoke into his earpiece. "Okay, guys, are you ready?"

Eugene, Katrina, Novena, and Mei-Ling gave him an affirmative, and he took a deep breath. He stepped out onto the stage and up to the podium. The crowd's cheers filled his ears. He smiled and waved to them, showing them his gratitude.

"Thank you. Thank you very much. I'm here to tell you that we have successfully beaten back the attack on this station!" The crowd erupted once again. Cid let them cheer for a few more minutes before he silenced them. "I called all of you here today to tell you that we have accomplished more than just a simple victory. I want to point out the main forces behind this effort.

"First, I would like to introduce Novena, General Blake, and the general's wife, Katrina Tarr-Blake." The viewscreens stationed around him flashed on, showing the three to everyone in the crowd and in different sections of the station. When the crowd saw them, they once again cheered.

"These brave souls led a fleet made up of humans, Twilights, Tigeras, and Telbins that evacuated the people including the children who were on this station." Another cheer.

He motioned for Jonathan and Thomas to join him on the stage. Just as they had done when Cid had stepped out on the stage, the crowd now cheered when the two admirals came out. Cid introduced the two, although no introductions were really necessary: Jonathan and

Thomas were famous in their own right, with all their accomplishments in battle known to the public.

"These two brave men successfully held back the invasion, giving time for an unexpected ally to arrive." At this point, Nesith stepped out onto the stage. The crowd paused for a short moment before they cheered, and Cid understood why: the Soliens were notorious for their stated reluctance to involve themselves with other species—or as they liked to call them, "warm bloods." And it didn't help that Nesith, the son of a former tribal chief, was a very notable Solien. Everyone was a little confused as to why a Solien would help them.

"Now that you have met your saviors, it is time for you to understand our enemy. While I explain them to you, many of you will become angry and wish to strike out; but please, *please* restrain yourselves." Cid explained to the people of Measha Station, made up of outcasts from all different walks of life, who the Wraiths were, how they were created, the destruction they had already brought, and what their ultimate goal was. He also told them what Wright had done to Jonathan, and even showed them the recording from the *Freedom*.

When he finished, he searched the crowd to see their reactions. Many of the Twilights looked nervous, afraid of what everyone else would do to them; and the Tigeras looked as if they wanted to kill the nearest Twilight and human. They didn't care that it was the Twilights' ancestors, or that it was Wright and the Imperial Guard, who were behind the attack. They were Twilight and human, and that was reason enough to attack them.

When the murmurs from the crowd turned into hateful words, then into screams of rage, Cid ordered security throughout the station to get ready to try calming the crowd down. He turned to Jonathan, Thomas, and Nesith. He also spoke into his earpiece. "Okay, you guys are up."

The three friends jumped from the stage into the crowd, and headed in different directions. They made their way to hover- carts that were awaiting them. They jumped on the carts, activated them, and flew up over the crowd. Eugene, Katrina, Novena, and other personnel did the same from their locations. They flew in the air and activated their bull-horns. The loud sound reverberated throughout the crowds, stopping their shouting and making them turn toward its source.

"Enough!" Jonathan yelled. "Look at yourselves! Look at what the Wraiths have reduced you to: *morons*, fighting amongst yourselves!" He waited a few moments for the crowd to take in what he had said.

When they settled down, he continued, "I know that you are angry. I was angry at my own brother when he had me tried for treason, when he beat Mei-Ling, and when he made a deal with the Wraiths." He paused for a moment. "I almost acted out in anger a short while ago, and it would have cost me greatly if I'd done so." He looked at the viewscreen that showed Novena. "Luckily for me, a friend stopped me and convinced me that what I was about to do was wrong and stupid!"

"And that is what we need to do," Thomas said. "We need to calm down and think about our next step. If we don't, then the Wraiths won't be the ones that will destroy us, it will be *ourselves*. We will implode from the inside out, and it won't be just *us*. No, the entire galaxy will follow suit, and the Wraiths will pick the bones."

"What do you suggest we do?" someone asked.

This time, Nesith spoke up. "There is only one thing we *can and must* do: put aside all the hatred and prejudices that we hold toward one another! If we do that, I know for a fact that we will succeed."

There were laughs, boos, and angry cries from the audience. "You want us to *work together?*" a Tigress yelled as he jabbed his finger at a human. "Against these *planet killers?*"

That ignited more screaming and yelling. Cid just sighed and thanked the Creator that no one had started a riot. If that had happened, the station would have turned into a bloodbath.

Jonathan, Thomas, and Nesith tried to calm the crowd down, but they were having no success, until there was a loud scream that stopped everyone short. All over the station, people looked at the screens and around themselves to find the source. They discovered that it was Katrina, who was breathing heavily, her eyes red from crying.

"Look at us! Look at us! We've just defeated the enemy, and we're already at each other's throats! Is *this* what you want? Do you all want to *die?* Fellow Tigeras, I understand your pain; I've lost *my* family too. And yes, I'm angry at the Imperial Guard for what they've done. But does that mean that I should hate all humans? My husband, whom I love more than anything, is a human, and he used to be part of the Imperial Guard! Should I just despise him because he was part of them at one point in his life?

"And what about Jonathan and Novena, huh? Jonathan also used to be part of the Imperial Guard, and his brother is the one behind all of this. Should we kill him just because of his brother? And Novena's people attempted to play God and now we are *all* paying the price, so let's just kill them, too. Let's just destroy each other, like mindless monsters!"

She began crying harder now, barely able to control herself. Eugene suddenly showed up and took his weeping wife in his arms.

Novena was the next to speak. "People of the galaxy, yes, the Twilights *did* attempt to be like the Creator, and we paid a great price for it: the Wraiths turned on us and almost completely destroyed us. If it weren't for the Nexus, we would have been completely decimated. They were really angry with us, and they had a right to be, but they forgave us and gave us a chance to redeem ourselves."

"So we should just forgive them for what they've done and not be angry with them?" someone asked.

"Of course not. You guys have every right to be angry at the ones who did you wrong. All of you do. But if we don't forgive them and separate our enemies from our allies, then I have no doubt that the *Wraiths* won't destroy us; *we* will."

There was a pause before Eugene spoke. Katrina's head was still buried in his chest. "I don't know about the rest of you, but I don't want my children growing up with the Wraiths after them 24/7 and with all this hatred around them." He looked into the eyes of everyone around him, and into the cameras that were projecting his image throughout the station. "Is *this* the future that you want your children to have? To *experience*? Because if it *is*, then there won't be much of a future for *any of us*, or for *them*."

The crowd was so quiet that you could hear a pin drop. There was not a person from any specie that wasn't touched by what had been said.

Some people started crying, and, spontaneously, people throughout the station started to comfort each other. Many apologized; others shook hands and smiled.

Cid was amazed at what he saw. Things were still tense among everyone, but it was a start. He looked off to his left at Mei-Ling, who was out of the crowd's view. She had tears in her eyes, and Cid knew why: her father's dream of a unified people was starting to come true right before her eyes.

JONATHAN WAS ABOARD THE *Freedom*, overseeing the repairs of the Dreadnaught. The work was going smoothly, without any problems. There was still a lot of work to be done, but he was confident that the majority of it would be completed by the time they reached their destination. People from the entire station were helping the crew. The summit they'd held that morning helped everyone put their differences aside in order to help out against the looming threat they were facing.

He also had a meeting with Cid and Thomas about the Stingers that had started to become self-aware. Cid told them not to worry about it just yet. He would put out feelers to keep an eye on it, but they had others things to worry about.

Jonathan wanted more people on this, but Cid was right. They had a war to deal with, and they needed to focus the majority of their fighters on that.

As he watched the repairs from the viewport in his stateroom, Jonathan heard the hatch behind him open. He smelled a familiar perfume, and knew who it was. "Hello, Mei-Ling," he said with a smile.

Mei-Ling walked toward him and stood beside him, gazing out the viewport as well. "This is amazing, Jonathan: all these people, from all different walks of life, working together and enjoying it! It's my father's dream coming true!" She paused for a moment, listening to the music that was playing throughout the ship and outside. "I like this band. Who is it and what's the name of the song that's playing?"

"The band is Creed. The song is called 'One.'"

She smiled. "How appropriate."

"Everyone else seems to think so, too."

They stood there for few moments, silent. "Where is everyone?"

"Thomas is overseeing the repairs on the *Zeus*, Sara is recovering and Ryan is with her, and I believe William is helping out with the Tigeras refugees pouring into the station."

Ever since the battle against the Shadow Fleet had ended, refugees from the main Tigeras home world were starting to pour in. They could have gone to any of the other planets that the Tigeras had settled, but the majority of them had no family to go to. They would go to one of the other planets eventually, but until arrangements could be made, they would stay on the station.

"And what about you? Where did you come from?" Jonathan asked.

"I just came from a meeting that Cid, Eugene, Katrina, and Nesith are having with President Martinez and representatives from other races via long-range communications."

Jonathan smiled. "What's it about?"

"Did you know that Cid broadcast the entire public assembly over the whole galaxy?"

Jonathan looked at her in shock. "*Really?* Is that what the meeting was about?"

She nodded her head. "Apparently it has caused quite a stir throughout the Ashlon Republic, the Tigeras and Telbin Empire, and the Twilight Continuum. Other governments are responding to it as well."

"What did they say?"

"That Measha Station is becoming a symbol of people from various races putting their differences aside and working together to reach a common goal. It's becoming quite inspirational."

"Is that a good thing?"

"Oh yes, Jonathan, it's a very good thing."

"Then why aren't you with them?"

"Right now we're at recess, and Cid told me not to worry about the rest of the meeting, but to come see you."

They turned toward each other. Jonathan looked deep into Mei-Ling's eyes. "I'm glad you did."

Jonathan never thought he would ever hold her again and feel her on his skin and smell her hair, but here they were, against all odds. He looked into her almond-shaped eyes and saw all the love that she had for him, and what he felt for her was beyond words.

Mei-Ling said, "Make love to me, Jonathan."

Jonathan was caught off guard for just a second. Then he saw the passion in her eyes, and he felt the need to be with her, to feel her under him, and to take all the love that she could give him.

MEI-LING DID NOT SAY a word as she took a step back and began to take off her jumpsuit. As she watched Jonathan do the same, she felt her body began to get hot in all the right places. She had not been with another man since he left, and this moment that she was experiencing was well worth the wait. He came to her and led her to his bed. She said, "I love you. Now and forever."

He laid her on the bed and started kissing her neck, working his way down to her breasts, gently kissing them. When he kissed and bit her nipples, her body shook with passion as she let out a moan of pleasure. He kept kissing her, down to her belly and below. When she wrapped her legs around his shoulders, she began to scream with pleasure. When he was finished, and she took hold of his cybernetic arm and pulled him on top of her. As they made love, Mei-Ling knew this was real, that from now on, no matter what might happen, they would always be together. They made love for a long time until all their energy was spent.

MEI-LING HAD BEEN SLEEPING peacefully when the comm rang from Jonathan's desk. She looked at Jonathan, who was still sleeping. Deciding to let him sleep, she stood up and grabbed a shirt, putting it on as she walked to the desk. As she answered the comm, she wondered who would be calling this late at night. When the unit came alive, Cid's face appeared on the small screen.

"Hi, Cid, why the late call?"

Cid looked like he was about to bust a vein in his forehead.

"There you are! What have you been up to? No, don't answer that: I can guess. The leaders of some of the galaxy's smaller governments have just named me the president of the newly formed Nova-Star Republic!"

"Whoa! Whoa! Slow down, Cid, and start from the beginning. What are you *talking* about? What is this Nova-Star Republic?"

"It seems that the public assembly we had earlier had inspired people to take the concept of unity and cooperation much further than we ourselves had envisioned. People are contacting their representatives from all over the galaxy. They see what's happening on Measha Station as more than just the symbol of hope described by the leaders we talked to earlier today. The people want to unite their various governments into one. *Imagine*, different species under *one* government! Really inspiring, huh?"

Mei-Ling's voice got caught in her throat. Once again, she saw her father's dream becoming reality. "This is great, Cid. But why do you look overwhelmed?"

"Because, as I said, these leaders want me to become the *president* of this new government!"

"*Really?*"

He nodded. "Apparently, they feel that I am the most respected person in the galaxy—that people from all species will trust me the most." He shook his head in mock annoyance. "That's what I get for sticking my nose in other governments' businesses, and for having a station where anybody can go and be free with few restraints!"

"How long do you think it will take to form and structure this new government?"

"I'd say close to a year, or longer. We're talking about joining several governments into one. A lot of amendments, constitutions, and countless other things have to be decided on." He rubbed his forehead. "This is going to be one big headache!"

Mei-Ling laughed. "Looks like you have a lot of work ahead of you."

"Oh, I wouldn't start laughing just yet, my dear. I told everyone else that if I were to accept this crazy job, I would want *you* as my vice president—" Mei-Ling was struck speechless. Before she could reply, Cid continued, "—and that I also wanted Jonathan as the head of the space navy!"

Once again, Mei-Ling could not speak. "Why would they *agree* to that, Cid? We're from the Imperial Guard. Why in the world would they let us be a part of the new government?"

"Well, Mei-Ling, they've seen the footage from the *Freedom*, and the video showing what had happened to you during your punishment. That, coupled with what Jonathan has done for everyone since his exile, and what your father has done to try to rid the Guard of racism and make everyone equal, has convinced them that you have the best intentions for the future of the new government. Now I'll let you get some rest. Tell Jonathan I want the two of you in the main conference room at noon today. We have a lot of work to do. Good night."

Cid's face disappeared from the screen. Mei-Ling's heart raced with excitement as she turned around and ran to where Jonathan was sleeping. She jumped on the bed, laughing with delight.

Jonathan woke up and looked around, confused. He checked the clock. "Honey, it's two in the morning. What's going on?"

SCOTT T. WRIGHT SAT in the park outside his temporary quarters, thinking about all that had happened during the past two weeks. He had lost his closest friend, Albright, and suffered his first big loss in the new war. None of the ships he had sent to Measha Station had come back. One-fourth of his fleet strength was lost, and the remaining ships were guarding Earth 2 and searching for Measha Station.

His thoughts turned toward his brother. He did not know whether or not Jonathan had survived the battle, but he wouldn't bet against him. He smiled when he remembered Brougth's face when they'd received word that their fleet had been destroyed, and that they couldn't confirm his brother's death. Brougth had been *sooo* pissed! He didn't know what the Wraith hated more: that the attack was a failure, or not knowing whether Jonathan was alive or dead! He told them not to underestimate his brother, and now they were paying the price.

Scott's inner musings turned serious. He loved his brother, but he couldn't let those feelings stop him from achieving his goal. If it came to it, he knew he could kill his brother.

Abigail called him back into the house. He stood up from the bench he'd been sitting on and made his way into the house, heading for the dining room. When he arrived, Brougth was already there. Abigail was waiting by his chair. They took their seats.

Wright looked at Brougth and smiled. "I *told* you not to underestimate my brother!"

Anger covered the Wraith's face. "Don't worry, I will not make the same mistake again!" Brougth paused. "How much longer until construction on the superstation begins?"

Wright's smile increased. "They tell me that construction will begin in a month."

Brougth nodded. "That's good. Soon we will truly be the most powerful body in the known galaxy, and your people will be one again."

Wright raised his glass. "To uniting humanity!" The two commanders toasted their alliance.

IT HAD BEEN A week since Measha Station had left for the Sorus Cluster. They expected to journey for another two weeks, trying their best to avoid the Shadow Guard and any hostile aliens.

Sara Albright walked down the grassy path, her sandals leaving small imprints in the ground. She carried nothing with her but the clothes she was wearing—cut-off shorts and a blue tank top, with her swimsuit underneath.

She had received a call from Ryan to come to Bio-pod 5, a pod that contained beautiful forests, with small lakes scattered throughout and striking beaches.

She made her way through the pod, to the designated location. From her hover-car, it was just a five-minute walk. As she entered a small clearing, she stopped and gasped at the breathtaking view. Exotic trees and flowers surrounded her. Off to her right, at the edge of the clearing, was a waterfall that fed into a small spring.

Near that spring was a small table loaded with food and wine, and two chairs. In one of those chairs was Ryan.

As she came toward the table, he stood and pulled the other chair out for her.

My, my, what a gentleman. I'm surprised."

"I'm *full* of surprises."

She smiled. "So I see."

As Ryan poured the wine, Sara looked at the food on the table, at her surroundings, and at the man across from her. She didn't know how things could get any better.

WHAT THE HELL AM I *doing*! Ryan screamed in his head. He had a plan, but for some odd reason, he'd forgotten it. Some spy he was! As the two lovers started to eat, he decided that all he could do was play it by ear. Hopefully, he would be able to hold a conversation without acting like a total idiot.

As they neared the end of their meal, Sara smiled at him, her white teeth shining bright. Her beautiful smile seemed to make her mocha-colored skin and her green eyes stand out. She was one of the few people that had seen his dark side and still loved him for the man that he was. She did not judge him; she only loved him.

He was so caught up in her beauty that he didn't realize that he had gotten to his feet. As he made his way to Sara, her expression turned to one of puzzlement. "Sara, we've known each other our whole lives," he began.

She nodded her head, waiting to see where this was going.

"For the past few years, our friendship has turned into something more. I didn't know how much it had grown until I was on Earth 2, when that blasted Wraith rammed his tail through me."

She made a face, and he decided not to go too deeply into that. When she'd found out what had happened to him, it had really upset her.

Ryan continued, "After that, I thought a lot about my future, and with whom I wanted to spend it."

Ryan reached into his pocket and pulled out a small jewelry box. As shock and tears came to Sara's face, Ryan got down on one knee. "Sara, I want to spend the rest of my life with you." He opened the box and inside was an engagement ring. "Sara Albright, will you marry me?"

Both of Sara's hands covered her mouth as she gasped for air while weeping happily. She nodded her head ecstatically while screaming, "Yes!" She jumped off the chair and into his arms, planting her lips on his.

After a few moments, the two lovers separated. Ryan took hold of Sara's hand and placed the ring on her finger. She gave him a small kiss and started moving backward with his hand in hers. She pulled him with her toward the small spring. As they reached the edge of the spring, Sara kicked off her sandals and took off her shorts and tank top, revealing the blue bikini that she was wearing beneath.

Ryan smiled and took off his sandals, shirt, and shorts as well, until he was wearing just his swim trunks. The two laughed and kissed while falling into the water. Neither knew what was going to happen in the future, but until then, they were going to have the time of their lives.